THE MAGELLAN

PROJECT

WILLIAM J. BREIDINGER

1

THE MAGELLAN PROJECT

Copyright: 2013, by William J. Breidinger

For Phyllis, my Fiddy
For Collin, my No. 1 son and Scientist
And to my friend, Carole Lazore

All persons indicated in this novel are fictional. No character is meant to be an embodiment of any specific individual, rather a conglomerate of

personalities and characteristics of the many
wonderful individuals I have meant in this life.

Cover: Original art by William J. Breidinger
Printing: Max Graphics, Cortland, NY
Editing: James J. Daly, Esquire

Hardcover books can be purchased directly
through the author at:
PO Box 127, Homer, NY 13077 or
wbreidin@twcny.rr.com.

Published in the United States of America.

ISBN: 9780615891552

Prelude

Old cultures give way to new frontiers.   Yet, the past challenges those who would change the world.

Nine people from vastly different paths are inexorably drawn towards a remote chain of Islands on the Mid-Atlantic plateau.   They are all plunged into mystery and mythology as scientific experiments seek to change the course of history and the direction of the planet.

After a devastating separation, Chris returns to his beloved southwestern Colorado to find that his friend in Silverton has disappeared.   Other friends he had known are either dead or missing. The cases are cold.   As he fights to regain some kind of life and build a new foundation, he renews an old friendship with Ann, a successful Attorney in Denver.   Little do they know what awaits them.

Far off in the Acorean Islands, the top corporation in the world embarks on a historically dramatic project, isolated on tiny the island of Graciosa, encompassing the newly developed resort of Atlantic Sun. As the project evolves; Chris and Ann, seafarers of WorldGreen, and officials of the Portuguese government, itself in turmoil, find themselves magnetically forced into a deepening mystery and the discovery of the millennia.

PROGRAMME

CHAPTER ONE   Freedom

CHAPTER TWO   Visions

CHAPTER THREE   Politics

CHAPTER FOUR   Durango

CHAPTER FIVE   The Western Slope

CHAPTER SIX   Leadership

CHAPTER SEVEN   To believe in this
                            Living

CHAPTER EIGHT   Arrangements

CHAPTER NINE   The Habitat

CHAPTER TEN   Quebec City

CHAPTER ELEVEN   Jamestown

CHAPTER TWELVE   The Foreign Legion

CHAPTER THIRTEEN   Castello Blanco

CHAPTER FOURTEEN   Undersea Discovery

CHAPTER FIFTEEN   Graciosa

CHAPTER SIXTEEN   The Ante-Deluvian
                            Era

CHAPTER SEVENTEEN   Atlantic Sun

CHAPTER EIGHTEEN   Home Invasion

CHAPTER NINETEEN   Sea Cruise

CHAPTER TWENTY   Resolutions

CHAPTER ONE

Freedom

"Bring the ship in line, synchronize at fourteen degrees north, northeast, then level out at fifteen hundred feet."

"Roger, Control."

The specially engineered Huey helicopter cut its starboard jet, then on a rapid ninety degree turn, cut the port as well. It hovered on its fore and aft propellers, squaring off directly above, away and due south of the island shrouded in the mist below.

"OK, very good, now set to remote and prepare for release on our count. Ready, five, four, three, two, one, now."

"We're on beam now, Control."

"Alright, gentlemen, sit back and enjoy the ride."

The two pilots eased back in the bucket seats as the helicopter gradually descended towards the gulf below. The digital display and gauges smoothly coded the effects of the tractor beam emanating from the island just on the near horizon.

At the control's helm, the technician's eyes danced across the hardware, constantly monitoring the laser's output, the tube's drawing strength and the computer controlled signals housed within the artificial beam's shield. He turned quickly to his supervisor who stood directly off to his left, overlooking the control station and the display.

"Chief, we've got some kind of interference on the beam, atmospheric, I think, but it's causing some fluctuations on the command sequence signal."

"Ramp up the beam tube."

As the technician re-aligned the energy output for the laser, the tube inside it, regulating the control signal, the two pilots thought they noticed a jump in acceleration, accentuated by a bump in their downward glide path.

"Control, are we still on line?"

"On line and coming in strong." The Chief's comfort

level had been just slightly disturbed.

Again, the technician turned, this time quite distraught at the turn of events.

"Chief, the beam's increased power has eroded the connection. I don't know if I can hold it."

"Cut back on it then, dammit. Can't you get this thing stable?"

"Yes Sir. It was fine all week on simulation and robotics. I don't know what the problem is."

He turned to reduce the strength.

"Jeezuz Christ, I've lost the connection."

"Damn, cut the beam off," The Chief immediately switched the headset, "Sea Hawk, power up, right now. You're off line, I repeat, you're off line."

"Oh shit," the pilot screamed as the helicopter tilted and dove headfirst towards the reefs below. At the low altitude and at the speed of the descent, there was no chance that the ship could fire up the jets and erect itself in flight before it would hit the deck. Even as the propellers turned and the engines began their ignition, the plummeting copter sent two screaming men to their deaths on the coral outcroppings of the island's lagoon.

The crash was spectacular, propelling smoke and fire upwards in a voluminous spray of sea water and foam; the sound of impact a colossal thump and explosion in the calming waters of the shoreline.

In an instant, Chris shot up from the sleeping bag.
"What the........!"

His heart was racing, pounding in his ears and throbbing at his temples. He looked about, the night sky coolly quiet in the surrounding hills, light shafts of moonlight dancing off the dew laden pine boughs that bent the light in the early morning breeze. Barely a sound came to him, save the grunt of his German Shepard, who now rose on his forelegs and began to rumble up his warning growl.

"It's okay, buddy, it's alright. Just another one of those dreams. Too much Star Trek," 'or pot', he thought, laughing to himself as he rubbed the massive dog. Still, he could not dismiss the dream altogether. Chris had been in the counterculture up to his neck from early on and he knew dreams could represent many things. One, it could have been a premonition, of something in the future. That seemed unlikely. What the hell would he ever be doing involved with a helicopter. Two, it could be something from his past, maybe a past life. That seemed ridiculous, since it seemed a futuristic dream in the first place. Third, it could represent upheaval in his life. That could be, but it didn't seem like anything he was doing could ever be quite so dramatic; and last, it could be a release from stress. He didn't think he had an ounce of stress. That didn't make sense. Maybe, in the future, it would come to him, but for now, it held visions in stark contrast to the real world he lived in.

This was a serene peaceful morning in the highlands. Light blue tinted the crest of the horizon and the darkness of the greenery lightened with each passing second. Crystalline drops of rain hung onto the fat leaves of the hardwoods, dropping with a light patter to the ground.

He looked over at his partner, Buck, who was dead to the world. The night before had been tough, the good-bye party before the two set out for Colorado. The 'gang' had turned out and they had hit the street early, cruising to their four favorite haunts and ending up with a porch party that drew the cops twice. By four a.m. they had whipped the last dog, the metabolic shutdown had arrived, and they crashed randomly at his friend's apartment. It was a great time, but not an auspicious start to a journey that was supposed to begin early.

Chris patted Bezo on the head. The one hundred and ten pound mixed Shepard-wolf finally calmed down. The animal had a strict code. If he thought that Chris was in danger, he would growl once and if the situation didn't mellow out, he would attack the offender, regardless of the situation. Chris constantly had to be aware of his canine's disposition, for Bezo was not one to mind the directions of others very well. And he was a fairly ferocious dog when it mattered.

The two had forged their bond in Colorado three years earlier, when Chris had found the animal starving, near death, in the small mountain town of Nederland. Nederland sat at the end of the snow-capped mountain stream that filled the reservoir that supplied Boulder's water. The alternative style of life had solidly planted itself there, ninety three hundred feet above sea level, twenty miles from the city; without much regard to employment or even the basic necessities of life. The young people homesteading in the town were challenged to provide for themselves and their animals were continually turned loose when it became a choice between the residents or the pets getting what food was available. It was a huge problem. He probably saved the animal, but in a way, Bezo had saved him, too. Since then, they had been inseparable.

Chris chuckled again as the dog closed his eyes. Bezo had sensed they were going for a big ride, but patiently had to wait better than half a day while Chris and Buck sobered up enough to get their shit together and get out of town. In the semi-lucid moments when Chris raised his head off the couch, only to determine that he was still not able to get up, the dog would look at him as if to say "You asshole, you've done it again and now I have to sit here and wait, and wait, and wait."

Looking around the forest and through the mountain laurel that covered the Pennsylvania mountain ridges, Chris assured himself that the start he had given himself was nothing but internal and that there was still an hour or so before the dawn would fully clear the hills to the east. Just as he started to doze off again, the first sounds of the Doves and Woodpeckers greeting the first rays of the morning sun came chattering lightly to his ears from the nearby woods.

The journey west had been a seed implanted on a hot summer's day. The two young men had been painting a summer camp on Skaneateles Lake, a job that required almost as much time lounging off the dock as it did completing the actual work. Chris remembered the day, a beautiful summer afternoon in August when the lake was finally warm enough to swim in, a balmy sixty eight degrees. He and Buck had talked about the future and Chris had mentioned going back to Colorado. For lack of a better explanation, he had told Buck that the constellations appeared to be twice as big at ten thousand feet and the air was so crisp that every breath snapped the senses alive with a new found clarity. He had not mentioned a far off love that still kindled the fire of passion within him.

Buck had remembered that day, too and when the two were both laid off from their respective jobs in the middle of February, they made a pact to take the unemployment and run. That would get them six months of income while they looked for work out west.

It seemed funny to Chris now that they actually had left. Nobody believed they would, not his family or his current girlfriend, nor the many friends they both had in common. No one really thought they would go, but with but four hundred dollars, give or take, apiece and the hope that the interstate claims would start coming in by the end of the seventh or eighth week, they had determined to make a break from upstate New York. Neither one of them knew where they were going, how long they would stay, nor what they would do when they got there. Chris never felt freer in his life. It was absolutely joyous.

Packed up, clearer of mind from the mountains slight overnight breeze, they sped down Interstate eighty one into the lower reaches of the Shenandoah valley. Their inexhaustible spirit of freedom gave way to a festive atmosphere. It had been fueled by the hitchhiker they picked up in Maryland. The passenger had plied the two friends with the tastiest joint they had smoked in weeks. When the vehicle sidled over to the shoulder to let the traveler out on his way to D.C., the smoke lifted out of the van like a small fog.

"Thanks for the ride, Man,"

The brother swung out from the side doors and hoisted his pack onto his shoulder.

"Stay cool," Buck added, then swung the beat up Chevy ten panel van back onto the superhighway.

"Great weed, Man. Jeez, I'd like to get a bag of that shit."

"I am really high. On one joint. I wonder where he got that?" Chris fumbled with the tapes, then popped in

13

Hendrix's Cry of Love. As the guitar wailed and the bass pounded from the two huge stereo speakers that were bolted to the platforms built on the inside of the panel walls, the van crept up to cruising speed.

Purchased for three hundred dollars a month ago, Chris's '65 van was a magnificent piece of engineering that seemed perfectly suited for a cross country trip of unspecified duration. It had a floor and walls that the rust hadn't yet breached and enough space to house all of their worldly possessions, the dog, and in a pinch, afforded them makeshift housing in nasty weather. The fact that the clutch was held together with a bent thread rod and that the accelerator had a tendency to stick, or that the thing rode like a tractor on the highway did not in the least detract from the trip or their intent.

They had built in a great sound system and recorded tapes for months. In the last week before the trip, they deferred van improvement in favor of aesthetic beauty. As a result, while the mechanics of the vehicle shook and shuddered, the driver side panel of the van caught the eye of every passerby, a huge mural of the Tetons zipping past them.

The van caught a wide curve that separated the two sets of lanes. For several moments, the northbound lanes were completely hidden. As Buck held to the passing lane, Chris took another toke, then snapped forward.

"Jeezus Christ, Buck, this is a two lane road."

Buck hit the brakes, snapped the steering wheel to the right and the van fishtailed across both lanes, wobbling and screeching into the dirt on the shoulder and uncomfortably bouncing the two young men until it finally came to a stop. The road was silent for a moment until other cars roared down both lanes. Chris began laughing uncontrollably.

"You son-of-a bitch," Buck roared.

"Ah, you should have seen your face," Chris howled, "I knew you were as stoned as I was."

"I'm getting a beer. You drive."

"Get me one, too."

*

The sun's warmth felt great on his face. It was about time. It seemed like March had lasted three months. There had been a hint of spring, and then, seemingly without pause, the snow storm of a week before vanished into the heat of an early summer. Montreal was definitely a different world than New York City. It was a lot colder, for a lot longer. Anyway, he was free. That was the important thing. He looked down at his copy of the "Daily News". It was a week old, but it didn't matter. He was happy to have it. It was just one of those things you missed and didn't realize it until you couldn't have it anymore. Oh, he could've gotten by with the Montreal paper. He still would know how the Mets were doing, but it just wasn't the same. The "News" was sensational; New York at its best, or worst, if you cared, and he didn't. He just loved the headlines, the fanaticism, or maybe it was the veracity of life that laid itself out on these deliciously tacky pages. Only in New York.

Joe Hackett looked up long enough to take in the rest of the lunch crowd; except that it wasn't lunch for him. This was part of his daily ritual on the nice days; up at the crack of noon and out to a small cafe on Sherbrooke Avenue or DuVal Street for coffee and a cigarette, maybe something to eat once he got himself situated.

He lit up another Marlboro, the pack a recent acquisition from his care package from home. He'd probably go into the Pub around three and grab a sandwich. That didn't cost him anything. He was the head bartender, part-time manager, and jack of all trade's at Winston Churchill's. Unless he took the day off, he was usually in by then, anyway, even though the crowd and the shift didn't start till five. There was always something that needed tending to and he could get mentally organized for the evening to come.

It had been five years since the draft notice had come and he had made the difficult decision to leave the city and head north to Canada. He would never fight in the war after the invasion of Cambodia. To hell with them. It didn't seem to matter how many countries they invaded over there or how

15

many people they killed doing it.

He felt bad about the whole thing. He had to leave his family, his friends and make his way by himself; not even an old lady to make the trip with. It was tough, but he'd done it. He felt bad for his brothers who were going over there, many he knew already were not coming back. And for what? To keep the oil companies in business? To back up the French, who screwed it up in the first place? To support a corrupt regime in the middle of a civil war that the people there didn't even want? It was bullshit, all of it. Too bad he had to be branded a traitor at home, one who deserted his country. He didn't see it that way.

A patriot is one who gives up his life for his country. Many of his brothers had done so physically. He had done it mentally. His life back in the city was gone and he could not go back. Some would say it was a matter of convenience, but that wasn't it at all. It wasn't an easy life up here. He would never have a career here and he knew it. And life, well, it was just different. At least that Cox shucker Nixon was gone. Tricky Dick, the prick, resigned in shame. He'd raised his mug high to the TV that night at the pub. God damn him for eternity for what he'd done; or not done, for that matter. If he'd just gone out and won the damn war, maybe it would've been different.

Joe put the coffee cup down and waved to the waitress. She was a cute little thing with a delightful shag haircut. He was trying to get her into the Pub. Actually, he was trying to get a lot farther than that. 'That's the one good thing about being up here', he thought, 'the women are fabulous and as an ex-patriot, I do have some bohemian charm.'

"What's your name?" he asked.

"Do you think I'd tell you my real name?" She grinned."

"Joe Hackett, nice to meet you." He tilted his head slightly and tipped his fingers as if he had a hat on over his shoulder length hair. "I've been here quite a few times, now, and I see you working here. I like this place. It's nice."

"We like it. It gets real busy, though, like now." She was impatient and leery of lingering too long with any one customer. Jobs were hard to find and she didn't need to catch hell.

"I can see that. I won't keep you. I work over at Winston Churchill's Pub. You should stop in, you'd like it. It'll be a good night tonight."

"Maybe I will. Nice meeting you."

He got up as she turned away. A beautiful derriere, he thought as she worked through the tables. The French language put such polish on even the most mundane things, not that the shape of a beautiful woman was in the least bit mundane, but Joe had come from a rough neighborhood in the City and to get along with the fairer sex, he had to learn a great deal about manners and decorum. He was naturally attracted to many women, and they to him. Joe stood six-two with a trim physique and dark, neck length hair with a thin moustache. He was an American ex-patriot, which added a certain interest, and he liked to party. His sharp features seemed to work well in these social environments, so he never feared for lack of company. But his decision to leave the United States left him in a permanently impermanent situation. It made it hard to sustain any relationship when he could not stand on any solid foundation, now, or in the future.

He drained the last bit of his coffee and wondered what it would be like to spend a whole morning at cafés, watching the world go by and pontificating on the politics of the day.

He stood up to his full stature, brushed off the crumbs from the muffin, and left a very nice tip, from one service worker to another. The brothers and sisters understood that. You just did it. He picked up the paper with care. It might be another three weeks before he'd see another one.

*

The trenches just weren't working. The tarp was doing its job, holding the water off and running it to the channels so feverishly dug three days ago when the rains hit, but the intensity of the storm filled them to overflowing.

17

"Son of a bitch," Chris muttered to himself. He ratcheted through the sleeping bag, the pack, the pile of extra clothing and food and finally the small wooden storage box to find the folding shovel. He put on the poncho and eased out from the meager shelter into the enveloping drizzle. As he got up, the dog started.

"No, it's OK buddy, we're not going anywhere."

The Shepard sat silently, but warily. Bezo had no intention of racing out into the heavy rain. He didn't like it much, either.

Vigorously, Chris dug another channel away from the tarp off the existing one, doubling the water flow away from the north side of the plastic tarp he had fashioned into a lean-to. He did the same on the other side, then swung behind the structure to deepen the back trench. Mud, water and pine needles flew off from every stroke amidst continuous swearing and mumbling.

Satisfied that he had contained the deluge for the time being and could keep his equipment, ground cover, and clothing dry, he ducked under the tarp and carefully took the poncho off, trying not to get anything wet. If there was one thing he learned in all the years of Boy Scouts, it was to keep warm and dry, the latter more important than the former to him. He maintained that swimming would be a great sport if you didn't have to get wet.

The plastic container he used as a cup was virtually empty, so he refilled it from the half gallon wine jug. He was making a good dent in it today. It didn't matter. There wasn't anything else to do. In fact, just about everything that could have gone wrong, had.

They had been at this national forest campground now for three and a half weeks. That was right after the van broke down and had to go in for a major repair that the mechanic in Longmont didn't seem to be able to get around to doing. They had to beg an acquaintance to give them a ride up to this place four miles outside of Nederland, well up into the front range and although there weren't many folks in it, the area ranger was getting downright testy about them being there. Buck kept telling the guy they would leave when the van was fixed and every day, he came back with the same question. It was like the Pope and Michelangelo and it was getting old.

That was just the tip of it. Chris had other motives in this excursion back west, most notably his desire to rekindle his relationship with Sheri, the woman he lived with two years earlier. It had always been his intent to send for her, but one job after another went down the tubes and his plans to build a house had ended up as dream fodder, nothing to hang on to. In retrospect, he should have never left, for now, she had returned to her ex-husband. She still saw him, but he knew things had changed dramatically. It was just a kick for her. And now, he was thirty miles away with no wheels.

Worse, Buck had his old lady flown in from the east. That had complicated things, especially since they didn't have the van. Chris felt bad for them and gave them his new tent to sleep in. They were in it now, a hundred and fifty feet away through the pines, the fog and the never ending rain; while he dodged the deluge under the tarp. So much for being the nice guy. Well, it really wouldn't do to have the two of them suffering while he was sheltered. That would have been too much guilt for him to deal with. Damn guilt. It always got in the way.

He took a gulp of wine and realized he was getting drunk. Piss on it. What difference could it make? It wasn't going to make the weather any better; it wasn't going to end the ache in his heart; and it wasn't going to get him out of the campground any sooner. Sobriety just seemed to add insult to a bad situation. Having given it considerable thought, inebriation was an excellent state and should be continued ninety-nine percent of the time. It reminded him of his days back in New England, at the height of the revolution. They used to joke about acid. What if you gave a kid acid for fifteen years and then stopped giving it to him. Wouldn't reality be a trip? What a concept.

He was dwelling on the impossible, the idiotic. He grabbed the poncho again and fumbled through his things for his cowboy hat. He secured the dog, knowing that he'd be pissed, but better off than traipsing through the rain with him.

"Buck," he hollered out through the drizzle.

19

"Yeah," came back the muffled reply.

"I'm goin' to that bar in Rollinsville." He didn't wait for an answer.

It was a long mile to the three story bar and rooming house that made up about twenty five percent of the village. He would be damp, possibly wet through by the time he walked there, but at least he'd be dry and in the gin mill. Whatever was going on there had to be better than what was going on here. He wouldn't worry about how he'd get back or in what condition. That would take care of itself and he probably wouldn't remember it anyway.

*

The heat beat down on the mountainous spine that was central Portugal. The midday sun oppressed the landscape with its passionate, hot embrace, seemingly pounding the senses with the hundred degree temperatures. The dry, light brown earth drifted in the breeze, the heat adding unwanted sting to the granular mist that the occasional gusts tossed forth. Sparsely set green trees and scrub brush claimed what land they could in the barely arable land.

Anybody with an ounce of sense hid from it. It was Siesta time. And Siesta was not some rule that the villagers had to abide by. Siesta happens. The body just knows that after lunch, in this heat, the brim of the hat must surely make its way over the brow, the shade of the nearest tree or porch covers the being, and serenity covers the soul.

Juanita knew, that in her father's case, the serenity was helped along with the beer he had for lunch. After Siesta, the man would make his way down to the Cantina and that would pretty much do it for the day. She hated that. Half the time, he would come home and knock her poor mother around. She was a fine woman who cared deeply for her and her brother. It was a hard life here with him and she had barely been able to fend off her father's advances. After the incident with the knife a couple of weeks before, he'd pretty much backed away from her. She was full grown and a beauty to boot, a rose in this thorn bush of a village.

She stealthily walked past the man who called himself her father, he nestled against the adobe shack and went into the kitchen area where her mother finished cleaning up the midday meal.

"Mama, can I go up the canyon?"

"Sure, little one, but take your brother, he has nothing to do."

"Do I have to?"

"What would you want if you were him?"

"Alright, alright."

She took Alvarro by the hand.

"Come on, you bag of stones."

The seven year old smiled and his radiant face beamed with the crooked teeth of his unstructured youth. They left the house and walked up the hill behind it, into the canyon that sat at the base of the mountainous ridge. Well into the canyon, the wash displayed some of the water that was deeply embedded in the recess, sided by trees and brush. It was here Juanita found joy in this simple life, hiking up the gorge to the pool that sat at the bottom of the faint waterfall, now barely dripping from the last of the summer's spring. It would take a good rain to make it well up again. Perhaps a tropical storm would come.

She worked her way along the beaten path as Alvaro scrambled to catch up until they reached the well canopied and hidden swimming hole. Juanita disrobed and dove into the refreshing water. Alvarro followed, only to his knees. He could barely swim, but liked to wade in the water while his sister swam in the cool, ever swirling pool that kissed the hard rock formations. She swam until she could feel the chill, then came out to lie on the rocks, allowing the sun to dry her naked body. Alvaro took some notice, but at seven, he was only slightly interested in the anatomical differences between himself and his sister. Mostly, he just enjoyed being with her.

After the suns deep rays dried her, Juanita put her clothes back on, walked back up the path and sat with her brother underneath a large shade tree. From that spot, they could see the ridge as it extended northward to the deep canyons like Braga Canyon some fifty miles north. Juanita knew her area well. She was an explorer, a bit of a tomboy, and took every opportunity to know the land around here. It was, in her estimation, a much better use of time than anything else she did.

"Someday, Alvarro," She waved her hand in a sweeping motion, "We'll go beyond that ridge, far, far from here, where no one can harm us."

The boy had heard this before and sullenly played in the dirt.

"We'll go to America, like our cousins and our Aunt and Uncle. We'll have a real life, and a big house. Just you wait and see, Alvarro."

"Can we take Paco?" He asked, with his charming grin and boyish innocence.

"Yes," she mused, "We can take the dog. We can take whatever you want."

*

Buck entered the San Juan Tavern with a full head of steam. It had clearly been a tough night. Chris saw him pass Marvin at the door and work his way through the crowd to his corner of the bar. He was ready for him.

"Hey, Pard. What'll it be?"

"One of them milkshakes and make it a stiff one."

Chris had the blender set up right at the end of the bar next to the well, so he quickly mixed the Smith & Currans, pressed the button and as it ran, poured a couple of drafts for the two customers next to his friend. It was the Saturday night dance and with a hundred people in the Tavern, he had to work and talk at the same time.

There were all manner of young and old, from all parts of the country. Like Chris and Buck, they had ended up in Silverton, liked it and stayed for the season. Some came specifically to work at a business, like Lois, who came from California to run the pottery shop, like Nancy, from Minnesota, who worked at the Timberline Trading company and Richard,

22

the Navajo, who ran the jewelry shop. Then, there was their friend, Skip Conboy, who came from Philadelphia. Skip had a brush with the law there and decided this was as good a place to hide as any and a safe place to make a life. There was Stormy the waitress, Vern the miner, and John, fresh from Prudhoe Bay in Alaska; Craig, Ron, Gregg and Tom, wildcat miners who came in from the Eastern slope; All there by chance and all there to have a good time.

Buck snarled as Chris returned from the blender.

"You look pissed off," Chris nodded to his friend as he gave him the drink and pushed back the cash.

"I got three tables of Texans and I don't think I got a three dollar tip out of all of them combined. And this one, man, I worked my ass off for. Sixty bucks for the four of them and they stiffed me. I hope their Winnebago falls off Coal Bank Pass, the bastards."

Chris tried not to laugh. When they first pulled into Silverton, Buck had drawn the short straw and had to go to work first. At the time, the Acropolis Restaurant had the only openings in town. But that was early June and as the town geared up for the summer season, other jobs opened up and Chris picked up his gig at the San Juan. He knew he had it better than his friend, but not by much.

"Hey, Buck, we ain't here for a long time, just for a good time, right Rick."

The man they called "Mountain" Lyons pounded his shot of Tequila and gave out his patented roar. Buck laughed as he finished off his drink.

"Give me another one. Looks like a hot night here tonight."

"The band's great. Just about everybody in town's here, plus some wonderful looking girls came in on the train. There's a cute little blonde down there who's holding up that end of the bar and she's been looking at me all night, but this damn job keeps me backed up and I can't even get out for a dance. What sucks is that I get to watch it all happen and don't get to do anything about it. Hold it for a minute, Pard, and watch the tap, I gotta go change the tape."

Chris went to the center of the bar, pulled out the

Fleetwood Mac tape and put on Van Halen. The band would still be out another ten minutes or so and he wanted to keep the place rockin' till they came back out. That wasn't much of a problem. When they had a dance in Silverton, folks came down from the slopes. The miners, the tourists, the bikers, and the locals all came together to raise hell and they all got along together real well, most of the time. Since they'd moved there in late May, after the van was finally repaired, they'd had a wonderful two months in the town. It was an accident. They had been on the way to the Grand Canyon and had come through Silverton because Chris had heard it was a cool town three years before. They fell in love with it and changed their minds on the spot. The summer season was about to unfold and the service work was plentiful. Besides, they had only about Thirty dollars left between the three of them. That was a big factor.

Chris poured a couple of drafts on the way back and Marvin was waiting next to Buck.

"Got another one for you," Marvin handed him the automatic .45. The biker was right behind him. Marvin was the bouncer, if you could call him that. It was the protocol of the town that if you had a "dance", you had to hire an associate Sheriff to man the door. It was just part of the deal. Marvin was a slightly rotund middle aged man, dressed in his official butternut gray uniform, complete with the accompanying black utility belt, which contained his whistle, cuffs, mace, and a sidearm. Chris doubted he had ever used any of the items. Marvin just wasn't the type.

"Let me know when you're ready to leave and Marvin will give it to you on the way out."

The biker headed towards the band and Chris placed the pistol under the bar.

"Damn, I just hate those things. Why the hell do they bring them in here?"

Buck smiled. "Yeah, and a damn lot of good it does to give it back to him when he's drunk. He could just stand outside and shoot it."

Just as he felt he had one disturbance out of the way, another one started up. At the table next to the fireplace that

24

was made out of an ore car, a tall muscular Mexican fellow bolted upright, smashing a pitcher in the process. In an instant, four miners were on top of the guy, pushing him towards the door. Chris didn't catch it all, but he did see Marvin spray mace in the Mexican's face. All that did was annoy the man further and he slammed Marvin against the door jamb.

Now, the four miners went after him, shoving the Mexican out the door and into the street. Marvin was in a panic and made his way directly to the bar.

"Chris, you gotta do something."

"Jesus, Marvin, you're the Deputy Sheriff. What am I supposed to do?"

"You gotta stop them or they'll kill him."

"Damn. Okay, I'll get the dog. Buck, watch the bar, don't let any of those guns loose. Marvin, you'd better get a hold of Floyd."

Chris flipped the service door open and pushed his way through the crowd to the door. Once out, he quickly opened the sliding door of his van that was parked directly in front of the bar. He pulled the massive Shepard out by the collar.

"C'mon, buddy, let's go."

The pair made their way around the corner to the main street and found the four miners about a block down, stoning the Mexican in front of Romero's. As Chris and the dog raced passed them in the enveloping dark, he could see the man was in a bad way, lying in the gutter with his hand up to protect himself from the rocks that were pelting him without mercy.

Chris placed himself and the dog between the two parties, about twenty feet from the miners and about fifteen from the bleeding victim, still holding onto the animal's collar.

"I'm not going to let you guys do this."

In the next split second, he pointed to the Mexican and said, "You. Get out of here."

"Chris, you ain't going to stop us," the biggest of the miners barked out. It was Gregg, one tough son of a bitch, and although Chris knew him and liked him, he also knew he couldn't take him.

As the beaten man worked his way to his knees, the four men attempted to move closer. Chris sidestepped to block the advance.

"I can and I will."

"That dog ain't gonna hurt nobody!"

"You still gotta get through me and I'll get at least one of you, and the dog, well, the first one of you that gets within three feet of me is going to have him draped all over his neck."

It wasn't bullshit.

The four men hesitated. The Mexican bolted down the street, as fast as his ruptured body could move.

"C'mon, Chris, that bastard was molesting the girls in town all day. We got a right." Gregg had moved forward a little, but when Bezo rumbled in fury, he stopped dead in his tracks.

"Not to take the law into your own hands. I'll tell you what. You've already given him a lesson. Why don't we go back to the bar and I'll buy you all a beer. Fair enough?"

There was a deafening silence as the five men faced each other. The quiet in the town was disrupted only by the distant din of the saloon up the street and the brisk, gusting wind that pushed its way into the valley from the mountainsides beyond.

"Damn it, Chris, why have you got to be such a pain in the ass?"

"Ahh, cause I'm the best bartender in town and cause I'm a long haired freak. Heh?" He raised his arms in an upward gesture, momentarily forgetting about the dog.

"Hold on, buddy."

Gregg backed up and turned to his friends.

"Ah, the hell with it. Chris?" He turned back, "What are your gonna say to Marvin?"

"Marvin's a dick. He didn't help this situation, not one bit. And, he's a sandbagger, and a sandbagger doesn't get any free beer."

The five men laughed and walked back up the street, Chris in the rear, clutching his four footed friend with a shaking arm.

*

Chris worked ninety hours a week in the first month there, splitting his time between two of the five bars that were open during the season. He planned to take a weekend off and see some of the rest of the State, perhaps go back out to the Eastern Slope and have a visit to Manitou Springs. That would have to wait a bit, but he did want one evening off, to catch the belly dancers at the Grand Imperial. Any entertainment in Silverton was exciting, but to have something like this from out of town, that was truly special. Bob Bryson, the owner, told Chris he could take off after nine and he would cover for him, but when the day came and the evening wore on, Bob was busy trying to make time with the sandy blonde who just got off work from the Chattanooga Café. By ten p.m., Chris knew Bob had no intention of letting him leave. He was on the hunt and couldn't be bothered. Chris was boiling and fifteen minutes later, had put up with enough. He walked over to the table and dropped the bar rag next to Bob.

"You told me I could leave at nine."

"I'm busy."

"So am I, and a promise is a promise. I'm out of here."

Chris turned on his boot heels and walked out. Bob was too stunned to say anything at the moment and had a bar room full of patrons with no one to serve them.

The next day, slightly hung over with visions of belly buttons, shifting skirts and clanging bells in head, Chris went in as usual at Handlebars for his day shift. It took three cups of coffee and a good half hour to get the place ready to open. By then, Chris looked fairly normal. He could take a good beating. After two months of day hiking on the eastern slope and climbing around Silverton, he was arguably in the best shape of his life. He was six one and one eighty five, fairly well tanned and weather beaten by the high peaks sun and winds. He never thought of himself as good looking, but several women apparently thought he was. His shoulder length blonde hair and bright blue eyes set him apart from

27

most of the locals, but it was his constant laughter and off beat sense of humor that attracted them most.   It certainly helped the bar business.   It would have been nice, though, if he could have found some other kind of work; or not so much of it, that he could actually spend time with some of the girls he met.

Unlocking the door and airing the place out, he wasn't open for much more than forty five minutes when the first passengers of train number one out of Durango arrived.   Not far behind the first entrants, two of his new friends, Craig and Ron came in, four days out of mountains, grinning like cats with canaries in their mouth.   They had both worked at Standard Metals and had gotten laid off a month ago.   They had turned their talents to wildcatting and were quite successful at it.   Craig pulled up a satchel on the bar and took out a rock the size of a soccer ball.   It was striated with gold and silver.

"Look at that baby.   Ain't that a beauty?"   Craig's smile went from ear to ear.

"That rock will fetch us two to three grand."   Ron added.

"That'll make a huge dent in my tab."   Craig allowed, which was good, because his tab was now clearing two hundred.

"And we got a ton of fresh trout. Great dinner last night." Ron was clearly amused.

"What did you use for bait?" Chris asked naively.

"Blast."   Ron added.

"Never heard of it."

"Dynamite, Chris.   We tossed some in Little Molas Lake on the way back."

Ron rubbed his chin.   "Now, it's either an Old Miner's trick or and Old Fisherman's trick, and I ain't sure which one it is, but it always brings up the fish."

Dynamite was a way of life with these guys.   Like all wildcat miners and those that worked at Standard Metals in Silverton or over in Ouray at the Ouray Mining Company, they had access to dynamite.   It was absolutely necessary in hardrock mining.   Miners operated hydraulic machine drills. These machines consisted of an encased motor and hydraulic pump connected to a hose the led to a five foot long pulsating drill that weighed in around seventy pounds. Massive segments of rock in the shafts were perforated with a dozen or more pilot holes, dynamite then inserted, fuses lit and the rock blasted to hell in hopes that gold or silver shards appeared or the blasts led to the exposure of rich veins. The hydraulic machine drills did the rest of the necessary chiseling and the process was continued, perforating the next set of pilot holes. Men who did this kind of work tended to be very strong. Chris's friends were no exception.

Craig was six foot six and two hundred and fifty pounds with just a small paunch from his robust life style. Ron was a wiry five foot ten and approaching middle age, but was as taut as mountain cougar. They both knew the work well.

"We got to get this to the Assay Office and then cash out. When do you get off, Chris?"

"I get out at seven, supposed to be at the San Juan at eight. I'm sure I pissed Bryson off though. I'll find out when I go in."

"We'll come with you." Craig ventured, "I'll stop back here and pay you off, then we can go drink over there, with your usual discount, of course."

True to his word, Craig came over at ten of seven, paid off his tab and the two met Ron at the Bent Elbow for dinner. The three waltzed into the San Juan just before eight. Bryson met them before Chris got halfway to the bar.

"What are you doing here?"

"Going to work."

"The hell you are, you're fired."

Chris was caught off guard, but not totally surprised.

"Well, good luck Bob."

Chris started to find a corner of the bar to get a beer, but Bryson blocked him.

"And, you're not drinking here, either, ever. Oh, and neither are your friends." He pointed directly at Craig and Ron.

"You know what, Bryson? I can get another job. You're always going to be an asshole."

Chris waved his buddies onward to Handlebars, Craig was so pissed off that spittle was dripping from his lips. Ron had no expression other than an intense frown that refused to go away.

"He can't throw us out," Craig yelled as they walked up the street. The spittle was getting worse.

"He just did and he owns the place, so piss on him. We can still drink anywhere else in town."

They proceeded to pound beers at Handlebars, then shots at the Miners Tavern. By one a.m., Chris was so loaded that he didn't care about anything and actually had to be helped over to his friend Dave's house.

But Craig and Ron had taken great exception to being thrown out. They worked when they wanted to, played where they wanted to and were used to having the freedom to come and go as they pleased; drink and relax where they pleased.

At two thirty a.m. that evening, having worked up a good case of indignation, they decided to get even.

"We'll teach that son of a bitch." Craig pushed his friend in misdirected anger.

"And show him who really runs this town." Ron added.

They bundled up some dynamite, climbed up to the second story roof of the San Juan, set the dynamite and lit the fuse. After scurrying down the escape ladder in the back, laughing hysterically, they just managed to get away from the building as the explosion tore off the back half of the roof, leaving a crater half the size of a baseball diamond. By sheer luck, no one was killed.

By eight a.m. the next morning, ATF agents had arrived in the village out of Denver. When the distress call came in, the agents left immediately and at high speed, drove the four hundred plus miles in a little over six hours. Unauthorized use of high explosives was under the jurisdiction of ATF and no one took such infractions lightly. Within hours, both Craig and Ron, quite hung-over, were taken into custody.

When the ATF Agents found out Chris had been with them, they determined where he was and decided to interview him. An agent came to Rich's house around noon with Marvin, his gun drawn when he came to the screen door. Chris was still asleep on the couch, but Bezo met the Agent at the other side of the screen. Face to face with the wolf dog, who was growling rather ferociously just beyond the thin mesh, the agent slowly put his gun in his holster.

"Guess he's not in, right now." He said to Marvin.

"We might best catch him later on," Marvin added.

Around two p.m. Chris awoke, his head pounding and he went outside for some fresh air where two agents waited in a black SUV. He had no idea who they were or what the decal on the Blazer stood for or what they were doing there. They waved him over and Chris cautioned Bezo to stay in the house for the short time.

He went over as bidden and they motioned for him to get in the car. They explained to him what had happened and then concluded.

"Chris, we know you didn't have anything to do with it, we just wanted to hear what you had to say about what led up to it."

Chris explained what had happened on his end.

"I got really drunk. Rob had fired me at the San Juan because they promised me I could go see the Belly Dancers at the Great Imperial Hotel and an hour and a half after he said I could go, I finally got pissed and left anyway. He told me I was fired when I went to work last night, so I went down to my other bar with Craig and Ron and we got smashed. We'd been thrown out of the San Juan by Rob. I thought it was funny, what a jerk the guy was. We went to two other places and I ended up getting walked home by Rich. That's all I remember until now. I guess Craig and Ron didn't think it was funny."

"There's nothing funny about blowing a hole in a residence with dynamite. It was a miracle nobody got killed."

The other agent looked at Chris and added. "That's all, Chris. Like the man said, we know you didn't do anything, but we may need to talk to you later on so don't leave the State."

Chris was visibly shaken after the meeting. He grabbed Bezo, went back to camp and prepped his backpack for a long week out. He left the van with Buck and told George at Handlebars he was going away for a few days to sort things out.   He would go see some of the rest of Colorado.

The next morning, Chris got out of the tent, put on the backpack and walked out with Bezo to the edge of town at the Wye of Route 550.   It started to rain, a little at first, and then gained speed. They were getting very wet.   He stuck out his thumb.

About twenty minutes later, a station wagon pulled over and a middle age woman rolled down the window.   Her husband sat compliantly behind the steering wheel.

She smiled at Chris.   "I felt sorry for the dog."

*

Chris sat in the large oak chair adjacent to the circular table near the door and the black ore car.   He had just put a fire in the converted tram and opened the door to let the smoke out and the fresh air in.   The bar was quiet, as it always was, when it first opened.

He liked the silence in the place, the full of the day ahead of him.   In some ways, it was like a microcosm of life; peaceful and quiet in the beginning, like now when the warmth of the sun inched through the large double doors of the Tavern, chasing off the cold, sifting breeze that tugged at his collar, forcing him to back up closer to the tram and the crackle and smoke of the fire.   Then, passengers from the train would drift in, some to look oddly at the place, just to see what it was, and some would come in for lunch.   Around noon, it would get extremely busy and then lighten up late in the afternoon.   The happy hour crowd would show up a little after four and the band would set up intermittently through the afternoon and finish up before they started at nine.   Then the dance, the party, that would last for hours, the place rocking and rolling, the timbers shaking from the ferocity of the dancing.   Then it would quiet down, the last of the determined pushed out the door.   He'd clean up, stack up the chairs, then sit for a minute and smoke a doobie. It would be quiet again, peaceful and serene, but full with the history of a complete day, a huge slice of life having been taken in, enjoyed by so many and lodged in memory. It was full circle.

He had been back a week from his hitchhiking adventure that included Crested Butte, Steamboat, Vail and Aspen. He got a great dinner at the Hotel Jerome and a four hour hike along I-70 through the Palisades. For every high, there was a low. He was glad to be back in Silverton. George was glad to have him back, too, because now he could have Chris for two shifts. In a town with but six or seven real bartenders, being the best didn't take a mixology degree.

Chris added a log to the fire in the Tram. In the distance, he could hear the sounds of horses making their way up the streets. He cocked his head back and tilted the chair to catch a glimpse of Mountain Lyons and two of his friends on horseback, dragging along five pack horses for the trek up to their claims in the canyons east of town. This was a shot in time, that a hundred years later, wild cat miners would still go off like this for four and five days, then come back with what they hoped would be sacks full of huge chunks of gold and silver. Of course, they would end up here at Handlebars towards the end of next week and they would get incredibly drunk and he would have a hard time not being a part of it. It was living in a myth, a time that, even now, seemed legendary. He loved this place.

Soon, the first arrivals would come, but Jack the cook would have to handle that today. He had to go over to the Sheriff's office. This was an unpleasant duty of tremendous proportions. It all had to do with the fight two and a half weeks ago and probably the explosion a few days later. He knew Floyd Martinson would not be a happy man.

As he entered the small two room office nestled in the county courthouse at the end of Greene Street, he was hearing the end of Floyd's oratory on the matter, and he had guessed right, he was not a happy man.

"So, what am I going to do with you guys, huh?" Floyd waved at Chris to come in and the bartender obligingly walked past Shirley, the secretary and dispatcher, to the lawman's private office. He could see Gregg, Tom and the two others, sitting on a bench and two chairs as they tried to pay attention and care.

"You still think this is a mining camp. You think nothing has changed here in a hundred years and it's okay to beat the shit out of somebody anytime it suits you.   And then, we have the bombing by Craig and Ron on top of everything else. Well, I'm here to tell you that none of this here is alright.   I know there aren't any charges here facing you guys, although I could write you up for disturbing the peace.   I won't, but, you guys have got to get it through your thick heads that this crap can't go on here anymore.   By now, the Durango Herald has picked up the story from the Silverton Standard & Miner and everybody knows what happened.   How's all this going to look for the rest of our tourist season, huh?   We got two, three thousand people a day coming in here and they want to come to a respectable place with the flavor of the old west, not assault and battery, explosions, prejudice, some asshole ruining their evening, and God knows what all.   Now get the hell out of here before I change my mind."

The four men didn't let the furniture get any warmer and left with a lot of yes sir coming out of their mouths. The Sheriff turned his gaze on the long haired young man in front of him.

"You got anything to add?"

"No sir, just coming over like you asked."

"Look, Chris, you seem like a nice enough young fella. This is a good town, but you can't do what you did either. Now, I know Marvin's a bit of a putz sometimes, but you should've waited for me to handle it.   Besides, it could have gone bad for you and that would have just made it worse. You've also had the poor intuition to pick some friends who could have gotten you into some real trouble'

"Yes sir."

"I hear you're leaving soon.   When are you going?"

"In another couple of weeks, when the season's over. I'd like to stay, but, well, with the summer season gone, the traffic's getting low and I don't think I'll be working in the mines."

"Yup. I know. You people come and go. Sometimes you come back, most times you don't. Well, good luck to you and Chris," He cut back on his authoritative manner for a moment, "...And thanks."

*

No one paid any attention to the Chevy Blazer as it rolled up Greene Street in Silverton. Even if anyone had been up that early to walk the main drag, they wouldn't have taken any notice. Four wheelers, many of them rentals, commonly came through the town to take the Alpine loop up through Eureka, Animas Forks and on to Lake City or to pull up into the mountains along the way to take off from trailheads. Hunters or wild cat miners often drove the vehicles deep into the cavernous valleys that lay outside of town. There, one could disappear for days or forever in the San Juan National Forest, a wilderness that extended virtually a hundred miles in any direction.

The passengers appeared no different than any others; Three men with the trappings of typical outdoor adventurers, save one distinct item, the cargo in the back of the off road vehicle.

The Blazer headed northeast out of the village, past the ghost town of Howardsville, then turned right up through Cunningham Gulch. They passed sheep grazing in the alpine meadows, the last of the season's abundance, then worked their way up the canyon wall to the back end of the gulch. The vehicle stopped in a casting of dust at the end of the beaten road and at the beginning of a slightly worn path that led up to the mountainous plateau that held the Highland Mary Lakes.

The driver, a medium built, gruff individual with an intense disposition, exited the vehicle and wiped his receding hairline with the red bandana he pulled from his faded jeans.

"Get the son-of-bitch out," He barked to the two men

35

who accompanied him.

The lanky fellow complied with due haste and cranked the rear door window down, pulling the tail gate open. The shorter of the two held back, but hoisted his .306 into position.

"C'mon, c'mon," The driver continued, "Get him out of the bag and let's get moving."

"Right, Boss."

The lanky fellow tugged at the huge canvas duffel and with great difficulty, extracted the itinerant migrant worker from his confinement. The shorter man leveled the rifle and motioned to the manacled prisoner to move on up the pathway.

"Get on it, Senor, move your ass."

"Lock it up, Luke," the leader gestured, "and let's get up to the mine before some damn hikers show up."

There was little real fear of that, though. The tourist season was over and the snow would show up any day now. The time between the end of summer and the advent of the ski season provided a pause for the community that lived on tourism and government jobs. There would be little traffic in the hinterlands.

The foursome slowly made their way up the trail that was already being reclaimed by nature. By the time they had ascended the fifteen hundred feet to the mine's entrance, the morning mist had lifted off the peaks and the snow pack of the late fall was clearly visible on the crests of the mammoth range. It would give one cause to stop and sense the natural beauty that only God's hand could have crafted, the shimmering peaks reflecting the early morning sun as it fought to rise above the passes of the caps that hid it, the sounds of the freshets cascading off the canyon wall, and the crisp air stimulating the lungs with that unexplainable freshness that could only be found there.

Yet, there was no such pause. The three men were but of one mind, one purpose and they set to it without regard for the natural order. The driver motioned for the rifleman to push the poor man into the mine's gaping entrance. The mestizo, a farm hand out of Bayfield, could not budge. He was terrified. What had he done? He could not understand it.

He had been sitting in a Durango bar the night before and now he was about to be shoved down a mine shaft or worse. He could not bear it and broke when the short man with the rifle was distracted by a large animal in the near distance.

He ran feverishly, clambering over rocks and the short scrub trees that barely held below the timberline. It was a great difficulty for his hands were still cuffed and his legs cramped from the long ride in the back of the car.

"Don't let him get away, Luke." The leader yelled at the tall fellow.

Luke started up the path behind his charge, but the crack of the rifle behind him stopped him in his tracks. Up ahead, the fugitive turned hauntingly, stunned and torn through the upper right torso.

"Mia," He cried, "No maas."

A second shot ripped through his right clavicle and he fell into the snow, the blood from the wounds coating the white covered ground and rocks around him. By the time Luke was upon him, he had given up the ghost, his last faint cries for his lost love muffled by the depths of his agony.

"God damn it, Jake, You screwed it all up. What the hell'd you do that for?"

"Got em pretty good, huh, Boss? He'd a been gittin away for sure if he'd got up over that ridge there."

"Getting away from what? There's fifty square miles of nothing up there. Christ, Jake, we could have tracked him easy enough. Look at this mess." He paused and thought for a minute. "This was not the idea at all. We were going to leave him in a mine shaft, so he got the message to get out of the San Juans for good, not kill him. Damn. Shit. Well, you shot him and you have to clean it up. Get Luke and drag the body into the mine, stick him deep in one of the unworked shafts in there, then get back out here and take care of this. Damn it, you clods, of all the stupid ass things to do."

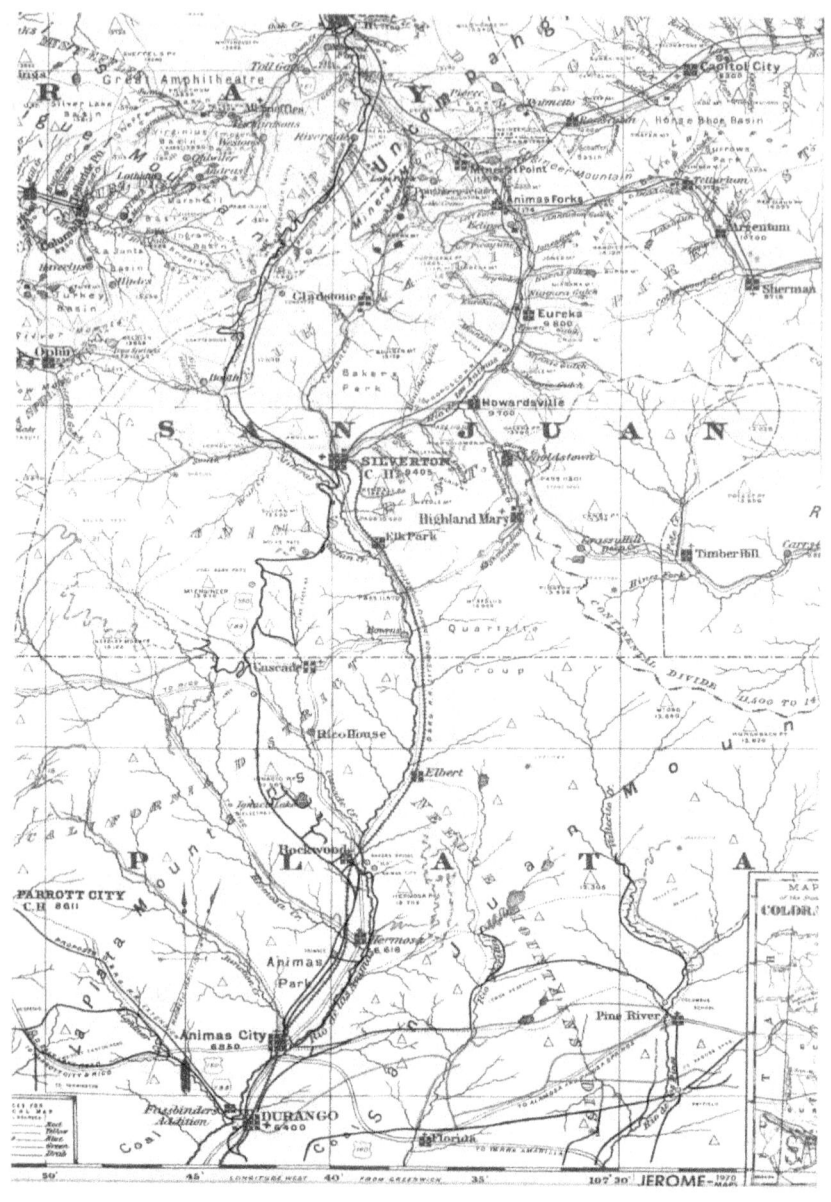

38

CHAPTER TWO

Visions

Craig Carpenter and Ron Aylesworth blew up a bar together. They were arrested together. They were sentenced together. They were sent to the prison in Canon City for seven and a half years together and when their time was done, they were released together. Production of gold and silver in the San Juans was over. Having no skills other than those of the Hardrock miner, they soon migrated to Vegas, thinking that with all the de-construction of outdated establishments underway, they could find work with a demolitions outfit.

It was a reasonable thought process, however, they soon learned that the ability to blow up things, place dynamite in pre drilled holes, or deftly make trout swim belly up in a mountain lake had no place in modern demolition. Occasionally, an odd job would come up where a couple of ex-cons who had such skills could be put to work, but the risk was tangible and neither particularly cared to go back to jail.

Ron, however, felt they had an ace in the hole. They had met a fuck up by the name of Luke in the LaPlata County jail in Durango serving the initial part of their sentence. Luke had worked for Brian, a real estate agent and developer. He was busted on a petty theft and then a felony drug charge. Luke had let the cat out of the bag that Brian had hired him and a friend to hijack an itinerant worker in attempts to implicate the whole of the wildcat miners in San Juan County. The job had gone bad and the migrant was killed. He also had a huge distaste for Brian, a man he called greedy, balding, ugly and fat, not necessarily in that order. He made it sound like Brian would be easy pickings.

Six weeks behind in rent in the one bedroom apartment they shared at the Mason Apartments on the southeast side of the city, Ron decided that a little extortion might ease the financial pain of little work and accumulating debt. The two found the address of the real estate agency and sent a certified letter to Brian Deming, Broker Associate and now President of Western Slope Development.

Brian Deming was a former football scholarship player at Colorado State. At six foot, two twenty, his was a good size for a college linebacker, but way too small to ever play in the pros. Moreover, his memory of his playing ability was much greater than the reality of it. He graduated with a BS in Business Administration at the tail end of the seventies recession and had no prospects for any job in the state, let alone the front range. He enlisted in the Army.

His three year term familiarized him with computers and specifically purchasing and requisition. He was good at it and was promoted several times, reaching the grade of Master Sergeant. Brian was in good shape when he left, but it was true that in the following years of building up a real estate business back in Durango, he had failed to keep any kind of regimen and had become a bit slovenly. A couple of weeks of required camp in the summer as a reservist would set him on the right course for a while, but he would soon revert to his old bad habits.

However, his unit was called up for active duty for the Gulf War. It was an inauspicious time for this to happen, as Brian had just entered into a new partnership and was starting a different track in his career. But, within a month, Brian was back into playing shape. He had toughened up considerably and led a squad of mobile infantry in support of a tank unit that made its way, inexorably, into Baghdad. Brian found that killing an enemy that was easily detestable to him was a rather fulfilling kind of activity. He understood that everyone always thought that the other guy would get it, but he also firmly believed it, and went about the work in front of him methodically without fear for his own safety.

He had only been home three weeks from his tour when the letter from Craig and Ron arrived. Ron could not have been more mistaken about Brian being easy pickings.

The demand letter wanted ten thousand dollars of hush money. Brian was to contact them at a specified time at a pay phone outside of Vegas. Arrangements would then be made. In the interim, Brian did his homework. He traced the possible sources of this problem back to Luke, and then confirmed the identity of cellmates at the time. Luke's big mouth and loose lips had been taken care of years before in a spectacular car crash outside of Durango.   But, Brian had not anticipated this kind of problem.

Further study also connected the two ex-cons with several others who were wildcat miners back in the day and Brian saw they were the very same he had tried to tarnish almost eight years before.

These men were dangerous and he could not have them following his footsteps into his new future.   He would deal with them straight up.

He made the call at the anointed time.

"Yeah, I'll have the money, but I won't meet you in Vegas.   You come half way."

"Agreed, but no tricks and you come alone." Ron answered.

"I wouldn't think of doing it any other way."

They arranged to meet in Tropic, Utah, just inside the Bryce Canyon National Park.   Brian's company had developed a lodge complex that was near completion and had just been sold to another outfit.   Brian's construction company still had equipment there and it was an ideal spot, close to the halfway point, and perfect for Brian's needs.

They met two days later in the late afternoon.   At an abandoned parking lot of the engineer's trailer office, a ten by forty converted mobile trailer, the threesome converged to conduct the business.   Craig was still an imposing figure, but heavier than his youth.   He carried a forty five in his waist. Ron looked almost the same as he did years earlier and he held a thirty eight, pointed directly at Brian.

Brian did not look like the person they expected to see. He looked like a pro wrestler, his muscled frame fit snuggly in a blue T shirt and carpenter jeans.   He carried a black brief case as instructed. They approached cautiously.

"I've got it all here," Brian nodded to the case.

"It better be."   Craig answered back.

"Are you sure you want to do this?" He asked them.

"Right on." Ron waved his pistol at him.

"And I can be assured I won't hear from you again?"

"Oh, yeah."

"Okay, then."

Brian feinted a toss of the case to Craig, which caused Craig to momentarily raise his hands, then threw it to Ron, who tried to catch it with his gun still in his hand. As Brian did so, his right hand slid down the side of his carpenter pants where he pulled out his palm sized twenty two and put two shots in Craig's chest before the big man could pull his forty five passed his belt. Ron tried to get the case out of his hands and almost got the thirty eight in line when Brian's next shot went straight through his skull and another followed in the neck.

Both of the miners were on the ground in the last throes of life when Brian put a bullet in the side of each of their heads, execution style.

It took Brian two hours to bury the bodies with a backhoe behind the make shift office and drag the car out to the pit, where he heaped tons of fill over the beat up Dodge the two men had come in.

This would be the end of this threat, but there was no doubt in Brian's mind that the others of that incestuous group could be a problem for him in the future. He would make sure that no situation like this would ever again come to pass.

*

Elaine Eberhardt took great pains to prepare herself for the clambake. It wasn't that she didn't look forward to it, not at all, but rather that she was taking her sweet time getting ready. She could go and actually have a good time there, but she really only did it for Chris and for his family. If she could delay and arrive fashionably an hour late, well, that was one less hour she had to be there and one more good hour she could stay at home. Besides, she had to look just so and it took time to pretty up.

Chris waited impatiently outside, checking the oil in the

car, then the other fluids; anything to keep him from going back in the house and killing that woman. She absolutely, positively drove him nuts and he would have thought that after fifteen years of marriage, he would have gotten used to the constant procrastination, the never ending attempts to jerk his chain.

When she finally appeared, he tried not to let on how irate he was about being late for his father's annual party. It wouldn't do any good and it would only set up a bad tone for the rest of the day. In some respects, he was a fully trained husband who had learned when to leave it alone.

The whole family was there when they pulled in, most of them hanging around the large in-ground pool or by the outside kitchen and brick poolside grill. The old man had set up a bar on the patio near the grill to the back of the pool and, of course, that was where Chris's best friend, Massimo Sylvestro Salustri, leaned in deep conversation with Chris's brother in law, Jim.

Elaine went into the house with the dish to pass and as she went, he lugged the two lawn chairs out to the patio. Chris knew she would be inside awhile. She would get caught up with his sister and it looked like the old man was inside hovering around in the kitchen. Still steaming from the late arrival, he headed directly to the bar.

"Jim, grab me a beer."

"One barley pop for Mr. Congeniality."

"Oh, up yours. I can't wait for you and Sandy to get married so you, too, can enjoy all this wedded bliss. Hey Maxie, glad you could make it." He shook his friend's hand heartily.

"I'll drink your dad's beer any time. He always gets good beer."

"Yeah, not like that A-1 crap we used to buy by the case out in Boulder."

"Or the fifty five gallon drums of plastic 'Magnat' wine. Jeez, we used to drink some awful stuff," Max added.

Jim stood, somewhat agitated, at the side of the little service bar, patiently waiting for the opening bull to pass.

"So, what was it that you wanted to talk to me about?"

43

"Oh, yeah, nothing really, I guess, just a decision. Maxie, you might be interested in this, too. I've decided to go back to Colorado for a couple of weeks in July."

"Family vacation?" Max seemed confused at the proposition.

"No, Elaine isn't interested at all. I've brought it up every year and she doesn't seem to care about it. I made the statement point blank last week that I was going, that I took the time off and she still isn't interested, so, I said 'It's been eleven years and every year I say I'm going back and something happens and I don't. Well, this year I'm just going.'"

"That doesn't sound like your old lady."

"Look, Jim, I know it doesn't either, but she really doesn't care about this and apparently, she thinks I'm not going to do it. You remember how it is out there, Max. I don't have to explain it. God, I still have dreams about the place. I'm flying around out there, like and Eagle soaring on the thermals, the mountains underneath. Hell, I even think I can smell the air in my sleep."

"Okay, so when do you plan on going?" Max asked

"First two weeks of July. Look, you know you guys ought to go with me. When are we going to get a chance like this again?"

"I'm in." Max added

"I'll check my schedule," Jim laughed, "I don't think I have anything heavy scheduled for then."

"Great, I'll get the atlas out of the car, show you what I've got in mind."

Chris went to the car and by the time he had returned, Elaine, Sandy and his sister had joined his brother and his friend.

"Maps again, Chris?" Elaine laughed. "All winter long, it's maps, maps and more maps. What now?"

"Just showing the menfolk here about the Colorado thing."

"That again," She cast a disdainful look upon her spouse, "I thought we were through with that."

Sensing the possibility of a stressful situation, Chris's

44

sister immediately excused herself.   The domino effect was almost instantaneous.   Jim and Sandy followed June and Max deftly exited to the backside of the pool to another group.

Chris paused for a moment, collecting himself.

"Look, honey, you know I'm not through with this; I'll never be through with this.   It's in my blood."

"Why aren't you taking me?"

"You've told me time and again that you didn't want to, that you don't like the high mountain passes at all.   In fact, you're terrified of them.   Honey, you know I'm determined to go.   I've gone ahead and planned it out and it looks like Jim and Max want to go.   That would be great for me.   You know I'm serious, so you have to decide once and for all, Do you want to go with me or not?"

"No, I don't want to go, but it pisses me off that you'll go without me."

"I'm sorry you feel that way, but I'm not going to be right unless I do.   There's no reason to be pissed off about it, it's just the way it is."

"And this is just the way this is," She gave him the finger so no one could see it and lurched off in a huff to the grill.

Yes, that **was** the way it was; a difficult marriage and by the looks of it, not getting any better any time soon.   Chris slumped back into a lounge chair to collect himself.   It seemed so easy for her.   She could just get mad, get so angry at him so quickly, then she'd be over it, like it never happened.   He couldn't do that.   He couldn't let the anger go away.   He was stuck with it.   It would smolder in him and as much as he wanted to let it go, it would still be there, waiting to rear its ugly head at any moment.

When he was younger, he used to run away, off to a bar somewhere and get drunk with some good time buddies. It was a world he was certainly comfortable with in his youth, but now, in his early middle age, it didn't seem to fit too well. He remembered one argument, not long ago, when he'd taken off afterwards, determined to get drunk and had gotten as far as the end of the road.   It dawned on him that he really had no place to go.   It was four o'clock on a Saturday afternoon and he was going to go get drunk and then what? Do any number of things he shouldn't that would only make it worse? Or perhaps, just go out and have a couple of beers and come back? He'd turned around and gone back to the house and confronted Elaine and in a half laugh said, "from now on, when I get pissed off at you, I'll be out in the camper." That did make more sense, but it still didn't resolve the problem of anger begetting anger.

He had a sense of helplessness about it all and in the end, swept it under this huge emotional rug, to be dealt with later, if ever. He choked down the last of his first can of beer, pushing it past the knot in his neck that his anxiety caused him. He wouldn't let it bother him, he'd just have to make a good day of it. Fortunately, the cooler was right next to him and an immediate, friendly solution was right at hand.

*

David Deeds looked out over the horizon of the shore line of his new island paradise. Every wave of the ocean tossed more cobbles up on to the rock strewn beach of the west side of the peninsula that jutted out to the North, the rattling sounds complementing the soft foamy murmur of the evaporating surf on the blackened sand. Down the dirt road that led away from the beach lay the burgeoning village of Praia, on the smaller island of two that comprised Graciosa, the old village of Praia lay at the optimal point of a perfect harbor. Praia was a would be resort town of peasant shacks and one mediocre hotel at the outskirts of the village. That could stay, he thought. His workers would need a place to live while they built the initial compound and the few villagers should take it well; the promise of work and a better financial future would come true. Of course, they would all have to be moved out later on as the plans fulfilled themselves.

The one and a half billion dollar package was a huge

amount of resource to part with to buy the whole of the small island, the commercial port facility, the rights to the entire village of Praia, and concessions at the airport north of Santa Cruz on the big island to build and solely use his own runway, but this was not simply some idle real estate venture. What he had bought, what he had required, was complete freedom. Originally, he had hoped to obtain something off the Baja, closer to the states, but the incessant drug running and violence all up and down the coast made that an impossibility.

Instead, Graciosa was the perfect second choice. It set in the northeastern arm of the Acorean archipelago, an Island chain in the middle of the Atlantic Ocean, a thousand miles west of Lisbon, Portugal and over two thousand miles east of the closest point in North America. The nine islands proper were part of Portugal, but were collectively an autonomous regional government. They were isolated but still had daily flight service out of Lisbon and Boston. They were the perfect blend of isolation and the ability to transport people and equipment while incorporating a solid working infrastructure and a permissive regulatory system. David Deeds needed to move without interruption or inquiry, so, in essence, he had purchased a small country. The President of Portugal had bought into it immediately. The money, the computers, the expertise he obtained to let this little known and less traveled Acorean Island go had been a marvelous exchange from his point of view. Other than the quaint fishing villages, the two islands of Graciosa were primarily consumed by national parks, wildlife refuges, conservancies, and a slow growing eco-tourism industry. It was the same on the other Islands in the archipelago as well. Only Sao Miguel's Punta Delgada could be could be considered an urban area; and that Island sat a good hundred and eighty miles to the south of Graciosa. On the Ilehu de Praia, the small island; a park had been placed there by the previous administration because they essentially didn't know what else to do with it. It was too far away to effectively develop commercially and even as a park with the small village adjacent to it, few travelers ever called upon its' shores. Those that dared to risk the remoteness and traveled there were forced to stay in the Plaza Esperenza in Praia and rarely thought of returning.

After feigned outrage at the possibility of environmental destruction, the Acorean Parliament approved the purchase.   As the Azores were an autonomous governing region within the Republic of Portugal and their legislature had to have final approval, it was no surprise that in the smoke-filled back rooms they rejoiced at having robbed the imperialist fools of some much wealth and rid themselves of a nine mile long stretch of rock; a jungle filled and desolate Ilehu that featured clusters of sandstone and hardened lava striated cliffs, a deep valley, and a high ridge that held the Franciscan Caldera.   This remote little island sat off the northern tip of the big island of Graciosa, the most north central of the Acorean chain.

To be sure, the island offered too little for one who sought traditional Atlantic beauty.   But that was not what David Deeds was looking for.   He wanted a corporate base, free from intervention and this place was just exactly what he wanted; relative geographical seclusion, one hundred miles from the next island, one thousand from the European coast, as well as secure access.   The location also protected the island from the ravages of the ocean.   The three other major islands lay south and west, providing a break against the gulf stream and providing the kind of calm, warming seas necessary to his aspirations. The local population would be tremendously loyal and would obscure his work.   He would see to that, but he would do it right.

This was the kind of power he had and although he didn't wield it unwisely, he was determined to get what he wanted and this island chain was a huge part of his dream.

"Geoff.   Bring up those topo maps, would you?"

The engineer shuffled through the rocks and sand back to the launch and returned as bid, three scrolls under his arm.

"What did you say earlier about the arable land?   I couldn't hear it over the motor."

"Well sir, from what I gathered we initially thought that less than fifteen percent could be used, but as I studied these maps, there would seem to be a huge midsection between those two ridges beyond there, that with proper equipment, we could bring it up to twenty, twenty five percent."

"We'll need some of that for the housing. That's my first priority. I've got to have that in the interior. At least that's what Brian tells me. I wish he'd have come in off the yacht today," Deeds looked off to the deep water of the bay where his two hundred and sixty four foot yacht, Moontracer, lay at anchor, "but he's still working up the real estate end of it. Damn, that reminds me, we have to go to the hotel. Geoff, bring the jeep off the launch and have Matthews come along. Pack up the bags, too. I want to do a stay over."

The man did as bid, while Deeds sat on a large rock that held a good view of the bay and the town from the cliffs. This would be a perfect spot for a hiking trail, someday, he thought. There was so much he could do with the place. But, buying the lands from Portugal was only one element of the process. It didn't clear the way to take these people's homes and businesses. He could use the Portuguese form of eminent domain and run them off and he might have to do that in some cases, but for the most part, he would buy them out or build them up to support his vision. He needed their loyalty and he needed them to develop a decent environment for his own people. It would need to be a symbiotic relationship if the grand plan were to ever work, and he needed time for that.

The hotel was first on the agenda. The three men wheeled the new Wrangler down the mud and rock cobbled streets to the three story building. David Deeds led them through the alcove to the front desk, a small affair aside an open room with two round tables and assorted chairs. The place beckoned back to Hemingway's time. It had an air of the mysterious, the avant-garde, but mostly an atmosphere of a time gone by, when expeditions out in to these remote islands were common.

The dining room, which provided up to thirty with included meals, set off from the lobby across the hall. The walls were painted of nautical scenes depicting exploration and the first settlement of the islands. The paint was peeling and the spackle falling from the cracked plaster and lath construction.   No doubt, it was grand in its day, but these days, most excursions were done almost completely off shore, the ships themselves providing all the necessities for any tourists or scientific teams with all the comforts of home and the advanced technological needs.

"Hello, Hello," Geoff called out to the sleeping manager behind the partition.   The man was sprawled out on a couch while a nonsensical game show blared out of a twenty five year old television. The man stirred, but not appreciably.

"Swear at him in Portuguese," David suggested.

"All I know of Portuguese is enough to live on, Sir, like for beer and sandwiches."

"Then pound on the desk and repeat that.   On the other hand Matthews speaks a little doesn't he?   Jesus, I really didn't give this much thought, here, did I?   Brian's PA is the fluent linguist in the bunch. Well, we'll do what we can until he gets here.   Ask Gary to come in and deal with this lout."

By now the owner had responded slightly to the din and was upright, rubbing his bloodshot eyes.   By the time Matthews arrived from the Jeep outside, the owner could entertain a conversation and did so earnestly, although he couldn't understand why they wanted eggs and beer so early in the morning.   Deeds asked Matthews to ask him how much.   The man responded with his suggested room rate for tourists, for which he fully expected to bargain down to his real price.   When Matthews repeated the question, mixing his carefully chosen words with hand gestures, the man soon understood that they were asking how much for the hotel. This was not a difficult decision for him to make; to go from doing nothing to doing nothing with money, but he had some difficulty determining an irrational price to give them.

"Two hundred thousand American dollars," he offered in his best broken English.   He awaited the counter offer that would surely come, but after a pregnant silence, soon understood that there would be no counter offer.   Deeds instructed Matthews to secure his personal operating account book, then turned to the rather amazed fellow and indicated that it was a done deal.   Deeds took the loose leaf ledger and scrawled his name across the check, then tore it off judiciously and handed it to the man.   As an afterthought, he pulled out a wad of one hundred dollar bills from his pocket and gave him a thousand dollars.

"Tell him to be out of here by tonight.   Have our ground crew brought in." Then with the excitement of a pumped up athlete, added, "and let's get started on this bad boy."

*

Crossing the deep of the Irish sea at night was almost suicidal, especially in the ten foot swells that surrounded the converted tug that had been deployed for this mission.   The hellish black, heavy cloud driven sky was exceeded only by the murky sea, each wave a pinnacle, a cap, a lid to the endless dark cauldron that set below them, churning with a tethered fury that could break loose at any minute.

Aboard the small, forty foot ship, the crew huddled inside, tentative and silently fearful.   There is no way to explain the helplessness that comes across a soul in the face of the true power of nature.   Those who favor extreme sport use the power, the skill of the being and place it directly in the path of the earth mother.   It is a contrived and controlled experience, born of ability and of the thrill.   There was no thrill here.   Nature scoffs at such folly; for to her, the elements that existed this night, were only but a taste of what could be, a minuscule surge of the immense power that could be unleashed at any moment.   This was what the crew feared, each of the five men who stared at the looming, white capped spires as they pushed relentlessly towards them.   If the seas got any rougher, this mission and their lives were in jeopardy.

The mission was straightforward enough for the radical activists, a search and destroy run to rid the sea of the ill-conceived oil deck situated in the Little Minch, the sea lane between Ireland and the west coast of England.   The deck was an ecological disaster in the making, a UNIOIL project that had been bullied through parliament. WorldGreen had not openly sanctioned this action, but did nothing to stop the associated splinter group from implementing it. For Joe Hackett, this was a crusade.

The team had purchased the weathered and sea beaten, converted tug from a commercial dry dock out of Londonderry. They made the minor repairs necessary to make it seaworthy for this mission alone; this was not an investment. They cruised northwest out past Barra Head, then harbored overnight in Hynish Bay on Tyree.

Once the oil deck's platform underpinnings were blown, they would not dare return by the same route, rather they would run forward further into the Minch and land on the eastern Irish coast, then scuttle the craft.

The engines churned, coughing at the strain of powering the boat further into the strait, catapulting the trawler across the caps and crests of the open sea until the vessel came under the leeward side of the Emerald Isle. Once deeper into the Minch, the cavernous swales flattened and the tumultuous waves chased at the stern of the boat, seemingly pushing it forward into the channel. The darkness hid any landmarks in the distance and the drilling platform would be cloaked in the sea lane were it not for the platform lighting that could now be seen flickering in the distance.

Now came the hard part, lowering the inflatable and crossing the strait with the C-4 explosives and mounting them on the deck supports. They had been assured that the work crews returned to shore each evening, such that their incursion would result in no loss of life. The strait was still swollen from the sea surge as Joe, Mack, and Devon shuttled the craft towards the mounted behemoth, uprooted from the channel like an alien smelter, an ominous silver hulk of metal, light and machinery. They fell silent as they neared it, each consumed with dread that this action represented to them, but filled with the greater dread of what the deck represented.

For Joe Hackett, the passage was interminable, but it gave him pause to think, about the audacity of this, and the path that led him here. In a sense, it wasn't a huge jump from anti-war activist to anti-corporate activist, from self-imposed asylum in Montreal to eco-terrorist on the Irish Seas, but it had taken him a long time to become comfortable with the radical left and the violent action that he felt was now necessary in this devolving society. In the new world order, corporations would be global masters, defining communities by whom they would hire and when, and in turn, defining our conflicts, much like the oil companies had done in Viet Nam and in the Persian Gulf. Perhaps, some of that was inescapable, but the destruction of the environment need not be and that, at least, was something he could hang his hat on. And this act was significant. It sent a clear message that they would not stand by and let it happen.

They approached the platform cautiously, then tied up on the nearest support. Devon taped the plastic explosive to the magnificent towered strut, then motioned to Mack to untether as Joe jerked the electric motor into gear. They repeated the steps at the other three corners, then added a massive pack to the drilling shaft for good measure.

"Get me the hell out of here," Devon yelled as they finished, "We've got less than twenty minutes before this thing blows."

Joe jerked the motor around and cranked it for all it was worth. The little motor strained to push the raft forth against the current, the whir of the electric now fully audible as it neared and echoed off the tug. They had barely gotten on board when the first explosion tore at the rig. It still stood. The second followed and it still held fast. But on the third, the huge frame slid and lurched to the side and the final two blasts tore the facility apart, the smoke, belching fire and steam rising high into the sky, illuminating the Minch for miles. This was no time to be spell bound by the site and Trevor Hagan, the helmsman, thrust the tug's engines to full speed. Hagan, an active IRA member, had no problem blowing up an English oil company's off shore rig, an act he considered patriotic at the least, but he was having a time catching his bearings, facing the tug into the darkening night in front of him while the unearthly flame and light from behind distorted his sight. He took his best readings and bearing, carefully watched the screen in front of him and guided the tug to the eastern shore of Ireland.

As they cautiously approached, Hagan backed off the engine, then motioned to the crew of four, who prepared the inflatable for its final leg.   Hagan hopped below decks, set the small, contained explosive and timer, then returned to the helm.   He locked the steering wheel in place with a "club", then set the engine to reverse.   Quickly, he joined the others and they set out on the raft for shore.   Minutes later, the tug's hull blew and the ship disappeared from sight in the pitch black night, barely visible from the distance as a rise of sea foam, a ripple of waves that escorted the inflatable's ride landward.

At shore, they slit the raft, folded the remains, weighted it with the motor and trudged along the shoreline until they reached the high cliffs Hagan knew awaited them. Back off the cliff's edge, where nary a countryman or traveler would wander, even on the most pleasant of hikes, they buried the craft and motor in the sandy, granular soil that held the thriving underbrush.

Now the crew of five followed a pathway along for about a mile, coming to a dirt road headed away from the coast.   Making the most of the night, they hiked without incident until the break of the morning sun when they pulled off into the fields to lay out their sleeping bags under some light forest cover.   At night, as preplanned, they would split up, then follow separate routes to shelter in the interior and coastal villages, eventually making their way back into Canada.

*

Alvarro Parros would turn seventeen in March.   He was finishing up his senior year at the high school in Villa Real, a long bus ride from his village.   He was a bright kid who had a future in front of him, if he could get to it.

It was a warm spring day when he got off the bus and shook off the dust as the bus pulled away.   There were five other kids that got off, too, and each of them went off in their separate directions. Alvarro worked his way up the path from the four corners to the small two room house he lived in. Hopefully, his father was still in town, or the next town, and his mother would be at the house and would be fine.

He missed his sister. She had been gone six years now, off to America to live with their aunt and uncle. His mother had seen to that. How she accomplished it, he never knew, but it was nothing short of a miracle in this village. He would like to follow her, but that didn't seem likely.

As he approached the house, he could hear a ruckus inside. He opened the door to find his father standing in the kitchen area with a long bladed knife, brandishing it at him with wave after wave of his arm. He was clearly drunk again and had come home early from his siesta to work out his aggressions yet one more time.

"Get the hell out of here," he snarled.

Alvarro could see his mother on the couch, bloodied and beaten; again. This time, she was almost lifeless. Barely a twitch came from her contorted frame.

He did as he was bid. He left the door open and went directly to the shed. Under a small canvas, he took out the old rolling block pin fire shotgun that had been his grandfather's. They used the old gun for hunting; or at least they used to when his old man had more sanity and he was a younger lad. He fumbled through the two shelves until he found three slugs for the gun. He loaded one and pocketed the other two. He knew he would only need one.

Alvarro returned to the house and pushed the front door further open. This would be the last time. He found his father standing over his mother, the knife still in his hand.

"Dad," he cried out.

His father turned and swore. Alvarro calmly leveled the gun and pulled the trigger. The blast to his father's chest blew him backwards over the couch. He would not get up.

Alvarro ran to his mother's side. She was still breathing. He ran to the neighbors to get help and soon, half the village was at the house. An ambulance would come from Villa Real; and the police. Alvarro would be placed in custody, but everyone in town knew the circumstances and anyone could see what had happened.

Still, some justice had to be served and once Alvarro's mother healed, he was released to her custody under certain conditions. Arrangements were made with the help of the relatives in the states, but he could not travel to America to be with the other side of his family. The crime prevented that.

However, tuition assistance was provided to send him to the University at Oporto where he would begin his studies, with the caveat that he be enrolled in the officers' studies program that would ensure his military service and automatic enlistment in the Federal Army. His punishment would be a mandatory service of six years in the army, a punishment he gladly accepted to be rid of his village.

Finally, his mother could have a free life, free from the bondage of that villain. He would make the best of his circumstances and study law. It was obvious to him that the double standards in their legal system were killing people like his mother every day and he vowed that, in the future, he would do something about it.

The killing was just beyond all measure, the sentence given him a blessing. He would remark later on that it was probably the best thing that ever happened to him; and, his mother.

*

The cinders from No. 473 blew out of its stack at each controlled burst of the engine. The power of the train was undeniable, but with nine passenger cars to haul and the steep grade of the Animas River basin to scale, she rarely exceeded fifteen miles an hour as it labored its' way along the river. As she rounded a bend, the angle of the engine was perfect for a voluminous spewing of smoke and ash upon the coach and open air cars behind. Chris caught a cinder in the eye.

"Shit."

"What?" Max followed.

"Got it in the eye. Jim, can you see this?"

Jim put down his beer and spread his brother in law's eyelid.   A trained paramedic, he was not without skills.

"Yeah, it's in the corner.   Hold still."   He took out a match, wet the end, then dabbed the moistened tab against the cinder and carefully plucked it out.

"Thanks, Bro.   Jesus, they weren't kidding about the soot."

"That's the last thing we need," Max groaned, "a blind, whining invalid on our hands."

"Especially when we have so much to do." Jim added.

That was an understatement.   Chris had attempted to pack in about three week's worth of adventure into six days. His motive was to do everything he didn't do eleven years before.   It was an impossible task.   The excursion on the Durango and Silverton Railroad was the first part of the journey.

They arrived in the hauntingly beautiful mining town midday, the second train out of the tourist mecca that Durango had become.   Chris led the trio to his old bar where they saddled up to the mahogany ridge.   The place hadn't changed much, except that it seemed like there were a hell of a lot more dead animals adorning the walls.   Actually, it was a bit disconcerting being viewed by all the stuffed fauna so unceremoniously draped over the restaurant's dining area.

Next to the threesome, an obviously inebriated man sat, hunched over, smoking heavily, propped up on the padded rim of the bar by both elbows.   Chris looked at him as his gaze drew up, bloodshot and reddened from his consumption.

"Hi.   I'm Rich, I'm the town drunk and the town musician."

"If that's civil service, I'm pissed."

"No really, man, I play at the Grand Imperial tomorrow," He sipped an iced whiskey with a water back, "I've been off and ah, drunk for three days."

"Uh-huh."

This was already too much information and the travelers were relieved when the drunk stumbled out the door.

"Christ, it's only 2:30 and the guy's loaded."   Jim

stated the obvious.

"Not like we ever did that," Max laughed.

"Yeah, maybe at Watkins Glen.

"Beer and Fruit Loops for breakfast. Yumm."

The three finished their lunch and headed over to the Livery. The signed on for a short, two-hour ride along the outskirts of the village; up off Anvil Mountain and towards the ghost town of Howardsville. As they rode the side of Anvil, the last train from Durango cleared the head of the canyon formed by the Animas as it left the 'park' and entered sight as it came into Silverton; it's shrill, unmistakable whistle echoing off the surrounding mountains.

Chris watched it turn by the station as it crossed the river into the village. He watched his brother in law and his friend up ahead of him, the horses loping at an easy gait through the alpine meadowland. The light mountain breeze tossed the white puffs of the meadow grasses heavenward and the sun cast its gentle heat on both rider and horse. He thrust out his arms by his side and tilted his head skyward.

'Lord, take me now.'

It had been a spiritual quest and finally, that became more real to him. It became a further reality on the trip to Mesa Verde. Among the cliff dwellings of the Anasazi, there was a sense of loss, a sense of magic and mystery. In the remains of the kivas, the trio could imagine the visions of the elders, hastened forth by the copious amounts of peyote ingested to bring them on. In an idyllic way, it seemed such a natural, almost necessary part of their life and the passage of time clearly indicated to each that there were, indeed, better ways to travel the path of life than that.

The last leg of the journey found them once again in Silverton; and not in the least to catch the fourth of July parade and the festivities that followed into the night. On the last day, the friends took a power walk out of the village, deeper into the valley. On the return, Chris motioned to Max and his brother in law to go on ahead. He turned up one of the many dirt side streets in the village and followed the numbered mail boxes until he came to a small trailer at the end of the street. He knocked on the door and Skip emerged, his gray hair fully invested, his tall trim figure slightly bowed and paunched from the eleven years distance and the hard life he had obviously endured in the mountain town.

"Skip, Chris Eberhardt. You remember me?"

"Yeah, sure," He studied the man he used know with obvious curiosity. "C'mon in. Want a beer?"

"No, no thanks." Skip took one for himself. "How are you doing? I know it sounds kind of corny, but I've been meaning to get back here all this time and I'm really sorry I didn't keep in touch."

His old friend nodded and got another beer and placed it in front of Chris, anyway.

"I'm doing Okay here, I guess. Worked at Standard Metals for a bit, till they closed. Got odd jobs here and there the last couple of years. Got three lots here. Guess I could retire off that. Yeah, I'm doing alright, and you?"

"Fine, but I don't get out here enough."

Skip got up, went to the refrigerator, sat back in an old reclining chair, popped the top off the second can and kicked back.

"It's not the same, though,"

"Yeah, I can see that. I knew the mines had closed and I guessed the town was in trouble. But the tourism still looks good."

"It's still not the same. That year that you and Buck were here, that and the next one, they were the best. The town was full of life."

"Best summer of my life. I still think about it."

"Well, up until you left, maybe. You heard about the murders, didn't you?"

"What murders? I didn't hear about any murder."

"Some Mexican. About a year and a half after you left. Some hikers found the body in a mine shaft. They tried to pin it on Gregg, Tom and those guys, but it didn't stick. Wasn't enough evidence." Skip chugged the rest of the can.

"No, I didn't hear a thing about it. It wasn't in any mail I got and I didn't subscribe to the paper after a year. I can't believe it."

"It's true. Those guys blew town after that. Of

course, they would've anyway, on account of the mines and the government.   And then, a few years later after Craig and Ron got out of jail, they were murdered out in Utah somewhere.   They said it was a mafia thing. "

"I never heard about that, either," and then under his breath, "there but for fortune, go I."

"It seemed too coincidental to me, even then, but three years after that, Gregg and Tom were found dead in Montana at the copper mines."

Chris nodded, "That would get my attention."

"Well, it got mine and my nephew just became the undersheriff here, so I've been kind of looking into it.   Did you know Buck went up there with them?"

"No, I lost track of him, too.   He came back east a few years back for a visit, but that's the last I heard of him."

"He got tired of resort work and went up to Montana to work at Lodges as a fishing guide.   I think he split time between mine work and guide work.   Nobody knows where he is."

"If there's anything I can do to help, Skip, let me know. Buck was my partner and a partner is a partner.   It sounds like you're doing what you can and I don't want to get in the way, but anything you need, just call me."

They talked awhile further, but Chris soon recognized they had little else left in common.   Time did that.   He remembered how they had partied together and he had seen how his friendships had changed over the years.   People grew and changed in different ways, at different rates.   And, everyone went in different directions. All the same, he admired his friend for his dedication.   Skip had made a life here where he could not and for some reason, that impressed him greatly.

And yet, he was so glad he had not chosen the same path.   His life was so totally different and had none of the drama that Skip was currently dealing with.   Still, Chris was a part of it, if only for the sake of past loyalties. These had been good friends at one time.

He could not help but be saddened by the news and the predicament in which Skip now found himself.   It was a damned hard life out here in the mountains. Anyone who worked there for any period of time could see how it wore on people. It was okay for young people, but as he got older, Chris understood how this kind isolation and the limited work would have strangled him. Still, Skip seemed to thrive here. He was a tough man in a rough place.

THREE

Politics

The large wooden doors opened to the spacious office nestled underground in the far reaches of the 'skunk works'. Jackie strode through with confidence and was led directly to Chester "Bud" McNaughten, CEO of the Rockland Group. Bud greeted her pleasantly, for her visit had been planned well in advance.   In fact, the meeting was more ceremonial than functional.   The minions had worked out the details over a six month period.

"May I offer you a drink, Ms. Guiterrez?"

She paused for a moment, taking in the luxurious, if not tightly structured environment.   Truly, this was a company still dominated by men.

"Yes, I think I might, if you have any decent single malt."

She would have preferred a chilled Chardonnay, but in this culture, that suggestion might have been perceived as a bit wimpy and she would not be perceived as anything less than she was, a power broker to be reckoned with.

"We have learned, Ms. Guiterrez, that our working world has to be very accommodating; to virtually all tastes and cultures.   But, I must admit, you do surprise me."

He walked behind the service bar, retrieved a crystal canister and poured the delicately bronzed bourbon into an elegant old fashioned glass.   He thought of handing it to her straight up, but dared not.

"Ice, perhaps?"

"Yes, if you please. Thank you."

This was a moment to savor and she relaxed into it. It was clearly a long way from home; a route that led through a Stanford MBA into a fledgling computer company in southern California.   As a brilliant minority professional, it hadn't taken her long to rise to the top of the cutting edge company.   At age thirty four, having fought and struggled her way out of poverty; having constantly faced obstruction based on race, gender, class and country, she had risen to Executive Vice President in charge of Corporate Resources. She **made** the big deals. Of course, she had to consult with David, and had to follow the corporate agenda, but she was the closer.

To sit here, sipping fine aged bourbon with the CEO of Rockland, about to consummate a nine hundred million dollar deal, well, that was heady stuff. And it wasn't just the money, it was the acquisition itself, the new prototype shuttle, the next wave into space. Now that was something.

"I assume you and the attorneys have gone over the entire proposal and specs. Are you empowered to complete the deal?" McNaughten ventured.

"Yes. If your CFO can give the transfer routing and account information, I'll punch out the remittance per the payment schedule. I just want your personal assurance that we will get what we want."

"You have it. The prototype will be half again bigger than the current model. That was one sticky item with DOD, I'll tell you, but your team certainly prevailed there."

Jackie was a little edgy on this point. Applying political pressure wasn't particularly her area of expertise. Brian handled that, and deftly. He had bulldogged Holmes and the rest of the Armed Forces Committee to support the change from the three-quarter variation originally designed by the Pentagon.

"I think, Bud,.....May I?" She crossed her legs in a knowingly flirtatious way, assured of his answer. Body language was one of the many tools she employed to attract attention. With men, it was too easy; like tossing a lure. She had the attributes. She had begrudgingly come to accept them. It was a ruthlessly competitive world and if it took a little sexual innuendo to capture attention long enough to connect with concept, process and implementation, then she was not above it. Men did it all the time, and usually, very badly.

"I think it was the investment, the technical contribution and the long term commitment that made it work. Washington wanted to privatize, but more importantly, wanted a working partner. We have our mission and they just wanted to progress to the next level as inexpensively as possible. With you guys on development and our long term relationship together, this was an excellent fit for everybody. Our question is, will we be able to get this thing out there in the next four years."

"Oh, I think we'll be ready. We've got most of the design work done, just to make sure we could do what you asked. I'm now convinced the mechanics will work as intended."

"Our contract points are very fine on this matter. You know that."

"We accept it."

"Alright, then."

She lifted her glass to his.

"Ching, ching. Let's get the CFO in here."

*

Chris Eberhardt enjoyed the local politics. He could. He was a civil servant who could detach himself from it, yet still be conspicuously involved. The functions of the body politic ranged from pounding the beat to the receptions, fund raisers, and hopefully to the celebration of victory. For his candidate and friend, Ron Beauchesne, the latter was all but assured. It would be his fourth term in the State Senate. This reception was little more than an acknowledgement of his fine work and another opportunity to raise some money for the campaign.

Elaine seemed to enjoy it, too. She like being involved in the community in some way, even though she was essentially a home body. This was an opportunity to meet and greet people in a splendid setting and the hotel had done a wonderful job in preparing for the party.

Chris worked his way to the bar amid the crowd of over a hundred supportive souls and returned in time to catch Ron and Elaine in conversation about Church, a commonality they shared.   Chris was still in his Zen search and organized religion was not exactly his cup of tea.   "Sunday Clubs", he called them, but only at home and then, the comment was not well received.

"It was really nice of James to lead us on this quest," Ron had referred to Chris and Elaine's son, who had driven the involvement of both of them in their renewed contact with the Catholic faith.   "If it hadn't been for him, I don't think I would have taken to it so well."

"We were very proud of him," Elaine added.

"Except now that he's in college, he's questioning everything, so God knows what he believes this week." Chris chipped in.

"How are you doing, Chris?   Is the new Governor treating you well?" Ron asked.

"So far, so good.   Of course, they haven't got to my level yet.   They did get rid of all the Commissioners, though."

"Yes, that comes with the territory.   I'll bet it surprised a lot of people though.   I'm sure most of them thought Eliot's successor could never lose."

"He really did lose touch with reality, especially upstate," Elaine added, "But Chris, you said you had civil service protection."

"As a fall back, yes, but as a Division Director, that's an appointment.   I can lose that and be blocked out.   You don't have any protection if they really want to get you."

"I'm afraid that's true, Elaine," Ron added, "but at least Chris doesn't have to run for office every two years. Speaking of which, I better go pump the flesh for a while.   I'll catch you two later."

As he left, a tall dark haired woman stopped the Senator and gave him a hug.   She talked briefly, then came over to Elaine.

"Hello Elaine," She said in a most pleasant voice.

Elaine was caught by surprise and hesitated for a moment.

"Ann?"

"Yes, I came in for the election.   A chance to catch up with the family."

"You look great.   What are you doing now?"

To Chris, the first statement was more than the usual obligatory greeting.   Ann looked better than great, she looked fabulous.   Her long dark hair cascaded to and around her shoulders, her face improved with age; the light brown eyes, dancing with speckles of green, her lightly emblazoned crows' feet accentuating the personality that had surely filled itself with laughter during the many years she had been away. She didn't look like she had added a pound since college, still thin and angular.   Ann was an acquaintance of Elaine's, but a good friend of Chris's sister, June, a delightful fact that Chris was enjoying fully as she had not yet recognized him.

He enjoyed observing the differences in the two women.   Elaine was a few years older, shorter, but exotic and fiery.   Her dark hair was curled and short, accentuating a lively face. She was cute as hell.   Ann was taller, soft spoken, but elegant. She had a smoldering quiet about her.   She had always been determined and driven.   She was classy.

"I'm still in Colorado, chasing ambulances."   Ann laughed and caught Chris's eye.

Elaine caught the look and apologized.

"I'm sorry, Ann, this is my husband, Chris."

"Chris," she repeated as she shook his hand, "you look familiar."

"I should, unless you've forgotten June altogether."

"Oh, my God."

"My fault, I didn't have a beard the last time I saw you and the hair's arguably quite a bit shorter, but what was that, almost fifteen years ago?"

"Not quite, I think.   You came with June to a UD football game, I remember.   You were out there for a while, too."

"Yes, on the western slope, in one of my visits back."

"So, what are you doing now?"

"Trapped in government, kinda like your brother."

"I always thought that was one of the more exciting parts of it.   For a lawyer, it's sort of the end game, in a way. Eventually, you want to create legislation and good public policy."

66

"I thought you were a Judge," Elaine inserted, trying not quite so delicately to reinstate herself in the conversation.

"I was, but the term ended and I didn't get re-elected so I'm back on the street, so to speak."

"Are you in town long?" Chris asked, realizing almost immediately that this was not a question he should have posed.

"Just another week, until after the election. My family will get tired of me being gone."

"So, you're married, then?" Elaine asked.

"Second time around. They say it's better."

Chris didn't say a word. Based on the look he got the last time, he decided he wouldn't venture forth on this. He could sense it was getting a bit awkward and was relieved when Ann excused herself.

"You should plan on coming over for dinner," Elaine offered as Ann took her leave.

Ann nodded, but Chris sensed this was an empty gesture by his wife and it was confirmed moments later as they finished the last of their drinks.

"I'm ready to go, if you are," Elaine said as she placed her glass on the nearby table.

There was no mistaking the intent and Chris simply agreed.

"I was going to talk to a couple of people, but I guess I can catch up with them later."

It wasn't until they got in the car that she let him have it.

"I saw the way you looked at her."

"What."

"Don't give me that stupid remark. Your eyes were all over her."

Chris had seen Elaine jealous over the years and it was not pretty, but he had a hard time with this, an innocent conversation. He knew he could, like any man, he supposed, respond to an attractive woman in a flirtatious way, but if he had, he was unconscious about it.

"Jesus, Elaine. She's an old friend, a friend of my sister. It would have been nice to catch up a little bit on her life."

"So, you're saying that I don't value her, or our own friendship? So, when did you take over anyway?"

"I give up. You win."

To Chris, that's what it boiled down to, winning. It wasn't that there was really an issue here. There probably wasn't an issue at all. It may have been something that happened months before, an argument, a slight, some thoughtless act on his part that he still didn't see that might be the root cause of all this. Some might call it the feminine mystique, but in his relationship, all he could see was anger directed at him for something. And the worst part was, there had to be a winner and a loser. If he did not acquiesce to losing at some point, it would bubble up into a heated argument and possibly into physical violence. All behind closed doors and all because she had to win. Yes, there were people like that out there. They should all have played on his jayvee basketball team, the one that lost every game. It would have taught them that winning isn't everything, that it's the game, the greater involvement of other people; that it was just fun and not a way of life. Having to win all the time must be a horrible burden, he thought, worse than losing.

He couldn't be Elaine and he couldn't imagine what lay behind it all. Sure, everyone felt insecure sometimes, but he didn't think that was it. And, he didn't think that played into the anger. It didn't make any sense. In fact, most of the time this relationship didn't make any sense and he wondered what he saw in it in the first place. Trouble was, he was beginning to forget what that was. It was easy to say they had been hot for each other when they were young, but you'd think that there would be some memory of the emotion, of the love that was supposed to be there, not just the lust of youth. It escaped him, and that alone scared him. Nonetheless, there was some powerful frustration here that was working its way to the surface; in her, in him; and he didn't know what to do about it.

*

Pedro Anabel Cavadas wiped the sweat from his brow. The late day sun beat on his forehead as he sat near the edge of the podium. He detested speeches. It was even worse that he had to give one, but he had long since learned that the way to power was littered with unremarkable oratory. The lies were commonplace, the content almost irrelevant to the fever pitch that he needed to create. For him, the pathway to the federal parliament was a mission borne of necessity, a life and death struggle for himself and his people.

Pedro's was an odd heritage at best. A Gallecho Basque with mixed French lineage from the province of Vila Real, he was descendent from the colonial occupation of the country by Napolean and the would be empire that grew in the cauldron of the European revolution. His parents were blessed by no small good fortune in his home province. They were both formally educated and had met as teachers when they had both returned to their native community. They had raised him to challenge authority and delve deeply into the social meanderings of law and oppression. It had come easily.

The road to the podium, though, had not come easy. Throughout the rebellious nineties in the North, he had been a guerilla captain, unknown to the Portuguese populace in general. In the year that had followed the cease fire, the mountain fighting had destroyed his own village, left his sister and two of his brothers dead and had virtually shut down the economy of the region. It had resulted in the poor becoming poorer, the people more repressed than before. During the four years that followed, it had become clear to him that the internal strife would never solve the problem. War was not politics by other means, but the complete failure of a nation to value its people, its diversity.

As he looked about the crowd of thousands before him in Oporto, the government square sealed and ringed by Federales, he sensed the agitation in the air. He knew he could ignite the crowd, but that was only part of what he wanted to do, he had to make them see it, see the whole thing as he did. The current administration under President Raul

DeSilva was so out of touch with the common people. It was a repressive regime that had a tendency to crack down on all aspects of free expression. Pedro Cavadas detested this government and was openly aggressive in his opposition. Still, he had to tread cautiously with a mixed crowd such as this one.

Pedro approached the podium, his linen jacket long since gone, his bolo tie loosened significantly. His small, wiry frame belied his physical strength and his determination.

"Brothers and Sisters. I do not come before you as a politician, but as a person determined to cherish Portugal, all of Portugal..." The crowd applauded politely.

"We cannot survive as a country if we implode on ourselves; and we cannot disenfranchise a people or a region in the name of a greater good."

Pedro was getting warmed up and the crowd was beginning to respond. He thumped the podium and raised his voice.

"Our assembly must open up and respect all minorities, respect Minho and Braga, respect Oporto, respect them by respecting all of us; RESPECT PORTUGAL."

Each pause in his speech, a calculated cadence, was punctuated by another thump as he played to the cheers of the crowd.

"Not because I say so, but because it is in their hearts, their minds, their souls."

He held up his arms to the crowd.

"It is not just about the poverty of we people. It is a convenience, a means by the government, to lose focus on the real problems of Portugal by applying oppression and tyranny here. As long as we cast about for demons, we will never take economic control of our own destiny. We must avoid the sorrowful pit of foreign capitalism's malignant grip on us. It only seeks to impoverish us all; uproot us from our communities and endanger our families."

He backed off, lest he lead the crowd to riot, gratified that the oratory was working. Now, he had to close it with the pitch and the obligatory humility.

"I pledge to you, my brothers and sisters, that if you

send me to Lisbon, I will carry your voice.   I will lead the fight for a compassionate Portugal, a Portugal that prides itself on its people; on their development; on their future; on their spirit. I will do this with you.   Please give me your support."

He backed up from the podium, bowed to the cheering crowd, hands clasped as in prayer.

"God bless your hearts, God bless your families.   God bless your spirit."

*

Chris sat in the lazy boy, slumped forward in anguish. It wasn't the wailing kind, the kind that sometimes flies out of a human body at a funeral, and it wasn't the kind that manifests itself in streams of tears, it was more the kind that invokes confusion, the kind that lays a soul empty, the kind that makes it impossible to move, to decide, to even dwell on the next moment.   It was that kind.   The quiet kind.   And even as he felt it, he thought on all those people he knew who had suffered this kind of anguish, the silent rage and pain that lay underneath the smile of a friend at work going through a divorce, the pain of a lost child, the death of a parent, a beloved pet; some agonizing fate that befalls everyone at some point in life.   He remembered how bad Max had done it, lived with it.   He remembered how Joanne fought for her life with it and how she still struggled with it.

He could see the destruction before him, the last quiet vestiges of rage; the broken glass, the debris from the table, the overturned chair in the kitchen, and what was left of dinner, at various locations from counter to floor.

It was his fault and he knew it.   It went back to the night before.   He had been working in the office room, looking up something on the internet, something totally unimportant and Elaine had come in.   They talked, then touched, then got interested and the next thing he knew, he was back on the futon, she fondling him until he was fully aroused.   The clothes were going off, bit by bit. She rubbed

71

her chest against his, teasing him until he couldn't stand it. Then she was on him, pulsating against him with ferocity. In the midst of her passion, she moaned, "Oh, babe, Oh, Ja...., Oh God." He was riding with it, enjoying every second of it, until they were both satisfied, virtually together, fighting to hang on to each other and not fall off the couch.

When it was over, he thought, 'What was that?' What the hell is Oh, Ja? It doesn't go with anything, not Oh God, not Oh Jesus, not Oh shit, not anything. It was just odd and it stuck. It wasn't until the following morning, in the half sleep of the waking dead that it came to him. It was John, Elaine's colleague at work. Maybe a guess, maybe not, but it all seemed to fall into place. John was the only male at work that Elaine spoke highly of; the rest characterized as rube-ish and closed minded. It would also explain why she was so often late from work.

Then, too, there was the location of the act. The office. It was too familiar, too easy to dismiss. After work, together in the office, she the aggressor...it was so logical to him now. In her passion, in an environment so similar to her, she had slipped just a little, just enough.

If he looked back on it, he could see it had gone on for some time and he couldn't shake the thoughts that intruded. Then, he remembered something strange she had asked a month or so before. "If I had an affair, would you want to know?"

"That depends," he had answered, "on if it causes you pain. I guess I mean that if it was something quick, it came and went, then no. If it was something that hurt you and you couldn't resolve it, then I guess I would. It would be something we would have to work on'"

It was so simple, so straight forward and he had meant it.

But after that, he had questioned his emotional ability to deal with it. He knew he should let it go, but he couldn't, and that, in the end, was the cause of all of this.

It would never be right and he knew it. Sometimes, a marriage can live on lies. It can even grow, outdistance them, and in time and forgiveness; in acceptance of people and the feelings that fill each of us, find stability, even warmth and the genuine love that had brought them together in the first place.   He had seen it in elderly couples who had gone through hell together and somehow managed to hold onto each other till the end.   Perhaps, they each held onto something of each other, something they could believe in, and that was enough.

But he could see that this wasn't going to be one of those marriages.   There was too much anger, too much hurt and pain behind them both to try.   It hadn't helped either that three months prior, the ax had finally fallen at work.   The Governor, possibly in a preparatory move to run for national office, had cleaned house.   Hundreds of career professionals had been let go, clearing the way for hacks and bag men to take their place.   He hadn't taken it well, and the economic stress had poured salt into old wounds.   It hadn't helped and he knew that some of his response to it had driven Elaine away.

He also knew he had to leave.   In the end, it was her house, her place, her friends.   He could start over, someplace else.   He had done it before.

'I can't wait here any longer,' he thought. 'If I do, I'll melt. I'll give in. I'll accept. And I'll be lost in this triangle, or the next.'

Slowly, his numbed synapses sparked enough for him to focus on the domestic tragedy around him.   He rose from the chair and walked out the door to the fifth wheel RV in the yard.   He would sleep there the night, then in the morning, after Elaine went to work, pack the things he cherished and needed, then leave.   The where remained unknown, but the start would be to D.C., where James, his youngest, lived. From there, who knew?

One thing he did know.   Freedom could be painful, but never taken for granted.   His thoughts went back to a time when freedom, full of choice, without a plan or a demand, had meant everything to him.

*

Brian Deming looked off the bow of the ship to the island ahead.   He would have to go over to Ilheu shortly.   He didn't like the field work so much anymore, but this was David's baby and the responsibility fell right into his hands.   As the number two person in the company, he handled all of the day to day and the furtherance of the vision.   He steered the corporation and its assets.

The Ilheu of Graciosa would be the new overseas corporate base.   The current headquarters in central California would still be the face of the Corporation, but everything for two phases of the new programs and actual scientific value would be run from here.

This was all part of David's vision for the future, based on some damnable utopian concept he still held from his youth.   Brian could only partly buy into that; but he could really buy into the control issue.   Here, the meddlesome regulations and rules of the United States would be impotent.   This was a country, and as such, created independence of form and action.   Brian loved that.   If anything, he was a control person, a man of action.   He was that way in the service and his philosophy had only strengthened over time.

His relationship with David was an odd one.   They had first met while skiing in southwestern Colorado some twenty years before.   On a Purgatory chair lift, they got into a conversation about business and the future.   The two couldn't have been more different.   David was a college dropout, a computer nerd on his way to California.   Brian was a graduate, a Staff Sergeant in the reserve, and a real estate broker in Durango.   He had some computer experience and a thriving business.

David had an idea about developing personal computers and had little seed capital.   Brian had a thriving business, focused highly on development.   He had been looking for an investment opportunity.   Over several runs and Apres ski, they cemented a partnership.   Brian agreed to finance the venture for a forty percent initial stake, provided they work together on the business plan.   It was a rocky road the first couple of years, but Brian believed.   When it took off, he had to sell out of Colorado and move to California to take charge of the business operations.   The company grew beyond his wildest expectations.

Now, he ran an empire and looking about him, the trappings of that empire pleased him.   Nothing like he was doing now had ever been done before or on any such scale. The plans for the island were mammoth and he had nearly a hundred contractors on land, over six hundred workers on the job, building the corporate nation of the future.

He sipped the last of his coffee as he gazed off at the Graciosian coast, eerily visible through the fog in the distance. He walked across to the helm, instructing the Captain to ready the launch, then returned to his office.

He was having a small problem with one contractor. He had to deal with that and get a push on the completion of the airport north of Santa Cruz.   Some people didn't like confrontation.   Not Brian.   He virtually thrived on it.   A former middle linebacker at Colorado State, he didn't respond well to people in his face and when he ran the show, things would get done on his terms.   He was ready for the fight.

He grabbed his blues, the contract in question and boarded the shuttle for the short journey across the harbor to the village.

CHAPTER FOUR

Durango

Chris shoved the gearshift in drive, switched to trailer haul mode and lumbered the diesel and fifth wheel up the driveway. He stopped at the end, turned to look back at the house he had built and the life he was leaving.   He had raised his sons there.   His life and work revolved around this place. He could see the lights in the windows in the early morning grey blue sky.   He slumped in the seat at the end of the driveway.   The commuter traffic to the city waited ahead.

Now, I have heard all of this from all my friends and what remains of my family and   realize that everybody will go home and say, "Gee, that was great, we really helped him." now all I have to do is suck it up and go out and do this.

I recall mother Theresa saying "Think about what you want to do", "think about how you're going to do it, then do it." Easier said than done; and I don't know if that should have a damn thing to do with relationships.   I have to free myself from that to ever accomplish a damn thing, to ever get out of this emotional funk, so if I think, perhaps, that the personal qualities of leadership ingrained in me could and should apply to this awful situation.

My mother used to say, work is an effective means of moving through emotional trauma.   In the midst of such upheaval in my life, perhaps I need to focus on the externals of work and building a successful community, but how? Where?   It can't be here, not with all this, this recent past; not with this drama and all these misstatements and outright lies that people will entertain as truth.   I am diminished in all eyes, and I have done nothing wrong.   I will have to start all over again and if that freedom isn't there, then I will have to create it.

For many of us, that's a joke and we'll never, ever be able to be aligned with the people, organizations or the communities in which we live.   The politics in my community have been so reactionary, so predictably stupid; and they will not change in my lifetime. So, I ought to find some place to live where I <u>can</u> be aligned and **have** some sense of community.

That's why it's so damned important to be true to ourselves, to find out what it is that is really important to us, our life purpose, and try to find alignment with that or there is no harmony at all.

I think of Mother Theresa again. In India, I think of a place which is spiritually focused and where each life has value. Perhaps, then, it easier to be true to one's self and one's convictions when each person has a tendency to bring value to you, where each action is blessed. If I live in a society where there are scapegoats and blame and that pervades the society, I can see, then, that it has so little value to me to work for it. There is no psychic return, and yet deeply, I know, that there can be building only if I engage in learning and loving partnerships.

So, I have to ask myself one last time, as I sit here looking back at this place I once loved, could I ever grow and prosper in this environment? Can I rid myself of my emotional baggage here? Can I be my Self?

Obviously, today, I'm very upset. The illusion of any control in my life has been completely shattered. I'm only capable of challenging my relentless emotions and my duality in personal happiness by trying to recognize the awful situations I let myself create or nurture. Love is so hard, so complex, that it breaks down all hope of driving my Self forward. Just as Akishnu faced his uncle in battle, the pain and the intellectual rationalization are so at odds that reconciliation is impossible. In any action, the energy is constantly compromised, sometimes causing complete inertia. For so long now, I have said that I have been comfortable with it, and yet sometimes it was so impossible to bear.

Fine, I refuse to sit in a damned waiting room, but if I'm forced to accept that everyone is where they are supposed to be, then I am, too. I will have to wade through that madness to pick out the light, that one spark to keep me going.

Alas, yet another redeeming conversation with my inner being.   The light shines a bit once again and I go forward, dragging this personage forward inch by inch.   Someday, when it ends, I will miss it, but then, what chaos awaits in the universe?   Only that which the pain of this life sustains.

Change is a must.   Change is constant, not always for better; not always for worse; but always a necessity.   I must go, I truly must go…

*

Chris pulled into Boulder late in the evening.   A week out of D.C. and two weeks out of marriage, his spirits were dampened by the sense of loss in his life and for a time that was no longer.   Boulder punctuated those thoughts perfectly.   Twenty some years before, it was a small college city.   There were open fields and cattle grazing between the campus and Denver, the same between the City line north and Longmont.
The vision that unfolded in front of him surely demonstrated the epitome of urban sprawl.   Gone was the prairie and the enveloping foothills of his memory.   The metropolis and suburbs of Denver now claimed the land to the college town and well beyond, reaching some thirty miles in virtually every direction.   In comparison to the past, it was unchecked destruction and he could not imagine how the infrastructure could handle it.
The people he knew in the area were long gone or simply untraceable with the one exception of Ann Beauchesne and he hesitated to call her.   His decision to return west was not based on any concept of connection with friends, but with his sense of comfort.   He loved Silverton and the Durango area and it seemed logical to him that in his time of need, this place that he loved would graciously accept him again.   He could be there in another day, but for now, he'd simply run out of steam.   The Chinook winds off the

mountains had been a huge drag on the truck and the fifth wheel and he could barely keep the rig out of passing gear. He was exhausted and just wanted to set up and crash.

He camped at the fairgrounds near the city and went into town for dinner. The street that used to support Shannon's, his favorite bar, was now a sprawling commons, filled with ethnic restaurants and coffee houses. He supposed that it was inevitable, but it still didn't set well with him. You can never go back, he thought. Then it dawned on him that the statement applied to everything, that he really was alone here and that starting over was not going to be an easy task.

In the morning, he summoned up enough nerve to give Ann a call. The call rolled over to an Assistant.

"I'm sorry Mr. Eberhardt. She's in court today. But she will be available tomorrow afternoon after one. Would you like to leave a message?" The gatekeeper was professional, if not genuine.

"No, not really. Just tell her I called. I'll be in Durango tomorrow. I might call then."

He hung up the phone and felt sorry that he'd made the contact in the first place. They had been friends and had a history. It had been platonic and there was no reason to think it would be any different now, but in a way, he felt that his presence would be an unwanted intrusion in her life and it was unfair of him to pursue the contact at all.

Regardless, he had a new life to build and Durango was as far as he was going to go to start it. Given some time and thought, he was sure his future would come to him. Go with the flow. Let the energy be unblocked and he would know what he had to do.

*

Ann Beauchesne completed her day virtually the same way she always did. She closed the heavy office door to her executive suite and lit up a cigarette. She knew it was an addiction, knew it would eventually destroy her health, knew she should quit and had done so several times.

Nonetheless, she touched the flame to the sleek 110. She didn't smoke that much anyway, she rationalized, and she just wanted to relax a little, have some quiet time before she went home.

She fumbled through the messages and smiled at the slip in front of her. Chris Eberhardt. What the hell was he calling about? It certainly wasn't legal help, but it didn't make sense for him to be in Denver or Durango either, unless he were on vacation with Elaine. Then, she wondered why he would have called if he were with her. She remembered their meeting last fall and it had seemed a little icy.

Perhaps he would call again. She had always liked Chris. He was a good man with a strange sense of humor. She remembered when he visited her when she was at law school and the one other time after that when he had passed through to the western slope. That was a long time ago and a lot had happened since then.

She had blown out her first marriage because she had relentlessly driven herself to succeed. She looked around the office and took another puff, a long drag this time. She could question all of it. Eighteen years in the profession with ten on the bench, not counting law school, had given her an appreciation of every side of law and its application. She had defended murderers and thieves, sentenced them, prosecuted them and at times persecuted them. Sure, there was bias on the bench and everybody knew it. Some people just pissed her off and God help them when they came in front of her for sentencing. You would think that people like that would learn not to end up in court, but some were just too damn stupid.

Now, she enjoyed a successful practice. Maybe too successful. She had taken the partnership because it was a low key firm. It offered steady pay, steady work; nothing glamorous. That was fine with her. But after only a year, she could feel the pressure building. It was her own damned fault, the nature of her being.

In deeper contemplation, she knew she had pushed it.

A classic type A, if the stress wasn't there, she had to make it be there.   And then, she would get all worked up about it. Why do I do that, she thought as she ground the half smoked cigarette into the gold leaf ash tray given to her by her father. Dad.   He pushed me and drove me into law school.   It was what he wanted, an extension of himself and what he could not be. I never really wanted this for myself.   I wanted to be a teacher.   I wanted to work with kids.   I wanted to have children.

She closed her eyes and caught the tug in her throat. Enough.   Paul would be waiting, annoyed, as always and there was still the dreaded commute.   She rose and smoothed out the mid-length skirt, a force of habit.   At the end of the day and before the ride home, what was the point? The wrinkles and creases had firmly set in for the day and could not be persuaded out.

She left the unfinished motions and orders on the secretary's desk and walked out to her convertible Sebring. This was a small luxury she afforded herself, although she could have easily bought a BMW.   She wasn't trying to impress anyone in either case, but there were times when the top would go down and she would tear it up through the canyons.

Today, however, would not be one of those times. The top would never go down on the commute to Evergreen. All that would do would be to accelerate the smog, dust and diesel fumes that would accompany her and the half million other people that made their way in, out or through Denver on any given day and she didn't need to add to the agony of the trip by having her eyes irritated to the point where she looked like the morning after.

She eased out onto I-25, worked her way southwest through one fender bender and turned off to face the mountains on the last leg of the forty-five minute commute. Soon she would be back in the quiet foothill village she called home.   At least, it used to be when she moved there six years before.

She caught a glimpse of a heavy cloud as it broke the crest of Mt. Evans.   She could see it had some girth to it and no doubt it meant rain somewhere, but the storms on the range were unpredictable and although it looked like it might shower, it could easily dissipate or just hover menacingly over the majestic peak.

She smiled as she thought about Chris. Durango was a nice town, quiet by Denver's standards. She had been there a half dozen times over the years and liked the feel of the place. Paul's son, K.J., had recently moved there. After flunking out of the University of Colorado, he'd gone from going nowhere fast in Denver to going nowhere slow in Durango. Paul was infuriated by it all, but she could see the wisdom in it. People made entire lives out of resort work and a life out of working to afford recreation and it didn't seem to dampen their enthusiasm or zest for life any. Quite the contrary, those kind of people seemed to be the most well balanced she knew. Compared to the gridlock she saw ahead, it seemed downright pleasurable to contemplate. Funny, she always thought Chris would end up like that. He never seemed to have the disposition to take life that seriously. Maybe that was why he came here.

*

David Deeds disliked staff meetings and rarely held them. If it couldn't get done via e-mail or a phone call, then a meeting wouldn't do it either. However, he conceded there were times when details were needed, when he felt the need to be satisfied that the work was actually moving in the right direction.

When he got the click, he left his private office for the spacious and simple, yet somewhat elegant meeting room adjacent to his suite. Decorated modestly with oriental art he had obtained from his several journeys to Japan, Hong Kong and China, the meeting room looked stereotypically more like a parlor from a tea house than a corporate venue. He rarely used this space and there was no phone in it, so often times, he would come in to escape the rigors of his business. Upon the rare occasion there was a meeting scheduled, the absence of a phone eliminated the interruption of contact for staff present. He detested that and it was his corporate rule that no cell phones were allowed there during meetings or conferences. If it was important enough to get together in the first place, then everyone should have complete devotion to the task and not allow calls to interfere. It annoyed everyone and signaled a false impression of importance for the receiver. That impression could be easily dismissed and if violated, was swiftly dealt with.

When he entered, Jackie, Brian and Detlev Augenstein, his chief financial officer were already sitting on the floor comfortably about the five by eleven foot redwood table that was imbedded in the floor, eighteen inches off the carpet. In embracing Feng Suei, David had elected to extend the counter culture values of his youth by having his meeting room begin and end with the floor. Staff and Board would sit on the thick carpet and allow themselves a different freedom of movement. It created an atmosphere of focusing upon the tasks as much as did to remove the shackles of the corporate structure. He hoped it would improve free thought.

He picked out two cushions and placed them near Jackie, lowering himself to their level. The process was as much a spiritual directive as it was a means to get at the table. Whenever possible, David liked to have a woman on his left side. It made him feel at ease.

"Brian, How about you start first. How's life on Graciosa?" David asked.

"Better every day, David. I'm getting so as I like it there."

"Are you off the boat?"

"Not quite. We don't have the executive suites done, but the punch list is only a couple of weeks away."

"The Habitat. What about that?"

"We ran into some problems with gulf stream's current shifts. I don't think anybody expected this much ebb and flow this far up the channels, but there it was and the structural integrity had to be quite a bit stronger. We expect to open it to sub transport in about three weeks, if we can get the kinks out of the mainland water supply process and the air quality where we want it."

"Okay, Brian, overall, what's your sense of it, today, now that you're away from it. Think back on it from some distance and with some objectivity."

Brian thought for a moment.

"I think it's everything we hoped it would be and probably more. The construction problems would be there regardless, but the site really is perfect, logistically and environmentally. We can operate smoothly, hell, we are operating smoothly already. The systems are up and running, services are coming in nicely and the weather has been phenomenally cooperative. It all measures up. The hotel and golf course are done. The overflow and staff housing lags a bit, and that is a problem, but we make do and when I return, that will get back on schedule." His voice picked up strength at the end. David nodded in approval.

"Jackie," David said, "How are we doing with the shuttle?"

Jackie looked to her right to get eye contact with David and turned sideways, backing up slightly from the table and shifting her legs from her version of the lotus position. Her loosely fitted, pleated midi draped alluringly across her knees. After years of mental seduction, she was oblivious to her graceful body language at times and it sometimes caught her off guard when the simplest of movements evoked response. She had David's full attention.

"I thought we might have problems with Bud. He was entirely too agreeable. But after four meetings and review of the project on the floor, I believe that the shuttle will be completed without controversy and on time. I think Bud just looks at it as another contract. Sometimes, I don't think he gives a shit at all. I am concerned, however, about the constant flow of NASA and military personnel in and out of the 'works'. We may have sold them on design, even on implementation, but I have serious doubts that what you have planned for the missions will go unchallenged."

"We'll need Brian's help on that." David turned to his right hand man.

"How much pressure do we have exert to move our agenda?"

Brian was a bit unnerved at the question.

"I can't really say. My guess is that we'll have to commit a substantial amount of soft money in the right places along with direct campaign contributions. We'll need to use the industry lobbyist and direct shmooz money there as well. It won't be cheap and there are no guarantees."

"Then that brings right into Detlev's corner of the world," David said. "Tell me, Detlev, about the capital costs on Graciosa, our cash flow, our political fund accounts and our balance sheet."

"Detlev looked up from his silver rimmed, shaded bifocals as he thumbed through his folder of print outs. He took two ledgers out. He didn't need them, the information was summarily implanted in his head, but he had them there for support.

"Sir, the Graciosa capital budget now exceeds three hundred and seventy five million based on our last postings. Of course, that will go much higher and with what Brian has said, I can't project costs from that. The operating funds I've folded into day to day administrative operations and that has reached four million, seven hundred fifty thousand plus, but there are stock options values yet to figure in the compensation category."

Detlev set the two ledgers aside and took out two other print outs.

"Cash flow has been increased over the time period because of earnings and dividend yield, most notably from our stock buy-back plan. That was very timely and brings us to the balance sheet, which is improved considerably in overall corporate value. In essence, Sir, we've outrun all of our costs on the project, including the approximate two billion of payments and goods provided Portugal for the inception of the purchase of the island. We haven't spent that much this year on political funding and we're under budget and we can easily transfer additional cash if needed. However, I do have one question."

"Yes," David said.

"I would like your permission to bury all of the Graciosa costs under the separate company established as the foreign subsidiary. Even though NYSE rules require standardized accounting practices, the manner in which they are posted as a foreign company will not come under our audit scrutiny and eliminate questions here. Also, that subsidiary will show huge losses as a startup investment and qualify for foreign investment tax credit. Since that is already in the new tax bill, we could benefit greatly on several counts."

"Do it. As a matter of fact, Brian, I think we should load up on our wish list. There's no reason, at this point, not to get everything we want for Graciosa. We'll regret it later if we don't and we should take advantage of every possible avenue of value gain here. It's one thing to make a Utopia and quite another to make a paradise. Let's make the paradise. We will want to savor our decisions."

*

Reinholt Thillo took the complimentary paper from the hotel lobby, grabbed a cup of decaf and set out for the beach just beyond the pool along the short, palm tree covered walkway. Irma wasn't up yet and he didn't want to wake her, but it seemed a shame to waste such a beautiful morning by sitting inside the hotel with the paper in his lap, rocking to and fro like an old fart, which he had no intention of becoming. Yes, he was sixty-three and getting on, but retirement was just beginning to bring back some of his youth and he wasn't going to miss out on any of it.

They had worked hard all their lives, building a small Baltic coast business into profitability and in these later years, benefitting tremendously from its sale and with the help of an excellent broker, investments in the DAX, they had ensured not only peace of mind for themselves, but for their children as well. This trip to the Algarve, the southern corner of the Iberian coast was the first evidence of that, something they had looked forward to for months.   Perhaps, if all went well, they might consider a winter place in the area, or possibly on the west coast, south of Lisbon.

He set out onto the beach and turned south at the corner of the peninsula. Their hotel was on the eastern most portion of the resort village of Lagos and soon he had come to the end of the development.   Back off the beach, construction for a new complex had begun, but as dawn had just broken, it would be a little time before the workers would be in full swing.   He could hear some background noise, perhaps a foreman or manager making their plans for the day and he paid it no attention as he wandered on a bit farther down the beach.

He sat in the sand, not far from the rising surf that seemed to call him closer.   He was unaware of the sounds around him, almost meditative in the quiet stillness of the relentless sea and the awakening of the village in the distance.

He did not notice the two men approaching, nor responded when he heard someone call out.   It was a guttural noise, a different language, and it meant nothing to him.   He did notice when one of them grabbed his arm and yanked him upright.

"Your money, senor."

Reinholt was staring squarely into the barrel of a crudely sawed off shotgun.   He quickly determined that the two men were desperate, and he would have easily obliged them had he brought anything with him, but all he stuck in his light cargo pants when he left was his room key and the five euro bill on the dresser.

"I don't have much," he said as he fumbled his shaking hand through the velcro pocket, "but you can have it all."

Meekly, he thrust out the five euro bill.

"What is this, a joke," asked the larger of the two in his own dialect.   His anger was clearly evident and he reached out and slapped his intended victim across the face.

"You think we are stupid?"

"Yeaah, stupid," said the other with the gun, his nearly toothless grin scrunched up into a threatening gesture.

Smarting from the blow, Reinholt tried to explain, but they would have none of it. The larger man backhanded him, then punched him as the little one jabbed him with the shotgun, harder each time. The bigger man, tiring of the physical assault reached for his knife, a five inch blade with a serrated hunting edge that he kept in a sheath on his hip.

At the sight of the knife, Thillo screamed. It didn't stop the blade from entering his abdomen, nor the smaller man from hip firing the shotgun that nearly tore the tourist's shoulder off. Now, his screams amounted to a death wail and he stumbled forward as the larger man shoved the knife into his lower back.

At the sounds of the disruption, a crane worker caught the sight and let a blast out from an emergency horn. In moments, a crew burst out from the compound and onto the beach, in time to see the assailants vanish back into the scrub up the hillsides from which they came.

Reinholt Thillo lay face down in the sand, blood pouring from the shoulder wound, his room key and a shredded piece of a five euro bill in his hand.

It was a miracle he lived, but he would never be the same. The German Government lodged an official complaint with the President of Portugal, Raul Salinas DeSilva, and then dropped it, inexplainably, four months later. Irma Thillo, angered by this lackluster effort, went on a one woman barrage against the Rathaus collective in Hamburg, enlisting the aid of the Hanseatic Parliament, the new small business and tradesman's Guild. It wasn't even the play of the racial overtones, in her mind, as much as it was the damnable indifference of the government to Reinholt's situation. She needed an advocate and an organization that could be proactive. He was damaged for life and nobody seemed to care about it. This wasn't what she believed in her country for, paid her taxes for, or worked all her life for in supporting this wonderful man only to have it taken away from her and nobody give a damn.

The Hanseatic League played the Islamic card for her and within two months, the issue was back on the

Bundestag's agenda, this time with the President's priority stamp on it. It was not to go away soon and after the spring Madrid meeting between the two Presidents, it was on DeSilva's priority list as well.

Lisbon was quick to act. The General Congress, Portugal's Parliament, swiftly passed a law, under DeSilva's guidance, that created a new federal police force of fourteen thousand. In addressing the Senate and Chamber of Deputies, DeSilva deftly parlayed fear, creating a sense of urgency and a need to act.

"We can no longer stand aside and allow outlaws, separatists, revolutionaries or jihadists to dictate policy. We cannot afford to stand aside and allow our progress, our business, our tourism to be set back by common thieves and murderers. We need to make our streets, our beaches, our villages, our resorts, indeed, all of our thirty one states, safe from harm, safe from fear and safe from violent tyranny, free from oppression.

This is why I support this bill and the creation of this federal force; to complete the task of eradicating this cancer from our midst."

Despite the power of the Socialist Party, the ruling party of the last thirty five years, behind him, the bill did not escape massive criticism in the Legislative Assembly. The Lower House of the General Congress had been taken over by the Socialist Democratic Party with the help of the Greens and the Left Bloc in the last election held in July. The party had swept legislative seats in the urban and suburban areas, even making inroads in the traditional socialist party rural strongholds, and commanded a strong majority in the three hundred elected seats of the Upper House. This breakthrough by the SDP had been built by the progressive election of several governors in the past decade in seventeen of the country's states.

The debate raged in the Assembly before passage and Pedro Anabel Cavadas led the charge. Recently elected to his second three year term, he had established prominence in the opposition coalition and now served as the Armed Forces Committee Chair. His commentary was unsparing and relentless.

"The administration's attempt to veil this as a business friendly, security issue is alarming, if not at least corruptive. If you pass this," he waved his hands angrily at his contemporaries, "You endorse a police state, a government accountable to no one, a government that creates a Gestapo and silences its critics with brutal repression. Oh, you may clean up the beaches. You have to do that just to clean up the appearance of this, but you know that this force will be used, perhaps in the most violent ways, to subvert our people and our democracy.

We have an army of forty thousand. We can expand it. We have local police forces. We can support them. There is no need to establish this force. I know it will be used to destroy legitimate opposition in my district and deny our citizens their due rights."

Pedro knew the Chamber would understand him. After the big eight summit agreement, the federal government had seized land in the Moelho, farms that belonged to the poorest of his people, people who had little else to lose. This action bore the revolt and now, the Basque supported Liberation Army had become a credible fighting force. Bloodshed was now the horrible face that had shown itself, almost daily, in his home district.

Regardless, the bill narrowly passed the Chamber. The Senate ratified it within weeks. Pedro Cavadas vowed he would watch this like a hawk and do everything he could within his power to stop it; strangle it by tying up funding in committee and making it the major issue in the next presidential campaign.

CHAPTER FIVE

THE WESTERN SLOPE

The RV park was just three miles north of the City of Durango. Even over the past twenty years, Durango had not changed that much physically, but had just pushed out a bit. That pleased Chris immensely. He did like things to stay somewhat familiar.

The City boasted a mere fifteen thousand souls, but the suburbs had grown quite a bit, sprawling into the canyons on all four sides. To the east and south, drumlin like prairie and mesa in the distance claimed the landscape, nestled with Santa Fe style homes. To the West and Cortez, rolling foothills were strewn out along the LaPlata and mountains before breaking into Arizona. That was more rurally commercial. To the North lay the gorgeous Hermosa Valley, its red rocked cliffs climbing three thousand feet above the fertile green layered valley cut by the Animas River. That area boasted new mountain home developments. From there further North, the valley ambled and swayed with the river into the San Juan mountains up to Silverton, his old resort town.

Two days after a late arrival, he finished up the setting of the site for long term camp. The awning, sunshade, ground mat and chairs all in place; the camper washed and tightened up where needed. He had spent a significant amount of time in 'camp' and whether it be a tent or a half million dollar diesel pusher, one spent a lot of time putzing around a campsite, although this was a far cry from a blue tarp strung between two trees. Still, the routines were remarkably similar. You started with a nice big cup of coffee, then a good long sit to look at the cliffs and the valley and to contemplate the possibilities for the day. His site was close enough to the Animas River to hear it gurgle in the distance. It was a refreshing and reassuring sound. Later, he'd take a short stroll down to the camp store to get a morning paper, the Durango Herald, then back for another cup. Down the valley, he could hear the shrill whistle of the Durango & Silverton train leaving the station. That was a comforting sound as well. It gave him a sense of belonging. Up the valley, an eagle shrieked as she cruised above the river looking for breakfast.

There would be some requirements of him today, but like most seasonal campers, he would have to think about what he might do for the remains of the day; after noon, of course. He sat in the lounge chair under the awning, coffee in hand when the cell phone rang.

"Chris. This is Ann"

"Ann, my God, How did you get my number?"

"Ah, Chris, this is a law office. You called my direct number, which I'm sure my brother gave you. Nobody has my direct number except my family and high profile clients. We bill at four hundred dollars an hour and so when a call comes in on my line, it's logged. You do know lawyers charge for phone calls and by the minute."

"Uh huh. Never let a possible billing slip by."

"Don't be mean. Where are you?"

"Durango. Got here a couple days ago and am settling in. I'll be here awhile. What's going on with you?"

"You stopped to see me, Chris, and I'm sorry I missed you. It would have been nice to catch up. You say you're going to be there awhile, what's going on with you?"

"A long story, better left untold, but I'm on my own now and, well, this place is special to me and I thought, better to be here than any place else."

"I have a thought. One of my cases has depositions in Durango next week. I was sending out a junior associate, but I can take that over. It's rather mundane, anyway, so she won't mind. That would get me a couple of days there and we could meet for lunch."

"That would be great. What day? I have such a busy schedule."

"Silly. Probably Tuesday. I'll call you. What are your plans for the weekend?"

"Annie, you're assuming I plan. I think I'm going to take the D&RG up to Silverton and I suppose I should probably do a little job hunting. Not that I'm in a hurry. And, as you might guess, as a former Division Director at the State, I'm a little overqualified for just about anything local anyway."

"That aside, no effort signals a complete change of attitude. I don't think you have that in you. In any case, have a good time, Chris, and I look forward to seeing you on Tuesday."

*

No. 486 pulled out of the Durango station exactly at 8:30 a.m. as scheduled. The station sat unobtrusively behind the elegant Strater Hotel, a fixture for a century in Durango's history. At a snail's pace, the engine, five windowed passenger cars and one open air car, plus caboose chugged noisily through the city, the whistle screaming at every intersection in the town.

Chris sat in the open air car with his overnight bag at his side. From experience, he had learned that the complete round trip of eight hours was deadly. Most people were exhausted for the return leg and couldn't enjoy it. He would stay over at the Grand Imperial Hotel, the grand lady of the village that had been there since the 1890's. Besides, he wanted a little time in Silverton right away.

As the train cleared the city, it picked up a little speed. At top end, it would only go about twenty five. It was narrow gauge and winding track, not at all harmonious for tourists with little kids at high speeds.

Up through Hermosa, he could see his RV resort in the distance. He would stay until at least late September. If you were going to start a new life, spring was the time to do it. There was a freshness and a sense of possibility in the air. It was, in spite of everything that happened, thrilling. The colors seemed to be brighter, the red rocks of the valley's foothills had come alive with the greening of the hardwoods, the aspens; the primary trees that filled the glades. The snow was melting from the mountain caps and visible from time to time, thrusting the white and grey smattered peaks into the crisp blue sky.

Seven miles up the line the train climbed and approached the cliffside hairpin, a seven hundred foot drop into the gorge below. Because the D&RG was narrow gauge, any look out the window seemed as though the train was completely off the turn, hovering in mid-air. Although an exhilarating view, it was unsettling to many as they gazed into the foaming, white frothed river below. It didn't bother Chris at all. He knew he was completely safe, until he wasn't. He was more concerned about the cinders flying out of the stack five cars up. There was a bit of a bad memory about that.

Up past Pinkerton and Rockwood, where the train took on water, the rail bed leveled out and hung to the edge of the river, crossing back and forth. The class four rapids violently pummeled the rocks in a sea of spray. Some adventurers paced along the opposite bank, looking for the perfect drop in.

After three hours of incredible views, the train pulled out of the gorge and into the 'Park', the wide open valley in which Silverton lay. Chris was excited about seeing the place, so long the time away. The train pulled into the station, bells clanging, and two hundred happy riders disembarked for an afternoon in this quaint, Victorian, western town that hadn't changed in one hundred years.

He strolled over to the Grand Imperial Hotel, the largest building, save the courthouse, in the village. The grand lady anchored Greene Street, the main drag of the town. He registered and dropped his bag behind the counter and made for the bar, a magnificent western styled mahogany behemoth with four center Grecian posts, each two feet in circumference, encasing three mirrors of an obelisk shape. It had been there as long as the hotel, hauled in by rail from the east. There were several tourists and locals there having lunch and he perched himself at the end by the picture window that looked out into the street. The view was as he remembered it; Kendall Mountain out past the river, a constant strain to look at as he ate his sandwich.

After lunch, he took a stroll, mindful that at ninety three hundred feet above sea level, he would have to catch his breath and pace himself as he slowly got used to the altitude. Notorious Blair Street still had the same buildings; the Livery, gift shops, four restaurants, but a couple of the names had changed. The Bent Elbow and Zhivago's were still there. Essentially, the town was just as he left it years before.

Back on Greene Street, he passed the Sheriff's office and decided to stop in. Silverton was a small town of about six hundred and everybody knew everybody. The Sheriff's office was not to be feared. Chris wanted to find out what happened to Floyd Martinsen, the Sheriff so many years ago.

As he entered, the dispatcher, a Ms. Tomlinson, looked up warily.

"May I help you?"

"Just visiting and wondered what may have become of Floyd?"

"Oh, he retired about eight years ago and moved to Grand Junction. He passed away last year."

"I'm sorry. He was a good man. Who's here now?"

"Our new boss is Scott Jackson. He's in the back, doing paperwork, which he hates. Would you like to speak with him? And what's your name?"

"Chris Eberhardt. I think I remember Scott."

"I'll ask if he'll see you."

Ms. Tomlinson passed the dispatch station and entered the private office and returned with a fairly round man with a full face and a half smile.

"Hello, Chris. I remember you from ages ago. I was a rookie deputy when you were first here and that was a tumultuous year. Come on back."

Chris followed him in and had a seat as instructed. After the obligatory small talk, Scott decided to get to the interesting history.

"You did hear about the murder of that Mexican fellow, Torres was the name, I believe. It was a rather strange affair. I knew you had saved him from a stoning, but apparently, he was destined."

"Yes, Skip told me about it ten years ago when I was last year. Said they tried to blame it on Greg and the other three. "

"Yes, but the evidence never pointed to them. Two fatal bullet wounds from a rifle that none of them owned and then the body left in a mine shaft that they occasionally worked; didn't make any sense at all and there was no other proof. We had to drop it and it is still unsolved. I try not to think about stuff like that, bugs the hell out of me. Besides, I was a rookie then and my opinion didn't matter that much."

"I heard those guys left town soon after that."

"Yup. You know, there was so much going on in that two year period. This was always a bit of a wild place; had the reputation of being a true western town, complete with a hundred year old attitudes about how justice was handled. The wildcat miners were a tough bunch. You remember them?"

"God, yes. Four, five days out, then drunk as hell for three; out of money, pack up and head back out again. Every now and then, they'd come in, all gaga about a big rock or a good trip out and they'd be out of town a bit, but right back at it, soon enough."

"Yeah, well, it was getting pretty stale here. We had bikers coming in as well and the two didn't always mix, but what really capped it was that dynamite business those two friends of yours did, blowing a hole in the San Juan. We had ATF all over the place and the town was pretty shook up about it."

"I remember, Scott. It scared the hell out of me, then. I was drunk and passed out and didn't know a thing about it till late the next day."

"Story was, after they corralled those two, ATF went looking for you. Marvin was with them. They got to the house you were staying at, guns pulled, and came face to face with that Shepard Wolf of yours, eyeball to eyeball at the screen door and the agent said to Marvin, 'Guess he's not in right now, we'll try later'. Laughed my ass off."

"They were nice to me when they talked to me; knew I had nothing to do with it, but they never mentioned the dog."

"Point is, Chris, people had had enough, especially developers from Durango. It was next to impossible to think about improved tourism, ski center development, etc. with stuff like that going on. When Standard Metals closed; and the mine over at Ouray played out, the government stepped in with all kinds of new regulations and the era of the wildcat miner was over. Everybody moved on and we settled into the kind of tourist mecca we had all hoped it would be. No

96

one regrets leaving the past behind. You made a good decision to create a life somewhere else. The transition here wasn't easy."

"Thanks, Scott, I've had a good career so far and am grateful for a decent life. And, I'm glad to see the town doing so well. It means a lot to me. By the way, is Skip Conboy still over on Blair Street? I missed him when we passed through here seven years ago. I'd like to see him."

"You hadn't heard? Skip was in a lot of pain a couple years back. Lower back pain, I guess. Well one day, he got up and went out into the mountains, and never came back. We sent out three search parties and never found him."

Chris sat stunned. He knew Skip was a tough guy, but that didn't sound like him at all. If anything, he might have fallen in a mine shaft. It happened. And, Skip was the kind of guy who liked to explore the caves, to find interesting artifacts or perhaps a left behind nugget. He couldn't imagine him just walking off to die. He remembered how much fun they used to have, how Skip and his girlfriend, Lenore would dance the funky chicken and how Skip actually looked like a funky chicken. Perhaps, there was more to it than just this. His wheels were spinning, but he wasn't hitting the ground with anything, just stuck in neutral in cold amazement.

"I'm really sorry to hear that, I really am," He finally blurted out.

"His nephew works here. You might want to give your condolences. Meanwhile, enjoy your time here. Come back any time. We love tourists."

Chris excused himself and couldn't help thinking that possibly he had just received a very diplomatic brush off with a slight hint of 'don't let any dust collect on your butt on your way out of town'. He finished his tour, another forty five minute walk in all, then cruised back to the hotel for a rest. It was still a tourist town and at night, it rocked like one. This time, pensive mood aside, he might really enjoy it. He wasn't behind a bar.

*

Ann Beauchesne's Sebring strained as it reached the summit of Wolf Creek Pass. She had taken the southern route around Walsenburg, through Alamosa to arrive in Durango. Even though it was late spring, there could be a chance of snow or late spring rock slide. It was wise to be cautious and take a more southerly route. It was four hundred and fifty miles in all, a lengthy nine hour trip. She'd had a good long time to think.

In a way, this excursion made little sense. She didn't need to do the depositions and seeing Chris might not be the best thing she should be doing at this point in her life. She knew she was unhappy; she knew this might be grasping; she knew she didn't need any entanglements, but she told herself she was just seeing an old friend and getting out of the office for a few days. Nothing wrong with that. It was a beautiful ride and time to think was precious. Don't over think it, just enjoy it. Life is what happens while you make other plans.

She arrived at the Doubletree just shy of seven, too late to refresh and catch a dinner out. She called Chris and let him know, briefly and precisely, that she was done in and would just call room service and catch him for lunch tomorrow. She flopped in, exploded into sweats and proceeded to thoroughly mess up the room, knowing she did not have to clean it up.

*

Chris was excited and anxious about meeting Ann for lunch. He didn't sleep well and got up early, drove from the RV park into the city and parked at the Courthouse. He was worried about so many things, mostly how he would look to Ann. He'd shaved off his beard, leaving only his moustache, and his hair was beginning to grow out. The fifteen pounds he'd added over the years and thought he'd be fighting with forever had melted away a little, aided by the upheaval in his life, but he hoped he could appear to be at least fairly attractive to her. He could obsess about that and probably ten other things.

So he decided that, while he was waiting, he'd go to the Durango Herald office and check out the old newspapers.

This ended up being an additional trip to the library, where he could examine records and papers on microfiche.

He thought he'd go back to his second time in Silverton and work forward until he found something about the murders. He remembered Skip telling him about them years ago and it dawned on him that Scott Jackson hadn't mentioned them at all.   That was odd.   In any case, he would have to start scanning when they figured the first murder occurred.   It had happened about six months after he left, but the body wasn't found until quite some time later.   It made it tougher to pinpoint the date.

Finally, he caught an article that indicated the wildcat miners were suspect and even though most had already left town, arrest warrants were issued.   In following articles, he noted some of the arrests, statements, police beat items and side features about the change in the economic dynamic of the region.   As he began to trace the time forward, he noticed many letters to the editor on the 'wild west' and the need for it to finally come to its natural end.

He would have to study it more.   In his past work as a Division Director, it had been part of his job to uncover violations of laws or compliance with statutes. It was part of his ingrained nature now and he couldn't let go of something once he'd set his teeth into it. The references ran forward almost three years until all the charges were dropped and the cases closed, unsolved.   This drove him nuts.   There were more than a few breadcrumbs on this trail and it seemed that any investigator could have traveled down the path way a lot farther.   He sure as hell knew he could.

So, there was quite a bit more that he wanted to read, but time had escaped him and he needed to head down to the Strater where he had promised to meet Ann.

It was another beautiful spring day, cool temperatures warming for the afternoon, the city lively as noon approached. Tourism hadn't even begun to start its season, but Durango was still a busy county seat and all manner of new construction saw the transport of contractors, work crews and materials thru and around downtown.   Chris remembered many trips from Silverton as 'Sun and Fun in Verdango

Beach', as they called it back in the day.

He was virtually shaking as he entered the lobby of the hotel and saw Ann sitting at a small table, coffee and paper in hand. She looked up, with a radiant smile and the speckled green eyes that always captivated him.

"Hello stranger, have a seat."

"I would love to, you look wonderful." To Chris, that was an understatement. Her radiant black hair swirled over her shoulder, hints of brown cascading on to her emerald green dress, a mid-length one piece that accentuated those great eyes and her slim figure. He couldn't imagine a more beautiful woman anywhere on the planet.

"Are we eating here?" she asked as she took a last sip of coffee.

"No, I thought we'd save this for some other time. I'd like to walk up the street to Farquarts. It's an old favorite of mine and I think you'll like it."

"Been there. Remember, KJ goes to school part time here and I've been here once or twice." She picked up her valise, left the paper and the two exited the charming Victorian lobby for a two block walk up to the restaurant.

"They used to have good pizza here," he mused as they entered. It still had the obligatory eccentric artifacts and wall art, posters and prints that had made it a funky anchor for Durango's party nights, in season or out.

"I remember it being kind of rowdy," Ann whispered as they were escorted to a window side booth. The restaurant was half full, a good lunch crowd, but not great. They ordered and as the iced tea came, Ann got right to it. She was never one to waste time on inconsequential matters.

"So what gives, Chris? You must tell me."

"It's hard to put into words, for me, at least. I get bundled up with all kinds of mixed emotions. Elaine had lost interest in me for some time; we fought a lot; we didn't seem to enjoy each other anymore; had different interests. I thought that was okay, you know. Relationships of longevity can withstand a lot, but when I knew she was unfaithful, I guess that just accentuated the rest of it for me. I wasn't a saint, Ann. Early on, I strayed, and I messed up a lot; so, I had a lot of patience, and guilt, I guess. We had one huge fight later on and I think I was so embarrassed and beaten that I just gave up."

"And drove all the way across country to get away from it? Most people just get separated and make a mess of it."

"I've always been good at running away. Suits me fine. What about you"

"I'm still married. I thought I was happy, but lately, I've been questioning everything. I probably was happy being settled. I haven't given it that much thought, but I'm here sitting with you, aren't I? Ah, here's lunch. Saved by food."

They each enjoyed a burger and chatted about Ann's work, Chris's job search.

"But like I said, Ann, I'm not in a hurry. I'll get unemployment for a long time and I don't want to take something just for the sake of it. Besides, I'm enjoying reconnecting with the area. You know, this restaurant used to sponsor one of Hardrockers' Holidays Tug of War teams. That was a big deal here."

"I remember seeing ads for it in Denver, the Holidays, I mean. It was a miner's festival, right?"

"Yup, had all kinds of events, like mucking, machine mucking, but the tug of war was the big thing and each of the towns; Durango, Silverton, Ouray, Ridgeway, even Telluride had a team. It had the elements of a world championship. Anyway, Farquarts always sent up a tough team. The year I was there we beat them in the finals."

It was close to two hours before they finally got sore from sitting so long at the booth. The waitress hadn't pushed them at all. It never got that busy, so she hoped they might pad on another drink or two before they left. She was to be disappointed.

The couple strolled out into the sunlight, the crisp spring air warmed by the midday sun and they stood awkwardly on the sidewalk.

"Do you have to go?"

"I should. I can be back by nine if I push it."

"But you don't have to, do you? I mean, after all this time, I really want more time with you."

She looked at him inquisitively. So sweet, and smart, and so cute.

"I guess I don't have to. I could check back into the hotel and take off tomorrow."

"How bout this? Why don't we go up to the hot springs for the rest of the afternoon, then you could come over to the RV and I'll cook you dinner. You can even stay there if you want. It has another bedroom. It's quite big you know. Do you have a bathing suit?"

"Yes. I always travel with one. I like to swim early mornings at the Hotel, when I can."

"That's great. So how about it?"

"Alright, Chris, but one thing at a time. I reserve the right to bail at any moment."

"Absolutely. As you wish."

They drove up Hermosa to the springs separately, then plied the hot thermal waters; different degrees in the three different pools. In the cool spring air, it was exhilarating, but a large amount of the time, they just sunned and spoke softly about little things, each not trying to admire the other in their suits. Both had reached early middle age in good shape. And maturity brought forth knowledge behind the quickened glimpses they each took. There had been a long attraction for both of them and it appeared that it hadn't weakened over time.

Arriving at camp, Ann was amazed at the fifth wheel. It was forty feet long and had four slide outs. Inside, it was cavernous, bedrooms on each end, large living room, kitchen and entertainment area, including a fireplace and work station for Chris's computer.

"It's bigger than an apartment. I can't think of this as camping."

"It isn't really. It's like dragging a house around; and it has all the same issues. I can tell you, though, the guest bed is very comfortable. I've slept in it several times."

"I'm not even going to ask," She grinned. "Chris, I've got to make some calls and get on the internet and it's kind of private."

"Okay, fine. I'll be outside, I'm going to do up some

ribs, so that will take a bit of nursing. Come on out whenever you're ready."

He grabbed what he needed and went to work. Ann came out about an hour later and Chris had the table set up and a bottle of red wine at the center. Ribs and grilled vegetables were just coming off the RVQ.

They had a lovely dinner as the sun set over the western ridge of the valley cliffs, the reddening sky dazzling the eastern valley slope's red rock with a golden glaze. The last train whistled on its way back from Silverton and horses whinnied at a distant ranch as they came in for the night.

"I could get used to this." Ann smiled.

"Yes, it can be very healing, but we'd better go in before the denizens of the dark get us."

"What denizens, Coyotes, Bears?"

"Bugs."

They entered the RV, leaving the door open, but left the screen door closed to protect them and yet, still allow the cooling mountain breezes to seep into the main room. They sat in the two easy chairs across from the fireplace and turned on the flat screen TV. It truly was like an apartment, with all the features you would want in a compact, highly structured space. But, in less than an hour, early fatigue had set in.

"I really don't have the energy to plod off to a hotel, Chris. I'll stay in the guest room, but no monkey business."

"No monkeys around here. Just let me make sure you've got everything."

Ann went to the car and brought in her bag. Chris made sure there were towels for her mini bathroom and the bed was in order.

"Anything you need, Annie, just holler, I'm only thirty feet away."

She settled in and Chris stayed up another half hour, then headed off to his master suite. He tried to sleep and wondered how Annie was doing. It was impossible to shake the images of her throughout the day. He wondered if she thought the same way. He tossed another fifteen minutes.

He thought he heard something. He got up and closed the main door, then heard Ann in the other room.

103

"Chris, everything okay?"

"Fine."

"I can't get this nightlight to work."

He went into the room. The light seemed fine. She reached up and kissed him, pressing her body next to his. He could feel her magic stir in him and he set his hands free as he kissed her lips, then neck, then ear. He was devouring her as he slipped off her top. So beautiful and a shape that was so much more than he imagined in her bikini that afternoon. He caressed her body as she clutched at him. Soon, he was pleasing her in every way he knew. She shuddered under his caress, then was completely his, and his again. They rolled back, exhausted, then kissed sweetly, silently, until they fell asleep, lips still touching as they drifted off into the netherworld.

After a light breakfast, Ann packed up and slowly prepared the car.

"You'll call me later today, won't you?"

"Yes, of course."

"And tomorrow?"

"Yes, yes."

"And the next day?"

"Absolutely. Every day."

"Good. I want that," she brushed her beautiful auburn streaked black hair across her face, then sparkled at him with those sensational eyes.

"Oh and good luck with your murder mystery thing. Remember, I can help a little in research. I do have access to an infinite amount of records."

"I'll remember; and I'll call every day, I promise. You know I don't want you to go."

"I know." She looked at that sweet face and could see the pain in it. "But I have to. That's just how it is."

They both knew they were acting like high school kids, but it didn't matter. They were too enveloped in their feelings.

Ann wheeled her Sebring out onto 550 south, skirted the city and headed east on 160 towards Pagosa Springs, the

104

passes, and the long drive home.   Tears welled up in her eyes.   She had been lying to herself all this time.   She wasn't happy and she knew it. Being with Chris had reopened her eyes to the thrill of passion and infatuation.   This was so missing in her life and now, having felt it once more, it pulled at her very being.   She could feel herself tighten and strain as she sat so uncomfortably in the car.   She pulled the convertible off at a scenic area to have a cigarette.   She leaned against the car, gazing at the valley below, looking back over the horizon to Durango.   She sighed. What would she ever do?

CHAPTER SIX

Leadership

I always knew I wanted to lead.   And, I understood exactly what that meant.   It meant that I would always have to accept that within in me; that it became part of my character, not just some trapping that I added on when I needed it.   It meant that I would have to be an example.   I would have to be a role model.   I would have to wear different hats at different times to move either the project or the people I served forward.   I knew it, I accepted it and I lived it.   I did not expect, though, that it would truly be like this.   I did not expect that I would lose my identity or the ability to go into the closet in the morning and pick out the persona that I wanted to be that day. It is more than just a job, I have become it, I live it, I am lost in it.   Its 24/7 with no daylight at the end of the tunnel. I must make decisions.   I must make bad decisions. And even if they are right, or even mostly right, there will be little to recommend them to most of the people I know, even the people I love.   I have aged so.   I can see it in my face, my hair, my posture, my demeanor.   I'm short with people.   I'm angry. And yet I do this with honor, because I am supposed to be here now, for exactly all those reasons.

President Raul Salinas DeSilva stared in disbelief and then felt the horror that stared back at him from the Communique. Sixteen dead, twenty wounded in a separatist assault in the northern province of Vila Real.   It was a coordinated attack on a police substation and military outpost, carried out by a band of insurgent rebels who demanded independence for a new state of Galicia, a region that encompassed Vila Real, Moelho and the provinces of coastal northwestern Spain. He buzzed his Executive Assistant and the intercom creaked back in its static tenor.

   "Get me Minister Pechorro.   Tell him it's urgent.   The utmost urgency.   Now."

She did as instructed and within fifteen minutes, Ferdinand Pechorro stood at the massive oak doors fronting the President's Office.   Ferdinand did not like being summoned nor did he respond well to urgency.   Barring a nuclear attack that he could actually see happening in front of his face there was no need to rush to do anything.   Bad things happened routinely in this world and no amount of speed would undo them.   It was better to methodically plan out how to respond and how to do it effectively in the best way possible.

As the stately doors rolled open, he once again gazed upon the opulence of the office.   Mammoth fourteen foot high ceilings with ornate carved cornices, gilded with gold trim and castings;   delicately designed wallpaper with overlaid tapestries from the Middle East;   fine china and ivory carvings from Japan and Manchuria;   all evidencing the colonial power of Portugal in its most successful decades. Sadly, it did not represent the Portugal of today.   It was meant to impress any visitor who entered, but had just the opposite effect on Pechorro.   His country was poor, full of strife and violence and it fed on the handouts of others in hopes it could revive an outdated economy.

"Come on in, Ferdinand," DeSilva gestured, impatient at even the fifteen minute wait, "You know about this?"

"Yes, of course. It came to us first."

"Is it the Liberation Army?"

"We don't think so.   We think it's a splinter group, one that espouses violence and doesn't particularly care about the long term outcomes."

"Have you responded?"

"No sir, not without your approval.   They hold both stations and possibly hostages.   We have some options for you, but none of them are particularly tasteful."

DeSilva thought for a second.   He trusted Ferdinand. He was ex-military, a general in the Federal Forces, and a determined fighter and strategist.

"What's your choice, Ferdinand?"

"Well, if it were my choice, I believe I would blow both buildings to hell.   We think there may be one or two hostages, but none of our people get hurt. The collateral damage is minimal. The buildings are both junk and our intel on the ground indicates it wouldn't be a great loss until new ones were properly built and staffed."

"And the other options?"

"We blast away until we have a breach, then send in our troops. We lose a few good men, possibly rescue the hostages and save the buildings enough to repair. We could also wait them out. I really don't like that. The political fallout is palpable, especially if they are able to broadcast out of the post radio station. Further, they may be able to entice reinforcements and we could have an all-out civil war. Getting them out of there immediately is the most important thing."

Ferdinand Pechorro liked his President well enough. He knew he was thoughtful and could make the tough decisions. He suspected which one he would take, but was then a bit surprised by the response.

"I'll rest on it overnight. In the interim, I want to start moving Federal forces into all of our areas of unrest. That's what we fought for the legislation for; to bring those new Federal units to bear on these problem areas. I want a full regiment up there with a full complement. You know what I mean. Artillery, air support, quartermaster, clinic; all of it. And I want another one in the Algarve, same thing. I also want another one in Oporto, but we have one with full complement there, so just the ground forces will do. And, it's time to put one in the Acorean Islands. Their legislature is just a little too independently minded for me. Their complement should include a new naval patrol squad."

"Yes, Sir. As to the current situation?"

"Okay, I'll speed it up. I'll give you my answer in a couple of hours."

Ferdinand was about to get up and go, then thought better of it. He sat, listening to a 17th century clock ticking and President DeSilva knew he was working on something.

"Mr. President. You know your opponent for election and some of his staff, right? Well, Pedro Cavadas's campaign manager is Alvarro Parros. I remember Alvarro.

He was a good officer in the service many years ago. A Captain when he went inactive. As you know, once in, always in. We could call him up. I like the idea of promoting him to Lt. Colonel for the regiment to go to the Azores. He'd be second in command and as such, wield very little power, but more importantly, we'd have him off the radar screen, out of the campaign and a thousand miles away from mainland. I think it would strike a serious blow to Cavadas' campaign, certainly disorient it for a while."

"Ferdinand, sometimes I think you'd make a better campaign strategist than a military one. That is just a splendid idea, just splendid. I'll make it an Executive Order. It can only be received as an honor."

"He will see through it, Sir."

"Accept an honor or go to jail for insubordination. Not much of a choice."

*

As per corporate protocol, David Deeds' Executive Secretary entered the board room first. The floor cushions had been replaced with plush leather office chairs, a clear indication of the new seriousness that pervaded the company's new attitude. The days of the counterculture were over. Those ideals had been ingrained into the corporate mission, but so had the trappings of big business, and EngenUnity was now one of the biggest. David wanted that evident in the surroundings of the office and the meeting rooms. As people grow and age, so do corporations and EngenUnity was now a fully grown adult.

David Deeds followed his Secretary in and sat at the head of the table, his favorite chair waiting for him. His staff were already there. He greeted them warmly, but there was a hint of a worried brow noted on his boyish face.

Per his usual agenda, he asked Detlev Augenstein to start with the financials. There, he had a base in reality and from there, planning could start.

"Are we in the blue?"

"Always, sir. That's not a problem, but some of our projects, our Research and Development are eating into our bottom line."

"Which are our major offenders?"

"Systems synergy is still a problem, but we planned on that. The Skunk Works is over budget, but we have many add-ons and change orders, but Graciosa worries me."

"New science, Detlev, is always costly."

"Yes, but It's not just the science. It's the labor costs, the transportation costs, materials, delays, etc., etc."

"Alright. I recognize what you're saying, but this is in our new missions, buried in foreign investment and overall, a small part of R&D. Since its all retained earnings, does it really have that much of an impact on the overall picture?"

"In the end, no, but at some point, if it keeps up, it's going to balloon on us and cause some real damage and, I'm afraid, invite a lot of unwanted scrutiny."

"Brian, your take on it."

"Detlev's correct in the escalation of costs. There have been several small problems that added together, cost a lot. For instance, delays in moving materials because they have to send some customs team out to the Santa Cruz airstrip to examine everything and it never seems to be convenient. They have to fly in from Sao Miguel. They want us to build and staff a customs house. And, then there's the airport. Our strip is half again longer and we provide our own maintenance. We're also bringing material and supplies in by ship and half way across the Atlantic is an expensive trip. Then there's labor, and I don't even want to go there."

David leaned back for a moment, then looked at Jackie, always on his left, and rocked his chair for what seemed to be an eternity.

"Let me think about that for a moment. Jackie, how's it going over at Rockland?"

"Delay after delay." She shifted uneasily at the abrupt change in topics. "Initially the one hundred and fifty percent size design scheme seemed no problem, but with the change philosophically to a space station type of operation with a pod vehicle landing and material hauling capacity even that size now seems overly cramped. The team has had to work out docking and uploading the pod and supply wagon, plus everything that goes with it. Taxiing back and forth presents fuel problems; and we still need sufficient passenger and living space. We are about on the same time line as when we started and we're a good three years into it. It also doesn't help that we have NASA and the General Services Administration constantly looking at what we're doing."

"I might be able to help with that, " Brian chimed in.

"We can get to that later," David interrupted, "Detlev, what would be the effect of operationalizing both components now, completely?"

"You mean, as ongoing businesses?"

"Precisely."

"First, you'd have to show some revenue and then all the expenses applied would be considered losses after the fact. All the expenses would be moved out of retained earnings and R&D; they would not be taxable as now, so as to cut our overall income and reduce our tax burden. It could save us millions."

"Then I think we're missing the boat, here. We're far enough along to capitalize on what we've already done. The Shuttle is mostly built, but faces redesign. We could open it as an adventure project; build displays around it; make it a working interactive museum, if you will. Jackie, could you work up something like that for me in a week or so?"

"Sure, Boss. No problem, but I'd like to talk to you about that privately."

"Okay, right after this." He turned to Brian. "Brian, we have the hotel and resort built and the staff housing for the contractors is almost done. We could expand the resort grounds and make use of Gibralter Beach on the east coast, right? So, let's add some real posh villas, each with a gorgeous pool and open the whole complex as a resort for Eco-tourism. We'll gradually shift the work crews to the central part of the island in newer construction later on. The resort itself is ready go, and for the Villas, If we start immediately, we could probably be ready in four to nine months ."

"That just might work, if we can get enough expert labor out there. I'll send Gavin down to Costa Rica and have him scout out the best of the Eco-Tourist Hotels and Resorts, just so we don't miss anything critical. Villas would be pretty much standard construction, so I'll have A&E start on the work ups this afternoon. Since the Habitat is offshore and fairly much ready for assignments, I don't think that presents a problem. We'll need to make some trails and a roadway, especially if we want to get crews, heavy equipment and materials over to the east shore, but that can be done immediately. I might have to bring in some pre-fab housing, initially, for contractors, but we can do it."

"Detlev, back to you. I can see the numbers rolling in your head."

"This is why you're the CEO, Sir. You think of things we don't. All this extra up front cost and most of the prior costs can now be built into the resort development. You can guarantee a loss for four to five years on paper. Then, even operational profit will still be a loss, factoring in depreciation. This beats the hell out of shelving R&D costs overseas."

"Then, I think we are in agreement that we have a strong enough working concept to initiate, so let's get to it. Brian, you and Jackie both want an audience, so I'll take you first."

The two executives waked into David's private office where his Executive Secretary was laying out draft reports for approval. Brian was still a bit disheveled from his journey. His appearance had deteriorated over the years due to a thirty pound weight gain and his refusal to accommodate that with properly fitting clothing. Still, there was no doubt in David's mind that Brian was sufficiently as powerful as he ever was.

"Gail, could you excuse us?' David gestured politely.

"I'll tidy up just a bit." She answered.

While she quickly finished her distributions, Brian had time to take note of the small changes in the office. As ex-military, he always used surveillance as a key to determining the nature of the situation. New to him in the past year was the model of the shuttle on the credenza as was a scale model of a domed city. On the wall, a new map of the Azores and on the adjoining wall, Project schedules for all six of the major initiatives the Corporation was currently working on. This was a working office, devoid of much decoration save a few paintings of Italy and pictures of resorts. David never had plants in his office. He paid no attention to them, referring to his space as that where plants go to die. Gail had quickly learned not to put any Flora in there after discovering she would have to go back in and save them later.

Brian's long standing relationship with his Senior Partner was always evidenced by very frank discussions.

"Dave, I didn't want to say anything in front of the others, but we have one additional problem that we need to deal with," David nodded, "and it's political. The local Acorean legislature is somewhat autonomous, as you know, and the Chair of that legislature, Gustave Pacarno, does not like us very much. I believe he felt pressured by the Federal Government to make the deal and has held it against us ever since. And, even though we are one hundred and eighty miles from Sao Miguel, he feels that we are destroying the Islands' character. He can't show or prove anything to that effect, but just doesn't want a large American Corporation footprint in his chain. I think we will have to pressure him."

"Brian, I'm sure our significant new investment for Eco-Tourism here will persuade him. I think this will just go away after we start the new developments."

"Dave, you always think that money and new ideas will be enough to handle the situation. For some people, that just doesn't work. Some people need to be coerced, even corrected if they cannot change their opinion. I think this is one of those guys and I think he needs some significant behavior modification. I may be the junior partner here, but you put me squarely in charge here with autonomy. You will just need to let me do what I do best."

David Deeds always knew that Brian Deming was a tough operator. He knew it when he partnered with him twenty five years before. He knew it and accepted it, because that was the one area he could not master, toughness. And business needed to be tough. He needed

Brian and Brian knew that as well.

"Alright Brian. It's your call. You know I always ask, though, that the full range of thought be given and the full measure of possible consequences be evaluated."

"As always," Brian tapped a two finger mock salute and departed rapidly. He had a lot on his plate.

Jackie Guiterrez popped her head in the door before Brian could close it.

"David, my minute, please."

"Enter." He really liked Jackie and when private sessions were required, always had Jackie come after Brian. A Cool Breeze after a Tropical Storm.

"David, I've never asked. It wasn't my area of assignment and obviously, I have my own issues with mine, but Brian scares me a bit with the Graciosa Project. What exactly are we doing?"

Deeds looked at her and smiled. She'd been professional and polite enough not to inquire, and he supposed he should open up a bit. She could put two and two together, but he didn't want her going off in a wrong direction.

"You are right in that this is not your area of assignment," David smiled again, "Jackie, what we are doing is that we are building the world's largest and deepest undersea habitat. It will create new technologies, a whole new science about living in challenging environments."

"But why?"

Now, that was the question. And it needed to handled delicately.

"For a new kind of eco-tourism, of course. A true look at the undiscovered ocean," he paused for a second, "No, Jackie, that's not it at all. Climate change will dramatically alter our world in the next hundred years. It is expected the seas will rise five feet by the end of the century. Do you have any idea what that will do to Billions of dollars of real estate and world business? If we prepare now, we may be able to save most of it. This Corporation is going to be on the front end of all of it. We will know how to protect all that can possibly be protected, and, of course, profit unimaginably from it."

That was an acceptable answer for Jackie, and far reaching. She had always admired David's vision. He was the epitome of the new corporate leader. He thought years ahead and always managed to get his team to share that vision. He got the best out of everybody.

*

Chris was going to be late for the call if he didn't hurry. He wheeled the truck into the RV resort, easily breaking the five mile per hour speed limit, kicking up a bit of dust and garnering a nasty look or two from some of the other residents. He liked being in a relaxed state when he called Ann and he wanted to be sitting in his living room sprawled out on the couch when he did it. He had been rigorous as he promised. He called her that first day after and then, every day after as she had wanted. It would be quarter to five, just before she closed up the law office for the day. The conversations vacillated over just about everything from current events to politics to work or non-work as in his case. Just the sound of her voice was reassuring and thrilling. He looked forward to it. And she, as well. Today would be a bit different. They were planning a getaway together and were working out the details.

He quickly hopped into the RV and punched in the number.

"Annie."

"I knew it was you."

"What's happening?"

"Nothing."

"Oh come on. You know very well. Where are we going and when?"

"There's a concert I'd like to see over in Aspen and there's a cute little Chalet type resort in Snowmass we can stay at. I can meet you there Friday. I'll take the afternoon off and I can get there by four, four thirty."

"I'll be there. Oh, I probably should know the name of the place."

"Crystal Peaks Chalet."

"Okay, great, I'll see you then…"

"Where do you think you're going?"

"I wasn't really, I was just excited."

"I haven't had my time on the couch yet."

They talked on for another hour and the relaxation of it put him right to sleep after they hung up. He woke up at seven and decided to head back into Durango for a bite and a few cold ones.

He liked going to the Strater. The Diamond Belle saloon was a lively spot for the somewhat over twenty crowd with a piano player who did a lot of ragtime tunes. The place was packed and he was lucky to find a spot to stand at the end of the bar under the interior balcony. It was just like you would expect from the Old West, the kind of interior second story balcony John Wayne's stunt man would go sailing over in the ever necessary saloon fight scene. It was beginning to feel like summer now and the tourists had begun to arrive. Many stayed at the Strater and many would come by for the early entertainment after debarking from the train just two buildings down.

He loved the ambiance. The ornately carved wooden bar towered over the crowd with its one huge centered mirror, the gorgeous mahogany ridge angled toward the end, the large wooden chairs to sit in perfectly situated and the reddish brown paisley carpet that accentuated the saloon hall look all blended together to give it that perfect feel. He also particularly liked the one waitress with the dimpled cheeks and long sandy, pony tailed hair who worked there on Wednesdays. He learned her name was Lena, but all he did was say hello. He also knew that his feelings belonged elsewhere.

It was a mature crowd, which he appreciated, and he had gotten to know one of the bartenders fairly well. Chris came from the cultural revolution where a good bar was a home to a certain crowd and you could get very comfortable being there after a time. He was beginning to get that feeling here, but, yet, something just wasn't right.

He had developed a relationship with Annie and it was

beginning to impair his social adventures.   He had no reason to base any hope on it.   He was free, but she was not and it was unrealistic to think that was going to change any time soon. But, over the past month of phone calls, conversations and plans, he had let his heart loosen a bit and he found now, that it hurt in a lot more ways than he imagined.

Somehow, the magic wasn't in the evening for him and after his third beer, he decided he was really lonely in a room full of people having fun.   It was time to call it a night. Tomorrow, would be better.   Maybe he'd go up to Silverton and have lunch.   That would be good.

*

The Albatross II, a hundred and twenty foot Russian built ice breaker, unceremoniously left Vancouver Port just as the sun's first rays peered over the mountain peaks to the East.   Gulls shrieked at the departure and swooped about the stern looking for perhaps some little snack left behind. Joe Hackett looked out the back window of the Helmsman's Bridge and watched them swirl around.   Like the inside of a dryer.   He chuckled to himself.

Joe had come a long way from Montreal and his terrorist forays in the North Sea. In his fifty plus years on earth, he had finally come to terms with who he was and what he had become.   He did not hate his former country any more, but he had no desire to go back.   He did not hold a grudge, but had developed a very fine sense of what is right and what is wrong.

His days as an eco-terrorist were short lived.   It was too dangerous.   And while he was good at blowing things up, he had an overriding guilt that he may have killed someone. It was a nagging dream sequence that came to him from time to time. He knew he hadn't, and he was proud of that, but it came to him in his dreams, this idea that he was responsible for a murder and had buried the body in some deserted place. It had to have been in another life, because it surely wasn't in this one.   Nonetheless, these dreams haunted him and he was glad to leave that life behind.

What those forays did for him was crystallize his hatred for multi-national corporations. He detested them with a passion. The majority of them cared little for the environment. They didn't care how many natural resources they devoured. They disregarded nationhood as an inconvenience and acted like their own little colonial empires. If they were compared to people, as they liked to be legally, they acted like psychopaths. Worse, there were state owned corporations, like the Chinese had, or the Japanese industries that filled the pockets of their officials. They had the full power and blessing of their respective governments and had no shame whatsoever.

He had joined WorldGreen six years before. He had always been around boats, down on Long Island and even in Montreal, where boating on the St. Lawrence Seaway was big business. He'd earned his first tonnage rating there and joined WorldGreen shortly thereafter.

The Vancouver Office was a small operation. It existed primarily to support the Albatross II, one of the two former Soviet icebreakers in the fleet. The ship was docked at the city's port and ran into the North Pacific to intercept whaling ships. The Albatross II weighed in at a shade under one thousand tons and carried a full complement of staff at thirty two. The WorldGreen crew numbered twenty six, including Stephanie, the Biologist and RN. He was particularly fond of her. He would make his way to her that evening and every other when the chance came. Nine others on board had particular skills, but the rest were needed to run the ship, and, in a pinch, run interventions on the high seas.

Joe was considered a Commander, just as in the Navy. He was second only to the Captain, a gruff, sturdy short man whose size and shape belied his strength. Captain John Danforth was as tough as nails and not one to mess with under any circumstances. He never said anything that wasn't of value; ergo, he never said much at all.

Joe stepped out of the cabin, slid down the stair rails to the foredeck and took in the city as it slowly disappeared. They had just cleared the Harbor and with Vancouver Island straight ahead just forty sea miles in the distance they began the slow turn down into the sea lanes that would take them past Victoria, then around and through the Straits of Juan De Fuca that separated the Canadian Island from Washington's Olympic Peninsula. Oddly, the wide channel reminded him of the Minch so many years ago. But this was a peaceful venture. The sun cleared the mountains and blinding rays streamed warmth across his face. He went back in to get his sunglasses and hat.

"Cap'n John. The usual?"

"Mostly. We set out for Kodiak and sit about four hundred south at the Gulf of Alaska, then move westward later towards Attu. We'll find them. We always do."

"Good, we'll be ready for them."

Joe went back out of the cabin, back down to the foredeck and did an overview inspection. The pursuit boats appeared to be all tied properly, ropes coiled as they should be. Storage bins had been fully stocked prior to departure, including the weapons bins. They hadn't needed to defend themselves yet, but they needed to be prepared just in case. This might be described as a peaceful venture, but it wasn't entirely up to them.

He went down to the galley and grabbed a cup of coffee. Everyone was in the process of preparing for the journey and double checking equipment and supplies. It would be a full day and night of travel to fully clear the coast and he would get a good portion of the night shift. He took the coffee up on deck and took in a deep breath of the sea air. Soon, he would go to his cabin and try to get some sleep. He'd get up just as the sun would set and they would still be in the Straits, with the Olympic Peninsula and its stunning mountain range off to their left. He would enjoy that view and the orange, red, then lavender and purple hues that would span out over the range and the Pacific in the distance until it was his turn to take the wheel. The sun always put on a show off the coast. It would add an inviting panorama that would accentuate the thrill of the chase.

CHAPTER SEVEN

To believe in this living

I am committed to my profession, to my job, to my marriage, my church, my friends, my community. I should be committed. I have been raised on guilt. I know why people have affairs. They do it because they are missing something. Anybody who says they don't need anything is missing something. I am. I am not full. I have needs. I need to be touched, to be cared for, to be listened to, to be, for some part of the day, the most important person in someone's world. I did not think of spending my life in the throes of a dull routine of the same old shit day after day. I remember the John Prine song. How can a person, go to work in the morning, come home in the evening, and have nothing to say. I have nothing to say.

Ann sat at the corner of her desk, a cup of coffee in one hand and a cigarette in the other. The motions, orders, statements, pleadings and assorted correspondence all lay on her desk, some in neat piles, others in disarray. She couldn't get to them, didn't want to face them. She stared out the office window to the front range, the foothills that reached near the city.

It had been a wonderful weekend. She had arrived in Snowmass early Friday evening and they went out to a nearby pub for very basic food and a little wine, then back to the chalet where they made exquisite love and rested, bathed in shafts of moonlight that filtered through the second story window. It seemed magical to have such quiet talk with a living silhouette. She could only make love in the dark, but the moonlight was unavoidable, and yet, entirely acceptable.

The next day they had squeezed in a short round of golf, then back to the resort to the spa and some sunbathing. They ordered in, a delicious room service dinner. That was a special treat for her. And then, they wanted to repeat the evening before, but were both exhausted and soon gave in to sleep.

Their passions re-emerged after coffee and a morning cigarette.   It lasted till nearly checkout time and when it came time to go, she cried.   Couldn't we stay longer, she had said. But how could they, he had said.   Not that they didn't want to, but she had to go back to Denver, and while he had nothing to return to in particular, he had to go back to Durango.

Here, back in her real world, she could feel the wheels coming off.   Her marriage was essentially an arrangement, two people living in one house separately.   They hadn't slept together in over a decade, separate rooms, a story apart. Paul wasn't hardwired for sex either.   He didn't seem to care about it.   That left Ann in a home with little joy, and little prospects for much more of it in her lifetime.   It was tearing at her.

She had fallen in love with Chris and he with her. They knew the minute they laid eyes on each other.   The smiles on their faces, the way their eyes danced gave them away.   The energy they shared together was unmistakable, the difference between loving someone and being *in love* with someone.   It filled her heart.

Now, reality was a problem.   How to deal with this. Chris had said the problem with being in love was that people felt they had to do something about it.   And, that was just not necessary.   He quoted an Indian friend who had said, "sometimes the purpose of a human being was to just be". All well and good.   Yes, but one has to think about it.   For the time being, she could just let it be, but she had the feeling this wasn't going to go away, the dread, the guilt, the feelings of shame. Yet balanced against joy, love, laughter and sexual fulfillment, there really was no contest.

She needed to clear her head.   She put the butt out, sat the coffee cup on the desk and strolled out of her office. Her two legal secretaries stared at her.

"I'm going out.   I'm not sure when I'll be back."

Her manner suggested that any further conversation about appointments or calls would not be received well.

Somewhere out there, he's walking around: the campground, the city, maybe back up in the mountains he loves.   Probably dwelling on that old unsolved case, or maybe just fishing, or maybe having an early lunch.   God, I miss him.   Shut up, Ann, you have a life.

I'm not going back today.   I think I'll drive up the canyon.

*

Chris was bored.   Without Ann around, he felt like a flat tire, deflated, unable to move, ugly and a problem.   He rode his bicycle for an hour in the morning and decided to go to Durango and visit the library.   He would read some more microfiche, go out for lunch and finally head back to camp for the afternoon.

He was looking back through the film forward from the dynamiting of the San Juan and remembering Sheriff Scott Jackson's voice speaking about the changing times, the need for the Village and County to separate itself from the hard drinking and fighting days of the Wildcat Miner.   Here and there he would see a headline about a new Kendall Mountain ski development area and an editorial on the wild west and a theme began to emerge that Scot had alluded to: the development folks wanted the miners out, wanted to clean up the place for good and wanted to build a wholesome family oriented winter center that would rival Telluride.

He started seeing articles and artist's renderings of what the new resort village would look like and the name of Western Slope Development Corporation came up time and again.   It was the driving engine of the planned project and had been seeking permits and meeting with local jurisdictional boards for approvals.

And after years of articles in the microfiche, it all just sort of evaporated.   He sped through paper after paper and found nothing. The only thing he managed to pick out was the name of a spokesperson, Michael McMahon of Durango.   He jotted the name down and decided that he was hungry.   He hadn't realized it, but he had spent four hours looking at the film and it was now two o'clock.   He went over to Farquarts for a burger and a beer and decided afterward to go back to camp and check out what he could on the computer.   Then, it would be time to call Annie.   He looked forward to that and found himself smiling.

It started to rain slightly as he left the restaurant.   The wind was picking up, too.   It would be smart to hurry back and roll up the awning.

Engrossed in the search, he forgot the time.   It was five o'clock and he should have called fifteen minutes before. He picked up the cell and hit the speed dial.   Annie answered in a feigned anger.

"You're late."

"I know, I got sidetracked."

"You're not allowed to get sidetracked.   I'm just about ready to get buggin' out of here."

"That's a visual I'd love to see."

"Don't be mean.   What kept you?"

"I've been researching microfiche and data bases trying to figure what went on here, you know, what would make murder and a few false arrests palatable around here. But I'm at a loss.   I feel like I hit a brick wall."

"What's the issue?"

"Well, it looks like a real estate company, Western Slope Development Corporation, was behind all the potential development up in Silverton and the major agitator for the social renaissance of the town.   But it just disappeared and I can't find a thing."

"Hmm.   You know, dear, that corporations have to file annually with the AG's office among other things, and that the State Department handles all the corporate documents, such as the original incorporation papers, etc. "

"Annie, I wouldn't know where to look."

"I guess that's why you want me around after all," she paused for a moment, "and if they did disappear, they would have to file dissolution papers as well.   I can search those data bases for you here if you want."

"Could you?"

"It'll cost you a dinner.   And, you have to come here."

"Say When."

"Next Wednesday."

"I'd happily do that ten times over."

"Alright, then. I'll talk to you tomorrow. I really have to go."

He sat back down in the chair next to the computer and looked around the camper. The rain had turned into a steady downpour that made a heavy patting sound on the rubberized roof. At times, it was comforting, but at others, loud and annoying as hell.

The camper was like a hotel room. Everything was okay here. He didn't need to be there. He remembered all those years ago up in Rollinsville, when the rain drove him out of a lean to and he walked a mile to the only bar in the village. At least now, he didn't have to walk.

He thought he'd take the short drive up to Tamarron, the golf and condo complex. They had a nice bar up there and it was an adult resort, filled with full time vacation home owners. It might be lively.

He drove up to the hotel and a valet took his truck. He headed straight to the bar to find only two people in it. Dead as a door nail. He ordered a bourbon manhattan and walked out to the covered deck that overlooked the upper Hermosa Valley. The rain had stopped and the clouds cleared the peaks. In the far distance, he could see Engineer Mountain in the fading sunlight. He remembered cresting Coal Bank Pass right next to it years ago in a surprise October snowstorm. That was one scary night. He didn't think he would live through it.

He sat in a wooden chair toward the end of the deck and the last remnants of rain pelted the tin roof above him. It sounded better than in the camper. He sipped the drink, remembering that snow storm and how by the time he'd hit Molas Pass, seven inches of snow were on the road and he had nearly bald tires. He had slid in low gear seven miles down the two thousand foot drop into Silverton with but large rounded stones protecting the edge of shoulder as the guard rails; it must've taken an hour and the whole time, he kept telling his Wolf-Shepherd 'We are going to die here, buddy'.

He chuckled at that. It was a crazy time. Not like this was so much more sane.

He ordered another drink and sat outside again until the oncoming darkness obscured the view, thanked the bar tender, then took the truck back down 550 into the city. Perhaps a stop at the Iron Horse would pick him up. He wished it were Wednesday already.

*

In the end, the solution to the mother ship's shuttle craft and cargo transporter was nothing short of genius. Bud McNaughton was grinning from ear to ear when he laid it out for Jackie.

"You see, the idea of the shuttle or the pod, if you will, being inside was highly problematic. So, we did a complete redesign based on function and aerodynamics."

"Yes, Bud, and it cost us a year."

"I know, I know, but let's forget about that for now. This is so much better, I can't believe we didn't come up with it sooner."

He waved to two assistants who went to the storage room and pulled out an eight foot long model of the new prototype.

"Look at the back of the top of the ship here. This looks like a deflector on a semi, with a window behind it. This front part of it is the cargo carrier, molded to the shape of the shuttle. The window here is in the front end of the shuttle part itself and note the engines are in the back just in front of the tail fin. It is also molded. They are attached together and detachable from the Space Craft either together or separately."

"But the tail fin," Jackie objected.

"Yes, that was an issue at first, because we also wanted to use the pod as a thruster for the ship, as an auxiliary engine when attached. It's actually multi-functional in this manner, providing additional power when needed, but also low speed thrust, or, for lack of a better word, trolling. We simply unlock the tail fin and fold each side down and you actually have an extra set of wings to use as the pod jets fire out over them."

He demonstrated how the fin worked.

"Our model testing indicates it will work fine and with the added fins on each main wing of the craft, stability as a whole is not an issue.   It is actually enhanced."

"Finally, access can be achieved to each unit, inside and out.   We can load the cargo carrier from the hold inside. And we'll fill it full from the outside prior to launch.   You get maximum cargo, maximum free space, additional power and maneuverability."

"This is just outstanding," Jackie mused aloud.

"Do you need approval to go ahead?" Bud asked.

"No, I have full authority here. But we have more to ask of you. We have decided to make a working museum and set of displays to open the project for the public, for a fee of course.   For starters, this gem here is more than I could have hoped for. I want a full size replica of this cargo carrier and the pod, sans engines, electronics, or components for a walk thru. That and maybe a shell of the Ship with mock up?   Then, some inter-actives, etc.   I think you get what I mean.   Can you do that?"

"Did you bring your checkbook again?" Bud laughed.

"I always bring my checkbook." Jackie grinned.   It was a smile that Bud had never seen on this pure professional.   It lit up the whole building.

Still grinning, Jackie exited the skunk works and walked out to her car, cell phone in hand.   She couldn't wait to call David.

She waited impatiently and he answered on the seventh ring, just as she was about to funnel her excitement into voicemail.

"Jackie?"

"Yes, Boss.   I have great news."

"Let's have it."

"They've got it worked out.   The new design and prototypes are just astounding.   They'll be able to provide the models for an inter-active museum and they tell me they can have all this done in a matter of months. I know they'll have tests to do and all, but they should be ready next year."

"Good. I want another one."

"What?"

"I want another ship. I want two. We want to be able to cycle them."

"What do you mean, cycle them?"

"One arrives six months after the other; in continuous rotation. Now, go back in there and tell McNaughton that's what we want. And get a price right away. He should be so flabbergasted that he may have a weak moment and we'll get it on the cheap."

"Yes, Sir."

Jackie shoved the phone in her purse, stunned. What had she gotten into? Things just weren't adding up. She had thought they were running two separate scientific enterprises, each developing newer, usable technology that the corporation would then create whole new markets for, but now it seemed the fusion of the two was inescapable. Had she been out of the inner loop? Her focus had been solely on the shuttle, without thought to the Habitat or its future purposes.

Jackie had come a long way from a simple upbringing, but all the education and professionalism in the world would not obscure the nose on her face. She had a good dose of reality as a child and no amount of gamesmanship or chicanery could get past that test. Still, she believed in David Deeds and his visions, no matter how obscure to her. And, she was a trooper. She would continue the task laid before her right to completion.

She turned on her heels and headed straight back into the building.

*

The Albatross II turned thirty five degrees and steamed full speed at twenty two knots westward. It lay a hundred and

128

twenty miles south and southwest of Adak Station and had been out to sea for two weeks traveling in whale hunting lanes known to the Japanese. They had dedicated satellite support from the base in Canada.

Joe Hackett had overheard the radio as the operator picked up the signal from Vancouver. A Japanese whale factory had been sighted about four hours distant and this was the second encounter they had since the left port. The first was relatively uneventful. The Albatross's harriers had raced around the Japanese ship and after an hour of disruption, the factory had moved away, peacefully.

Thereafter, the Albatross II had refueled in Adak Station and provided a couple days of shore leave for the crew. Adak did not have a lot to offer, but it was a welcome base just the same. Years ago, it was a major naval air station that had over six thousand service men and women covering the Alaskan Coast and Aleutian Island Chain. During World War II, it was the base from which America recaptured Attu and the westernmost islands from the Japanese.

Over the years, the need for the base reduced, the Navy began downsizing until 1997, when it closed the base. Most of the assets were transferred over to the Aleut Corporation, which then owned everything, including the roads, except for the airport. That was retained by the State of Alaska. It was a major air strip, on a par with most international airports, and flights left twice weekly. That was good to know since the Albatross and other ships needed to airlift crew to Anchorage and the hospital from time to time.

There were three major docks that served the fishing fleet and other transport ships and one Sports Bar, the Adak Station Sports Bar and Grill (ASSBAG), It was the only one left. The bowling alley and even the McDonalds had called it quits years ago.

Joe chuckled when he thought about it. He and Stephanie and several of the crew had gone down to the Bar and had tied a good one on. The young crew men and women, all dedicated and decent kids, had gotten smashed and could barely stumble back to the pier and on to the boat.

Laughing all the way back, they had agreed they had gotten assbagged in Adak. Assbagged and Asstagged. They were singing that when they got back onto the Albatross, giggling incessantly when the night watch yelled at them to shut the hell up.

He was still laughing about it when they got the update. High winds, typical of these cold northern seas, picked up and the swells started to crest over ten feet, slowing the boat to a crawl. Captain John had a scowl on his face, but as usual said little. He steered into the swells, taking them a few degrees off course.

"Joe, I'm going to lay off."

"Sir?"

"The reports say it'll get worse and even if we caught up with the bastards, I can't send those kids out in the harriers in these swells."

"Right, Skip; and they can't work whales well either."

"Good point. Find me a safe haven, Joe. Get me a reading off the GPS and chart it for depth."

Joe Hackett checked Capt. Danforth's readings and got his nautical chart rolled out and spotted East Cape Island, about ten miles to the Northeast. They had been following whaling routes but had steadfastly held close to the Aleutian Island chain throughout the voyage.

East Cape jutted outwards of the chain and behind the Island, Joe noted a deep anchorage that would keep them out of the swells and the bulk of the wind. It lay in the wide channel between East Cape and the Island named Garelot, a five thousand foot plus mountain thrusting out to the sea in the middle of the Volcanic chain.

Joe gave the skipper the coordinates and took up observation on the foredeck. The wind and sea spray cast up a mist that met the light fog as they turned about to seek their anchorage. On a good day, he would have been able to see the mountain in the distance, but not on this day. As they drew closer, he suspected it would rise out in front of him; an old nautical benchmark no longer in use in the age of modern technology. Thank God. The Aleutians had been a ships' graveyard for centuries.

Joe gave up a deep sigh. There would be no telling how long they would have to sit there, but their quarry wouldn't be going anywhere soon either. It was a cat and mouse game and it was called off for the day.

CHAPTER EIGHT

Arrangements

The two fishermen left the docks of Santa Cruz, Graciosa an hour before sunrise. They were fishermen from fishermen from fishermen; generations of Azoreans who lived by and from the ocean. Dark skinned and wizened from constant exposure to the sun and sea, they lived a hard life based solely on the catch of the day.

Just the first hints of the morning had come to color the sky with faded orange streaks that tinged the black and dark blue starlit night, encroaching on the shades of gray. They hoped to be in place as the sun rose, the best time to haul in the first of their catch. Their boat was little more than a large Bateaux, a square stern thirty footer latched to the old twelve horsepower motor that propelled it and with a single mast fore to handle the small sail that could take advantage of the wind. But, as usual, little wind pushed at their backs as they shoved off from their tether in the village's bay. The sail would stay tied to the mast, unless the afternoon winds picked up, and the motor rattled and spit as the boat lumbered forward against the light chop.

They had decided to take a different course to the banks southeast of the island, an area they seldom fished and hadn't been to for months. The course would take them on the far side of the Ilehu of Old Praia, the smaller of the two Graciosan Islands, then out easterly, looking toward the coast of Iberia, some thousand miles away. It would take them the better part of an hour to get the two nautical miles past the Ilehu to the sandy banks, some two hundred feet in depth, where they believed the fish had now migrated to.

As they passed the small island, they could see the new hotel and villas, the new landscape, the huge dock under construction and the improved sea walls. The village lay to the south of the new construction and the smoke from early morning fires had just begun rising from some of the rooftops.

They could hear an occasional rooster in the distance.   Dogs barked at the crowing in the light fog that hung close to the water's edge.

They had heard of the resort, but had not been this close to see the vastness of it.   Nothing like this had ever been built in the entire island chain and certainly not envisioned in the two islands that comprised Graciosa.   To the two fishermen, this was startling.   They looked at each other and shrugged.   This was an unknowable thing and they shouldn't let it bother them, yet it was still fascinating.

As they approached the banks, they could see a large barge with a huge crane on it in the distance around the eastern end of the north point of the Island.   It easily dwarfed their boat, tenfold, and sat squarely where they had planned to fish.   Curiosity drove them onward, even though they now knew they would have to alter their plans.   As they got nearer, it seemed as though the ocean itself was lit.   There was a soft green light emanating from the sea floor.   This was wholly beyond their comprehension and as they closed in on it, the lights in the ocean became brighter and more distinct, and their fear heightened.   By the time they were within a hundred yards of the barge and the lights fully lit the ocean floor in several locations, they were in shock, too scared to go any further and completely unsure of what to do next.

The elder shook his head and waved backward towards shore. The younger hammered the boat around and opened up the throttle to full speed.   Silent on their rapid trip back to the village, there would be much to talk about in the café later that morning.

*

Alvarro Parros let out a sound he had not ever heard come from within him as he looked at the letter.   It was a cross between a yelp, a gasp and a groan. The others looked at him in disbelief and he excused himself to stumble into Pedro Anabel Cavadas' office. Pedro was flipping through reports, looking at the polling data that had just come in for the week. Less than two months remained before the election and he and DeSilva were neck and neck.

The incident at Moelho had tossed them into a dead heat. DeSilva was blamed for the death of six hostages and eleven of his federal troops in the raid on the police station and the army outpost. It hadn't mattered that five people were saved and the rebels killed to a man. It was considered a botched raid, ineffectually planned and decidedly horribly implemented.

To Cavadas, the working people's choice, the benefits of being the alternative candidate were immediate, but he would himself agree that he probably would have done no different if he were in DeSilva's shoes.

Alvarro showed him the letter. Pedro was astonished as well, but not terribly surprised. He expected no less from a determined opponent who would stop at nothing to be re-elected.

"Looks like a nice promotion."

"You know what it is ?"

"Oh, yes, yes indeed.   This is to get you out of the way and disrupt the campaign."

"Exactly. I must report to Oporto in two weeks to begin training with the balance of the regiment to be sent out."

Pedro paused for a moment.

"Alvarro, I'm thinking this might not be so bad?"

"How so?"

"First off, you're to be a Lt. Colonel. That's not anything to sneeze at. Secondly, the election's only seven weeks away. If I win, and I believe I will, I will be able to make you a general or a minister and that would appeal to a lot of people. Thirdly, the campaign is in high gear, in no small thanks to you, and there is little your absence will do to stop it from a successful completion."

"As in I'm not needed anymore."

"I didn't say that, but the situation is here and there's

134

little I can do about it."

"Pedro, this is like being sent to prison or Siberia, or worse. There won't be a thing I can do there. I'll be taking orders, buried in day to day crap while the Colonel drinks at the officer's club or hosts soirees for the local dignitaries."

"Alvarro, Learn what you can and make use of your time. I'll be in touch and your time will come. Not everything we foresee will come to pass and you may find this might be one of the most beneficial things that ever happened to you."

"Oh, come on, Sir, you can't be serious."

"But I am. Deadly serious. The Azores has been neglected by our government for decades. This might be a chance to look forward to doing something profoundly good. Let's embrace it. Can you do that for me?"

Alvarro looked down at his shoes and snapped his neck upright.

"You know I'll do anything you ask, but I still don't feel right about it."

"Make lemonade, Alvarro. Make lemonade."

*

Ann Beauchesne examined the corporate filings on paper held in the State department data base for the three year period that the Western Slope Development Corporation had been ambitious in its planned expansion of the old Purgatory Ski Center into Silverton. In addition, she pulled and copied the original Articles of Incorporation. She noted the seven board members and as an afterthought, googled each of them. Four were deceased and of the remaining three, information was sketchy, but available. She also found the Dissolution papers and from the Attorney General's office, the required filings under Sarbanes/Oxley. She stuffed all of them in her brief case as she left her office at five p.m. She was to meet Chris at the Downtown Marriott.

This was Ann's town and she explained to Chris that

she needed him to get a room there, convenient to her office. No one would have any suspicion of a rendezvous when an attorney, attired for work, arrived at the Hotel, briefcase in hand, obviously destined for a meeting with an out of town client.   She could not afford to have her reputation diminished nor her firm tainted by her behavior.   And even though she was fully aware of all the possible consequences of her actions, she couldn't wait to see Chris.

In her briefcase, she also had a nightgown, her favorite perfume and other beautifying essentials.   She wouldn't spend the night, but she would bathe and enjoy her lover, cleaned and refreshed.

She also had asked Chris to order in room service. When she got there and went directly to the room, dinner was waiting.

The smile on Chris's face went from ear to ear.

"Chicken Parmesan, as you ordered, Dear."

"And the penne?"

"Absolutely.   And a nice, red Zin."

"I hope this all didn't put you out too much."

"Not at all, Annie."

"And, after all, I am worth it."

"Oh God, yes."

They kissed and sat down for a delicious dinner.

Afterwards, she pulled the documents out of the briefcase.

"Let's get this out of the way.   I pulled everything I could think of for your little mystery hunt, here.   I don't have any current addresses on the remaining board members. You'll have to track them down if you want to talk to them. The AG's filings are fairly standard and they weren't too involved then.   The dissolution papers indicate the company was bought out by a Simisync Corporation.   I didn't go looking into that, either, other than the fact that it is California based.   You'll have to do your homework on that, too."

"Thanks, Honey.   I appreciate it."

"That'll be twenty eight hundred and fifty bucks, please..........or you have to come back each Wednesday for the next three weeks."

Chris laughed.   If this was considered a set-up, he'd walk into the trap a hundred times.

The drive back to Durango was a weary journey.   At eight hours plus, even spectacular views can become boring. Afternoon showers pushed through as he crossed Wolf Creek pass on the southern route homeward.   Still, he had a soulful smile and a contentment within him, steeped in joy.   He loved Annie, truly, and she filled him with wonder.   He had loved, but had never been 'in love'.   It was something they felt together, and apart, only the emotional and physical after aura of it, the memory of two souls perfectly cradled together. Just thinking of those eyes and that smile would bring waves of elation over him.   At times, he felt like he would burst.

But what was to become of it.   For now, he was escaping a mess; living far from the things that used to matter in his life; out of touch with his family, out of touch with reality. He should be working, but he didn't seem to be able to bring himself to take a job.   And, he didn't like what he saw out there.

Did he and Annie have a future?   She would have to make major changes in her life and he didn't even have his own legalities straightened out.   In the end, the best he could hope for was to live in the present; to enjoy that which was being given him.   He remembered Janis Joplin.   When someone comes along, who wants to give you love and affection, I say, get it while you can.   Get it while you can, Chris, don't turn your back on love.

Up ahead, past Pagosa Springs, the long and wide escarpments lay aside isolated mesas and the high plains of New Mexico; only to brush upon and end at the foot of the majestic San Juan Mountains.   In their vastness and unrelenting wilderness, they could seem daunting and treacherous.

In this heat of the late summer, Durango suddenly seemed cold and lonely.

*

137

Gustave Parcanto wrestled with the complaints in front of him.   As President of the autonomous region of the Azorean Islands, he ran the regional government.   Head of the Socialist Democratic Party, he was responsible for the day to day operations of the island archipelago within the framework of a multi-party system.   Worse, he had to contend with civil parishes on each island and the rule of law was dictated by the Republic of Portugal.   In short, he may have been the boss, but he had to bend to local administrations and bow to the Republic.

It made situations like this very testy.   Residents and the local police in Graciosa were complaining about the big American Corporation and its constant building program. The fishermen were incensed because the underwater construction was damaging precious fishing grounds and quite honestly, scaring the hell out of them.   The noise from the Ilehu could be heard twenty miles away in Santa Cruz. Tourists were now coming into the airport on Corporate chartered jets on their own runway and hastily shuttled out to the Resort without so much as a whiff of the village.   This angered the local businessmen who had been told they would benefit from the development.

The police had been out to the resort, entertained, and then lightly brushed aside.   The manager simply refused to answer to any order and the local court dared not issue any further orders for the fear of reprisals in some manner.

He had been Chair of the Legislative Parliament years before when the Corporation had received all the approvals to buy the Island, the airstrip lanes and warehouses; and had been there when all the permits for the Resort and Habitat had been approved.   In essence, they had given the company free rein to do what they pleased in exchange for the massive infusion of cash into their regional government.   This largess had been responsible for several new medical clinics on eight major islands, had improved police facilities, and had paid for building renovations to the Administration Buildings in Ponta Delgada and the Legislative Assembly building in Horta.

Leafing through complaint after complaint, Gustave

realized he had a particular problem that he should not solve. This should be a Federal problem.   This should be a Federal problem because he wanted to pass the buck.   He wanted them to take the blame.   He had always been a separatist at heart and would have loved the ability for his precious Islands to gain their freedom.   They could stand quite well by themselves without living by the whims of Portugese Republic a thousand miles away.   If the Feds would make decisions that made the local parishes or the regional electorate angry enough, that freedom might be realized.

It would take greater effort now than ever before. Gustave knew that within a month the balance of a complete regiment would be stationed on the three main islands.   He decided he would dump the entire problem on the Commandant in charge, Colonel Leon DeSilva.   The good Colonel was a distant cousin of the President and had been given this posh position, which included not only full pay, but a fully furnished villa on the coast that rivaled anything in Portofino, plus full expenses for travel and entertainment.

DeSilva arrived later that afternoon, dressed in his casual whites and entered the Administrative office of Pacarnto.   It was a bother to be taken away from his heavy schedule of café con leche on the veranda, then his trip to the marina, and finally, his weekly meeting at Club Naval, where the officers planned the coming weeks' business.   Still, a meeting with the Regional President was not wholly unpleasant and he was never disappointed with the civility of the meetings.

"Tea, Colonel DeSilva?"

"That would be nice.   One sugar and light cream."

Pacarnto so ordered and the two sat in the two burgundy leather chairs in the corner where the window overlooked the harbor of Horta.   The tea was set on the round cherry coffee table between them and they began their discussion.

"Have you heard from your cousin?"   Pacarnto always assumed that the two were in contact and the Colonel always played along, but the reality was that Leon DeSilva rarely ever had any contact.   He had been given the post as a reward, given enough benefits to keep him quiet and content, and successfully banished to the islands where he could cause no trouble for his cousin, the President of Portugal.

"Yes, yes. He is quite pleased at the progress here. He is especially fond of the improved business climate from tourism."

"Just the matter I wished to speak with you about. I have several complaints here from the local constabulary, businessmen, fishermen and local parish officials regarding the construction and disruption to the local economy in Graciosa."

"Hmm. Have you discussed it with the Americans?"

"No. I have determined that this should be a Federal matter. If we intercede, it might create an incident and with the new Federal focus and the regiment coming, It might be interpreted as a pre-emptive effort to side step the government's interest here."

"Am I to assume that you want me to treat it as a military matter?"

"Colonel, with the police in Graciosa removed from any control of the situation and given the environment in which we now live, I see no other acceptable alternative."

"Senor Pacarnto. I have only two boats attached to my command and until the new four vessels come, I am a bit handcuffed, but if you insist, I can send a crew and a patrol out to reconnoiter the situation."

"I do insist and perhaps that would be sufficient."

"We shall see. But in the meantime, I am somewhat pressed for time. I have my staff meeting waiting for me. Would you care to join us?"

"I would love to Colonel DeSilva, but alas, my duties." He waved his hand at the pile of documents on his desk, "and now that we have agreed, I will have to contact all parties and indicate that the army will be responding to their issues. May I tell them of a time of arrival?" Pacarnto was not about to let his big fish get away.

"I believe I could arrange it within a week. Would that be agreeable?"

"Perfectly."

They shook hands and Pacarnto escorted the Colonel to the door for his return trip to Ponta Delgada. As he left, the regional President smiled. He was very pleased with himself. He had dumped the whole problem on the Army and could now claim he had positively solved the situation.

As DeSilva left the building, he smiled to himself as well. The situation had played right into his hands. He now could effectively claim control over internal Acorean matters and ingratiate himself to the American corporation. This would truly please his cousin. He could wrest any local power from the regional government as needed, when needed. And, suddenly, he had become the most powerful man in the Azores.

*

Chris Eberhardt was working the search engine until he felt like the enter key was beginning to send smoke off his fingers. He had gone through all the documents that Ann had given him and had decided to focus on the original Board of Directors of Western Slope Development Corporation. If he could locate and interview a few of them, he might get a better picture of what actually happened back then.

Unfortunately, search after search brought disappointing results. Four of the original Board were dead. Of the remaining three, one, Mike McMahon, the former spokesperson, was in an assisted living complex with advanced Alzheimer's. The second, Charles "Whitehorse" Gamble, a former congressmen, was listed in the Durango area, but no current address was given, and the last, Brian Deming was reputedly to be in Southern California. This meant he had only Gamble to access and he would have to hunt him down. This was another area in which Annie could help. She knew a lot about regional politics and the history of the State as well as anyone.

He called her at the anointed time.

"Hi Honey, how are you?"

"Acck, busy."

"You're always busy."

"I know, I know. I understand I put the pressure on myself. I wish you were here. I could use some time on the couch."

"I'm free every week, you know that."

"This week isn't so good. I've got a Chamber dinner, Bar Association meeting and a United Way fund drive meeting and three cases on my desk, all demanding my immediate attention."

"It is good to be needed, Annie, but don't you get lost in it all? I mean, I've been out of all that for months now and I can see how you can get caught up in it and I also see how unnecessary our participation is in most of these things. The world really doesn't need us."

"That's easy for an unemployed person to say."

"Yup, you're right. It is."

"This is not helping."

"Sorry, hon, I'm a little pre-occupied. What do you know about "Whitehorse" Gamble?"

"Him? Oh, quite the piece of work. A very adept politician. Used his political base to get elected, then switched parties. It really pissed a lot of people off. I worked for him on his Senate campaign. I thought he was a really good guy."

"Do you know where he is?"

"He's been out of politics for some time. I think I heard or read he moved to Aztec, you know, in New Mexico, just south of you."

"How could I find him?"

"Try the Republican party headquarters. Hell, try the Democrats, too. They both probably know where he is. Once in, they never let go of you. You could tell him I referred you. Look, Chris, I could help more some other time, but I really need to go. Call me tomorrow, same time."

"Yes, dear. I love you."

"I love you, too."

Chris put the cell phone down and plugged in the charger. It was too late to make any more calls; he'd have to make contact tomorrow. Had it had been a month later, the campaign seasons would be in full swing and the HQs would be staffed into the early evening, but not now.

The next day he contacted the Republican Headquarters promptly at nine a.m., as soon as they opened. Yes, they knew Charles Gamble quite well, even though he was now in a different district, and yes they could give him an address and a phone number from their database.

Chris called ten minutes later. A gruff, older voice answered.

"Your dime."

"Mr. Gamble, my name is Chris Eberhardt, former bureaucrat and currently unemployed historian. Ann Beauchesne said I should tell you she referred me. I wondered if I might speak with you."

"You're speaking with me now."

"I meant in person."

"What about?."

"Western Development Corporation."

"What's to talk about? It died years ago."

"Actually, there's a lot to talk about and the development boom of the four corners. You're the only one left I can get ahold of and your perspective would be unique, if not crucial, to my research."

"Mr. Eberhardt, I'm a busy man, but I have a golf outing on Thursday at the Aztec Country Club and we should be done by two-thirty. You say Ann sent you? That's good. The old saying in politics is that nobody wants anybody that nobody sent. If you want to meet me at the 19th hole, I generally have a couple of beers afterward and I could give you a few minutes then."

"I'll be there, Sir. How will I know you?"

"Just ask anybody. They all know me."

At the appointed day, and with room built in for unexpected delays, Chris took the short drive of thirty some miles south on Rt. 550, shifting through the rolling hills and table top mesas into the small village that held the ancient Aztec ruins, still a sacred site to both the Navajo and Mountain

Ute Indians whose reservations abutted the town limits.

As indicated, the Golf Course was on the left entering the village, just off a county road. Chris arrived a few minutes early, went directly to the lounge and bought a beer. It was a hot dusty day with just enough wind to make a slice or a hook worse and he wondered how he would fare on the course as he sat at a small circular table on the outside deck. Immediately, a waitress came over, apparently sensing a problem from an unknown person attending the private club.

"May I help you?"

"I already have a beer, but I might need another one."

"Are you a guest here, Sir?"

"You might say that. I am here to meet Mr. Gamble."

"Yes, okay. He should be along any minute now. He has lots of visitors here."

Disarmed, she smiled and offered, "I'll be glad to get you that beer, just wave at me."

"Yes, ma'am."

Content in the knowledge that Chris meant no harm, she went about her business as the next foursome came in, a little worse for wear and tear from the hot, dry heat and sand spitting wind. The waitress motioned to the tall grey haired member of the foursome, who excused himself from the group and came out to the deck to meet Chris. The waitress was right behind with two beers. Chris assumed that was on him. He was right.

"Mr. Eberhardt?"

"Yes, Congressman." He stood to shake hands and they both sat simultaneously.

"Ex. Just call me Charles. You're old enough. So, you're Ann's friend, eh?"

"From childhood."

"If I had been ten years younger and had my health back," he grinned, "I would have done anything to have that young lady by my side. What an elegant and handsome woman. But, alas, twas' not to be. Ann was and is an exceptionally gifted, beautiful, professional and extremely proper. She would never do anything untoward in any way. She must see something special in you."

144

Chris wisely let that one pass.   He was sitting across from a very distinguished individual, one whose obvious eighty plus years had only hardened his character and tempered his intellect.   The fact that he enjoyed life showed in his healthy grin accentuated by crow's feet that came alive when he smiled.

"You wanted to talk about Western Slope, right?"   He took a long swig of his beer.   It apparently had been a lot drier out there than Chris thought.

"Yes. Sir. It seems to me that there were big plans and they were driven hard, then all of a sudden, the project was gone."

"Before we start, you understand my disclaimer; this is purely off the records.   Yes.   There was a huge boom in real estate then, and commercial development ran right along beside it.   Money was easy to come by and highly leveraged. There were also some government incentives," he winked slightly, "and then, the bottom fell out.   The big ski center and all those condos planned for Silverton never got off the ground.   In fact, there was nothing left for Western Slope to do."

"Well, what about the whole clean up the County thing."

"Pretty much driven by our COO.   As a board member, I didn't mind that, it was a long time in coming and as a politician, well, it's difficult to market any product with baggage attached to it."

"Who was your Chief Operating Officer?"

"Brian Deming.   Brian wanted to clean out the miners, the hippies, the land leases; pretty much change the whole cultural landscape in front of the development so that there would be no negative issues when the new ski village opened up."

"How determined was he?   I mean, would he have done anything illegal to get his way?"

"That's conjecture, of course.   Again, as a politician, I only engage in conjecture if it were to benefit me.   However, let's just say that Brian was half rough. He was ex-military and had a bulldog mentality.   He didn't let anything stand in his way.   I have no doubt if the financing hadn't dried up and the incentives not disappeared, we would have seen a remarkable resort village just booming up there. No doubt at all. You know, he ended up being quite successful with that big software/hardware company out in California, EngenUnity. I think he's a full partner now."

"Do you think he was capable of murder?"

Gamble paused for a long moment.

"Young man, everyone is capable. It's just a question of will and necessity. I wouldn't have ever felt that way. But, I suppose…No, I won't conjecture on that, there's no benefit to me." He grinned.

"Why, Sir, did you ever leave politics?"

"Hell, son, I can get more done on the Tribal Council than I could in Washington. You've heard all politics is local, right? Local with real money and only two factions to deal with, that's where the real action is. You want another beer?"

"No, Sir, I have to drive back. Don't want to end up in a dry gulch."

"Too bad. Well, I should get back to my friends. But stop by sometime and let me know how you make out with your story. I'll let the manager know your tab is good here anytime."

He waved gracefully as he re-entered the club house. He was one of those guys who could so effortlessly take advantage of you and yet make you feel good about it, a born Congressman.

*

Brian Deming was livid. He had just returned from the meetings in California only to find out from his resort manager that an army squad and naval detail had been sent to the resort to determine the many causes of 'disruption' in Graciosa that supposedly had been the result of the resort and habitat build up. This was not acceptable. They had an agreement with the government and he was not about to let some pumped up, stuffed shirt of an officer come around, strutting his stuff and making a nuisance of himself at his project, his resort. He had dealt with officers like that in the service and he had no damned use for them at all. He immediately placed a call to the Regional President, Gustave Parcanto, on his direct line.

"What the hell was the meaning of that?" He didn't even identify himself.

"To whom am I speaking?"

"You know damned well who you're talking to, Parcanto. Why was that 'Posse' sent up to my island?"

"The Colonel felt the need to take a look, Mr. Deming, I'm sorry to say."

"Well, so am I. This type of harassment just for the hell of it is not any part of our agreement and I'm going to put an end to it. What is this Colonel DeSilva's number?"

"I'll ring him for you, Mr. Deming and you can meet here if you wish."

"Tomorrow, then, at eleven a.m. would do. This is a private meeting, Mr. Parcanto. We'll discuss our resolution with you afterwards."

Brian Deming went to the Yacht, Moontracer, and met with the Captain at the resort's new commercial dock and arranged to take the company's tethered speedboat that would have been winched by davit on to the rear deck of the main ship on voyages, but now sat alongside the floating hotel for quick runs to the islands or for pleasure outings. The hundred fifty mile trip to Ponta Delgada would take about three hours in this craft and Brian loved racing it.

He left bright and early around seven a.m. The engines rumbled up to a cruising speed of about forty five knots and the sleek, cigarette styled cruiser popped across the waves on plane as it quickly left the commercial dock behind in a sea of spray. Two hours and forty five minutes later, the boat glided into the harbor at Ponta Delgada and under the instructions of the harbor master, crept into the slip assigned at the city marina.

Deming reached for his brief case as he prepared to disembark, then thought he wouldn't need it for the meeting. He changed his mind at the last second, grabbed the case and left for the municipal complex.

The president's office sat in one of five governmental buildings that surrounded a small piazza with a fountain in the center, a fine place for workers to gather for a lunch or a morning coffee. He went to Parcanto's office ten minutes early and was motioned by the assistant into the private meeting room where, to his surprise, Colonel Leon DeSiva was already waiting, attired in his dress blue uniform, regaled with all manner of sash and cord.

"Unless I miss my guess, you would be Colonel DeSilva."

"I am, Sir, most pleased to meet you."

They shook hands politely and sat stiffly across from each other.

"I required this meeting, Colonel, because of the recent visit to my resort by your troops and the navy escort."

"Merely, a formality, Senor Deming. There had been some complaints. We just wanted to make sure everything was in order."

"I can't have that sort of thing going on, Colonel. We have a resort to run and Federal troops showing up is bad for marketing. I'm sure you are aware of our investments in these islands and our agreement with the Republic. We need to come to an arrangement."

The Colonel stiffened just a little bit more.

"We are prepared to provide our own security force and the way I would approach it would be to retain all non-citizens who trespass and remove them; however, your citizens would be referred back to your custody for whatever action you would deem to take. That should take care of any complaint issues."

"That would be somewhat inappropriate since I am in charge of all the islands by decree."

"Colonel, you may want to re-read our agreement with the Republic, which clearly provides a sovereignty clause regarding our purchase. That said, I believe that rather than tie up the courts with this and waste both our time, we could come to a financial arrangement."

The Colonel was visibly taken aback, not because he

was shocked, but because this was exactly what he had hoped for.

"I suppose, Mr. Deming, that I should consider this in respects to both of our positions.   What do you have in mind?"

"A lump sum payment to the account you designate for five hundred thousand dollars with a monthly stipend thereafter of two thousand per month for the next five years. In return, your forces will stay away from our island, our habitat or any of our facilities, including the airstrip and warehouses in Santa Cruz.   We will continue to support the customs office, etc.   This will all be written out contractually, which I have taken the liberty of drafting."

He reached into his briefcase, pulled out the two page contract and a corporate check for five hundred thousand dollars made out to Colonel Leon DeSilva, unsigned, with a memo for facilities and services support and handed both items to the Colonel.

"Review these now, Colonel and I will gladly sign that check if you sign the contract agreeing to these terms."

DeSilva knew exactly what he was getting into.   He could be crucified for this.   However, he also knew that he held his position at the behest of his cousin.   And, his cousin was in the political race of his life.   He could very well lose and Leon knew he could be replaced in months.   Gone would be his villa, gone his lavish lifestyle, gone, his leisurely routine.   The check that sat in front of him would mean the ownership of that villa and the monthly stipend, the means to afford a comfortable living regardless of what happened to his position.

If his cousin lost, he would be surely replaced and quickly forgotten.   There were so many other fish to fry that he would go unnoticed, possibly forever.

"I think, Mr. Deming, that this would be a sound policy and we should proceed."

He took the pen and signed the contract.   In turn, Deming signed the check and handed it to the Colonel.

"Colonel, my staff will be in contact with you to make the follow up arrangements to your satisfaction.   I'm sure everything will go smoothly.   It has been a pleasure meeting you and I hope you don't mind if I say that expect to never see you, or your men, again."

"Absolutely, Sir.   The pleasure is all mine."

*

The Albatross II steamed out from the fog behind East Cape Island and entered the Alaskan Sea like a giant serpent gliding effortlessly across a steaming river.   The seas had calmed and the two days of Anchorage had been a bit of a respite for the crew.

Now that the swells were a manageable three to five feet with light winds at eight knots, the ship could unload its inflatables in pursuit of any whaler they came upon. These hard shell, inflatable twenty footers were not unlike the larger Coast Guard versions used in warmer climates. Coupled with ninety horsepower outboard motors, the "harriers" were fast and highly maneuverable.   Generally, a crew of three was needed for the tasks of pursuing the moving factories, cutting harpoon lines, freeing whales, and criss-crossing the shipping lanes, slowing the factory ships' pace to a crawl.

Joe examined the ropes and pulleys to determine that no snags existed and that the four inflatables could be dropped without issue.   Accidents were unacceptable and often dangerous, so great care was given to the maintenance of the boats and their attachments.

The Albatross hit full speed of twenty four knots and lumbered across the sea for four and a half hours.   The ocean varied little in its sway and spray, the winds held to a light breeze, and gulls shrieked aft of the ice breaker as it headed to deeper water.   The island chain had slowly disappeared in the distant fog that clung to the land like a Velcro strap.

Radio reports from Vancouver had indicated that a Japanese whaler had been in the area three days before and it was a known fact that they would not leave a successful hunting ground until the hold was full. Satellite images were inconclusive because of the foul weather and the shipping lanes were quite busy this time of year with tankers, large fishing vessels, and even cruise ships plying the waters.

Just after the crew finished their lunch, a hulk was sighted in the distance. The Skipper adjusted his course and picked up his intercom.

"I think we've got one. Let's get prepared. All hands to stations."

The crew responded almost instantly, dumping dishes in the bus station and moving quickly to pick up gear on the way to the deck. Stephanie went directly to the first aid/nurse's room and picked up four kits, one for each boat. Joe left the foredeck and joined the Captain in the wheelhouse.

"That's definitely a whaler," Joe motioned with his left hand as he looked through the field glasses.

"Looks familiar to me," the Captain added.

"I hope it's not the same one we collided with three weeks ago. We had a tough time running them off."

"Yeah, I didn't like those bastards one bit. They were a nasty bunch."

They closed to within five hundred yards and Joe could make out the ship.

"It's the Hokandu. It's the same damn boat. And they've snagged one. I can see the line."

The skipper grabbed the intercom.

"Prepare the harriers. We're going in. It's the Hokandu again. Suck it up."

Sixteen young men and women moved to the inflatables, threw in their gear and began the process of lowering over the side. At three hundred yards distant, the Albatross slowed and the boats were dropped. Once released, the mother ship would close in for a quicker pick up, but the harriers had to do the close order work, especially with a harpooned whale caught at the back of the floating factory.

Two boats set out for the bow and began the criss-crossing pattern that would slow the ship while the other two boats headed for the whale. One crew of four would try

151

to cut the harpoon line and the other would try to remove the harpoon from the whale, always a risky business.

The Hokandu's gaping hull was open in the stern, readily waiting for the whale with its wide elongated ramp set to bring the beast in for processing. There wasn't much time left to spoil the catch. The crew set to cut the line had two holding the line down with grappling hooks while another tried to cut it. The helmsman just tried to keep the craft steady in the swells as they went about their work.

The second boat had two crew members trying to remove the harpoon. They managed to roll the whale just enough to get ahold of the lance. If the wound wasn't too deep and the prong not hopelessly embedded, they might be able to pull it out. That failing, they would take a small chain saw and cut it off as close to the wound as possible, hoping that the whale might live and be able to purge out the remains later on.

Just then, the harpoon gun fired from the whaler. The weapon went directly over the heads of the crew engaged with the whale. It was meant as a warning and even as it dove harmlessly into the sea the Hokandu was beginning to turn. That brought the front two inflatables closer to the others, all on the port side of the ship and between the Albatross, which was closing at low speed.

Sensing that time was not on their side, the crews worked faster to free the whale. The harpoon had punched such a wide hole and the humpback had put up a strong fight such that with a few sharp twists, they were able to free it and quickly backed up as the whale rolled away slightly. It had been hurt badly. The slack allowed the second crew to cut the line seconds later.

The Japanese, incensed at the loss and this second encounter with the Albatross reacted instantly. Two men climbed to an aft deck and pulled off a tarp.

Joe couldn't tell if the mounted machine gun was an older version of the anti-aircraft deck guns used during WWII or a newer model. The rifle was specially mounted on the highest aft deck of the whaling ship and it didn't much matter which kind it was because it was firing directly at his crew mates as the harriers zigged and zagged past the broadsides and stern of the ship.

This just did not happen in real life and Joe was in a state of shock as he watched this event unfold in front of him. He was dazed by the stupidity of it. Yet, there it was. The gun was raining potential death at his people.

Fortunately, the rolling seas made accuracy an issue, and the automatic rifle's heavy rounds flew astray of his crew mates in the first few barrages. Still, it would be only a matter of time before deadly damage would occur.

Joe raced down the rails to main deck and clutched at the tool box on the starboard side of the ship. He ripped open the latch and pulled out the first rifle his hands came to as he heard screams in the distance. His people were being hit. He checked the magazine. It was full and he clicked the safety off. It was a lever action Henry .22 that had a twenty two shot clip. It would have to do.

Joe turned quickly and could see his crewmates diving for cover in the boats and one set trying to pull one of the young women into the inflatable.

Joe took aim and began to fire. He hoped he would get lucky. The swells would make any shot inaccurate, but if he kept up fire, he might hit one of the antagonists. His first four shots went high, the next five low, hitting the plate walls and rails about the gun, but his next five found flesh and bone. He saw one of the Japanese spin backwards, probably a shoulder hit, but the other doubled over. That was a torso shot and that stopped the fight.

Joe fired again until he exhausted the clip, then stepped quickly over to reload. He didn't hear any more firing as he grabbed another clip, and could see the Hokandu limber up and its stern rear ramp start to close. They had had enough and were pulling out. Meanwhile, his crewmates were still swirling in the sea trying to recover from this unprecedented confrontation.

Once all the boats were rescued and hoisted aboard, Stephanie greeted the crew men and women with her emergency pack. She hurried the wounded to the medical room, where she had four beds. She had five to tend to.

But the worst news was immediately evident. The young woman hauled back on to the inflatable had died and one of the men hadn't made it back to the raft. He was lost to the sea.

Nothing like this had ever happened in the organization's history. This cost of human life was unbearable, for this work was never meant to end in 'warfare'. It was God's work to save one of his most precious creatures and while the people involved were clearly dedicated, none of them thought they would have to give up their life to do it.

Captain Danforth radioed to Vancouver to let them know what happened. He then called into Adak Station. He apprised the Coast Guard of the situation and was ordered to return ASAP. The wounded could be treated and evacuated as needed. Danforth then ordered Joe to find a storeroom that could be turned into a makeshift morgue.

Twenty minutes later, Stephanie arrived at the wheelhouse. One of the wounded wouldn't make the journey to Adak. He would have to be airlifted. Danforth got on the radio again to the Coast Guard and they authorized a helicopter rescue that would be there in an hour. Stephanie hoped there would be enough time.

Joe went below decks. He was shaking. He could not believe what had just happened and he was sick about it.

I have killed someone. I don't actually know for sure, but I feel it in my heart. This is the greatest dread of my life. I have always been against violence, always. That is what took me to Canada all those years ago. I could not ever see myself killing anyone. I know it morphed into something else later, but that was where I started from and that was my destiny. I lived as an ex-patriot and had given up a whole life I could have had, all because I could not stand the thought of taking a life. And, now, I have done that. I feel like I betrayed myself, that my whole life up to this point was a sham, a lie that I covered myself with. How can I forgive myself? I know I may have saved others' lives and I know I had to do it, but now that it is done, I have to carry this in my soul for eternity. How do other people do this? How do they live with it? God help me.

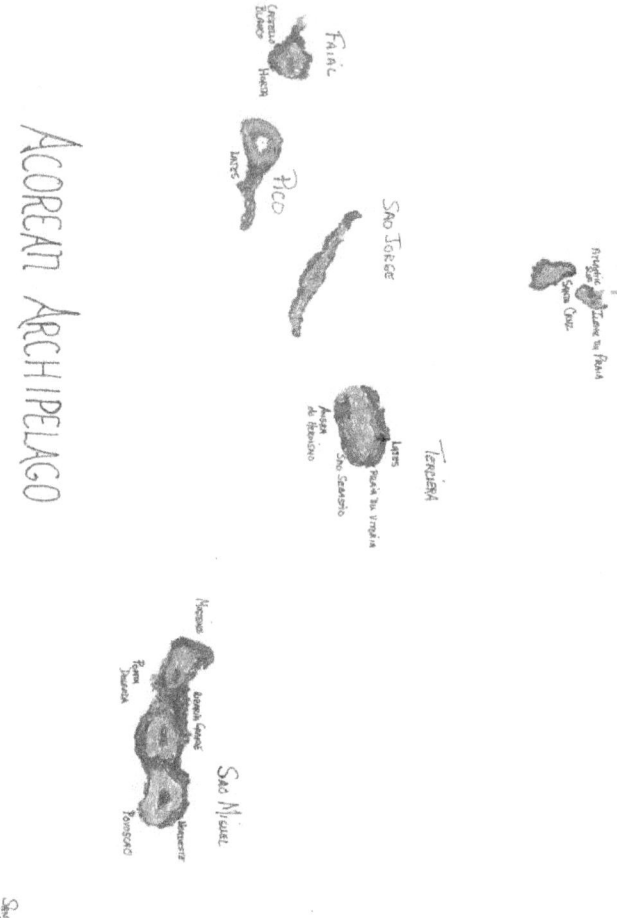

AÇOREAN ARCHIPELAGO

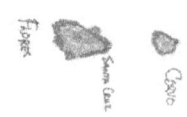

FLORES

SANTA CRUZ

CORVO

FAIAL

CASTELLO BRANCO

HORTA

PICO

LAGES

SÃO JORGE

GRACIOSA

NORDESTE

SANTA CRUZ

GUADALUPE

LAGES

ANGRA DO HEROISMO

SÃO SEBASTIÃO

PRAIA DA VITORIA

TERCEIRA

MOSTEIROS

PONTA DELGADA

RIBEIRA GRANDE

NORDESTE

POVOAÇÃO

SÃO MIGUEL

SANTA MARIA

CHAPTER NINE

The Habitat

Dr. George Thomas Preston led the first team into its new home. They had met on the commercial dock at the resort and were escorted on to the submarine that would take them to the Habitat. The boat was especially designed to carry eight tourists at a time and had a cargo hold to carry material and equipment, so it was fairly large and spacious for an eco-tourist sub.

There were windows larger than standard portholes and observation plexi-glass lites on either side of the walkway that allowed them to see the sea bed in the distance.

With him was his wife, Suzanne, also a PHD in Oceanography from the University of Rhode Island's Program, who specialized in Atlantic Archeological studies and Dr. Solomon Charles "Chuck" Frost, whose Doctorate in Ocean Engineering and advanced work in Biologic Oceanography with URI led to the development of the Inner Space Center, along with the Habitat's chief engineer, Wayne Trudeau, who came from a major Californian Development Corporation with a hydraulics and mechanical engineering background, specializing in Marine and Navy structures. Wayne served double duty as the ops manager for the Hotel complex as well.

Dr. George Thomas Preston had received his degree from Florida State University, met Suzanne, whom he alternately called Suz or Suzie, at a conference in Key West years later, got married, and they were the first couple to live in an undersea habitat twenty years ago at the John Pennekamp facility off Key Largo. They lived there for three months in the largest undersea habitat in the world at the time.

But nothing prepared them for what they saw beneath them. The complex dwarfed any other known undersea habitat fivefold. A large U shaped building lay ahead of them with a covered central courtyard that was then connected at the ends of the U with a huge domed Atrium. Wayne Trudeau began the accompanying narrative to what they were seeing.

"First, we scraped the sea bed to lay down the foundation, using the robot subs, divers and the crane/construction barge.   Then, we lowered modules into place and cemented them with the newly developed adhesive.   The three center modules forming the backbone of the U are the lab areas, where you'll be working and collecting the required data.   The five modules on each side are living quarters and study space and the courtyard is a common area to view the sea above and to allow for a bit of exercise."

"The Atrium is our proudest achievement.   This is meant to be an undersea garden and greenhouse.   We built it with blocks, specially designed structured insulated panels (SIPs), not unlike Legos, that snap together to form the arches and high density plexi-glass was fitted in at each stage, all sealed with a clear version of the adhesive. The Atrium can withstand eight times the pressure that it is likely to bear, so we feel confident that nothing short of a nine point five earthquake could move it."

"Additionally, we placed an outer rim of concrete footing around the Atrium. Since we occasionally, in geographic terms, have tremors, we felt that an exterior shell may be needed in the future.   We don't anticipate this as yet, but, it would have been much more difficult to add it later. Better to be safe than sorry."

Wayne completed his narrative as the sub settled onto the docking station and the Captain went thru the sequence of locking, connecting, and securing the hatchways that led to the entrance at the center of the lab modules.

Dr. George Thomas Preston entered as the Captain motioned him onward.

"Well, Suzie, this is home for the next four months. Hope you'll like it."

She looked at George, then Trudeau.

"Wayne, you say we have internet and television?"

"Yes, ma'am."

"Then I'll be just fine, George."

Dr. Frost examined the lab critically.   Modeled after

the Inner Space Center at URI, it still was much larger and more sophisticated, as he had demanded. There were three large screen monitors, wall mounted, with another half dozen surrounding them.

There were two rows of computers, each attached to a sensor array. Other control units with screens hugged the base of the walls around the lab, housed in the three large sections at the base of the U in the Undersea Habitat.

NOAA and the Oceanographic studies programs had focused on 'Telepresence', the ability of remote vehicles to photograph ocean floor sites and transport their associated video, plus sensory data via satellite to computers at a command center in some standard, constant location. That could either be on a ship like NOAA's Nautilus, or at an on shore site such as the center at URI. The Habitat, however, focused on the data of the seas affecting its own structures, including molecular changes in its interior and exterior atmospheres. Telepresence would be used later on as the activities of the Habitat expanded. And, in addition to the scientific data collected, the center was also host to the new Eco-Tourism business and Telepresence was a star attraction for two tours a day.

These were necessary distractions for Drs. Preston and Frost. But they had a long list of performance standards to meet during their tenure there and two particular molecular studies were required: One, the manufacture of water and two, the disposal of waste. These were, obviously, critical to any continued sustained human presence in any such environment.

The next phase of construction for the Habitat was the Desalinization Processing Building that would be attached to existing piping. This would convert sea water to drinking water and would replace the current Island to Habitat water line. After hearing how the Habitat was originally constructed, Dr. George Preston insisted on a remote operation vehicle (ROV) to map the sea floor.

"It appears that no scientific precautions were taken in the construction of this Habitat". He directed his comments to Wayne Trudeau.

"You see, Dr. Preston, that Mr. Deming is quite determined. He could have cared less what was under the sea floor when we started the building just as long it passed stability and integrity tests. He wanted the structure built and he wanted it done right away."

"I have noticed in my relations with the man, that he is not particularly considerate of proper protocols."

"No, he's not. He is a bottom line guy who will not accept less than what he wants."

"Well, we can't have that in the future," Dr. Suzanne Preston advised. "This is a scientific community here and we need to do things by the book in the future. As an ocean archeologist, I don't want us to miss out on anything significant, no matter how insignificant it seems to Mr. Deming. We'll insist on the mapping before we start anything else."

Wayne Trudeau nodded his head. He reported directly to Deming and knew Brian would not like delays, but also knew that the facility existed for a greater purpose and the scientists were there for a damned good reason and Brian would have to accept that. He didn't, however, expect him to be particularly pleased about it.

*

Alvarro Parros reported to the base in Oporto for his three weeks orientation. This was not to be a basic training. The two companies were seasoned troops and he was the commander of these forces until they arrived in the Azores. They were to get used to the command structure and facilitate their readiness to leave with four additional ships at the end of the month.

Oporto was the first capital of Portugal and the second largest city in the country. Originally settled in the 4th century by the Romans, Oporto was conquered by the Moors in the eighth century and then one hundred and fifty years later liberated. In the fourteenth and fifteenth centuries it became a shipbuilding center and home to the seafarers who would become famous as explorers.   The son of the first King John was Prince Henry the Navigator, who in 1415 led forces along the coast of Africa, the first of their colonization efforts.

The city, then, had a long history of exploration and naval operations.   In Oporto, the newly designated regiment was stationed at barracks at the old navy base on the north side of the Douro River as it opened to the bay.   The structures dated back to the late eighteenth century, damp stone lodges that the British took from Napolean's French in the assault of 1809.   In fact, the Portuguese government leased the buildings from the English for the housing of the detachment.

As troop commander, Alvarro wasn't obligated to stay in the primitive shelters.   He had a small stucco one story home next to the grounds, adjacent to the park overlooking the bay. He appreciated the well-kept red tiled houses that lined the river and the bay that provided a stunning view from the slight hilltop that rose from the water line. He enjoyed his walks to the compound, filling his lungs with the moist sea air that constantly wafted in from the Atlantic. At least, the stay would not be totally disagreeable, although he chafed at the prepared routine and soon to be finalized exile to the Island Archipelago.

The training included a familiarization with modern anti-terrorist tactics, house to house warfare, and operations of the four vessels that would take them to Punta Delgada.   It was during these periods that Alvarro had the ability to get to know fellow officers and establish a bond with the ship commanders.

The ships were purchased by the Portuguese Navy from the US Coast Guard.   Four Point Class ships, decommissioned ten years ago, had been transferred to the base.   These eighty two foot ships were replaced by a newer class for the US that could house the modern Coast Guard's staffing by both men and women, plus rapid deployment of boarding rafts from the stern.

The United States Armed Forces inventory was a veritable world-wide market place for arms and equipment.

In fact, it was the major export for the country that espoused peace, but constantly was at war.   Alvarro kept up on world affairs and was amazed that the US had voted down the international nuclear arms disarmament program, aligning itself with Syria, Iran and North Korea against the other one hundred and fifty three nations of the world in approving it. He had heard that one congressman from Utah had cited the second amendment to the Constitution as the reason he voted against it.   Alvarro did not know that the American citizenry should be allowed to have nuclear weapons and that puzzled him, but nothing about that country made sense to him.   If Pedro Anabel Cavadas were elected President, he would use the United States as the benchmark of what not to do.

The old point class ships, though antiquated for the US, were perfect for Portugal.   They weren't at war and weren't ever likely to be. They didn't need to rapidly deploy any boarding teams because there was no drug smuggling in the Azores, nor were there any pirates within fifteen hundred miles.   They weren't dealing with massive civil unrest, nor did they need to blockade the Island chain or plan an assault on some rebellious atoll.   They did, however, have four fine ships that could serve as a deterrent to any possible revolutionary activity and signal a strong presence to the Acoreans of the nation's determination to defend against separatists.

Each ship was well armed.   They had one 20mm cannon, five M2 Browning machine guns and one 81mm mortar.   That was a significant amount of fire power.   The ships could be run by a crew of eight, but had berths for thirteen and could transport another fifty servicemen in cramped quarters.

That still would be an ugly two day trip, Alvarro thought. Even at top speed of twenty six knots, it would take at least that long to get there and fifty servicemen plus gear and the crew would have to grin and bear it.   Fortunately for Alvarro, he rated a second officer's cabin but he would still have to put up with all the complaints.

The detachment spent three days on and off the ship,

learning its operations and weapons use. With a working navy crew of only eight, any incident or illness could have adverse consequences, and the ability of the servicemen and officers to reinforce ship activities was not only useful for the journey, but also for their assignment in the islands.

By the end of the last week, there was nothing else to learn, no additional assignments that made any sense and they were ready. Alvarro would miss Oporto and would like to return some day, but was now ready to take on his post. For better or for worse, the Azores would be his home for a while and like his mentor had suggested, he might learn something useful out of the ordeal.

*

The commuter train pulled away from the airport at the apportioned time, not a minute early, not a minute late. Brian Deming smiled at the conductor who promptly closed the sliding door on a dozen would be travelers who missed the last tick on his watch. He loved the Swiss. So precise, so unwavering; and the populace knew it and expected no less. They could be pissed off about it, but they would know that in exactly five minutes and forty two seconds another train would arrive.

Zurich was the largest city in Switzerland; a banking and commercial mecca that draped itself around Zurich See and sprawled northwards towards the Rhine Valley and the Bodensee. The Swiss were known for their privacy, confidentiality, and security; especially when it came to finance and international relations. Neutral forever, Switzerland was not above aiding and supporting all manner of international organizations, no matter who they represented.

Blackthorn International had recognized those facts as perfectly situational for all their needs and had established their headquarters there. Brian Deming needed to hire private security for his Island Ilehu du Praia, The eco-tourist resort, the Undersea Habitat and construction barges as well as the Airstrip and facilities in Santa Cruz, Graciosa. Blackthorn was his choice, but he felt compelled to discuss the deal in person and after four months on the Moontracer and on the resort, he felt the need to get off the Rock for a few days.

The train pulled into Hauptbahnhof, the central station and Brian exited out of the massive building's south facing entrance.   Opting for a walk on the nice sunny day as opposed to taking the bus, he strolled down Bahnhofstrasse, the main commercial and shopping district of the city.   He enjoyed viewing the latest fashions out of Paris, just weeks from the catwalks to the store windows and the jewelry shops and the bustle of city as all manner of the public walked emotionless to their appointments, all undoubtedly on time. They didn't seem to notice the ornate, turn of the century stone buildings, as he did, nor that the fashions of the day seemed to lack any semblance of color; all shades of gray and black with white.   Typical French, he thought, boring moody style with either a hint of heroin chic or massive depression.

He turned right at the Burkiplaz, the marina and water transit post on the See and walked lake side another four blocks towards Todl Strasse. He looked southward to the mountains at the end of the lake that still had some snow on the caps some thirty miles distant.   In his four day stay, he really should make a trip down there.

Across the Quai, 112 Todl Strasse stood, a magnificently ornate six story stone structure with gold leaf cornices beneath the eaves of a Mansard style roof.   Even the dormers evidenced elegance.   That would be where Blackthorn would be; top floor in a penthouse style layout.

He entered the building through the main door and headed to the elevators.   It struck him as humorous that there was no security to greet him.   It was either obviously superfluous here or the Swiss just did not give a damn.

From what he could tell, the office consumed the top floor.   He entered a lushly decorated waiting room, full rust colored carpet and comfortable leather chairs.   A Secretary handled phone calls from a headset behind a solid wall with a thick plexi-glass sliding window between them.   No doubt it was bulletproof. He didn't need to tap and she recognized him from the photo that lay on the file in the center of her desk. She buzzed him in.

Brian went into a large meeting room that featured a conference table and eight or ten chairs and photos covering the walls that exalted the operations of Blackthorn. He noticed that none of the shots involved violence; they were simple pictures of uniformed men and women in various locales with the nomenclature clasped to the frame: North Korea 1994, Thailand 1997; Somalia 2002; Sudan 2004, etc. They were meant to impress, but Brian Deming knew they could have been taken anywhere.

Colonel John Magruder entered from a side office. Thin and fit for someone pushing sixty, he was reputedly the great great grandson of the Confederate General Jeb Magruder who faced and fooled McClellan in the Peninsula Campaign. The two had never met, but had talked and emailed.

"Pleasure to finally meet you, Mr. Deming."

"Call me Brian."

"Yes, Sir." The Colonel was either deferring to a higher authority or just following a pattern of customer service formed long ago. Brian couldn't tell. He motioned to a couple of chairs and they both sat.

"You've indicated to me, Sir, the basics of your needs, but not the details."

"As I've mentioned, its relatively straight forward security, 24/7, but without concern for full strength nighttime ops, nor any black ops. It's a resort and we don't expect any serious confrontations, but we do have an agreement with the local magistrate to control our own grounds, deport those who don't belong, and return to their hands those who they should prosecute or remove. That said, I think we still need some weaponry."

"Then, we don't need to assign rangers," Magruder added, "Just trained security who know how to use force and how to properly transfer troublemakers."

"I also want air security, and I have thought about this a lot, so I think we need a couple of armed helicopters with a pilot each and I'd like a third for some testing we'd like to do. I think we could use a couple of patrol boats as well."

"Do you want these on a lease basis, Mr. Deming?"

"Yeah, that would be fine. I don't suppose any of those leases could be extended or include and outright purchase?"

"Yes, of course, that would be standard contractual stuff for this business."

"One other critical consideration."

"Yes, Sir?"

"Whoever you assign to manage this platoon has to report directly to me. He can advise you, and you can call me, but he has to take my orders on the spot. I can't have it any other way."

"Understood, Mr. Deming. I think we can do that. We've had those kind of arrangements before. And I have just the guy for you. Captain Charles Kane. I've taken the liberty and asked him to be here to meet you." Magruder called out to his secretary who tweeked her headset. Within ten seconds, a tall, muscular dark haired, fully uniformed Blackthorn Officer and ex-marine entered the room, a large sidearm attached to his belt.

"Mr. Deming. Glad to meet you and look forward to working together. Charles Kane; but the men all call me Candy, cause I'm so sweet." He shook his hand in an iron grip and the same was returned.

Deming smiled. There wasn't an ounce of sweetness in this guy.

"Former topkick, Charles?" Deming asked.

"Yes, Sir, how'd you know?"

"E-6, Reserve, Gulf War I."

"We're going to get along just fine Mr. Deming."

Deming was thrilled. Magruder had played it just right, thinking ahead on the assignment well before the ink had hit the paper. The meeting confirmed his intuition and that was why he had insisted on a face to face."

"Can you draft me a contract today?"

"I'll have to pull together some figures on the equipment, but yes, I can have it together tonight and send it over to the hotel."

"Send Candy over with it; and we'll go hit the red light district for some brews.   I think we might have a few tales to tell.   Oh, and one other thing, Colonel.   I want the team in place in a week.   The copters and boats can come a little later.   And make sure the lads have multiple arms and more than sufficient ammo.   I want to be fully prepared."

"Consider it done, Sir."

*

Chris got the call from June right after he finished talking with Ann.   June sounded shaky, but Chris knew she had a stiff drink in her hand, a double manhattan, he guessed.

"Aunt Grace died this afternoon, about three o'clock."

He knew it was coming, but it still saddened him deeply.   You couldn't find fault with the loss of one who had lived a full ninety five years, but she was such a sweet, gentle soul, and she would be missed.   And, he had the opportunity to say goodbye months ago.   She had been in the home for over three years, while Alzheimer's slowly took away her memories and her awareness.   It was a depressing place to visit, not so much for Aunt Grace, as she seemed happy and content, but for the others, who were so totally lost.   Chris could only think of the once brilliant minds that had been so unavoidably wasted and what they might have been like. Now, many were virtual zombies, encased in the human form without any sense of consciousness.

The last time he saw Aunt Grace, she did not know who he was.   She called him her sweetie and sang to him…"Let me call you sweetheart, I'm in love with you.   Let me….." It was so odd that she could remember the words of the song, but not the people around her.   He hoped he would die in his sleep, perhaps with a wonderful dream.

"June, you're the Boss here.   What do you need to have done?"

"You know the house is a mess.   She never threw out

167

a thing. After the services, we'll have to be there and start the process."

Chris groaned.   He knew this could take months. Really.   There was stuff in there that went back one hundred and fifty years.   It had been their grandfather's house before Grace's and everything since the Civil War had been moved from the old farmhouse into the General Store in Portsmouth and then, into the large, shake sided cottage in Jamestown.

"There's another complication, Chris."

"What could be worse?"

"As you know, Aunt Grace wanted co-powers of attorney, so that idiot cousin, Valerie shared some responsibility.   She moved into the house, then rifled off some of the contents, claiming it was her right or that the items belonged to her.   We're missing cash, a lot of jewelry, cameras, baseball cards, our grandfather's gold pieces and Morgan silver dollars, that I know of."

"It figures.   She is an arrogant snob who has this sense of entitlement.   She'd rationalize anything if it fit into her scheme of things. What does the attorney say?"

"He represents the Estate.   He says we need to find another lawyer to take on the matter of this evil."

Chris thought for a minute.   "I know just the guy, if he'll do it.   John Willie.   He was a frat brother in college, has his own law firm in Providence.   John has handled some, shall we say, delicately colorful high profile cases."

"Well, we will need someone like that."

"June, this is such a mess.   I knew it would be and I guess I thought it wouldn't happen for a while yet.   Christ, we'll have to live there.   I don't know how else we can do it. God knows how I can clean it up enough to be livable, with all that junk in there. And, Annie isn't going to take it well."

"Annie?   You don't mean my Annie, do you?"

"Yes, June, I do.   It's a long story and it'll have to wait until I get there.   Meanwhile, I've got a lot to prepare for to get ready to leave."

"How soon can you get back?"

"I'll need a week to take care of stuff here, then probably five, six days to get back.   We'll need the truck, of course, and I can't be without wheels. So, I'm driving.   I'll have to put the RV in storage.   God, death is such a pain in the ass."

CHAPTER TEN

Quebec City

Captain John Danforth was stuck at the dock in Adek Station. He wouldn't be leaving anytime soon, half his crew was missing. Stephanie had been assigned to the clinic, to assist with the tending to the wounded who had not been flown on to Anchorage. She would leave in a week or so for Vancouver and at some point, additional crew would be sent out to aid the skipper in a return voyage to home base.

Joe Hackett had been sent on to escort the severely wounded to Anchorage and the casketed dead to Vancouver where other arrangements could be made. Once there, he had been asked to move on to WorldGreen's Canadian Headquarters in Quebec City. He had no idea what they wanted and hoped it wouldn't take long because he'd like to be back in Vancouver when Stephanie arrived.

He took a cab from the airport down to the river at Port Royale where the offices lay adjacent next to the historic district near commercial docks. Since WorldGreen operated a small fleet of sea going vessels that were primarily registered in Canada, Quebec City made perfect sense. It was first settled at Port Royale directly at the point where the river narrowed severely, but also blossomed outward. The settlement, fortified in the early sixteen hundreds, could control the traffic on the river at that point, and yet, it was a deep water port as the river widened dramatically as it flowed seaward to the Gulf of St. Laurent. Great Lakes Tankers commonly plied the waters thru the Seaway from the west, making their way to the end of the river near the tip of the Gaspe Peninsula. The river was a full seventy five miles wide when it reached the bay. It was so wide that It wasn't uncommon for whales to swim upriver one hundred miles as far as Tadoussac.

Joe waited a full twenty minutes before the Director could see him. It apparently was a busy day there, not the least because of the incident a week prior up in the Alaskan

Sea.

"Sorry, I'm late, Joe. We had a fund raiser in Montreal and the traffic back was awful." Director Whiteford definitely showed signs of weariness.

"That's okay, Sir. It isn't hurting me at all to rest a bit here and there. I kind of appreciate it, lately."

"Don't get too comfortable, Joe. We have something for you." He waved to Joe to walk outside. They crossed the street and sat at a bench next to the pier.

"Ever since the shootings, I can't get a minute without the phone ringing. We can talk here."

"I will say one thing, though," he went on, "If you really wanted a lot more money coming in, arrange a shooting. Our donations have quadrupled in the last week and more coming. I would rather, of course, not to have anyone killed nor have any wounded or injured. What can I tell the families? Nonetheless, that is the side effect."

"Do you want me to go back?"

"No, we have another job for you. Apparently, there's a lot of commotion in the Northern Azorean Islands, Graciosa to be exact. We've gotten a lot of chatter about the destruction of fisheries, bizarre underwater construction, the inability or the total indifference of the Portuguese government to look into it. Some unknown corporation is behind it, using an Eco-Tourist Resort and a holding company as its cover. We want you to take a couple of people and go look."

"It doesn't sound like much, why bother?"

"Because nobody seems to care and we're supposed to; because it's another case of a multi-national corporation over stepping government, using its power to ride roughshod over a native culture. Besides, somebody hates this company and I got a five million dollar anonymous donation to go look. Will you do it?"

"Why me?"

"Joe, you handled yourself very well last week; probably saved a lot of lives. We need somebody like that, someone who can keep their cool in a dangerous situation. You've been a Commander for a while, so it's not an unlikely

171

thing to make you a Captain."

"But why us? Don't get me wrong, a five million dollar donation is great, but if somebody doesn't like them that much, why don't they or their company just hire somebody to check it out?"

"Too traceable. There'd be a contract, a direct line. Somebody would find out, even if nothing went wrong. They obviously know more than we do at this point, but they don't dare go any further. We're in the save the seas business and we get thousands of donations that just appear as revenue on the balance sheet. And this isn't America, where large donations, even to Non-Profits, have to be reported. No, Joe, we are a perfectly logical choice for someone who wants to know a lot more about something like this. So, are you in?"

"I do hate multi-nationals. I kind of wanted to go back to Vancouver, but I guess another month or so won't make much difference."

"Good. When can you start?"

"Well, we can't fly out there because we'll have to carry a lot of gear, especially if we end up diving."

"I already thought of that. We have arranged for a trawler, a Grand Banks seventy six foot Aleutian."

"That's funny."

"Why?"

"I just came from the Aleutians. Anyway, I'll want some modifications."

"Like what?"

"For starters, I want a couple of .50 caliber mounted machine guns. I saw what they did to us out there and if we're going to run into trouble, I want to be able to defend ourselves; and not just a little bit."

"Okay, but we can't do that kind of work here. You'll have to take it to Halifax for that kind of refit, but there may be other stuff as well. You can decide, the checkbook is fairly open on this. The boat is docked over in the City Marina there," Whiteford pointed down the shore, "Slip 124. Your mechanic is already there, Bill Hafner, but you'll need a couple of other crewmen."

172

"One question."

"Yes?"

"Is this a clandestine mission or are we open?"

"I'm playing it by ear, but probably clandestine if we're mounting guns."

"I'm not telling you then who else will be on board, but if I can find him, I'll pick him up in Ireland. Meanwhile, I'll go see Bill."

They shook hands and parted. Whiteford advised him to return the next day for documents, cards and cash. Joe walked along the old colonial waterfront the half mile down to the Marina.

Bill Hafner was a bit of a legend at WorldGreen. A Viet Nam vet, Air Force Captain who was stationed in Okinawa during the war, Bill was a missile base officer who specialized in Nukes and high end weaponry. For five years, he flew in missions in and out of the Far East, ran WWIII simulations, and learned how to work on high tech equipment. At the end of his second tour, the Air Force decided they would send him to Minot AFB in North Central North Dakota. Bill did not want to go to North Dakota. He liked Okinawa. He loved the Asian culture. So, Bill transferred to the motor pool, where he learned everything he could about engines, from jets to four cylinder jeeps; and he enjoyed his continued stay In Okinawa.

However, eighteen months later, they shipped him off to North Dakota anyway. Furious, he managed to stay a little over a month, then one day, he signed out a jeep and clad in full dress uniform, drove the hundred miles up to Antler, parked the jeep at the Border crossing, informed both sides that he had a top secret meeting with a Canadian officer, showed them a stamped and sealed envelope and calmly walked into Saskatchewan, never to step foot on American soil again.

From Winnepeg to Toronto and then Quebec City, Bill became the best diesel mechanic that WorldGreen could lay their hands on. He had been with them fourteen years. Normally, he would not have been available for this type of mission, but was in between projects and therefore the next in line.

Joe approached the slip to see the affable man leaving the engine hold and climbing topside. He still had all his hair, wavy grey that swirled out from under the Greek fishing hat he religiously wore. He was pushing seventy and had rounded out over the years, but it didn't look like he had lost a step.

If he didn't recognize Joe, he had at least expected him.

"You the new Skip?"

"Joe Hackett, at your service."

"Bill Hafner."

"I've heard a lot about you."

"None of it good, I hope."

"On the contrary, quite the opposite."

"Then my work here isn't done. So, what would you like to look at?"

"Do you know anything about this mission?"

"Something about going off to Portugal to save sea bass. No, I don't know shit."

"You're probably not far off. There's a secretive holding company that's messing with the Azorean chain and some of the fisheries there. Nobody seems to know what that is except for the fact that they have an Eco Tourist resort and some kind of construction undersea. And somebody really doesn't like them, so we've been funded, if you will, to go have a look."

"That means trans-Atlantic. That's not going to be easy. Come with me."

He took Joe down into the guts of the seventy-six Aleutian.

"We've got twin CATS, C18, 1015s. Good solid diesel engines. We cruise at sixteen knots, not fast, but this is a trawler and you know these are for efficiency and distance. That said, we hold twenty nine hundred gallons, but only a range of about eleven hundred miles @ 2000 rpm. That's a bit short of at least two ports we have to get to."

"Can we improve that?"

"Let's walk through."

Hafner took him through the salon down to the

174

staterooms.   There was the master suite, midships; the 'VIP' stateroom in the bow, a guest suite between the two and an aft cabin for a crew of two.

"We only need three of us," Joe stated, "so the crew quarters could go.   Can we get another large fuel tank in here?"

"Yeah, you could rip this out, but we'll have a weight problem, so we'll have to add some buoyancy.   That could push us up to seventeen hundred miles, which should get us from St. John's to Faial in the chain, but it's a stretch."

"Two things, Bill.   First, we have to go to Ireland and pick up our third crewman.   He will be especially useful."

"That's the northern route.   Hope we have a lot of time.   What's the second?"

"We have to mount some hardware.   I want a .50 caliber on the bow and one behind the pilot house here.   We have to go to Halifax."

"Halifax Iron Works and Drydock," Bill grinned. "Only ones who can refit the trawler for the added fuel and provide the guns.   My, this is going to be a fun trip."

Hafner truly looked excited.

"I hope not too much fun, Bill.   I'd like to get us back all in one piece."

Joe enjoyed his two days stay at the Frontenac Hotel courtesy of WorldGreen.   It gave him a chance to get a bit of café time.   It reminded him of his days in Montreal.

Checking out after a breakfast on the Veranda overlooking the river and Port Royale, he took his duffel and rolling suitcase and hopped aboard the Funiclear that took him down the steep grade to the Port.

Exiting the terminal, he stopped into the office to pick up his documents and then was off to slip 124, where Bill Hafner awaited him.

"Mornin', Cap'n"

"Anybody who owns a boat is a Captain.   Just call me Joe."

"Okay, Joe."

Hackett threw his bags on board and crawled over the

175

railing onto the boat.

"I forgot to ask, Bill, are you married?"

"Yep, going on twenty three years this time, to my lovely wife Renee."

"Did you tell her how long we'd be gone?"

"I told her a week or two and I'd let her know if it was going to be any longer."

"Bill, you know very well we'll be gone at least a month, maybe two."

"Yeah, I know."

Joe couldn't help himself, he laughed.

"You know what they say, Joe. It's better to ask for forgiveness later than permission up front. Besides, she won't miss me that much. What about you?"

"Oh, uh, no, I don't have anybody really. I just have never been in one place long enough to actually set down roots. That and relationships just never seem to pan out. The longest I had was, like, three years. And we never got along that well."

They finished loading all the gear, including the diving equipment, which they hoped they wouldn't use and managed to set out a little past noon. It was a late start.

"Cap'n Joe?" Hafner came up to the pilot house after they made headway into the channel, "since we can't get that far today, how about we stop off in LeMalbaie?"

"Any particular reason?"

"Three actually: Good harbor and pier, eighty nautical miles downriver and the Casino at the hotel. We'd get there about time for a late dinner."

"I can see why you're legendary, Bill."

They pulled into Charlevoix just as the first hint of darkness tinged the sky, tied up the boat, cleared the harbormaster and forgave the idea of dinner and went directly to the Casino. It sat adjacent to and across from a small valet drop off area from the magnificent hotel that bore the name Le Manoir Richelieu. It was a sister hotel to the Frontenac, one of many built by the Canadian Pacific Railroad and now one of the majestic resort hotels in the Fairmont chain.

Joe was up seventy bucks when he decided to go lounge in the hotel bar. It didn't take long to return his winnings and he was beginning to feel a little self-conscious and a little out of place amongst the well-heeled residents. He stopped to tell Bill he was going back for a night cap on the boat and went down to sit on the aft deck; to have a brandy and watch the lights twinkling along the river and down at the small city on this coast line.

He went to bed around eleven. Bill came in at twelve forty two. He knew this because Bill banged into every immovable object on his way past Joe's stateroom to his. This was either going to be a great trip or one he could shoot himself over.

*

Chris pushed open the screen door to the front porch of the two-story shake sided house on Marine Avenue. The early morning fog was just thick enough to obscure the young sun, covering the orb like a shroud so as to barely feature its outline. The white picket fence that surrounded the property was dotted with late blooms, the Dahlias his favorite. His Aunt had carried on the family tradition of gardening and had delighted in raising Dahlias and Coxcombs. They added so much beauty to the house and decorated the fence and property line with a kaleidoscope of color and shape.

He could hear the foghorn from the lighthouse at Beavertail in the distance and the sound still fascinated him. He remembered living off campus years ago and hearing the forlorn blare that sought to save ships from the deep. Centuries of ocean life where his family had lived and worked since the sixteen hundreds had given him a deep land and sea memory of the place that spanned far past his meager years on this earth.

Out west, the Aspens would be turning, covering the mountain sides with a blaze of yellow and light red. He missed that, the smells of the mountain air, his daily forays into Durango, but mostly, he missed Annie.

Jamestown was a fresh breath of quiet compared to the bustling summer season of the western slope. Summer homes dotted the island that still featured working farms and housed a small but adequate business district. It was uniquely self- sufficient and doggedly protective of its character. No tree could be removed without approval. He appreciated that because the island always looked the same to him as when he was a kid and visited the old homestead of his grandparents.   .

It had been two weeks since he arrived at the house. June would not stay there, preferring the hotel on the bay side facing Newport. It could be said that the best view of that City was from the Jamestown docks; all the beauty and none of the noise. It was helpful to Chris to not have commotion in his life at the moment. He needed to focus. It took the better part of the first week just to clean and repaint the bedroom, plus repair and freshen up the bathroom just to be acceptable for use. Old people couldn't help themselves when it came to keeping up a house. His Aunt had tried, well into her nineties, but she couldn't see well. Coupling that with the inability to physically do the work and the house had pretty much gone to hell. It was stock full of newspapers, magazines, boxes, bottles and the kitsch of the better part of two centuries. He had ordered a dumpster to be placed in the yard so he and his sister could start the process of tossing out the junk. Some of that would be painful, but not everything could be an heirloom.

Thank God the master bedroom opened to the second story porch that overlooked the west side bay. Here he could sit and gaze at the water and Narragansett a mile and a half distant. He could see the isthmus that connected the main portion of the island with Beavertail to the south. He could hear its foghorn wafting through the fog in the evening, see its light harken out to the bay. It gave him a place of repose and a sense of peace.

He would take the short twenty minute walk down to the coffee shop on the docks. He walked past Chopmist Charlies, where he would probably have lunch and then past

Sympatico, the Italian restaurant where he would enjoy some wine in the outdoor patio surrounded by the tall space heaters that chased away the early fall cold.

June met him at the picnic table on the docks behind the restaurant there. Boat owners were busy winterizing their boats and preparing to dry dock them. The fog began to lift and the sun warmed them while the bay quietly woke to the business of shipping and recreation.

"Let's review the plan." She was business like as usual. In the past year, June had let her hair go to feature some of the natural grey that infused her strawberry blonde hair. Even though she had fought it for so long, it had given her the distinguished look of a well- heeled Mother Earth matron. Chris swore the girl was born to embrace the hippie generation but then her calm sophistication and age defying good looks belied her years.

"I hate review. However, I still plan on going up to Providence this morning and meeting with my friend, John."

"The attorney, J. Giles. Like the band?"

"Well, yeah, I guess. Not the same time frame, though. If anybody knows the criminal mind and how to deal with it, it's J. Willie. Do you have the inventory lists?"

"Yes, that was one good thing Grace did."

"It's a start. I know the estate attorney doesn't think much of our chances of getting most of the items back, but we have to try."

"Meanwhile, I'll meet with him later this afternoon regardless and try to nail down the accounts, but I can help for a while with the trash."

"Let's go have some fun chucking shit." They finished their coffee and June gave him a ride back to the house.

That afternoon, Chris took the forty minute drive up to Providence to the heart of the inner city. John's office had moved to the first block of North Main Street, three blocks from the Capital and just a block off the river. The four story stone and glass structure sat squarely adjacent two parking lots near two blocks of similar small commercial buildings and retail outlets.

Chris chuckled as he first noted the Irish Bar on the first

floor.   How would John Willie ever get anything done?   He took the flight to the second floor where the new sign, J. Giles and Associates hung over the door.   He entered and a charming woman smiled at him.   John had been expecting him and came directly out.

"Chris!"

"J. Willie Giles!" They shook hands heartily.

"Yvette, this is one of my oldest friends, Chris Eberhardt.   We used to ride bikes together in college. C'mon in, let me give you the tour." He opened the partition door and brought Chris into the four office, two conference room flat. He met Mike and Sean, the   two associates, then went to John's office that overlooked the street.   Besides the chairs, there were two statues, one of Fleeting Victory and the other of Poseidon.

"What, no law books?"

"Everything is digitized now, Chris.   There all on the computers."   John piled up some papers to make things look neat, although Chris could tell from the adjacent meeting room with files, briefs and depositions strewn all over the place that John was in the middle of a fairly big case.

"So, you want me to whack an evil cousin."

"That would be nice, too, but we'd really like to get my Aunt's stuff back."

"What all did she take?"

"Fortunately, Aunt Grace made lists of her important things.   Here's the jewelry list and my sister, June, has put an asterisk by the most precious things.   Here's the furniture list, same notations, and then the general stuff.   Plus, we have this document here that's in Portuguese and neither of us can read that."

John looked at the document first.

"It looks legal and might be a deed, but I can't read it either.   I know someone who can or can find someone who can.   You remember Jack Connelly?"

"Our brother at the house?"

"Yeah, Jack's a professor over at UMassD.   It's right near New Bedford.   He had to take a sensitivity course on the Portuguese while working there?"

"Why's that?"

"There's a huge population of Portuguese there, all descendent, for the most part, from the early settlers in the late seventeen hundreds and the early eighteen hundreds. They were the navigators and sea wise sailors who guided the whaling ships. No doubt, your Aunt's side of the family came from those early settlers. Jack will find someone for sure. I'll email him and then fax a copy over. Now, this other stuff, these lists."

"Yeah?"

"This is how this generally plays out. I send a demand letter for an Accounting for all this, copies attached, under her term of Co- Power of Attorney. She then has to get a lawyer and then she denies she has any of it. I then submit to the court. The court requires a hearing. Eventually, the court decides to order the accounting. Both sides present. Hers is faulty as hell and we demand another one. She stalls, hires a new attorney, demands an extension, blah, blah, blah. This goes on for a year. In the meantime, she sells or fences all the stuff, on E-Bay, whatever, and she really doesn't have it a year and a half later when the court may get its sorry ass around to ordering a search."

"Beautiful, I want to go back to where I shoot her in the head."

"No, Chris you can't do that. What about your family? What about your eternal spirit?" John was laughing.

"At least I know I'm going to hell and my job will be to stick a pitch fork in her ass every five seconds."

John laughed again,

"No, really Chris. There is another avenue we might take."

"Like what?"

"The Robin Hood scenario. We take from the rich, or the undeserving in this case, and give to the poor, or the deserving."

"How does that work?"

"Without telling you too much, we wait until her Attorney answers and she denies that she has any of this stuff. Then we send in some Russian Plumbers over while

181

she's at work, armed with wrenches and these lists, and, for a small fee, wala, your stuff is returned. She can't and won't go to the police because she's already denied having the stuff in the first place. There really isn't any crime here because one has actually been prevented."

"Then can I shoot her?"

"No."

"That's okay, Willie, I don't even have a gun. Don't even like them."

John gave him the time projection of about three weeks and Chris left the office, beaming. Something was finally going to go right.

Three weeks later to the day, a grey panel van with the name of Mischikov Brothers pulled up to a small cottage style house in North Kingstown. A week later the truck would say Mandrakov Brothers and the week after that, the Wistikoff Brothers. There was a lot of grey paint in the world and stencils were cheap. Three men in tan worksuits entered the home with little effort, empty tool boxes in their hands. An hour and a half later, all the small items were in the boxes and three pieces of furniture shoved in the back of the van. For good measure, one of the men took a wrench and broke two traps on two separate sinks. Chris's cousin would be calling plumbers as soon as she got home.

*

Joe Hackett got up about seven a.m. as the sun beat through the salon window and through the porthole windows of his master suite. No alarm was ever needed for this work; it went by the natural rhythm of the day. He went up to the salon and put a cup of coffee on. About twenty minutes later, Bill Hafner came up, looking a little worse for wear.

"How'd you do?" Joe asked

"Up six hundred, lost four, gained one, cashed out up three hundred, less shot cost."

"You all right?"

"Cup of mud and I'm good to go."

182

Joe pulled out his charts.

"What do you think?"

"We should try to get South of the Rocher Perce. That takes us out of the mouth of the river and around the Gaspe."

"Any decent anchorage?"

"Not really until we get to the City of Gaspe, but that's just too far.   Perhaps we can get as far as Carleton.   There's a nice little bay there, but it'll be late."

"Okay, we'll shoot for that."

Bill went down for another cup of coffee.   He brought one up for Joe as well.   They were just passing the Saguenay River.

"Went on a couple of missions up there," Bill pointed. "We monitored the activity of Green Sharks."

"Never heard of them."

"They get to be about twenty six feet.   They go upriver because the water chasms are so deep; glacial cut about twelve hundred feet."

"Are they a docile breed?"

"Naw, they'll eat you.   But there's not that many of them and most people don't swim the river here or up in the fjords."

"Fjords?"

"The glacial cuts go both ways.   The cliffs around the river run upwards of two thousand feet.   They're beautiful, but not easy slopes to maneuver on.   A lot of folks vacation up at Lac du Saguenay.   There are some nice beaches there and it's much more shallow.   The Green Sharks don't go up that far."

Bill took a long sip of the coffee and gazed fondly as they passed the river mouth and the City of Tadoussac.   The hills on either side of the river were beginning to grow higher and as the flow widened further, it became more of an estuary than a river.   Four nautical miles further, they began the cross to the southern shore.   In the distance, Joe thought he saw disturbances in the water.

"Whales?"

Bill grabbed the binoculars, then handed them to Joe, who balanced his elbows on the wheel to look.

"Looks like a pod.   What do you think, Bill?"

"Just wait."

Joe cut the engines a bit, but held course.   The whales were undeterred.   Ships didn't bother them.   They swam right around them.   As they approached, they would   breach alternately.   Bill counted about sixteen.   They swam by, on either side of the boat, rolling gently with the incoming tide.

"This is why I do this."   Bill grinned from ear to ear. "Where else can you work and see stuff like this."

"I remember taking a tour up this way years ago with a girl-friend," Joe added, "I knew only a smattering of French then and the guide would go on and on in French.   I could only pick up a few words.   Then, for the four or six English passengers, he would say- And this whale has just dived." He chuckled at the thought.

Bill went back to the stern and watched the thirty and forty foot Minkes occasionally flip their tales as they calmly continued their journey upriver. They then completed the crossing and set off a quarter mile from the southern shore of the estuary.   Joe could see the highway undulate over and around the hills, then drop to the shore line and hug the edge of the river.   He had never been down this far and was amazed to see the size of the cliffs as they chugged on towards the sea.   He looked at the map and noted the Chic Choc mountains hung back from the shore line, reaching an altitude of four thousand feet.   He had seen the Pacific coast, but never thought such similar coast lines existed in the East, especially along the St. Lawrence.   It reminded him of the expeditions out of Vancouver and the Olympic Range. Though not as dramatic, there was still a familiarity about it all.

He choked back the feeling of homesickness.   He looked over at Bill, who leaned on a side rail, watching the shore intently.   This was like a vacation for him.   Joe decided he better adopt that attitude.

*

At four thirty, Ann picked up her phone and called. She wanted to leave early and couldn't wait any longer. Chris picked up almost instantly. He seemed harried.

"Let me go up to the deck," he said, "where I can hide from all of this,"

She could tell he was frustrated, if not angry.

He got to the second story porch and pulled up an Adirondack Chair. He hated the things; could never get his long frame comfortable on it or around it.

"You okay?" She asked.

"If you like messes," he replied. "It just seems, Annie, that I've been making a mess of things, living in a mess of things; probably just my existence is a mess of things; and it's been going on for months."

She didn't like him depressed. It wasn't like him to be like that.

"You can stop that right now. This is your destiny. I know you don't like it. I don't like it. But, you're moving toward something and it has to be good, because you've passed so much that hasn't been."

He knew he was upsetting her and vowed to stop it.

"I'm sorry. I just miss you and I wish I could see you."

"I know, so now it's my turn." She paused for a moment. She didn't like to express her feelings. It made her feel vulnerable and she didn't like that feeling at all. But, she had made a decision and she would stick to it.

"I didn't want you to go. I told you so. But you had to. I didn't think I would feel like this. I thought I could weather it and go on and live my life the way I'm supposed to, but it's not working, Chris."

Now, it was his turn to be silent for a moment.

"What can we do, Annie?"

"I'm coming to Jamestown. I told Paul. I'm taking a couple of weeks to clear my head. I need to know how I truly feel."

"How did he take it?"

"Honestly, Chris, he could have given a shit less. He just isn't like that. I mean, he cares for me, I'm sure, but he's never been passionate about it and he just likes his comfortable life.   I think the only thing he'll miss is having someone make a dinner now and then.   I almost think he has someone else, but I don't know how."

"You're serious, aren't you?

"Deeply."

"I can't tell you how happy this makes me.   God, Annie, this just changes everything.   I can't wait to.....oh shit, I have to clean out another room and make a working kitchen. Aagh.   When are you coming?"

"Friday.   Three days, Chris."

"Oh my God.   I'll have to work round the clock."

"Don't worry about it, honey.   We can do it together."

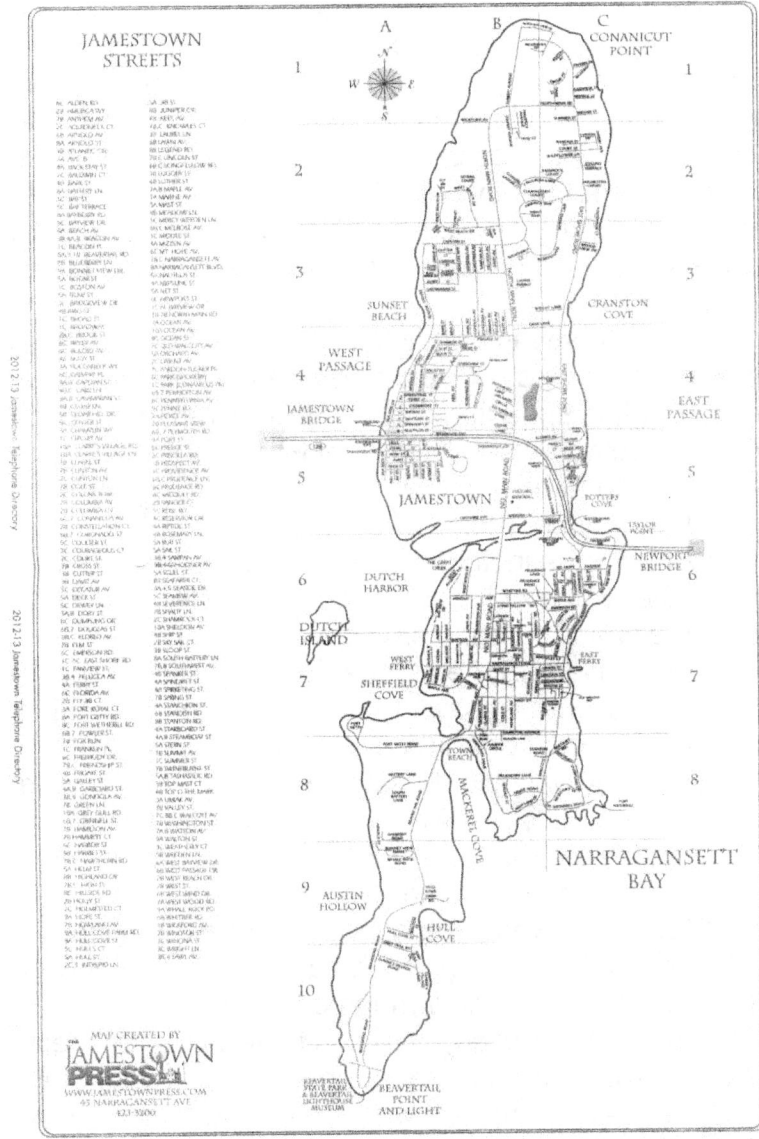

CHAPTER ELEVEN

Jamestown

Six weeks into life in the Undersea Habitat had begun to take its toll.   George was stressed about the work load and the progress.   Suz was beginning to get cabin fever.   Unlike George, she could not work 24/7.   She needed down time and had the routine of washing her hands of her work by around six p.m.   This gave her time to read, watch television or search the web.

The library was getting a bit slim for her tastes and television was a joke.   Cable had been put in, but there were only two English speaking stations that came in out of Lisbon; all of them routed by satellite out of Ponta Delgada.   The fare was pedestrian at best and utterly boring.   She spent most of her free time on the internet.

Her hobbies included antiques and she particularly fancied jewelry, the older and odder the better.   In their many travels, she would rather visit a pawn shop than a Boolchands.   Here at the Habitat, she could only browse the internet to see what was out there.   She was beginning to acquire a great deal of pent up demand.

Routinely, she would scroll through E-Bay to see what was available.   But, that was it.   E-Bay was difficult enough to deal with in the States, let alone Europe; and to attempt to obtain anything at the Habitat would be idiotic.

"You know what would be fun?" she questioned George one night,   "To go on Amazon.com and order a bunch of stuff and see how much gets here."

"Suzie," he replied, "We can't even get mail delivered and the stuff we send out never seems to get back home."

"Precisely.   I think it would be a riot to be emailing them and continuously asking them where our packages were."

"You are a sick puppy.   Is this place getting to you?"

"I'd be lying if I said no."

"Well, patience, dear, the ROV should be arriving soon and that will revitalize our stay.   In fact, I think we will have way too much to do.   But if you really want something, try to get it delivered to the resort.   There's a chance you might see it before we have to leave and then you'd at least have it."

"I just might.   It would give me a little entertainment and some satisfaction in knowing we were still part of the outside world."

"It'll get better.   The 'Neptune' should be here anytime now.

Almost on cue, the "Neptune II" arrived two days later. It was a huge machine; thirteen feet long, six feet wide and seven feet tall.   It had to be delivered by ocean freight to the barge, then dropped to the landing next to the sub port by the crane.

Primarily designed for ocean mapping and discovery, it had been one of the requirements of the Drs. Preston for taking on the job.   They would not work in an Undersea Habitat without proper scientific equipment nor proceed without proper scientific processes.

George Thomas Preston was an arrogant man, but he was also brilliant, and he demanded this concession directly from David Deeds.   Deeds had balked, primarily because Brian Deming was in charge of the project, but there were scant few Oceanographers who had the credentials he needed to pursue and meld his two programs.   He agreed reluctantly, knowing it would cost him some time and the added aggravation of a few arguments from Brian.

Suz engrossed herself with the vehicle sensors and navigation.   Neptune had a gyro, a pressure sensor, CTD, and optode, temperature probe, USBL navigation, Doppler navigation and Altitude, plus forward looking sonars.   For mapping, it had the standard imaging suite, an array of six variant lights, and a high resolution mapping suite.   If there were anything under the sands, the sea bottom floor, Neptune would find it.

George contented himself with coordinating and configuring the data array and the Telepresence.   He could either follow the entire mapping process on screen direct from the Neptune or have imaging and data uploaded via satellite. The latter would be more helpful later on when the Neptune would be sent out to one of the nearby abyss that surrounded the island chain.

Within a week, the Neptune was ready for its first chore, the mapping of the construction site for the desalinization plant.   The plant was to be set thirty yards from the Habitat and the intake and outflow pipes were already in place out to the site.   In this close proximity, Neptune was tethered to the Habitat and the imaging sent directly to the computers in the lab where George and Suz would monitor them and obtain the green print out quadrant cluster that would give them the site information they needed.

"Finally," Suz exalted, "We can begin something exciting.   I really hope this is interesting, because you're right, George, this place is getting to me."

*

Ann's flight into Warwick International was ten minutes early.   They'd caught a tail wind in from Denver and taxied to the gate about the same time Chris would normally call her.

He was waiting at the TSA entrance. His grin went from ear to ear when he saw her.   She was wearing a white, long collared blouse and black pinstripe slacks that draped slightly over her short heels.   Even this casually dressed, she was the most stunning woman in the airport. Her smile was radiant and her eyes beamed when she saw him, a stark contrast to her, he in jeans and a T-Shirt.

They hugged and he kissed her on the neck.

"I'm glad you didn't go all out to meet me."

"I didn't bring a suit."

"I'd much rather see the real you."

"You want to go out for some dinner?"

"Chris, dear, I've been up since four am.   I've been in a plane for five hours, three in a layover and it wasn't the best departure I've ever had.   I just want to get to the house and take a bath and then maybe I can think about food."

In his exuberance and joy in seeing her, he hadn't thought about what she might have gone through to get here. She was changing her life for him and it probably hadn't been pleasant.

"Sure, we'll go straight back. We can be there in about twenty five minutes."

They grabbed her three bags from the carousel and headed out to his truck. Chris lifted the two heavy suitcases and the suitor into the box.

"Planning on staying awhile?" He jested.

He shouldn't have said that. She was getting quite angry.

"What do you think? Some wild weekend? Just drop a marriage for a couple of weeks and see what happens? What are you, some kind of wise-ass? Don't be mean."

"I'm sorry," He truly meant it. "I don't mean to be a jerk. Sometimes, I don't know when to stop trying to be funny. It's just, well, maybe a little uncomfortable, you know."

"Well, get used to it, Buster. You started all this and now here we are."

"Annie, I'm sorry. I know this is what I want, from the bottom of my heart."

"I'm here, aren't I? What does that tell you?"

They turned off at the end of the Verrazano Bridge and came in the back way to the four corners, then down to Marine Avenue and pulled into the driveway a half hour after leaving the airport. Annie's jaw dropped.

"Chris, this is like my little girl's dream house."

"What?"

"It's that little New England cottage overlooking the bay. It has the perfect white picket fence. It..." She was out of the car before it had fully come to a stop. She was almost running around the side of the house, "It's a real gazebo, and an arbor. It's like a tea house back here."

"Look at this," she added, "all these flowers mixed in with all these weeds. This will take forever."

"My Aunt hadn't been here for months, but these beds were beautiful at one time. She loved the gardens so much."

She had circled the house.

"And this front porch. It's darling. Even the wicker

chairs and love seat are perfect."

"One of the first things I did. That and the second floor porch. Being in the house early on was awful."

He grabbed the two bags and opened the front door for her. It opened into a large living room that was completely filled. Each corner had an etagerie with porcelains or plates on it. There was a Victorian couch against the wall covered in pictures and framed documents. There were two overstuffed chairs that matched, a rocking chair and another cushioned sitting chair, two marble topped Lyre end tables and a marble topped coffee table. Against the farther wall stood an upright piano, music bench and a music stand that looked like it came from Paris.

"My Aunt played piano at the Church. She kept her music in the stand. Oh, and I haven't touched this room at all, just haven't gotten to it."

The dining room was adjacent to it and it was clearly revitalized. There was a corner hutch, a buffet, a secretary cabinet and a dining table with four chairs. A grandfather clock sat in the corner nearest the living room. Its chime went off. The stairway was directly opposite the clock and across the open space between the two rooms.

Chris motioned as he took her bags upstairs.

"This is your room. I just finished it yesterday."

"You can put the bags on the bed, but I'm with you."

"I wasn't going to presume anything, Annie."

She tapped her foot, then gave him a kiss.

"You are such an idiot some times."

They went down to the kitchen, which Chris had tried to modernize in his three plus weeks there. Most of the appliances were fifty years old and he swore the toaster was seventy five. The yellow and white cabinets had been repainted beige and the smell of the paint was still somewhat fresh. Annie looked out the bay window over the sink and actually saw the bay and the exquisitely perfect sized yard in the foreground. The white picket fence gave way to a split rail for the back line. It was covered by shrubs and sea grass that held to the cliff edge above the rocky shoreline. In the distance, the shores of Wickford struck out from the mainland on the other side of the bay and the northernmost point of Beavertail was capped with small sailing vessels moored around it.

"Chris, I never thought…I never imagined anything like this. Your family was so blessed and I have walked right into a fantasy." She shook her head in amazement.

"I think I'll go get that bath, now," She added, "and then can we maybe walk in the neighborhood and get something to eat?"

"Sure, Honey, anything you want."

"I want to immerse myself in this."

*

Jackie's meeting was at eight a.m. in David's office. It was unusual to have such an early meeting; David didn't like them, so she figured this had to be important. Since she always dressed as the consummate professional, there would be little change in her preparations for such a meeting. Glamour, however, was always reserved for the most important events and those certainly weren't one on ones with the boss.

She entered a couple of minutes ahead of time; always her style, and sat as bidden in the chair next to David. Detlev Augenstein was also there, and the two men were looking at a print out when David turned aside to her.

"Jackie, we're going to make some major changes."

She sat silently. She wasn't big on major changes. They cost money.

"We're going to alter the next shuttle design."

"Why?" she stammered. "The first is nearly ready for a test launch."

"New science is the simple answer, but it's a lot more than that. A group of professors up in Washington have mastered nuclear fusion and have created a working prototype of a nuclear fusion engine. We're going to re-design the power plant with that new prototype."

"But, David," She protested, "That's a complete change from what we have on the board."

"Bear with me. I'm not suggesting we change what we've got right now. We'll get that one up and running. We know that will work. But the nuclear fusion engine will allow us to reach Mars in thirty six days. The engine we have now will take six months. And there's more than just the travel time. The fuel load is one tenth of the standard engine, meaning much more capacity for cargo. And just think, in the future, we can round trip two shuttles every month. We can build much more quickly. So, in the end, we'll actually save time, not lose it by making way for change. Consider it an add on. If the nuclear fusion isn't capable of withstanding trials, we simply build on the old model. We just need to incorporate new design and have it ready when it will work."

"You really are going to build a base on Mars, aren't you?"

"Yes, Jackie, we are."

Her silence was deafening.

"Look, Jackie, I know you've been guessing around this and that's what all this work has been about; the Shuttles, the Undersea Habitat, all of it. We're amassing the technology and ability to make a permanent settlement feasible. The Habitat is to simulate interplanetary life and its extremes. And, to gauge how humans can work and live under such situations."

"But why not just stick to the science and exploration end of it?"

"Good question and I've wrestled with it and the economics of it all. I believe down the road, maybe not today, that we'll unearth such a bounty from a settlement and the consistent supply and yes, trade, that we'll not only grow exponentially, but also set the real stage for colonization and the export of humanity. These are not small things."

"But why us? Why not the government?"

"Jackie, you know every year I go to the CEO summit. It's in Boston this year. You know we all compare ideas, compete with ideas; and we compare ourselves. We measure our success against others. But, do you know who

I measure myself against?"

She shook her head.

"Henry Flagler. He was a partner in Standard Oil, but he built the Overseas Railway from Miami to Key West. It was a huge investment at the time and people thought he was crazy. Worse, it took years to build and he was in his seventies when he started it. He never lived to see his major resort built in Key West, nor did he live to see the railroad become profitable, but he did ride the first train into the City and he believed that eventually trade would flourish between Miami, Havana and Key West. Sadly, the hurricane of 1935 destroyed the railroad, but within three years, the Overseas Highway was built over the railroad's infrastructure. It has been a massive success ever since. But, back to the question. When Henry Flagler was asked why he did all this, not knowing the full outcome, and knowing that he might not live to see the completion of any of it, he said, If I don't do it, who will?"

Jackie nodded her head and understood.

"And as for the government, you know what I think of their ability to do anything right."

"All that said," Jackie asked, "How are we in a position to actually do all this?"

"Give me some credit, Jackie," David went on, "I provided the venture capital for the scientists working on the engine. We are the major owners of the start-up company. Further, the science of nuclear fusion has other aspects for study that we need to address. I believe we have the means to study that as well. We'll get to that in a minute, however, there are other issues here, Jackie and I need your help."

"Okay."

"First, McNaughton's group will be tied up with the current modifications for some time, so we won't need you here. But there are other aspects to the program, such as the cargo and personnel landing craft. We need to work on the landing systems and the planned trials for our prototype. The perfect place to do it is at our own air strip, without interference. The obvious place is Graciosa. So, I want you to take that over," he paused. "But, that is essentially a cover, there's more. Detlev, show her the print out."

Detlev brought over the excel spread sheets. He pointed to two separate entries, pages apart. One was a debit of five hundred thousand dollars to a Colonel Leon DeSilva. The next was a three million seven hundred and fifty thousand dollar debit to Blackthorn International.

"You saw those," David pointed out, "Wouldn't that seem a bit odd to you?"

She nodded again.

"Brian is my partner and Chief Operations Officer. He has free rein over there and I trust him. However, that doesn't mean I understand everything he's doing and even if I can hide this from the Board of Directors, which I can; if I have to explain all this to an Auditor, I'd kinda like to know."

"So, I want you to go to the Azores. I want you to take over the landing craft assignment; I want you to watch and learn what Brian is doing and report back to me; and I want you to deliver this to Dr. George Preston."

He handed her a portable hard drive.

"This is the nuclear fusion process. It is encrypted and has some missing elements. Those have been sent ahead to Dr. Preston. When he gets this, he can add to his experimentation; Two parts hydrogen and one part oxygen," he mused. "The one thing we really, really need, but still haven't figured out how to make."

"Water."

"Yes. Ma'am."

Thirteen hours later, Jackie Guiterrez was on the red eye out of San Francisco direct to Boston. After a six hour layover in the VIP Lounge, she would take another red eye direct from Boston to Ponta Delgada, Azores. There, the private jet would zoom her off to Graciosa and a new suite at the resort. She would be going back to the country of her birth. She would be a wreck when she arrived.

For twenty two years, I have worked alongside and

competed against men.   I've had to be better in every way just to be treated fairly.   I have been unjustly accused.   I have been attacked because I had been blessed by good looks and a strong physical presence.   I have held myself above it all with all the dignity I could muster.   I did it to achieve, but I did it to be equal, to prove I could do anything just as well as any man.   I have played the part and I have succeeded, perhaps well beyond my own envisioning.   And I have come to this. Two of the brightest men in the world pursuing probably the greatest dreams of a century and I'm like the conductor on the train. It is running forward at maddening speed and I seem helpless to stop it.   At what point can I get off? Can I ever get off?

*

Three days past Du Rocher Perce, the Aleutian Grand Banks arrived in Halifax.   Joe and Bill had decided to call the ship "The Cormorant".   The Cormorant was a nuisance, especially in the Great Lakes.   It commonly nested in colonies and consumed thousands of pounds of fish.   Years ago, there was a huge colony on the Island of Galoo, due south of Kingston, Ontario and due west of Sackets Harbor, NY where thousands of birds were effectively destroying the commercial and tourist fishing industry in eastern Lake Ontario.   The DEC of NY, reluctant to do anything, waited just a bit too long to come up with a solution and one night a squadron of commercial and sport fisherman raided the Island and killed most of the colonies' inhabitants. WorldGreen had no time to intervene, and outrage was ensured, but it was just one more case of government doing nothing until radical actions became necessary.   Balance between human needs and nature's protection was a difficult grey area for all concerned and it amused Joe to think that, in one mission, they were out to save the whales; and in another, protect the fishermen.   The irony was not lost on him.

They expected The Cormorant to be perceived as a

nuisance. It would act like a nuisance. And, Joe thought, it would be most appreciated if it actually was truly a nuisance. It should have been WorldGreen's motto. The ship, then, was aptly named.

Halifax Iron Works and Dry Dock sat at the oldest part of the harbor of the city next to the original customs house. Halifax had a long history of ship building, outfitting and outright piracy. During the Revolution and the War of 1812, Halifax was home to the English Privateers who ravaged American shipping. They were licensed by the crown to steal, sink, haul away ships as prizes, and impress seamen into duty.

During both World Wars and especially in World War II, the Navy built its Atlantic Fleet in Halifax and fortified the town, covering the sea lanes along the coast. One of the greatest explosions in history happened in the bay when two ships collided in 1917. There were over eleven thousand casualties in the City, destroying most of the Richmond district downtown.

Halifax Iron Works and Dry Dock had lived through all of that. For two and a half centuries, the Company had been outfitting ships, installing armaments in refitted vessels, and it prided itself on customer service. It knew ahead of time that the Cormorant was coming in and had slotted in the repair dates. WorldGreen had prepaid half of the work in order to have the necessary parts available.

The ship was brought into the strap hoist that would haul it up, then roll it over and onto work stands in dry dock. Joe and Bill tugged off their bags; they would have to stay in a hotel for a week and walked off to the closest, the Delta Atlantic at the harbor front. Bill had wanted to stay at the Lord Nelson. He liked to stay at the best hotels, but Joe vetoed it; too far away from the ship and they would have to be there every day. Bill was finally and happily convinced when he discovered the Casino was right across the street from the Delta.

The first night Bill and Joe went to the Casino, won a little, had a few drinks and went back to their suite, but on the second night decided to hit a night club, Lucifer's, just around the corner.   It was to be a celebration for the successful first leg of the journey.

Bill waved for a waitress as they sat at a table midway between the bar and the front door.   A young man came over and took their order, two Smithwicks on tap.   The two sailors discussed their upcoming trip.   It would take a long two weeks to get to Galway, Ireland.

"Why can't this guy just fly here?"   Bill asked.

"It's complicated."

"No, it's not. You get on a damned plane."

"Trevor Hagan is not going to get on a plane.   One, he doesn't like them.   Two, he has no phone.   And, if he did, he wouldn't come here if I called him.   You have to see him and talk to him."

"Why is he so important for this?"

Joe leaned forward.   "We worked in the IRA together. We blew up a few things.   There's no better helmsman than Trevor.   Best navigator I ever knew.   Knows more about explosives than anyone I know and he speaks a little Portuguese, which certainly will come in handy.   He's tough as leather and I never saw even so much as a speck of fear in him.   If we're headed for trouble, and I suspect we are, there's no one I'd want more to cover me than Trevor.   Trevor is one of those people who understands that for good to triumph over evil, it has to be just as ruthless.   And, he has no qualms about that.   I did the right thing in the Alaskan Bay, but I wouldn't trust myself not to waiver if things get out of hand. Trevor won't do that. No offense, Bill, but I don't know your capabilities.   I want this guy and the only way to get him is to sit down with him over a Guiness and talk it out. Besides, it's sort of on the way."

"Ireland is on the way?"

Joe waved his hand sideways.   Bill grinned and waved again to a waitress.   This time a buxom young dark haired woman in a form fitting halter top came over to refresh the pints.   She bent over, her body enticing in every detail, and Bill whispered in her ear.   She bolted upright and slapped him hard across the cheek.

The next thing Joe knew, he was being lifted straight

up from his chair.   Four hands that looked like the paws of Gorillas had him and before he knew it, he was airborne out the front door, tossed like an old shoe.   He landed on the front porch with a thud.   Before he could gather himself up, Bill Hafner flew out the door and landed on top of him.   That hurt worse.   As much as he knew he was being tossed, he hadn't expected Bill right behind him.

"Get off me." He yelled.   He knew it was Bill.   He looked up to see two giant men, the size of NFL linemen pointing at him.

"And stay out."

Joe looked at Bill as they brushed themselves off.

"What the hell did you say to her?"

"I dunno."

"C'mon, Bill, Jeezus.   What did you say to a waitress in a nightclub that could get us tossed like that?"

"Something maybe about being a suckling; and maybe about some silicone; I'm not sure."

"You're going to get me killed."

"No, I'm not.   You're my friend, Joe."

"Hell of a way to treat a friend.   I hope you got a lot more."

"Actually, I don't.   And at my age, new friends are hard to come by."

Joe stood his full six foot two length and brushed back his wavy black hair, now turning grey at the temples.

"I'm not all that much younger than you, Bill.   I'd like to stick around for a while.   How about we just go over to the casino?   You can't get into too much trouble there, can you?"

*

Ann finally unpacked her two bags and began to organize a closet and a dresser.   She took out a manila folder, nine by twelve, an inch thick with documents.   She tossed it on the bed.

"Chris, come here a minute."

Chris came in from the bathroom, his toothbrush still sticking out of his mouth.

"Is that any way to greet a lady?"

He stuck the toothbrush in his pajama pants.

"I give up." She frowned, then laughed. "I did some research for you, as you asked, about your friend, Skip Conboy. There are copies of police reports in there for you, along with some other interesting reports on missing persons, possible homicides, all cold cases. After you find the time to digest it all, we'll talk about it. Meanwhile, can we take a walk down to the Pier and get some coffee. I'd just like to watch Newport and listen to the ocean for a while."

"We can do that anytime."

"Then now is just as good. You know, I've lived in Colorado for twenty plus years. There's no ocean there, not even a lake big enough to fill up the bay window over your sink. It may be all the same routine to you, but I am thrilled, Chris Eberhardt, and I shouldn't even have to tell you that." She smiled.

"I am duly chastised, and there is nothing here that needs to be done right now anyway, ah, ever for that matter. Although, we do have to go see John Willie at the end of the day."

"Who?"

"My lawyer buddy from college. He's helping us with the estate. I want you to come with me."

"You want a second opinion?"

"I would appreciate your insight. And June's going up with us."

"I can't wait to see her. I love your sister."

They sat for a good hour at the picnic table behind Spinakers, sipping on cappuccinos under the umbrella, looking over the docks and the marina, occasional boats departing for fishing or just a jaunt on the bay. Newport sat peacefully on the other side, two miles to the east. Of course, it looked peaceful from where they sat, but the town was inundated with tourists and the college kids had just come back and it was nothing like peaceful at all. Like Chris had said, the best view of Newport was from the docks at Jamestown.   She loved it; the wind, the smell of the sea, the sounds, the early crisp fall air. It captivated her senses.   It was just lovely here.

They went back to the house.   June pulled in from Albany just after noon.   She pulled into the driveway behind Chris's truck and got out.   Chris and Ann were sitting on the porch in the wicker love seat.   Ann shot up. Her old friend had let her hair go light grey.   It was cut in a short French style and it seemed to give June even more grace.   Ann went directly to the car and the two hugged.

"So wonderful to see you, June."

"You, too, Annie.   You look radiant. But, I have to say I'm so astonished to see you here with Chris."

"It's all your fault, you know."

"Me? How?"

"If we hadn't been best friends in high school, I never would have had a crush on your brother.   And, if you hadn't brought him to my brother's fundraiser, we never would have met again."

June looked sternly at Chris.   "I had nothing to do with him and Elaine."

Chris pointed a finger at his sister.   "Elaine had everything to do with Elaine.   You know damn well we fought for years and it didn't take much to blow it wide open.   Elaine found that easily enough."

"And you?" June's stern look was slightly modified for her friend.

"There's a time, girlfriend, when a pointless life must come to an end. I thought I was marrying someone different, someone smart, thoughtful, but in a wise and eccentric way. In the end, he was just plain stupid.   But come on, let's go take a walk on the beach. You're so damned lucky to have this."

"Let me change," June smiled. "And then you can tell me all about it."

*

202

At four o'clock, the three left Jamestown for the forty five minute drive to downtown Providence. John had wanted them to be the last appointment for the day. Chris suspected dinner at the Irish Pub. They arrived just short of five, parked behind the four story building and went up the center door that split the pub side from the dining room at O'Malley's.

The three entered the offices on the second floor and were escorted into John's office. He greeted Chris warmly, stared in awe at Ann and smiled his devilish grin at June. Chris swore there was a wink in there somewhere, but John Willie was a master at hiding the twinkle in his eye that sparked his indomitable spirit. The three sat in front of his desk, in front of and underneath the towering statue of Poseidon.

"Well," John started. "Mostly good news." He pulled a box from his lower right desk drawer. We got all the jewelry you listed. The furniture is downstairs in a storage room, but sadly, better than half the coins are gone. They would have been easy to move, anyway, so I'm surprised we got any of them."

Chris, Ann and June leaned forward. There lay the most important pieces Aunt Grace had owned: Her string of pearls, her florin on the gold chain, two diamond rings, a gold wedding band, her talisman star and three cameos. The costume jewelry lay in another tray and a half dozen gold coins and a few Morgan silver dollars sat in a third.

Ann looked them all over and picked up the talisman star.

"What is this piece?"

"We've always called it the talisman star. Aunt Grace called it her lucky star." June added.

"Aunt Grace said it was the oldest thing in the family, handed down from her grandfather's grandfather." Chris chimed in.

Ann fondled the talisman that hung on a white gold chain. It looked like a small opened, angular Japanese lantern with a diamond crystal inside. She had never seen anything like it.

"And, you are lucky to have any of this," John noted,

"We gather from the accounting and from conversations with her attorney, who by the way, is a good friend of mine, that your shirttail relative had all these things on E-Bay."

"Thank you John, you don't know how much this means to us." June said.

Chris swore he saw another wink and hoped Ann didn't.

"Oh, and that document.   Jack Connelly faxed back the information we needed.   He says to get your ass over to Portsmouth and visit him.   No excuses." Chris nodded at John's declaration.

"This is a deed for a property in Horta, Faial.   It appears to be a farm residence, a villa of sorts, that your family has had for some time.   We believe it has been rented out for decades, but we can't find any lease information. Someone will have to go there and straighten it out.   I've talked with your estate attorney and he says you can't close the estate until that's settled."

June looked at Chris, her stern face showing again. Chris looked just as sanguine.   He knew what was coming.

"You know I can't go, Chris, you know it."

"Oh God," He groaned. "This just keeps getting worse. How the hell do we pay for all of this?"

"It's a necessary estate expense, Chris," John went on. "And your Aunt left quite a bit of money.   It won't be a problem."

"It could be like a vacation, Chris," Ann added.

"You're not thinking of…."

"Oh yes I am.   I'm not letting you get away with this. I'm going."

"I'd say we could use a drink," John smiled.   "How about we go down to the Irish Pub and catch some dinner."

Chris burst out laughing.   They got up to leave, then Chris had another thought.

"By the way, Willie, suppose you're reasonably sure some guy killed somebody twenty some years ago, and suppose he offed a couple more later, and then made one, maybe two of your friends disappear.   The information that's there is circumstantial; the guy always seems to be somewhere around the incidents. You don't really have any real proof, but you're damn sure he did it. What can you do?"

"Hmm.", John scratched his temple, "If you had enough circumstantial evidence, you might be able to convince a jurisdiction to bring charges and then hope the media and the social media, you know, Youtube, Twitter, Facebook, etc. catch on and something shows up that can really get him, but that probably won't work. You could just take him out, privately, of course. You could just forget about and let God sort him out later; or, you can wait until he screws up."

"Annie, would you agree with that?"

"You want your second opinion now? Okay, you're ugly, too. How do I know? I haven't done criminal law in years. I'm out of touch, but what John says is accurate. It's just that a guy that's been this careful and covered his tracks so well is unlikely to screw up. He's a real pro and has the power and money to wash out his problems."

"True," John added, "But even a fifty two time winner is going to lose sometime. The question is whether or not you're going to catch him when he does."

"Okay, I feel like a beer, now. Shall we?" Chris put his arm around Annie and June walked side by side with John. Chris thought he caught her in a wink as well.

Chris leaned over to Annie, "I think June really likes John Willie."

"I think so, too."

CHAPTER TWELVE

The Foreign Legion

The four cutters pulled into Ponta Delgada's port, passed the breakwater and into the basin where the Navy had a small base.   There was barely enough room to dock the four ships and they tied up at a small cruise ship dock the Navy leased from the City.   It had been fifty hours, two overnights and more grousing, swearing, and fighting from the contingent of the two companies than Alvarro ever heard anywhere else in active duty.

The base consisted of merely four buildings, weather station excluded that sat just off the Avenida du Don Henrique, the main drag along the shoreline of this jewel of a city in the mid-Atlantic.

Two city blocks to the west lay the Army's buildings, adjacent to the old Forte De Sao Bras.   The sixteenth century fort was made of sea shells and a rudimentary concrete and mortar mix that served the port well in its day, but became outdated when ships began using heavier ordinance that could pummel the walls to ruins.   Still, it served as a fine backdrop to the modern Army post.

Colonel Leon De Silva had called for an assembly at ten thirty a.m., barely an hour after the four ships had docked. Lt. Colonel Alvarro Parros marched his four companies along the Avenida to the parade ground in the center of the five large buildings that encircled the grounds that made up the Base.

DeSilva stood at a podium at the head of the parade grounds, dressed in full regalia in his finest whites, gold braid everywhere with epaulets to match.   Alvarro felt a bit out of place as second in command in his field blues, a light blue short-sleeve shirt with dark navy blue slacks.

DeSilva spoke through an electronically enhanced microphone to the assembled regiment.

"Soldiers and sailors of Portugal.   We are now a full and complete regiment.   We are charged with the safety of the populace of the Azores.   We are to support our government and the regional autonomy of the Islands.   That does not mean, however, that independence minded individuals or groups will be tolerated.   To that end, we shall have a presence on all the Islands.   Two platoons from Company B will be sent with a cutter to Faial and Pico where you will protect the two Islands and the legislative assembly in Horta.   The other platoon will be sent to Flores and Corvo with another cutter.   Two platoons will be sent to Sao Jorge with the third cutter and the last two Platoons of Company C will be assigned here as reserve with the final cutter.   That will provide us with six platoons and two cutters for Sao Miguel, Santa Maria, Terciera and Ponta DelGada in particular.   We'll make provisions for additional housing here at this base.   Each of your Company Captains will report directly to me.   Lt. Colonel Parros will remain assigned here and assist me in troop support and supply as well as daily administration.   Captains, you have your orders.   Dismissed."

DeSilva waved to Alvarro to follow him.   Alvarro reached him behind the podium as they strolled toward HQ. They shook hands.

"I want you to come to lunch with me." DeSilva said dryly.

"At your command, Sir."

"You can call me Leon.   I expect we'll be friends and that we'll be working together a long time."

Maybe and maybe not, Alvarro thought.   The news in Oporto just before he left was that with three and a half weeks left before the election, Pedro Anabel Cavadas was in a dead heat with President DeSilva.   Alvarro might not be here that long.

On the other hand, the Colonel was probably hedging his bets.   He probably was advised by the Defense Minister of Alvarro's status and was going to be nice to him until after the election.   If Cavadas won, Lt. Colonel Alvarro Parros would probably be long gone and not a problem.   If President DeSilva won, Lt. Colonel Parros would probably be here forever, in which case he would still not be a problem, but would have to be neutralized in some way.   Regardless, no harm should come to him.

But, down the road?   That might be a different case.

They walked over to the Yacht Club at the marina where DeSilva spent most of his time at the Club Naval.   It was his version of the Officer's Club.   They passed the public pools, the Sao Pedro basin filled with sail and fishing boats and entered the club.   They took a table overlooking the basin and the slips filled with ships of all size.   The breakwater that jutted out from the basin held a cruise ship on the outside dock, its cargo of tourists distributed about the island on the many available tours.   The inside dock held the four cutters.   Alvaro would have to retrieve his luggage after lunch.   He could see two of the boats reloading their contingents, preparing to leave for the other islands.

DeSilva ordered tea and began his prepared presentation for his new second in command.

"This will not be difficult duty for you, Colonel."   He was flattering in his salutation.
"I really don't need an assistant, we have things under control here, but here you are and we shall make the best of it."

Alvarro nodded as the tea arrived and they ordered lunch.

"Now, here is your assignment.   You are to review all quartermaster requisitions and insure that our troops obtain all the supplies we need.   The quartermaster is good, but review will tend to eliminate any possible chicanery.   You will also supervise daily drill, then tend to administrative duties such as complaints, etc.   Any policy decisions will, of course, be made by me."

Alvarro could barely keep the weighted sigh in check. This would be a test of his mettle to withstand the boredom that was being pushed upon him.

"As you know, all company Captains report directly to me, so the chain of command is not strictly in force.   Still, the fact that you are the Lieutenant Colonel of this regiment will imply that your direction will have been authorized and sanctioned by me, so you must exercise great care in your orders and command.   Is this all clear?"

Alvarro nodded. "Very, Sir. I will endeavor to support this command as well as possible."

"Good. I'm sure we'll get along fine. I've arranged for you to be billeted in the Commandant's house at the base. I have my own place down the coast and have no need for it. The commander's home is very nice and you should be very comfortable there."

Ah, a posh prison, Alvaro thought. How lovely. And the rumors were true, the Colonel had a luxurious villa on a private bay overlooking the sea.

The two finished their lunch amid pleasantries and DeSilva excused himself.

"Take the rest of the day to get settled in and report to me tomorrow here at eleven." He exited crisply in his full dress uniform, looking every bit the Commandant, got in to his chauffer driven Mercedes and sped up the Avenida along the coast.

Alvarro retrieved his duffel and two suitcases, dragging them along the sidewalk back across the basin and the pools. He had never been to the islands and was amazed at the sea of whitewashed homes, churches and public buildings. There was a mixture of red and brown tiled roofs and brown trim hugged many of the homes and churches, evidencing the specific style of the city. Beyond the city limits, foothills rose to small mountains that created an island long ridge that held two lake filled calderas east and west.   He hoped he would have time to visit Furnas, the one that had a village lake side in the Caldera. It was supposed to be a marvel. The island sported palms and fronds, all manner of tropical plants and flowers. It was a sub-tropical climate and it stayed warm and humid year round.

By the time Alvaro reached the Commandant's two story Spartan home on the base, he had sweat through his clothing and completely drenched, entered the air conditioned foyer to catch a chill. He would go upstairs to shower immediately. He returned the salute of the private, who apparently was his aide stationed there and as he banged his suitcases up the stairs, he noticed the map of the Azores on the south wall of the foyer. Then it hit him. There was no contingent assigned to Graciosa, none at all.   Every island had at least one full platoon and a ship assigned to it, but not Graciosa.   What sense did that make?

He shook his head as he went up to cleanse himself. It didn't make any sense.

*

The waterfront of Halifax fading in the distance, Joe felt a great relief to be underway again.   It had been nine long days waiting for the tank and flotation modifications at Halifax Iron works and Dry Dock.   The two .50 caliber guns mounted one on the foredeck above the salon and one aft of the pilot house had been cleverly disguised by vent covers designed by Bill Hafner. After meeting with Halifax staff, Joe had selected the MAGMIRS .50 calibers.   They were modern, light weight, maneuverable and represented all the fire power of the earliest models.   The feed belt and two hundred clip magazine for each were tethered to the base. For camouflage, they used the existing mounted pedestal for the base and covered it with sheet metal, then put a vented circular cap over the guns themselves that were held by hinges and clipped into place with a latch and bolt.   To fire, Bill simply had to undo the bolt and latch, flip the lid over and the guns were freed to swivel in any direction or tilted airborne, if necessary.

Nine days was also much too long to stay in Halifax with Bill.   They'd managed to get thrown out of four clubs, in addition to their own lounge in their hotel.

"Have you got something against waitresses?" Joe finally asked.

"No, not really.   I just think they're fun.   They can take it.   Besides, I'm almost seventy.   They know I'm harmless."

"No, they don't, Bill.   Ever since Viagra came out, no man under the age of a hundred is harmless and they know that, for sure.   You come on as a creepy old guy with a boner who might do anything to them.   That's why we've gotten the

210

snot kicked out of us three times."

"I hadn't thought of that, Skip."

"Just keep it in mind.   If you pull any of that stuff in Galway, you're liable to end up in a pen with Pig Flynn's hogs."

Bill nodded and then grinned.   He couldn't help himself. After all these years, he was still full of it.

They hugged the coastline out past Cape Breton, then cruised along the southeast side of Prince Edward Island. The red rock cliffs that rose from the sea became visible as they altered course for St. Johns, Newfoundland, their next port on the Journey.   They would pass by St. Pierre and Miquelon, two islands still held by the French that were actually considered a province that sent legislators to Paris. Bill was lobbying hard for a mooring there.

"I suppose it would be possible to end up in a French jail on an island in North America", Joe mused.

"C'mon, Joe.   It's not that bad, really it isn't." Bill had an affectatious way about him and Joe had to admit that he was a hell of a lot of fun to be around.

"One night, no fights, no waitress bashing, no hassles with the locals."   Joe forced his most stern look.

"Agreed."

The two docked in Miquelon the next day.   They bought duty free presents, liquor and a couple of items for their respective ladies that could otherwise only be bought in Paris or ordered and shipped back with astounding tariffs. They escaped the town unscathed and after a fuel stop in St. Johns, continued northeastward along Greenland's coast.

At sixty three degrees latitude, the Cormorant took a right turn for the direct trajectory to Reykjavik, Iceland.   The harrowing part of the journey had begun.   It was almost fall and the continuing climate change ice melt in the Artic meant that icebergs and floes had increased.   It was also at the top range of the newly refitted capacities of the ship, which meant a continuous run to the northernmost capital of the world. Auto Pilot ran the ship while Bill and Joe took turns on watch

211

for ice sheets and tips of bergs that could cripple her hull and send her to rest next to the Titanic.   At sixteen knots, it took six days to reach the island and they took two days rest before setting out for the Faroe Islands of Denmark, halfway between Reykjavik and northwest Scotland.   It would be another five day haul.

The seas rose on the fourth day, swells exceeding eight feet, which rammed hard on the seventy six footer. It was an effort to stay on course and Joe cursed the North Atlantic for its unyielding treachery.   Bill seemed to take it in stride.   He was a better seaman than Joe, or, he had come to just not give a damn.

Seventy miles outside of Torshavn, the starboard engine began to cough.   Bill was at the pilot house with Joe when it happened.   Amid about twenty shit, shit, shits, Bill bolted to the engines downstairs at the rear of the hold.   The ship was big enough to give him walking room around the 1015 Cummins Diesels and he listened intently to the coughing from the ailing beast.   It coughed, spit and then stopped altogether.   Bill had seen this before and guessed an EGR valve, but he wouldn't know until he took it apart. That would be a top engine overhaul and that would be a huge problem, but the more serious problem stared him head on. They would now have to limp into the Faroes in high seas with one engine.

Joe already knew he was underpowered by the time Bill got topside.   He was beginning to counter steer to keep on line and the boat heaved, bashed by waves front and side as they crept onward.   Normally, it would take four plus hours to hit port.   Now, at top end and the risk of blowing the other engine, it would take seven.

"Got any last thoughts, just in case?" Joe ventured.

"I wish all the waitresses would forgive me and I wished I had them all." He grinned. "Don't worry, Skip, the ship was built with the tolerances to make the journey.   It is well within its ability.   Maybe not the ability of the passengers, but she'll manage just fine. We'll get there.   Just stay alert and we'll bounce on in there in no time."

It was good to have an experienced man on board.

Joe steadied himself and reached into a calm that helped him force himself to stay within the present and look ahead clearly. He told himself he was sailing directly in front of him, not at the waves ahead of him. He could focus.

Six and a half hours of rough seas later, they limped into the bay, the ocean held back by the passage through the Island chain on the way to its biggest city. The bay was unique in that the city actually held two small bays in the large inlet. There was a short, glacial rock peninsula that jutted out from the waterfront which featured a cornucopia of red warehouses and buildings, connected in row house style. On one side, the commercial bay, housed the international Ferry and its parking lot. That was the main connection to Great Britain and Iceland. On the other side, the recreational docks, filled with sail and power boats of all kind.

The Cormorant docked at the Torshavn commercial facility, directly across from the Ferry Terminal. The seas had taken all the fight out of Joe and Bill. There would be no outings on this day. Shore power connected and all utilities set, they each took a shower and crashed. They would deal with the engines tomorrow.

*

Ann began packing her suitcases. It seemed to her that she had just unloaded them, which was true. She had only been there two weeks. Now, they were going to be on their way to Horta in the Azorean archipelago. She was beginning to think she was nuts. She had left her marriage, her work, and in some sense, her identity to follow this man whom she barely knew. She would now have to reconcile the image of the man she held in her heart and the reality of the person she had come to know. It was a lot more complex than she originally had thought, but that was the problem with infatuation and endearing love. There was a bridge to cross beyond desire and sex and joy to the land of commitment. There were a lot of aspects to commitment, especially when mature partners had a lot of baggage behind them. It was okay to drag along a suitcase, but not a freight train.

Fortunately, neither she nor Chris seemed to have much more than a daypack left.

Chris came into the room as she gently folded a pair of slacks and he put his arms around her waist from behind, pressing her to him. She tilted her head back to touch his, her hair streaming across his shoulder.

"Are you okay?"

She turned and kissed him. It was a soft kiss, light and gentle, but with a touch of sadness, a light sifting sea breeze across the lips the bespoke of the possibility of rough seas ahead.

"Chris," She looked at him with those piercing brown eyes, the green flecks dancing in them. It always stunned him. "I don't know if we'll ever be together in the end, but I've come all this way and I intend to see it through. I didn't expect all this, all these changes and I understand why it's all happening, but it is not the best of circumstances to be building a relationship in. If we could be a little more settled, then I would have a greater grasp of my feelings and where we are going."

"I know. I don't like it either. I thought we'd be settled here for a while and I hadn't realized how wonderful it was here. The memories of youth fade when the realities of the mature adult are required to find new perception. I hadn't realized how this place would affect me, and I know you love it here, too. You don't have to go, you know. You can stay here and take care of the place. June would be around to help here and there."

"No, I'm going with you, Chris. I came here to be with you and I intend to do that. How do I get the full measure of you when you're gone away from me? No way."

"And, you were the one who said we could make a vacation out of it."

"Don't you say 'you were the one' to me. It just pisses me off." She smiled and gave him a harder kiss. "Let's go see how badly you packed."

They went across the hallway to the other bedroom where Chris had his things laid out. On top of the large suitcase lay a gold chain and the Talisman Star lay attached to it.

"You're going to take that"

"I was going to pack it, but I've decided I'm going to wear it. I'll look more like a tourist."

"Are you feeling a little girly?"

"Annie, guys wear shit around their neck all the time. Out west, they wear turquoise chokers and silver chains. In the Keys, shark tooth and leather or Spanish coins from the Atocha or coral beads. And look at baseball players and their gold chains. It's almost ritualistic. Besides, Aunt Grace always called it her Lucky Star. I don't know why she did, but she did. We can use a little luck. I was going to pack it, but I'm afraid it will disappear if I do. I'd rather have all that infused luck right next to me, along with you. As God is my witness, with these two charms, I'll never be unlucky again."

"Okay, Katie Scarlet, I get it." She kissed him again. "You know what you're doing here?" She gazed at the two bags, stuffed to the hilt.

"I like to be prepared. Old Boy Scout thing. Not having enough sucks and too much doesn't matter."

"Well, we better clear one of these off and get some sleep. Four a.m. comes awfully early."

"And going to Logan is no picnic either. But the good news is we'll be in Ponta Delgada in time for a late café lunch. I'm looking forward to that."

*

Jackie was still buckled in her seat as the plane sat on the Tarmac waiting to dock. She was engrossed in her past.

Twenty six years since I left my country. Twenty six years, a whole lifetime ago. God, how I hated the place. Of course, this isn't like the central highlands of Northern Portugal. These Islands are a totally different world. I had heard

215

stories of how the Acoreans hated the mainlanders and how the mainlanders detested the Acoreans. I wonder if any of it is true, probably just a bunch of bullshit to make people feel better about themselves.

I wonder if the old village is there. I don't think I want to see it. My poor mother. Thank God for her. She saved me. Sending me off to live with my Aunt and Uncle in New Bedford gave me a whole new life; a good home, an education at UMass and then on to Stanford and my career. She saved me from that dreadful, abusive man that was my father. I hope he rots in hell, his genitals constantly being burned and singed and then stabbed with a butcher knife. I know he killed her. Not physically, but he just did. And my poor brother. I wonder where he is, if he is. I lost track of him so long ago. I hope he's had a good life. I hope he didn't grow up to be like my father. I hope he ran away.

Still, I should be grateful. I got away. I know my mother wanted that: for me to have a chance at a new life, a good life. Maybe, after all this is over with, I'll fly over to Oporto and drive up to the village. It might bring closure. I hated that place. I hated the house. I hated my father. I hated that name, Juanita. I'd like to stop hating my past.

The unfasten seat belt sign lit up and Jackie grabbed her carry on and computer bag and walked down the steps to the tarmac. It was a small airport, just one main building with multiple entrances. There were no causeway extensions and there really was no need for them. The weather was so rarely bad that the expense would not have been justified. Once down the steps, she walked toward the terminal and saw a man in a dark suit with a sign with her name on it. She half thought Brian would meet her there, then scoffed at the idea. He was much too arrogant for such a menial task. Of course he would send a staffer to pick her up.

The man introduced himself and directed Jackie to a twin engine six seat private jet that held a small meeting room in the cabin. It sat one hundred yards off to the right of the terminal near the freight hangers. She boarded as requested and sat in one of the posh aisle seats, which of course, was also the window seat.   She was pleased to see a small kitchenette at the back of the meeting room.   She would have the benefit of a cup of coffee on her short journey to Graciosa.

The pilot turned to her with a semi-toothless grin.   He wore a Blackthorn Uniform.   She was his only passenger and he gave her a thumbs-up and began to start up the engines. Once the volume was enough to drown out the sound of a human voice, he began to taxi out towards the outer runway designated for freighters and small aircraft.   Once airborne, he banked right to the north ninety degrees and settled in at about five thousand feet, just enough to clear the mountain tops for the half hour plus flight to Graciosa.

Jackie's first glimpse of the Sao Miguel was short lived, but at this low altitude, she could easily make out the hillsides, dotted with beautifully cultivated farm fields, properties separated by hedgerows and tree lines.   Over the mountain tops, the sea appeared again and in the distance Sao Jorge stretched like a carpenter's pencil across the ocean.   It was a five minute cruise to its shores and Jackie could make out the black sand beaches of this more remote island as they cleared the eastern side of an outstretched promontory.   She noticed what she thought was a Coast Guard Cutter steaming around the point. She shook her head.   That couldn't be right.

The island held the same fertile farm fields that Sao Miguel did; elegant pastures for sheep and goats and small plantations for fruit trees.   The jet banked right again, just shy of thirty degrees and swept out for the final twenty minutes to Santa Cruz, Graciosa.

This was surely a different Portugal, one totally at the mercy of the Atlantic Ocean and the Gulf Stream current.   It was so much more tropical than the mainland, which, at the same latitude, suffered from blasts of winter in the region where she was born.   She could remember from her youth how insufferable that cold could be in their three room home.

This looked like a paradise and Jackie was now beginning to look forward to this assignment.   It would be wonderful to live and work in this place, especially in a full scale resort.   Her Suite awaited her and the first thing she would do would be to go down to the pool for a swim.

Bill was right, as he usually was when it came to engines. The EGR valve was indeed the culprit. And since both engines had over three thousand hours on them, he decided to replace both EGRs, just as a precaution. To disassemble the top end of the twin engines, he used the salon as his parts station, laying out the pieces in order. It was like a mine field in there. The parts had to be special ordered and flown in. That was going to take another couple of days.

This presented two specific problems for Joe, one long term and the other, immediate. The long term problem was the delay. This was going to cost probably eight days altogether and so the trip was extended to the point that if they were in the Azores for more than two weeks, another trans-Atlantic voyage was out of the question. The winter seas would have set in and storms would be too prevalent to brave.

That meant he would end up flying Bill home and then he would basically have three options: One, he could stay out the winter, which did not seem an acceptable choice. Two, he could hope for an additional assignment down through the Canary Islands or the west African coast, which seemed unlikely; or, Three, he could leave the boat with a broker and fly back himself. He didn't see that as the preferred choice either, as the company had spent a great deal on refitting the ship. But all this was the long term problem.

The short term problem was what to do with himself. Bill was busy all day for the past three days and would likely stay so. At night, he was exhausted, so Joe would go find some take out, have a couple of drinks and bring dinner back to the boat for Bill. They had to eat on the aft deck, the salon cluttered.

Torshavn was not a hotbed of dazzling urban life,

scarcely twenty thousand people with but limited nightlife, restaurants and pubs, yet it was still Denmark. On Sunday, Joe decided to go to the city park, where the young and old alike were enjoying a nice, crisp early fall day.

He ambled around until he discovered the pungent smell of an aroma familiar. A half-dozen young people where sitting around a bench and a large adjacent rock in a tree shaded area of the park, smoking pot, playing a guitar and singing in relative tune. He approached them cautiously as he did not want to frighten them. They stopped singing when he arrived.

"Would any of you speak English?"

A young man with long wavy hair and frazzled beard answered.

"What can we do for you, Sir?" He and his friends gazed warily at the tall stranger. He didn't look like a covert agent, rather a seasoned seaman with a few miles on him. And any law enforcement officer would have spoken Danish, not English, so he didn't seem a threat. Besides, personal amounts of marijuana were not even a misdemeanor in this country.

"I was wondering if I might purchase a small amount of reefer from you all? Maybe a quarter ounce if you can spare it?"

The young man laughed and the others joined him. They invited him to sit. The lovely blonde sitting cross legged next to the young man opened her satchel and pulled out two baggies, the larger one about the size of what Joe was looking for.

"Okay?" she asked.

"Yup."

"Eighty," she added.

Eighty Euros for what used to be a nickel bag, Joe thought. Inflation surely had crept into the market over the years. He nodded in agreement and handed her the money, she the bag to him. He stuffed it into his shirt.

They invited him to stay and he sat for a couple of tokes with them and they shared their thoughts, the young people extremely interested in Joe's occupation and mission.

Several indicated they'd like to do exactly what he was doing. Joe thought about his past and couldn't begin to tell them how to go about doing it.

Joe excused himself and thanked them voraciously. It had been some time since he had some decent pot. He walked over to the other side of the park, pulled out some papers and rolled a thin joint. He would be smoking a lot in the next week. He shouldn't have this stuff on him in Ireland and certainly not anywhere near Spain or Portugal. They would confiscate his boat and put both he and Bill in prison. No, while Bill was playing with his engine, Joe would be getting high and amusing himself in this quaint little city.

He took three good tokes on the joint, then snuffed it out. That would do just fine for the time being. He set out for the small café, one of two down at the harbor and the only one open on a Sunday, The Glaemon, which sat on the backside of one of the many red warehouses on the point. It was on the opposite side of the commercial dock where Bill no doubt toiled on his troubled engines. Joe was quite pleased with himself as he knew he could not be seen by his partner. It was neither good fortune nor bad that he was an easily recognizable man.

He sat down at one of the umbrella covered tables and ordered a glass of chilled white wine. The waitress, a pert, short haired blonde smiled at him profusely and returned with a nicely filled glass. He thanked her and she turned and went back to her station inside.

That is simply a fine example of femininity, he thought, fumbling over the word femininity in his head. God, this is beginning to remind me of Montreal again. A flood of memories returned. Lordy, Lordy, it would be nice to be forty; or even close. He would have been much more brazen; and had a lot more energy. Somehow, now, all that didn't seem to matter that much. He chuckled, then giggled, then laughed until the tears filled his eyes.

CHAPTER THIRTEEN

Catello Blanco

On the fourth day of Alvarro's not so glamorous tour of duty he decided he should take his mentor's advice and learn all he could while stationed there. He set up a meeting with Gustave Parcanto, President of the Autonomous Region of the Acores at his administrative offices in the Government building at the east end of the city. As Parcanto had to serve in both the offices in Horta and Ponta Delgada, he routinely split the week at the two state buildings.

This would be a private meeting, he advised Parcanto, and that the meeting and their discussions would not enter the realms of Colonel DeSilva's knowledge.

He set the meeting up for 12:30 p.m., a time when he was sure DeSilva would be enjoying his daily luncheon at Club Naval. In his short time on base, Alvarro had readily ascertained the rigorous routine the Colonel had established for himself.

He arrived at his base office at 9:30 a.m., more or less, had coffee sent in with pastries, sifted thru the mail, tossing the most aggravating and pointless of items into a pile that would arrive on Alvarro's desk. He would issue the orders of the day to his master sergeant, his office manager, and review his emails before departing no later than eleven for his scheduled lunch meeting. He wouldn't return for the day, preferring to resume his review of military affairs at his Villa on the veranda overlooking the crashing Atlantic as the waves pounded the rock strewn base of the Cliffside that held the gorgeous three story mansion that crested atop the heights.

Alvarro's only concern was how to get to and from the offices unnoticed. In the end a bicycle rented the day before, a light suede jacket and a soft kepi style seaman's cap complemented his navy blue slacks to make him appear reasonably non-military enough to depart unseen.

The Regional Government Building was yet another

whitewashed three story building just off the Avenida Du Don Henrique, built in the classic Greek style with scrolled columns in a cream color that just offset the tiled portico underneath.   He locked up the bike at the supply entrance in the back and made his way to Parcanto's office on the third floor.

After passing thru light security, he was ushered into the President's office. Gustave Parcanto was a man of medium build, light grey receding hair that sat wherever it wanted to around his thick browed forehead.   He seemed more like a college professor than a politician, his bifocals hugging the bridge of his nose.   It gave him the air of an intellectual, which, in fact, he was.

"You risk much in this." Parcanto's greeting offered.

"Not as much as you might think." Alvarro returned.

"How so?"

"I doubt you know my story and possibly Colonel DeSilva doesn't know that much either, but I'm guessing he knows enough."   Alvarro cleared his throat.   The risk here was that Parcanto might be in league with DeSilva, but it might not matter.   Based on what he had heard in his short time in Ponta Delgada, that should not be the case. Parcanto was not a true separatist, but did want as much autonomy for the Province Acores as he could possibly gain.

"I was the campaign manager for Pedro Cavadas.   I also had retained my commission in the service in the reserves, so President DeSilva himself issued a proclamation that recalled me and sent me here as second in command."

"I see." Gustave's wheels were already spinning.

"It was obviously meant to disrupt the campaign, just one more thing that the President could do help win the election."

"How did Mr. Cavadas respond to this?"

"He took it in stride, as he always does, and indicated to me that I should use it as an opportunity to learn.   That, Sir, is why I am here."

"And what do you expect to learn, or hope to?"

"I want to know what's really going on here and I'm especially curious as to what might be going on in Graciosa.

President Parcanto relayed what he knew of the resort, the habitat, the corporation and the private security that existed for the corporate owned properties, including the airstrip at Santa Cruz. He told Alvarro how the complaints had come in and how Colonel DeSilva took that off his hands and had dealt directly with the corporation and the local constabulary.

"I'm not saying anything foul is going on up there. I don't know for sure. Our people who trespass are gently, but firmly returned to the local police. The tourists fly directly to the Santa Cruz airstrip now, bypassing us here completely. That, in itself, is counter to our original agreement. We were to benefit here from the tourism and we haven't.

"If foreigners are out there uninvited, I don't know about it. But it is disturbing in the sense that whole area is being operated as if it were totally independent of us. And it is even more disturbing that I have a full regiment posted all about the rest of the Islands."

"I could see your point," Alvarro noted. "An autonomous region shouldn't need military oversight. This is the kind of thing Pedro wants to eradicate. It does nothing but increase tensions and ignite insurgency."

"Do you mean if he is elected, we could be rid of this suppression?"

"Absolutely. I've been with him since the beginning, so I know he means it when he talks about a Portuguese Confederation. There is strength in the commonalities: and shared economics, taxation and judicial systems benefit from union. But distinctly different regions have distinctly different needs and he feels that supporting the kind of asset building that recognizes that, thru independent thinking, is the best way to improve the country."

Gustave Parcanto took it all in and looked at the young man across from him. He was a God send in one way and a big problem in another. Alvarro seemed to sense the caution that filled the room.

"Mr. President. My situation is precarious. I won't lie to you about that. I live in a half glass full and a half glass empty environment. It's 50/50 either way. If Pedro wins the

223

election, I will be going to Lisbon to serve and I can be a great benefit to you. If he loses, I will be buried here, probably both literally and figuratively. I may need your help. If the worst happens, I will try to escape the Islands and get to America. I have a sister there somewhere. But in the meantime, could you educate me? I want to know all I can."

Gustave reasoned for a minute, and concluded. "I will help you. You are a bright, articulate young man and this country needs many more of you. We can keep meeting when you can, but are you sure it will be safe for you?"

"No, not entirely, but I don't think the Colonel will touch me, at least for the next three weeks. And then we'll know for sure."

They parted graciously and Alvarro donned his cap and coat, slipped out the back to his bicycle. He quietly pedaled out to the Avenida to make his way back to the base.

In a black Renault across the street, two men took note and slowly made their way out into the traffic. Commandant DeSilva would know about it within the hour. That would be a card he would hold to use later.

*

Trevor Hagan lived mostly on his thirty six foot diesel powered sailboat off the Claddaugh Quay tied to a mooring about fifty yards from the docks. He also owned a small two story house in upper Salthill where he slept and entertained only occasionally and where he had a basement that had enough firepower to equip an entire squad of commandos. Trevor used to frequent the King's Head Pub halfway between his house and the River Corrib at the docks, but more recently he made his social headquarters at the Roisin Dubh Pub, closer to his boat and just off the quay.

Trevor was what they called an afternoon man. Any time after noon he might appear for a lunch and stay for the afternoon, if he wasn't on a job of course. But, generally, he came in at four thirty, had four or five pints, then a Jameson on the rocks and finally, but noisily, disappeard to his beloved three master.   He would eat on the boat, grab something on the way, or live off an appetizer at the Roisin Dubh.   Trevor liked the young girls working at the Dubh.   In that regard, he was a devotee of George Burns, another good Irishman to his mind, who, in his nineties was asked why he still liked eighteen year old girls.   George had replied that he liked them well enough when he was eighteen.

Trevor was invisible in Galway.   He lived by an alias and worked undercover with great skill.   Years of practice had taught him to keep to himself, work only with the best of professionals.   After the destruction of the UniOil rig in the Minch, he had gone with Joe into Canada, where he stayed out of sight for six months.   He returned with new identification and a new history to a new hometown and went about his business quietly.   He provided support, planning, technical help, and logistics for the IRA and other environmental groups, but mostly remotely.   Few knew him as Trevor Hagan.   That was an identity he wanted to keep for his old age.

Joe knew very little of this.   He remembered Trevor had created the new identity, but it hadn't dawned on him that he would still be using that now, nor could he remember exactly what the last name was.   It was something like Dylan Kelly, or Cavanugh or Callaghan, or Kerry, or something like that.   He hoped it would come to him.

They approached Galway Bay directly from Torshavn in the Faroe Islands by way of the Isle of Lewis for a quick pit stop.   Galway was the largest westernmost major port in Ireland.   It was an interesting City with a sorrowful past.   The English sent ships into the deep water bay to load up rebellious Irish prisoners and send them off to the Australian Penal Colony.   As a consequence, there was still little love for the English in Galway, a fact that Canadians would also need to concern themselves with.

Commerce had improved dramatically with the building of the new docks on the south side of the river, and cruise ships were now common to the populace.   The people of Galway loved Tourism, because it brought in so much money, but did not particularly like Tourists.   The cruise ship crowds clogged up the city and crowded into the pubs making it quite difficult for the locals to enjoy their repast. Most felt that if they could just send out some tweed hats, mugs of beer and T-Shirts, they could just stay on the boat. Better still, they could form teams of residents to sit at tables on the docks and drink pints and the tourists could photograph them from the ships.

Four weeks after having left Quebec City, the Cormorant cruised into Galway Bay. Just before they docked at the pier, Joe dumped the small amount left of his nickel bag into the ocean. He had smoked most all of it, but wasn't going through customs here with any trace on board. He never shared it with Bill, fearing for whatever beast that might unleash and he was sure Bill hadn't caught on to his new hobby of old. Bill might just have thought Joe was a little slow and maybe a little more content on the voyage in.

Once tied up, they had more than enough afternoon to scout the neighborhoods. They tried two pubs near the base of Salthill without any luck, then ambled into the King's Head. By then, it was time for a pint, so they sat for two and talked to the bartender, who wasn't much help until Joe showed an old picture of himself and Trevor together back in Montreal.

"That looks like a fella we know, lot younger though. If it's the same guy, he's got a scruffy grey beard now. Name's Kerrigan. Dylan Kerrigan. He used to come in here a lot, but since he bought his boat, he now calls the Roisin Dubh his living room."

They thanked the gentleman and graciously left a nice tip. They went back down the hill to the river, crossed the bridge to the north side, where the Roisin Dubh sat one block off on a corner lot.

Inside, dimly lit ball lights hung in the ceiling, accentuating the raised relief cherry panels. The bar was beautiful and harkened back to the days of Irish grandeur. Clearly, the Dubh had done well by tourism and the cruise ship trade. Once their eyes adjusted to the light, they could make out the patrons. At the end of the bar towards the kitchen and directly next to the waitress station, Dylan Kerrigan hoisted his last pint for the afternoon. He was about to order his Jameson.   He had said something funny to the handsome tall waitress who had just arrived with a table order. She burst out laughing.

"Man after my own heart," Bill snickered, "We'll get along just fine."

Without saying a word, Joe sat down next to his old colleague and ordered two Smithwicks on tap.   Dylan turned about to bitch that there were plenty of other stools at the other end of the bar, took one look at the stranger next to him and his jaw dropped.

"I'll be damned. It can't be.   Joe Hackett in me favorite pub. Lord be praised."

He was grinning from ear to ear and Joe couldn't help but break into a laugh.

"Dylan Trevor Kerrigan.   What's a beat up old reprobate like you doing taunting that lovely young lady there. Don't tell me I now got two of you to deal with."

Joe introduced Bill to Dylan.   Dylan was at least ten years younger than Bill, but looked five years older.   Time, the line of work and pub life had not been that kind to Dylan. For a tall man in his youth, he had shrunk a couple of inches, bouts with arthritis and the dismal Ireland weather taking their toll.   He wore a light brown jacket over a black shirt and slacks, enough to keep the fall chill off him.

"What brings you boys to Galway?"

"You, "Joe answered as he motioned the three of them to a table out of earshot of the other customers. "We're on a mission for WorldGreen to the Azores.   It sounded dicey enough that we added some heavy arms for the trip, refit the boat.   I got into a hell of a mess early in the summer out in the Aleutians and I'll be damned if I get surprised again.   I insisted on you, Trevor, uh Dylan, sorry, because you were the best I've ever worked with."

"How do you know I'm still in the business?"

"Pig's ass.   Of course you are.   What the hell else would you do?

"You have a point.   But, if you're serious, I don't come cheap."

"Not a problem.   We have a generous supply of funds

to work with. I knew this was the only way to get to you. You'd have to see me in person to take on the job.   Will you do it?"

"Seeins how you come all this way to face me and seeins how I don't have anything on my plate that can't be pushed back a bit, I guess I could do an old friend a favor, for about 40K of course.   Now, let's polish off these drinks and we'll go up to the house.   Leave a nice tip for Colleen, there, Joey."

He ordered the best bottle of Jameson the bartender had and took his two new partners up to his house where they drained the bottle and talked into the night.   In the morning, a bit bleary and a little worse for wear and tear, the trio set out to load up the necessary items for the trip.

Trevor tossed out his suitcase, added enough clothing for a couple of weeks and then took them into the basement where he selected a high powered .50 caliber Barrett Rifle, an AK104 and a 110, a sawed off double barrel, and two pistols, one with a silencer.

"How will you get all your guns aboard?" Bill asked.

"Very easily.   I'm a golfer, not a good one, but I play a couple times a week.   I have some friends who I can go out with most anytime.   I make it a point to tell folks I play in tournaments in other countries just because I like to. Sometimes, I take my car, sometimes my boat. I have a large golf bag with a snap over cover.   Depending on what I need, I can pack that sucker with a whole lot of firepower and all the ammunition I need.   No one thinks the wiser when I walk down to the wharf with a golf bag."

"And it works?"

"Wonderfully.   This big .50 cal. Is my Driver.   Long range and right in the middle of the fairway, every time. The AK110 is my fairway iron.   I tend to slice a lot with it.   The shotgun here is for chip shots.   I can't miss. And this .38 with the silencer.   That's my putter.   It goes thwack, glup, glup right in the cup.   Of course, I don't use them if I don't have to and I haven't had to in years.   I try to stay on the backstage, if you catch my drift."

They packed the golf bag as Dylan instructed and he

228

stuffed his rolling suitcase.   Bill carried the golf bag and
Dylan rolled the suitcase as they walked through the early
evening's last light down to the Cormorant and stowed away
the gear.   They got off the boat and went back to the Dubh for
drinks and dinner.

"One more thing we need," Dylan noted over the last
pint just before they left the pub. "We gotta get a couple of
bikes."

"Bikes?" Joe queried.

"You know, those little wheeled, folding type.   Dorky
dock bikes, I call them."

"Whatever for?" Bill added.

"Nothing screams boating tourists like those little bikes.
And they actually can come in useful.   We'll get a couple in
the morning before we leave and tie them up to that aft vent
cover that hides the gun.   That'll be just the thing."

*

Chris and Ann left Logan in the pouring rain with forty
five degrees, not much higher than Chris's least favorite
weather, and arrived in Ponta Delgada five hours later to
sunny, seventy five degree temperatures with a light sea
breeze.   It was a beautiful fall day.   They had enough time to
get something light to eat at the Terminal food court and then
boarded the Dash 8 for the flight to Horta.   The thirty- two
seater was nearly full which surprised Ann because she had
read extensively on the islands before the trip and assumed
much smaller aircraft and much less in passengers.

The flight took an hour and fifteen minutes as the twin
engine prop roared thru the sky at ten thousand feet.   It was
completely clear and Chris could make out the runway as the
plane banked for its final descent.

"Annie, you better know where the life jacket is."

She bent over him to look out the window.

"Oh, my God.   We have to land on that?"

The runway was nestled between the bulk of the Island

where Horta lay around its expansive bay and a round hilled peninsula that was connected by a wide isthmus. The airport seemed an afterthought, two wide lanes that appeared to be only about a football field in length, the sea at each end, directly at the end of the isthmus.

The landing gear down, the plane came in way too fast for either of their liking and they gripped to the arm rests, white knuckled as it hit the pavement. The thunderous screech of brakes and rumbling tires were accompanied by the gale force created by the flaps as the pilot expertly hauled her to a stop, but truly only a hundred feet from the end of the runway and the rocks that would have bashed an errant ship before it catapulted into the sea.

"If you'd have gotten me killed here, I would never speak to you again," Ann moaned.

"You wouldn't have to," Chris added with a huge sigh of relief.

After a short wait, they debarked and took a taxi to the Hotel Atlantic, overlooking the bay and the old docks of the city. Horta paled in comparison to Ponta Delgada, but it was the second largest city in the Azores and featured the same type of architecture, white washed buildings and churches with red and brown tiled roofs with an abundance of brown trim.

Checking in at the hotel, Chris received a message from Luis Recife, a contact arranged by Chris's old college friend, Jack Connelly. Luis would meet them in the morning at nine a.m. and take them to the farmhouse just outside Castello Blanco where his ancestor's property lay. Chris would depend heavily on Luis for translation and to tend to the business that would be required. In the interim, they needed to adjust to the five hour time change.

Once settled, Ann began to go over the itinerary. Chris suggested some wine at the café downstairs and they took the brochures and travel documents with them.

"Two days here," Ann noted, "and you think that will be time enough?"

"To get things at least ironed out the way they should be, yes, but if not, we can stay another day or two and change the reservation for the resort."

"Chris, this is the Tropical Natur Azores, The Atlantic Sun resort.   I don't think we can change without a penalty. Their reservation rules were rather specific."

"I'm sure we'll be fine."   He sipped the house Verdelho wine and looked out at the old docks.

"This used to be a whaling port," he sidetracked. "Jack tells me that's how my ancestors got to New Bedford.   The Portuguese were the navigators for the whaling ships and either my family had one or were related to one and they came to New Bedford to master the ships of the fleet there. "

"There's no sign of that now," Ann ventured. "All I see out there are mega-yachts.   I read where this is the trans-atlantic port for ocean crossings.   I wouldn't be surprised if we saw a famous person or two down there.   Do you want to take a walk later?"

"How about tomorrow after the meeting at the farm?"

"Okay, ancient, worn out, mostly retired person.   What else would you like to do with the evening?"

Chris looked at this wonderful, beautiful person who sat across from him and did not let his thoughts stray.

"I would think another glass of wine and then I have something in mind.   Maybe you could help me find a pair of socks."

At precisely nine a.m., Luis Recife arrived with a local barrister and the four met in the lobby as planned.   Through Luis, Chris presented the deed to the farm, the property and the out buildings indicated at Castello Blanco.   The barrister nodded.   They took a minivan taxi for the four mile ride out to the southwest side of the Island where the small parish lay.

A half kilometer passed the main intersection, they took a dirt road on the right that ran up the gently pastured slope away from the shore line.   Along the road, worn split rails lay haphazardly, barely resembling a fence until they came to a farmhouse some six hundred meters from the main road.

It was a fairly old two story house, somewhere in the neighborhood of two hundred years of age, according to Luis, and the white washed paint had faded over a long period of time giving it a parchment look. The roof was the same scalloped style brown tile Chris had seen in Horta and the well-worn weather beaten shutters had held their own and still looked operable. The windows, where closed, were multi-paned and no glass was missing, but most of the windows were open, especially on the second floor, where the sea breeze could whisk thru them.

At the rear of the house a single story extension came out at a right angle, a clear indication that it was an add-on, which had many more windows than the main house. Annie figured it to be a kitchen and she was right. Nestled in the interior corner, a cistern was built to capture the run off of both roofs. Luis explained that the home had indoor plumbing and a well put in during the sixties, but additional water was always needed for gardens and animals alike.

A small piazza adorned the space between the two wings in front of the cistern which featured a fountain, which hadn't worked in over fifteen years. It lay twenty meters from the kitchen door, where the tenants emerged.

Luis introduced Armondo and CeCalia Teresina. They both genuinely smiled at Chris and Ann. Neither spoke English, so Luis explained that Chris was the new Patron and had come all the way from America to see them and the house. Chris introduced Ann as his personal lawyer. She gave him an elbow in the ribs.

"Then, we're on the clock. That'll be four hundred Euros." She tapped him again.

"Take it out in trade, or dinners, or wine, da di di da di di da da." He beamed at her.

Armondo suggested that the men tour the grounds and CeCalia invited Ann to see the house. Ann agreed, for women of totally different cultures always had a way to make themselves understood.

Armondo led Chris around the front to the west side of the house where a small orange grove filled the property. Chris gazed at the sea to the south, but the trees blocked any view to the west, except for the rising slope in the distance. Walking around to the back, the four men examined the finely sculpted rows of the vineyard, which curled around to the eastern side of the property. Towards the end of the vineyard portion of the property, a small building stood where some grape processing was done.

Luis explained that the orchard and vineyard had been here probably about eighty years and Armondo's family had rented the house for two generations. They harvested the grapes, made some wine for home use, and carted the rest to the Co-op in Horta for processing. The orange harvest was sold directly at the market in town. The money they raised was theirs, of course, and the rent paid was very nominal, sent to Aunt Grace monthly.

Chris explained the problem to the three other men, of how rent for the past year had been siphoned off by the evil cousin. The barrister nodded vigorously. He immediately understood the problem. Moreover, now that the house was in the Estate, greater controls were required and that was well understood, too.

Chris further explained that while he and his siblings had no intention of either selling the place or removing the tenants, that a lease would now be required and a modest increase necessary in rent that he promised would result in upgrades to the property. He enlisted Luis and the Barrister to assist in that endeavor.

As they turned from the vineyard to the open lawn in front of the house, Chris stopped still for a moment. The aroma of the sea wind caught him and he felt it oddly familiar, yet he was sure he had never smelled that scent before. It was probably the scent of the oranges from the grove mixed with the salt air. He had never been to an orchard next to the ocean, so this had to be new, but it was so enchanting. Over to the east, he could see the mountain of Pico rising out of the ocean, a hint of snow on its peak. He must remember to tell Annie that it was the highest mountain in the world, although four fifths of it sat beneath the ocean's surface.

Ann waved from the kitchen, then came out to meet them.

"This is such a nice home, Chris. The Teresinas take great care of it. There has to be three kids because three of the four bedrooms upstairs are filled with their things, organized chaos, I would call it, but still there is a neatness about it. They have to be at school. The kitchen is ancient, but perfect. Come see." She grabbed his arm to lead him in.

Ann and Chris came into the kitchen ahead of the three men and CeCalia bowed graciously and waved them forward. It was clear most all of the eating was done here, a large table for six constantly in the process of the next meal. And, Ann was right, the kitchen was perfect. It was clear that decades of use had made it uniquely functional for its occupants.

Ann took Chris down the short hallway past the half bath on one side and the small library on the other to the two larger front rooms. A formal dining room was on the west side facing the grove. It looked like it had never been used. The parlor room or living room faced it and that was where the evening entertainment existed, a television that was hooked to the dish outside and a family sized couch facing it. There was a card table and a board game sat there, half finished. The four large windows, two front and two on the side, gave an expansive view of the lawn and vineyard, respectively.

Chris noticed a portrait and went instinctively to it. By now, Luis and Armondo had caught up, Armondo chattering to Luis. Luis tugged at Chris's sleeve.

"The original patron, Armondo says," Luis pointed. "He says that they still feel him here and dared not take down the picture for fear of disfavor for the house and the fields."

It was Chris's great great grandfather. He found himself clutching at his neck, holding the Talisman Star. The picture in front of him had to be at least one hundred and fifty years old. In actuality, it wasn't a picture, but a finely sketched penciled portrait, typical for the time before photography became the norm. It was faded and slightly stained and the pleasant looking man with grey hair and beard wore the Talisman Star around his neck. Chris shivered.

"Annie, I'm getting some awfully strange feelings here."

"Come back to the kitchen, honey, it's always safe in the kitchen."

They returned to the table and the latent smells of the breakfast eaten hours ago and reluctantly Chris went about the business they came for.   The lease was signed and fully explained.   Through Luis, Chris went on to explain how things would work in the future.

"First, we are very pleased at how well you've taken care of the place on your own.   The fact that your family has been here so long is testimony to that care and we honor it. Second, from now on, the rent goes to Luis, who will be the property manager.   It will be held in a segregated account here for the Estate and between the three of us, we will decide what improvements will be made and Luis will ensure that they are made and I am well advised on the progress.   All Estate expenditures have to be approved, so it may take some time, but the house will get nothing but better.   Finally, I will work with my other heirs to find a way to make your investment of time and care here permanent in some way. We have no intention of taking over the house nor in disenfranchising you after two generations."

They shook hands, left copies of the documents and returned to the hotel in Horta by late afternoon.   Back at the room, Chris was clearly stressed.   Ann suggested they go to the restaurant, have a wine and take in the bay.   They sat aside each other at the table, a light afternoon sprinkle just wetting the umbrella overhead.   Ann looked intently at Chris and noticed his eyebrow slightly furled.   He did that when he was worried, or stressed.   She remembered June telling her about that.

"What is going on in there?"

"This just might work, Annie.   I see that it could.   My sister cares nothing for this here; it's an albatross for her, so I could probably buy her out for a song.   Now, Jamestown is another matter.   That has real value to her, so it's a stretch, but there's enough in the inheritance to cover both and still leave me with something.   You'd have to take the bar in Rhody to practice, but I'm sure that John Willie could use you or at least refer you to a great firm, but, in any case, we could live in Jamestown; we could build this place up and maybe even add a small two story addition.   I'd take care of the

Teresinas, but it's not uncommon in Europe to have different families own parts of the same building.   Down the road, I could see us spending the winters here, helping process a little wine, enjoying the sea and our hobbies in our old age. We could truly enjoy it here."

Ann leaned over and kissed him.

"You said we, Chris, you said we."

"Yes, yes I did.   Didn't I."

*

Brian used the company jet directly off the Graciosa runway in Santa Cruz.   David's connecting flight from Chicago put them both in Boston within an hour of each other. The CEO summit was being held at the Marriott Waterfront near the Federal Plaza and Fanuel Hall.   David had reserved his suite well in advance, but Brian was a late registrant and could barely get a deluxe room at the Inn.   Over a hundred CEOs from around the world would attend.

David took a cab that dropped him off at the government center.   He walked past some of his old haunts from his MIT days, taking a side trip down Charles Street where one of his favorite places, Your Father's Moustache, used to be.   It had a different name, now.   Funny thing about old places like Boston, the people come and go, but the buildings remain and the names change.   It is different every time, and then it's not.

He backtracked to the waterfront, past the Union Oyster House.   Betty no longer had her Rolls Royce parked out front.   He wondered whatever happened to that beautiful old yellow behemoth.   As a college kid, he stood in awe of the thing.   Now, he could own a thousand of them.

He arrived in time for the evening Plenary Session. Ellison of Oracle was the featured speaker.   David would speak the next day at the dinner.   Registering on the Concierge floor, he noted several old friends and representatives from around the globe: From Europe; the CEOS of Siemens, Volkswagen, Nestle, and Mercedes; from

Rio; Petrobras and Banco Santander Brazil; from Japan; SONY, Honda, Mitsubishi, and Samsung; from the US; Dell, Apple, Ford, Exxon, and General Electric. The list was endless and his memory poor at remembering all the names. There had been a lot of changes in the last year as well.

As CEO of EngenUnity, he was now head of the largest market cap company in the world and Brian as COO held almost equal status among the best in the business. But Brian wasn't there to commiserate with his peers. He came solely to meet with David to discuss the future of his partnership in the company. His arrival an hour later meant he missed the opening of the conference, but he cared little for any of it. He would be out again in the morning.

Brian didn't bother to register, but went straight to the concierge lounge for a drink and paged his partner. David got the blip just as he left the session. Maria and Joan from CNBC waved at him from the registration desk. They wanted an interview. That would have to wait. He waved at them and made his way to the Concierge floor. He met Brian in the lounge and each took a drink down the hall to the Suite.

"Brian, you know why I asked you come?"

"I've got a pretty good idea."

"I'm concerned about the delays in the projects and the costs. I will have to make some explanations. From your end, why the delays and why the extraneous costs?"

"Dave, we are dealing with multiple problems, some of your making. Giving the scientists the authority to investigate and research the undersea was a mistake in my opinion. It's halted construction on the balance of the Habitat. The other big issue is that of dealing with a foreign government. Our deed creates autonomy, which is ironclad, but we couldn't afford to have the military prowling around, hence the deal and the private security. It's been better for business, but causes headaches when we have to remove radicals from the resort and the bay areas. Still, I'd rather have it that way. Besides, as Jackie tells me, the propulsion issue has the Shuttle on hold, anyway."

"That's not entirely true, we're only making room and time for some changes. It's worth the wait, and the scientists have their order of things, just as they do at the Habitat. Besides, discoveries may be valuable. That said, I'm just not that comfortable with the way things are being managed in the Azores."

"Neither am I, Dave. I'm not comfortable with any of it anymore. It's fine that our Corporation rakes in cash like leaves on a fall day, but this dream of yours is going to break us. I just don't see where we will derive all this revenue from the billions in expense. Besides, your dream isn't mine. I'm not one of these people who says I dream of things that never were and say why not? I'm the kind of guy who sees things as they are and decides they're okay just the way they are."

"I'm sorry you feel that way, Brian. We've been partners a long time."

"True. And, because of that, I have prepared a proposal that should be agreeable to you."

He handed David an eight and half by fourteen manila envelope. David took out the proposal.

"You want me to look at it now?"

"Please."

David looked over the eight page document. It was simple, concise and addressed Brian's points with clear accuracy. It even anticipated concerns that David would have. It was pure Brian, neat and clean; well thought out in every detail.

"And you're saying here, Brian, that we still retain all intellectual property, patents and discoveries that the Habitat produces and all testing results will be shared."

"Exactly."

"I'll take it back to Counsel and have them review it. If they find no ambiguities or raise any red flags, I'll sign it and we can begin the process of transfer. Are you sure you are serious about this?"

"Deadly."

ACT 14

The Underseas discovey

Dr. Suzanne Preston handled the joy stick. She still called it that from the days when her kids had an Atari. It maneuvered the Neptune II on the sea floor as she watched the monitors from the six different mounted cameras. George was looking at the streaming data and Dr. Frost was making notes in his experimental log. Wayne Trudeau was waiting for the sub to come and pick him up to take him topside to meet with Brian. He didn't look forward to that. Brian had just returned from Boston and had seemed in a good mood over the phone, but meetings with Brian were never about niceties.

Dr. Suz, as she was referred to by her colleagues, positioned the ROV at the nearest corner of the marked desalinization site. She began to move it slowly at quarter speed, closely watching the monitors. The sensors noted some minor debris in the sand, but George wasn't paying much attention to that. He did note the sand depth at about three feet, then some firmer footing beneath it.

At fourteen meters in, Suz stopped the ROV. She had something on the screen. George noted the anomaly in the data.

"Use the sweeper," George offered, careful not to ignite Suzie's somewhat delicate temperament.

Suz adjusted the blower mechanism, which forced sea water onto any object and then lightly blasted the object. When the sand settled, she directed the hydraulic brush which gave shape to a large urn.

"It's an Amphora," she noted.

"What's that?" Wayne asked from the other side of the lab.

"An ancient wine cask," Suz replied. "Ships carried a lot of wine in this type of ceramic vessel."

"Oh, we ran into a few of those when we built the

239

habitat.   Brian said they were nothing but shitty old pottery and we dozed them out of the way for the footers."

George groaned.   He knew what was coming.

"God damned useless bunch of jerks," Suz ranted. "Could you guys do anything right?   You just have no damned idea do you?" she paused for a moment.   Her diminutive frame seemed to have grown perceptively.

George thought he could almost see spittle on her lips.

"Amphora are wine casks and they were carried to supply the crews with enough wine to stay happy on long voyages.   Any concentration of them indicates a possible trade route, or an ancient port or mercantile center.   Ninety percent of all ocean exploration is dedicated to this theory and the discoveries have been not only rewarding historically, but financially as well.   And you clowns totally ignored them.   No wonder we live in the dark ages of our past.   We have you asswipes to thank for it."

"Sorry," was the best Wayne could do.

"Let's get on with it, Suz," George added.   "It won't happen again, now that we're here.   Alas, history is littered with humans doing exactly this: bulldozing over the past."

Suzanne grunted as if in pain, and redirected the Neptune past the relic.   Another eight meters forward and George asked her to stop.

"The data seems to indicate a hard surface about a meter down.   Let's send down the probe."

"Okay."   Suz stationed the Neptune as level as possible, dropped down the drill, which housed a retractable head for sending data back to the console.   At a shade less than a meter, the drill hit a thin coat of lava, the tailings of a last floe, not more than three quarters of a centimeter thick. The drill popped thru it and sank into a thick mud as the sensory tip was activated. George stared at the data in disbelief.

"No oxygen readings, Suzie."

"Anoxic soil?" she responded.

"That's not possible," Dr. Chuck Frost exclaimed as his head popped up and his logbook dropped to the floor.

"I'm looking at it, Chuck." George noted.

240

Wayne looked confused again.

"There's only one other place on earth where that exists and that's in the Black Sea. How did it get here?" Chuck asked.

"Any number of ways, I suppose," George pondered. "The petrified lava shield obviously covered it and the two islands here protected it and the sea current isn't that great here, but truly, I can't answer that question."

"What does that mean for the desalinization plant?" Wayne asked.

"It means, Wayne," Suz interjected, "that your plant will wait quite a bit.   Anoxic soil is the perfect preservative. Entire wooden ships have been found in it, untouched by bacteria and sea rot. It means we will carefully excavate the area and we will uncover, perhaps, priceless artifacts. It is," she paused, "a spectacular discovery.   We couldn't have dreamed of better outcome here."

"Wayne, we're going to need the Robotic Excavation Dredge down here." George stated.

"The RED?   I'll have to get Brian's okay, but yeah, I'll get it."   Wayne was clearly embarrassed and had no means to say no.

"Tell him there's money in it for him.   That might help."

*

Jackie enjoyed one day.   Brian had been in Boston and after she emailed David, she had nothing to do but relax. She had one of the two Governor's Suites on the eighth floor, the ends of the horseshoe shaped complex that overlooked the largest pool she had ever seen and the ocean directly out from the end, where she had a sixteen foot balcony.

The pool had a sunken bar, two massive waterfalls, bridges and coves, and a hot tub up in back of the largest waterfall.   The grounds were perfect, all manner of tropical plants and the eighteen hole golf course behind the hotel featured an island in the adjacent cove where a short walking bridge connected the 19th hole Grille and club house to the mainland course.

Beyond the course, several nature trails were laid out; an interior rainforest trail that catered to short nature hikes, a seaside trail that meandered along steep cliffs around the North point to the East side of the island, and a full day long trail that went back up into the volcanic mountainside to the Franciscan Caldera, a beautiful lake filled cone with gentle grassland about half way around its shore.   All three had idyllic stops and picnic areas for long or short term use.

Jackie smiled.   This was the kind of place that God would build, if he had the money.   She was suddenly proud of her company and the vision that built the place.   Of course it was David's vision that drove the company and Brian was the bricks and mortar guy that made it happen.   Together, they were a powerful force and she wondered if separately, they could have ever done this well.

She went down to the lobby and out the private entrance for staff that led to the old hotel, the one first bought on the island, that now served as the administrative offices for the complex.   Brian was in the first floor board room and Wayne Trudeau was just leaving.   He nodded to her on the way out.

Brian looked pissed off, but that was the way Jackie remembered him most of the time.

"Ah, Jackie, you're looking well.   Are you enjoying your stay so far?"

"Yes, Brian, I am.   This is much nicer than I expected. It's really quite grand."

"Good. Now, could you tell me what you're really here for?   I've gotten the memo from David and after seeing him, understand that you will be conducting the tests on the laser guidance systems.   However, we could have easily done that without you.   So, what gives?"   Brian was always direct, a bottom line man.

"I'm also here to pass on encrypted scientific processes on a portable hard drive directly to Dr. George Preston."

"And that we could have handled securely as well, too. You've seen my security staff here; we could have sent a courier to deal with that.   So, what else?"

There wasn't any advantage in belaboring the point that she was sure he already knew.

"David wanted another set of eyes and ears here on the ground.   He wants my take on the progress here."

"Delayed and costly, yes, I know, and he and I have discussed it and I just got another damned delay today. They want to scrape and map the undersea construction site for the salvage of artifacts.   You know, I don't mind anymore, really.   What the hell, the salvage, if it proves out, could be worth millions.   It wouldn't be the first time.   Hell, they got millions out of the wrecks of the Espadarte and the Santa Margarita."

"That said, Jackie, more delays and more costs.   If you want to stick around and report back to Dave, fine.   Just don't get in the way.   We've got a lot of work to do around here and this resort is a full time business."

Jackie bit her lip.   She was highly agitated.

"Sometimes, Brian, you can't seem to be a team player and you miss the big picture.   Do you know why David calls all this the Magellan Project?" She didn't wait for a response. "Because Magellan was the greatest Portuguese navigator of all time.   Perhaps, this being part of Portugal had something to do with that.   But, it was actually about the vision of world navigation and discovering the whole planet, the new worlds to be conquered."

"But Magellan never made it, did he?" Brian interrupted. "He got killed somewhere around the Phillipines."

"Exactly, Brian, that's the real point.   David knows that he probably won't live to see the fruits of his labor, the discovery of new worlds; nor will he be around to see the benefits of planetary colonization, but he has the vision to understand the value of it all, what it will due for the company, what it will do for the country and what value it will have for all mankind.   That's the difference between David and you and me.   He sees things we don't see."

"Yes, and when you see things that others don't see, it's easy to gloss over the things you don't want to see; like delays and cost overruns and unanticipated expenses or

243

government interference. Jackie, visionaries are a lot like highly educated intellectuals. They are fine when their vision, their credo or their philosophies remain intact, undented in any form, but they become rigid as hell when they have to deal with facts that don't support their hypotheses."

"Things are going to change around here, Jackie, sooner than you may think. So go ahead and accompany the tests; they're scheduled for Friday at eleven. Today's Wednesday, so you've got plenty of time to prepare. You can go with Wayne and the tourists on Saturday and see Dr. Preston. He's tied up with tours and equipment delivery to the Habitat until then, anyway. I don't really give a shit how you spend your time here. Just don't get in the God Damned way. I mean it."

*

Captain Charles "Candy" Kane set about his disposition of forces for the day. He had three helicopters, Bell Hueys that were originally Iroquois models refitted from combat duty, all bright orange with huge sunbursts emblazoned on each side and the letters Atlantic Sun Resort printed brightly across the front. Not evident to the casual observer were the machine gun ports on each side of all three of them that had been specifically left there during refit.

He would send up two this day, overlapping each other. The third was in the final stages of preparation for the laser guidance system test to be held at the end of the week.

He also had four boats, all triple outboard Boston Whalers, but sent out only two at a time. They were each manned by two security guards, each armed and they covered the North, West, and Southern side of the resort island. The East side faced directly to the Atlantic and did not generally have any traffic that would be of concern. On land, he had five other guards, one of whom operated the communications center at his headquarters. In all, he had fourteen, including himself.

With the helicopters, he had a good look at the whole island and out to sea in every direction.   The boats were the interceptors and they had done a fine job in turning back curious tourists, fishermen, and an occasional protest group from the main island.   By Kane's count, they had sixty three interceptions since the program began.   Most of these were disgruntled locals for various reasons, but at least a dozen involved foreigners who had to be removed back to other islands or sent home.   Atlantic Sun charged them for their return trips if they didn't have them already and the resort couldn't have given a damn less about their protests. It was either that or face charges in Portugal and that meant a short term jail sentence, at least.

The day set out to be routine, except for the seventy six foot Aleutian approaching from the east out of Lisbon, now fifty nautical miles from Graciosa and still unseen by the air patrols.

"Bill, plot me a course that takes us south of the island and puts us in between it and Sao Jorge."

"Roger that, Skip."   Bill double checked the charts and called out, "Five degrees to Port, Joe, that should take us toward the line you want, then, when you see Graciosa due North, cut right eight."

"Your plan?"   Dylan inquired.

"I want to anchor off the southwest side of the big island and take the Zodiac in for some intel.   And, I don't want to go to port just yet and I certainly didn't come all this way to walk into their security, which I am now understanding, is fairly formidable."

"Let me go in alone, first," Dylan offered.

"Why just you?" Bill asked.

"You may remember," Joe interjected, "that Trevor, ah Dylan. God, I have to get that right or shut up in public; that Dylan speaks a little Portuguese, which is part of why he's here."

"Hard to believe, Bill, but I was once a high school kid, who was an exchange student to Rio in my senior year.   I was immersed in the language and the culture and I've been back a few times on business over the years.   I can get by.

Besides, my wizened craggy features give me a look of an authentic dock monkey, which of course, I basically am."

Bill grinned. Nothing like a good self- deprecating humor to brighten a day.

"We'll bring it around the island and anchor directly opposite the Village of Santa Cruz.   There will be a road there." Joe noted.

"I'll take one of the damn dorky bikes with me and peddle in.   I'll find out what I can from the fishermen." Dylan added.

Three and a half hours later, the Cormorant anchored a hundred yards from shore in twelve foot depth, just off short cliffs that sloped gently up to a road where boulders were positioned as guardrails.

Dylan used the electric motor until he was within twenty feet, paddled the rest of the way in, dragged the bike up the slope, bitching at the thing all the way up, then folded it into use for the ride into town.   His long frame made him look like a circus clown as he disappeared around a corner.

Half way to town, he ran into a teenager with an old fat tired bike and it only took about three minutes to convince the kid that he would love the new five hundred dollar dock bike a hell of a lot more and Dylan was happily on his way to town, more authentic than ever.

He spent an hour on the beach talking to the fishermen who were tending their nets, repairing their boats or, perhaps, electing to take the day off from the sea. He bicycled through the small village of five thousand, where all the buildings were whitewashed with red roofs, and peddled into the airstrip northwest of the town.   He sought out the commercial flight availability and noted the private runway, maintenance building, and new customs station recently built on the interior side of the airport.

Dylan returned near dusk, dumped the bike off the side of the road and quietly motored the zodiac back to the ship.

"For starters, guys, the town appears sleepy and dull, but there's a strong undercurrent of discontent there.   The seamen hate the resort. They feel the Habitat is killing their fishing, and if they protest, or file complaints, they go unheeded. If they cross a certain barrier, they are apprehended and taken back, under guard and tow, to the local police. They get a fine. They don't trust the police, either. Last week, two men disappeared. The seas were a bit rough, but these were experienced fishermen. The villagers suspect foul play."

"Hmm," Joe muttered. "We'll have to get a better look at Atlantic Sun."

"Already thought of it, Joe," Dylan said, "I went to the airport and booked us a flight to Ponta Delgada and return. I could see the takeoffs and the landings. They take off to the west and circle around for their flights out. Incoming flights go out over the small island from the east to come in to the airfield. We'll get a good look at the resort going directly over it on the way back. Besides, we're tourists, and tourists take trips to the other islands."

"Any problems with docking at the village marina?" Joe asked

"None that I could see. I think we'll be fine. We're minus a bike, though, but some teenager is riding it around, and that can't look bad either."

"Well, let's go be tourists for a couple of days."

*

George and Suzie Preston were not only tops in their field, but were first class divers as well. That was how they met three decades ago and had shared that love ever since. It also was the dominant factor in their selection for the 'Ferdinand' or 'Ferd' as they had come to call the Habitat.

In anticipation of the housing of experts and divers, the Habitat had a transitional chamber built on at the port side entrance. This room was designed to mitigate the effects of the 'bends' that would be associated with the divers at this depth entering an oxygenated space. When the diver entered the sea water filled cavity, oxygen was introduced incrementally and water pressure lightened in a process that took about eight and a half minutes. The water was then drained and the divers could safely remove their gear. It took a little getting used to, but it was a life saver. This replicated compression/decompression stops associated with saturation diving.   This would not be considered recreational diving, rather commercial diving, which required specific equipment. All that had been brought to the Habitat in advance.

George and Suz prepared for the reverse of this process as they began their day with big RED.   They always planned their dives meticulously and had prepared for their stay in the 'Ferd' by obtaining specialized helmets for their dive suits that could be used with their Helix mix and include the communications they required.   At two hundred feet of sea water (FSW), they calculated they could physically work the site for about forty five minutes.

With so little time on plat, Dr. Chuck handled the console for both the dredge and the Neptune II, gently scraping away at the lava shield with big RED, then mapping out the anoxic soul with the Neptune.   While George and Suzie prepared for the dive, Chuck cleared and mapped a fifty foot strip and contacted the divers via their helmet headset. George and Suzie had just finished their time in the chamber and treaded lightly out to attend the two units.   They had been given a list of possible artifacts that might be there and Chuck would radio exact spots as they approached the lighted area scanned by the machines arrays.   Within the path, they began the task of spotting and digging.

Just as Suzie started to work her shovel, she felt a whoosh of water past her and looked up just in time to see the tail end of a Great White as the beast caught rays of light from the Neptune.   She screamed at George and they immediately went to the ROV and manipulated the light array. The twenty footer came back through the dark, but didn't like the bright halogens beamed directly at him. George set up a cross configuration that would hit him no matter where he came near.

"I'll watch the lights, Suzie and play lookout.   I don't think he'll be back though. If he does, I've got a stunner here."

Relieved somewhat, Suzie, started work on the first object.   It appeared to be something like a pulley.   She cleaned it off and put it in her bag. Four feet further, nestled in the recently uncovered anoxic soil, she found a small metal vase, dented, but intact and set that aside.   Not far from that, she uncovered a knife, slightly curved with a lengthy handle. She was very careful with that. There was no telling how sharp it might still be.

They were pushing thirty seven minutes when she got to the last item.   George cautioned her on the time and she thought twice about continuing but Chuck had told her it was a square shape and that was odd for an artifact.   She gently dug around the location and felt a light thud as she went four inches in.   Carefully, she scraped the soil aside to reveal the top of a wooden box. Excited in obvious disbelief, she extracted it ever so gently and placed it with her other treasures.   She called out to George and waved at him.   The dive was over for the day.

*

The Dash 8 left the Santa Cruz airport at eight am. Joe, Dylan and Bill had locked up the boat in the harbor and had joined nine other passengers on the trip to Ponta Delgada.   Most of them had come from the resort and from the bits and pieces of conversation that they could pick up, had rave reviews of the place.

The flight pulled in shortly after nine a.m.   The three men each had a day pack. They each had a pad and pens. Bill had a camera.   They set out to find a café to spend the balance of the morning as their return flight was twelve thirty pm.

Just past the terminal, the base, and the Forte De Sao Bras, they found a small café that set just off the Avenida du Don Henrique that overlooked the municipal pools and the parade ground.   A unit was marching in formation in the distance and the heat and drenching humidity was already accumulating in the city.

"Poor bastards," Bill muttered.   He had no love for the military, any military.

Dylan ordered coffee for the three of them and Bill was

about to say something to the waitress, took one look at Joe's face and decided better of it.

"Joe, you're the boss here, what approach do you want to take with this?" Dylan asked.

"Normally, WorldGreen is a confrontational organization. They get in the way, try to stop companies from doing damage to the environment or protected species. From what you've learned, I don't think that's going to work here."

"No, it won't. All the fishermen tell me the security out there is pretty tough. They are armed and board their vessels, tow them back to the docks. We cross a certain line on ship and they'll do the same to us; or we're in a gunfight."

"And the police do nothing, and we learn nothing."

"Right."

"Then, the other way WorldGreen works is to gather information to protest directly to the government in question; or, if that government is unresponsive, we present a case to the World Court in The Hague. Either way, we have to have some credible information to support our case or for further intervention."

"So," Joe continued, "We need a lot more information than we have. Getting a good look at the complex by air will help for a possible visit, but we need hard data, too. Dylan, you mentioned the fishing has been depleted. There has to be some hard numbers on that. This afternoon, check on the docks and see if there are before and after figures from a buyer, processor, official or whoever oversees the daily catch."

"I should also add," Dylan went on, "That the seamen tell me that the noise from the Habitat's underwater generators, the construction apparatus, and the lights emanating from the site has had a detrimental effect on the predators out there. All of that appears to disrupt their sensory reception and the sharks are particularly agitated. There have been several incidents in the normal fishing areas and a few of them have been particularly nasty."

"Then, I would check the hospital, too, and see what increases they've run into. Meanwhile, Bill, you could patrol

250

the docks and look for transient Americans, Canadians, etc.; anybody that speaks English and just feel them out. You might get some interesting takes on the resort. I'll try to get a room at the hotel this afternoon. They always have last minute cancellations. We need good drawings and some shots from the plane on our return, so I have a sense of where to start looking."

A light rain began as the humid air could hold no more moisture and soon accelerated into a heavy tropical storm. The soldiers scurried from the field, formation completely undone and the three men moved inside and ordered a refill.

Bill looked out the window at the rain as it crashed to the ground and back at the many other patrons who had shaken off the unexpected storm and now filled up the restaurant's interior.

"I think I'd like some pie. Anybody feel like pie?"

*

Dr. Suzie was almost afraid to open the wooden case. Whatever was in it was important enough to be boxed and it was apparent from what was left of the metal work plated on the wood, it was something important. Gently prying and lifting the cover, the case fought against its opening with a hardened arc, but finally yielded to Sue's persuasion. This was not what she expected. She expected jewels, gold or coins, but instead, there was one item, a medallion on a chain. It was fluted and circular with what appeared to be a piece of diamond imbedded in it. She laid it in the cleansing solution tray along with the pulley, the small metal vase and the knife until she was convinced the items were thoroughly saturated and seeped to as clear a finish as possible. She then lightly wiped the objects with an extremely fine abrasive cloth. She held up the medallion for inspection. She could make out markings on each of the flutes.

All four items were then put into the metal analysis chamber, one by one. The pulley was made of iron: the sword, steel; and the small metal vase was made of silver. The medallion, on the other hand, was made of electrum. This was astonishing. While the metal occurred naturally in the earth, it took a specific knowledge of metallurgy to understand its properties and to prepare it for use. The tubular medallion had to have a purpose to be made of this metal and to be encased in the ornate wooden box.

The next test was radiochemical analysis for age. Since the 'Ferd" had been set up to be the best undersea Laboratory in the world, if not the best lab period, it had been built with all the latest equipment, especially for sea exploration, archeology, and sub-atomic testing. Radiochemical analysis (RCA) was critical to determining the chemical and isotopic fingerprints of the artifacts.

Suzie laid out each piece to test independently while Dr. Frost was delicately cleaning the wooden case. He would carbon date the box later. All the items had been impacted in the anoxic soil, shielded by the volcanic layer for centuries. It would not have surprised anyone at the habitat that these items would be remnants of an ancient civilization.

Dr. Suzie adjusted the RCA for each and carefully ran the tests. Dr. George double checked the input and readings as the machinery ran. Once all four were tested, the RCA computer station printed out the table.

ARTIFACT	DATE TEST/SEQ.	CHRONOLOGY
Pulley	10/28 - RCA 1a101.6	11499
Vase	10/28 - RCA 1a101.7	11412
Knife	10/28 - RCA 1a101.8	11426
Medallion	10/28 - RCA 1a101.9	11435

"Can this be right?" Suz asked George.
"A ninety nine percent degree of accuracy, Suzie."

"You know what this means?"

"Yes, and we better email this and photos of all items up to Deming. We are soon going be inundated by all manner of intrusions.   We'd better get ready for it."

Graciosa

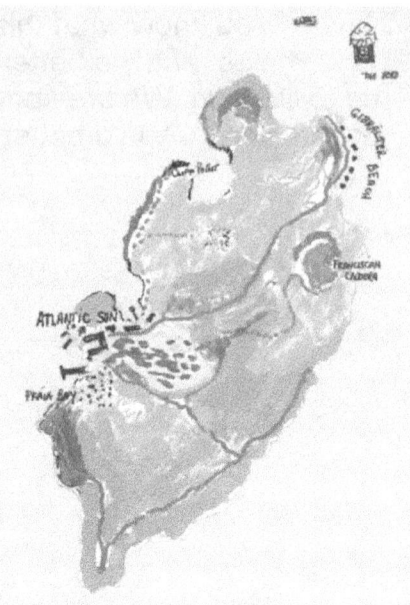

Ilehu Du Praia

CHAPTER FIFTEEN

Graciosa

The two lovers sat on the blanket they had borrowed from the hotel and looked out at the sea's crashing waves on the rocky shoreline below. Annie put her head on Chris's shoulder as they sipped from plastic wine glasses. Chris had called Luis Recife to ask him to contact the Teresinas to see if they would let them come up to the old farm for the afternoon. Chris wanted one more day to take it in without the cumbersome details of the estate business. The Teresinas agreed and they arrived with a picnic lunch and a white wine. Armondo took one look at the spread and would have none of it. He went back into the house and returned with a homemade vintage in a brown bottle that he insisted they take instead. Chris motioned for him to take the white wine in exchange, but Armondo would have none of that, either.

They enjoyed a fine salami, fresh bread from the market, and local goat cheese with the delicious Vordelho they had just been given. Sated, they just leaned on each other, tasting the aroma of the orange scented sea air that had so overwhelmed Chris the day before.

"I could vacation here," Annie whispered.

"I could too, Annie, but I think the Teresinas might get tired of us hanging around."

"Still, it would be lovely, wouldn't it?"

"Yes, but I remember visiting a commune when I was in my twenties. It seemed idyllic until you realized how much work there was to be done, and who actually did it and who did not."

"So, you're saying this isn't for tourists."

"It looks great and feels even better, but it's a hard life. My ancestors would have stayed if it were easy. It must have taken a lot to leave here to go to America and I suspect, even as things look so good today, it isn't easy for the Teresinas, either."

"Then you're just going to love Atlantic Sun, my darling.

All made for tourism and hedonism with none of your third world poverty guilt."

"Hmm. A little will go a long way. I'll force myself to enjoy it. But, I'll still probably feel guilty. Anyway, you picked it out and I'm sure it's just grand. The brochures sure make it out to be exceptional."

"I'll just like swimming and hanging around the pool with a good book."

They stayed close to two and a half hours and decided that was enough. They could hear Armondo out in the vines, gleaning the last vestiges of the crop to be sent to the co-op. Occasionally, they could hear CeCalia call out from the kitchen to her husband. It would have been nice to have learned Portuguese before they came, but there was so little time. In any event, they figured the kids would be coming home from school soon and the house would be abuzz with activity and it would be best to head back to the hotel and leave these good people in peace. Chris waved to Armondo and he helped them pack up by adding another bottle for their trip. Ann and Chris thanked him graciously and walked down the dirt cart path to where Luis would pick them up. He arrived about ten minutes after Armondo's call and took the pair back to Horta. Chris looked over his shoulder one last time at the old hacienda. He hoped he could someday see it again. In any event, he fixed a permanent picture into his memory. He would call on it from time to time.

*

"What we are looking at is the oldest use of metallurgy ever discovered. It predates the Catal Hoyuk works found in Turkey by thirty-four hundred years." George leaned forward in the chair to express his great concern to Brian Deming. Suzie and Chuck sat on either side of him in the office at the resort. "It means we have discovered the remnants of the oldest civilization known to man; an advanced society that knew how to manufacture metals, tools, ornaments and had

256

an excellent knowledge of geology and mineralogy."

"What are you telling me?" Brian probed.

"We believe we may have found Atlantis." Suzie answered.

"What?"

"According to Plato, Egyptian scholars had known about the civilization and had recorded the existence of two great city states prior to the 'cataclysm'; Atlantis and Greece. They apparently were commonly at war. These records were in the Library of Alexandria when Plato studied them in 400 B.C. Unfortunately, the Christians burned the library centuries later and the evidence went with it. The Christians of the day were a lot like the Taliban is now. If they saw a civilization, they felt the need to destroy it."

"In any case," Suzie went on, "according to Plato as recorded by Donnelly in his book, 'Atlantis: the Antediluvian Era', Atlantis existed one thousand miles past the pillars of Hercules, which we now call Gibralter. That places the site of the city, the country, right here."

"Further," George added, "These islands sit on the great Atlantic Plateau. There's a ridge of undersea mountains that stretches from Iceland to the Falklands. Right here is the one, the only undersea plateau. All these islands in this archipelago are the remains of the mountainous peaks of that plateau. Whether you believe in the volcanic explosions here from these old cauldrons, or, you believe in a meteor hitting the earth or massive earthquakes in the ridge that caused a sensational tsunami, this was the logical place for Atlantis, the country, to be, and the center of the great flood."

Brian was listening intently. He was truly stunned at what he was hearing. Dr. Frost took that as a need to fill in more information.

"Look, Mr. Deming, for years scientists have been focusing on the trade routes, evidenced by that useless old pottery you scraped over; and have been trying to make a case for the Black Sea sites, or Crete, or Santorini, but their problem is that these civilizations are only five or six thousand years old. How does that explain even the simplest fact that you have metallurgy in Turkey that's eight thousand years old. Where did that come from? And, it's before recorded history. Was there a blacksmith on the Ark?"

"And," George added, "The Ark was one of but many boats that escaped the doom. This is why cultures from the Greeks and Egyptians have similar epic sagas as those of the Delaware Tribe of North America and the Mayans of South America."

"And we're looking at proof," Suzie pointed to the pictures. "Thanks to the blessed find of the anoxic soil, we have probably the greatest find in history; right here. It's not just a few artifacts that we've found that lead us to this conclusion; it's the density of artifacts in the square footage uncovered. It is clearly indicative of some kind of settlement. We need a complete dig, an underwater excavation and extraction like no other, ever. Every artifact we pull up is priceless. Every one. Do you understand, Sir, what we are dealing with here?"

"Absolutely." Brian buzzed his intercom and asked for Wayne Trudeau and Commander Kane. Both arrived within minutes.

"Wayne, I want you to give our triumvirate here anything they need to do their excavation. Get more equipment, if you have to. Buy it or rent it, I don't care. Candy, I want extra surveillance and security for the site and the barge. You may want to contact Magruder and get more staff. We need 24/7 coverage and no outside interference whatsoever."

The three scientists nodded their heads in excitement. George thought for a second and indicated that they should report out their findings.

"I'll get a hold of Deeds this afternoon," Brian stated flatly, "and let him know what we've found. Still, let's keep this quiet until we have more surety. Agreed?"

They all nodded and left to get back to the 'Ferd'. Kane stayed.

"Candy, I can't tell you how important it is to keep this shut. No one is to know about this until I say so. You are now authorized to use deadly force and I don't care if it's the goddamned Portuguese army. Anybody butts in here, you take them out. Got it?"

"Clear as a bell, Sir."

Deming excused himself and left the office. Kane went back to his security shack.

As Deming crossed the compound towards the hotel, he passed Jackie on her way to the administration building.

"Brian, I just saw our three PHDs coming out, chattering like magpies. What was that all about?"

"Even more delays, more digging, more waste of time. Now, I'm going to have to inform David that we're excavating even more junk and not getting his plant built."

*

The daily flight from Horta to Graciosa was not a direct flight. It first went to Ponta Delgada, picked up more passengers, mostly tourists, and resumed flight to the two island community, arriving in Santa Cruz just past ten thirty a.m.

Chris and Ann walked down the steps to the ground and retrieved their baggage from the hold at the back of the Dash 8. They started up the tarmac when Chris stopped dead in his tracks. Out of the corner of his eye he noticed a helicopter take off from a pad on the near side of a separate runway adjacent to three buildings, all interconnected, but with differing roof lines. He tugged at Ann's halter in the back.

"Hold up, honey, something's going on."

"What," he had caught her completely off guard with the urgency of his tug.

"I don't know. I sensed this dread. It' surreal, I know, but it hit me like a psychic slap to the back of the head."

"What on earth are you getting at?"

"Something to do with that helicopter over there. We need to get closer. Let's take a stroll over. I don't think anyone would mind."

"Have you gone nuts?"

"Maybe, but humor me, please. God, I hope I'm wrong about this."

At the far side of the field, inside the annex to the Customs house that Atlantic Sun built, paid for, staffed and maintained, Wayne Trudeau explained to Jackie the depth of the experiment at hand.

"We've been able to produce an effective repulsion beam. Our tests have worked first at a molecular level, then with small objects and finally with a drone of significant weight, about equal to what we're going to test today. We feel confident we can now repulse gravity while controlling the descent of a helicopter. If we can do that, we can replicate a smooth landing for the cargo and passenger shuttles for a spaceship."

"But won't the gravity be different on Mars, or any other planet?"

"Yes, so the repulsion has to be recalibrated for that, and for the lack of air. We think we have that figured out, but first things first. We have to do it here."

"In layman's terms, Wayne, how does it work?"

"There are no layman's terms. Sorry. Some people would refer to it as a tractor beam, but no such thing exists or probably ever will. That supposes you'd be able to attach to an object and pull it in against its will. What we're working on is a gravity repulsion beam that will engage a craft and assist it to the softest landing possible, with or without its own power engaged. The device uses a Bessel laser beam that has clean borders. We were going to use a Laguerre-Guassau Beam, but it just didn't hold up. Inside, the beam a repulsive gravity field is created using gravitophotons produced by a ring rotating above a strong magnetic field. It allows us to attach to the object and pulsate it against the gravity force, under control, until it docks safely, in this case, to the heliport pad. Our chief Tech here, Raymond will demonstrate. Are we ready?"

The three techs operating the console of the Laser Guidance System all nodded.

"Then, let's get started."

Raymond radioed the helicopter and they took off, wind-blown newspapers flying in all directions.

"Bring the ship in line, synchronize at fourteen degrees north, northeast, then level out at a thousand feet."

"Roger, Control."

The specially engineered and equipped helicopter cut its turbine jet engine, then on a rapid ninety degree turn, held steady in sway above the coastline. It hovered on its fore and aft propellers, squaring off directly above, away and due south of the island shrouded in the light morning mist below.

"Steady and drop down slowly to three hundred feet." Raymond advised, "Okay, very good, now set to remote and prepare for release on our count. Ready, five, four, three, two, one, now."

"We're on beam now, Control."

"Alright, gentlemen, sit back and enjoy the ride."

The two pilots eased back in the bucket seats as the orange painted Huey gradually descended towards the helipad below. The digital display and gauges smoothly coded the effects of the Bessel beam emanating from the island just on the near shore.

At the control's helm, the technician's eyes danced across the hardware, constantly monitoring the laser's output, the tube's drawing strength and the computer controlled signals housed within the artificial beam's shield. He turned quickly to his supervisor who stood directly off to his left, overlooking the control station and the display.

"Chief, we've got some kind of interference on the beam, atmospheric, I think, but it's causing some fluctuations on the command sequence signal."

"Pump up the beam tube."

As the technician re-aligned the energy output for the laser and the tube around it, moderating the control signal, the two pilots thought they noticed a jump in acceleration, accentuated by a bump in their downward glide path.

"Control, are we still on line?"

"On line and coming in strong." The Chief's comfort level had been just slightly disturbed.

261

Again, the technician turned, this time quite distraught at the turn of events.

"Chief, the beam's increased power has eroded the connection. I don't know if I can hold it."

The Director screamed. "Cut back on it then, dammit. Can't you get this thing stable?"

"Yes Sir. It was fine all week on simulation and robotics. I don't know what the problem is."

He turned to reduce the strength.

"Jeezuz Christ, I've lost the connection."

"Damn, cut the beam off," The Chief immediately switched the headset, "Sea Hawk, power up, right now. You're off line, I repeat, you're off line."

"Oh shit," the pilot blurted out as the helicopter tilted. He tried in vain to get the turbine started, but with so little air space and time, couldn't get the blades moving quickly enough. The ship dove headfirst towards the reefs below. At the low altitude and at the speed of the descent, there was no chance that the ship could fire up the jet and erect itself in flight before it would hit the deck. Even as the propellers turned and the engine finalized its ignition, the plummeting copter sent two screaming men smashing into the coral outcroppings at the edge of the breakwater in the island's lagoon. The crunch and mauling of the metal against the rocks, the debris flying everywhere created a deafening sound of terror.

Neither Chris nor Ann could believe what they were seeing. Chris's mouth was wide open. At first he thought he saw someone getting out of the wreck.

"Don't let it explode." He gasped. "Please don't let it explode."

It didn't. Then, ten seconds later, it did.

The explosion was spectacular, propelling smoke and fire upwards in a voluminous spray of sea water and foam; the sound of the fireball a colossal thump and implosion into the calming waters of the shoreline churning up violent waves against the rocks as the flames shot skyward in a thick burst that hung overhead two hundred feet.

Chris held on to Ann for dear life. He was shaking like a leaf in a Nor'easter.

"I saw it, Annie."

She looked at him in amazement.

"It's right there. How could you not? Are you okay, are you hurt?"

"No, I saw it before. I mean I knew it. I was here. It was a dream, a long time ago. It came back a couple of times. But, I never figured it out. And, now, it has happened, right in front of me. I could've done something, I could have warned somebody, I could have...."

Annie grabbed him by the arm. He was still shaking.

"Let's get the hell out of here, Chris," she pulled him forward at a frantic pace. "You couldn't have done a thing. I couldn't have done a thing."

Jackie burst from the annex with tears in her eyes. This simply was not supposed to happen. How could she tell David about this? How would he react? This was one of the cornerstones of his project and it had failed beyond all belief. This was a huge set back. Wayne was right behind her. They would have to get to Brian right away.

As Jackie wiped her right eye on her sleeve, she noticed two people not a hundred feet away, one a tall sandy haired gentleman, a bit older than her, clearly affected by what he had seen and an exotic dark haired woman pulling at him across the tarmac. There weren't supposed to be any spectators anywhere. Where in hell did these two come from? In the end, that oddity didn't matter. She had a monumental tragedy to deal with, a setback that would cause no end of delay and no doubt, add real cost to the human cost so dreadfully lost. The tears filled her eyes again. She couldn't wait to get the hell back to the hotel.

*

263

Joe and Dylan compared their sketched drawings of the resort with the pictures Bill had taken from the plane and uploaded to the laptop. Done hastily in the flyover, each missed something the others had gained. The photos only caught a portion of the resort and Joe had sketched from back of the complex forward, while Dylan had sat on the other side of the plane and sketched from the beach backward. Once combined, they felt they had a reasonable description of the place.

Joe was able to get a room and decided to make it two nights, one day to case the place and be seen everywhere doing everything that a normal tourist would do, and another to pilfer what information he could lay his hands on. The three men sat down with their finished print of the complex.

"Dylan, if the place is being guarded by a security force, what can I expect to find, both in detail and in information?"

"First, Joe, this is a resort, so you won't see heavy arms, if any, on the island. They'll have those in the patrol boats. We saw a copter, too, and I'll bet that's armed as well. The main office will probably have a guard, probably one at maintenance and there's surely someone in the security office at all times, wherever that is. Otherwise, they'll be wandering around, although most will be with the perimeter defense or down on the docks."

"I'd pass on computer information. It's a nightmare of protocols with any security organization. Everything will be encrypted, password protected and you could spend days getting nowhere only to find the wrong files or that the information you want is in the cloud. Look for paper, look for old records, reports that look innocuous but contain something interesting. Some managements still like hard copies of reports. But, in general, it's a smash and grab, without the smash. And don't get caught."

"Right. And you're going to beat the town today and find out about the catch of late and what you can at the hospital."

"That's what we agreed on. Bill is going to schmooze the docks."

264

"And tomorrow, while I'm relaxing intensely, what are you up to?"

"Trevor and I talked about it," Bill added, "and we thought we'd take the Cormorant out for a little spin, out towards the barge and the Habitat and see how close we get before we get pursuit, then lay off a bit. Trevor thinks we should shoot at some sea birds for sport, just to see how they react to the possibility of return fire."

"I'm not thinking that's a great idea, but I'm not going to tell you that you can't. What did you just tell me? Don't get caught? Oh, and if I'm not back by Saturday noon, you know what to do."

Joe grabbed his bag, hopped off the boat and walked down the wharf to the water taxi that would take him to the resort. He noticed that while the man driving the taxi was wearing an Atlantic Sun shirt, he was not security personnel, rather a local, who appeared quite happy to have this new job. He made a mental note of that.

At the hotel, he registered, asked for and got a first floor room. That was particularly helpful for his plans. He immediately went for a late lunch on the outside verandah of the Mayan styled restaurant built outward off the backside of the pool in a grotto like setting. He made himself visible there for an hour and a half before walking the grounds out to the beach, then along the shore to the watersports rental building. All manner of boards, skis, floats, snorkel equipment, jet-skis, kayaks and other boats were available for rental as were parasailing adventures. Just beyond, the submarine that took tours to the Habitat had just returned to its dock, having completed the afternoon excursion. Surprisingly, the Security office sat well behind the water sports kiosk and adjacent to the larger older building which was the original Hotel du Praia. It was a one story addition with a tin roof that hung off the back of the converted three story building that had added a penthouse like top floor. As he walked the shrub sided pathway around, he saw the administration sign over the front door. They had seen the buildings from the air, but could not figure them out.

Out beyond the building, the golf course ran inland into

the valley between the northern ridge and the calderas, a maintenance building on his left as he followed the cart path and a long one story building with a tiled roof that looked like a Spanish style Super 8. A sign over its main entrance simply said "The Lodge". He could not think what that could be for; perhaps hotel overflow or hostel like lodging for the financially challenged eco-tourist, but there was no activity there, so he dismissed it for the time being.

Across the course, the 19th hole Grille stood across water, nestled on an islet sixty feet out into the cove connected by a walkway. That would be his next stop, to be seen there for happy hour, then off to dinner at the main interior restaurant, "Risotta". He might wander around later, but would leave his real work for late in the day tomorrow. Right now, a cold beer sounded damn good and he set his sights on the charming golfers' haven that would supply it

*

It was a quiet trip to the resort on the water taxi that took Chris and Ann to the small island. Chris was white and speechless, Ann hesitant to invade his aura, either by touch or sound. When they docked, she shook him a little as they debarked and he seemed to come around. They passed a security checkpoint which basically examined IDs and compared them to the days' guest list. It brought Chris fully back into the real world.

"Sorry, honey. I was lost in the past, somewhere in space I guess. It'll be hard to compartmentalize that memory."

"I know what you're thinking and it has nothing to do with you, really. I know it was awful and probably fatal, but these things will be sorted out. They have lawyers and judges here, too. It'll take some time, but if families were involved, they'll be compensated. If there was wrongdoing, the perpetrators will be found out and they will be punished. The systems usually work, Chris, so let them do their work. We are not here for that."

They walked, hand in arm, dragging their bags along the pathway from the taxi dock that sat past the submarine tour, past the watersports kiosk and along the beach path into the interior of the U-shaped hotel. Beyond the open beach party deck, they took a sharp left and followed the stone covered section of the path towards the Mayan restaurant set in the grotto area at the back end of the pool. The pool ran from the length of the party deck back to one of two waterfalls and the center section of the hotel. It was the largest pool Ann had ever seen and the setting was incredibly gorgeous.

Walking over wooden bridges that spanned eight foot canals connecting the grotto, the waterfall area, the main pool and the sunken pool bar, they entered the main lobby between the Mayan Restaurant and Risotta, the main hotel dining feature and made a beeline to the registration desk.

Chris dutifully signed in as Mr. and Mrs. Eberhart, forked over the plastic, and received the keys, the features and perks booklet, plus the hotel daily activities paper. They had a lovely third floor deluxe room with a balcony that extended out toward the waterfall and over the hot tub in the rock designed structure that held both.

"This is perfect, Chris. We'll just love it." She sensed, however, that Chris's enthusiasm might be quite a bit less than hers.

"Chris, I'm going to take a hot bath, get into my bikini, grab one of those robes in there and sit my large butt on the balcony with my laptop and enjoy the waterfall and finally the WiFi we haven't had in two weeks. Why don't you go to that pool bar down there and get us a couple of Pina Coladas and maybe a beer while you wait. Could you do that for me?"

"Sure, yes of course. By the way, your butt is perfect." He found a smile had grown on his face and by the time he sat at the bar, quaffing a perfectly chilled draft, he was beginning to think he might enjoy this trip after all. There was laughter around the pool, the pool bar was lively and there was a volleyball game going on in the shallow end towards the beach. He could see why people went on vacations like this. You could forget all that bothers you here.

He returned to see Annie intently at work with her

laptop.　He placed the drinks on the table on the balcony and gave her a kiss on the top of her head.

"Whassup?"

"You're not going to believe this.　I brought up the resort to check out everything here and I always go look at the amenities, the staff, etc. and I then went to 'about us', the Board of Atlantic Sun, which I like to do and guess what I find; and what links came up?"

"Where?"

"Look here."

There, staring him in the face was the picture of the President and Chairman of the Board, Brian Deming.

"Can it be the same guy?"

"That's what the links tell me.　You know us lawyers, Chris, we always check out the links.　Hell, that's half the process in electronic discovery.　See this link here.　It tells us that Atlantic Sun is a wholly owned subsidiary of EngenUnity.　You know from all the papers I gave you that EngenUnity bought out Simisync, which in turn had bought out Western Slope Development.　This is your favorite guy, right here."

"Get out.　I'm half way around the world and he shows up.　This isn't just a vacation anymore, Annie, this is a crusade thrown upon me by God and I don't think she loves me anymore.　Boy, I would just love to corner this guy for a half hour."

"A guy like that is not going to be around; not going to be one of the people we are going to see.　We're peons to him, tourists or customers who don't matter except for the money we put in his pocket.　He doesn't see us, doesn't want to see us and won't acknowledge any of us even if he did."

Chris nodded.

"He lives in a totally different arena, Chris.　He's an elite corporate giant, probably one of the top ten execs in the whole world and his realm consists of high finance, jet setting, luxurious surroundings whether for business or pleasure, and is consistently engaged in a barrage of verbal and intellectual stimulation.　He makes big decisions.　So, you can get the idea out of your head that you'll ever have a conversation with him about anything. You won't even get past a gatekeeper."

"Somehow, though, he has to be held responsible for what he's done, Annie. Things can't be right in the world, if he gets away with all that he did."

"I know, Chris, and I know you have a personal interest in this and it weighs upon you, but you can't feel that you are the one to clean it up. You're just not capable of dealing with something like this."

"I know you're right. I'm no hero. I don't think I've been in three fights in my life and they lasted only a couple of punches. I'm just an average guy who hates confrontation like everyone else. But, Annie, my sense of it is this: Deming wanted to clean up the Western Slope for new, high end development. He wanted the miners out. I don't blame him so much for that, those guys were a lot to handle. But, it certainly looks like he arranged for the killing of an itinerant Mexican Laborer. He tried to pin it on that group of four that I stopped from stoning the poor kid. Somehow, I'm guessing Craig and Ron found out about it and they ended up in a pit outside Las Vegas in a gangland style execution. Greg and two others of the four were found murdered in Montana. The last one and my old partner, Buck, have disappeared altogether. They're probably somewhere up in Alaska with different names. Then, Skip starts snooping around, because he heard about these cases from his nephew. Skip knew all these guys, too, better than I did because he stuck around and worked here and there in the mines. Somehow, Skip mysteriously disappears, just walks off into the mountains and is never seen again. I never believed that crap about a sore back. Not one minute. Did Deming do that? Was he getting too close?"

"Anyway, one cover up leads to another and another and another. Before you know it, at least seven guys are dead that we know of over a twenty year period. And, I believe, Deming is responsible for everyone."

"But you can't prove it, Chris."

"No, and John Willie is right. All you can do is wait around till he screws up, if he ever does. And that's what galls me. I can't do a damn thing about it and I feel helpless as hell."

"At some point, Chris, it has to unravel. It always does for the lunkheads I've run into, but this guy has the added assets of wealth, power, influence and a certain amount of immunity here. He's going to be a tough nut to crack. It'll take something unique to bring him down."

*

Just as he and Trevor had discussed several times over the years, an hour before dark was the perfect time for chicanery, especially in a place like this. The guests were out for dinner, or coming in from their sea side activities, or finishing up their round on the course. The staff were busy putting everything away, closing up shop. The office work was done hours ago and the encroaching darkness was enough to somewhat hide all that activity and still not cast suspicion on anyone walking around.

Joe walked around sailing adventures and the watersports kiosk and out towards the sub dock, then cut back between the pro shop and the maintenance building. As he suspected, the last of the carts were being punched into a pole barn and to his surprise, a security guard was talking it up with one of the crew. Earlier, he had seen another guard over at the kiosk, but that was understandable since it was managed by a rather attractive young blonde in a bathing suit. That meant he might have bought some extra time.

He circled to the north side of the administration building, where an old fire escape hung in rusted disuse. He could barely reach the extension, but with the relocation of a fairly large rock, was able to pull himself up, his feet gripping the wall. He had taken the precaution of taking off his shoes and socks and hiding them under a fern. Quietly, he could grip the wall and the escape without attracting any attention.

As he suspected, none of the windows were locked. There was still enough light to allow him to see the rooms and he carefully made his way to the fourth floor where a brass name plate was screwed into the door, Brian Deming, CEO.

The door was locked, but it was a standard lockset and he picked it in less than two minutes.

Inside, the usual office equipment lay about. Nothing exceptional stuck out to him. Hearing Trevor's words in his head, he forgave the laptop that sat closed on the desk and looked in the file drawer at the lower right of the desk. There were several manila folders and one towards the front was labeled Blackthorn. He took it out and lay it on the desk. Joe knew in advance that Blackthorn provided the security here and that was clearly evident in the uniforms they wore as well. He sifted thru the paper and found a printed version of a power point presentation. It was directed to both Deming and what appeared to be a manager named Magruder in Zurich. It was concise, though lacking in content:

- Interceptions: 38
- Returns to local jurisdiction: 23
- Repatriation: 19
- Interrogations: 12
- Missing reported by local jurisdiction: 2
  (Weather conditions presumed)
  It also contained a short narrative of other activities, basic stuff, that Joe didn't take the time to read. He stuffed the report in his hip pocket.

He went through the other drawers and found nothing unusual until he opened the top left drawer where he found the top stub check schedules for the Atlantic Sun account. He was losing his light and didn't have time left to review them on site, so he pocketed three rings worth and carefully closed everything up, locked the door and even more carefully, climbed down the escape, dropped to the sand, retrieved his socks and shoes, not bothering to put them back on. He made his way into the lobby, making a show of putting his footwear back on, then went to the pool where he took it all off again and shoved his feet into the water next to the waterfall. He was very pleased with himself and decided to go have a nightcap at the beach bar. He hoped what he had obtained would be enough.

Upon return to the Cormorant early next morning he found that his partners had done equally as well. Trevor had printed information on the fishing catch, down twenty two percent since the initial construction of the Habitat. Shark attacks had tripled since the beginning as well. Bill had found out that a couple of yachts had gone missing and one of the trans-oceanic travelers had remembered the name of one of them, the Sea Gall. That should be traceable.

The power point report that Joe retrieved had the inference of missing persons and that might be enough to prompt an investigation, but that was very thin. And the check schedules noted only local expenditures. Upon thorough review, though, they identified two payments to Colonel Leon DeSilva. Sadly, nothing else was written and without further proof, could have been meant for anything. Bill noted the check source and quickly understood something Joe missed.

"This is a Quickbooks account, Joe. It's great software for an organization like this, out of the mainstream of American accounting operations, especially in a foreign country with limited financial services and you don't need a CPA to run it, a damned good bookkeeper can do it all. You generate check writing off your own printer from the software and it keeps all pertinent information, including sub-accounts, on all revenue and expense items. Deming could even do it, and if he doesn't, I'll bet he's got a copy of it all, especially the monthly print outs and balance sheets. I'll bet he uses these schedules simply as a written back up in case the system goes down."

"How do you know so much about this stuff?"

"Look, Skip, I've been in the service, done business and non-profit work for forty years. I've picked up a little information, here and there."

"Nough said. So what you're telling me here is that I've got…shit. I've got nothing."

"Essentially, that's it. You really need that laptop."

"Damn, I'm going to have to go back."

CHAPTER SIXTEEN

The Ante-Deluvian Era

The second in command of the entirety of the armed forces of the military for the Autonomous Region of the Acorean Islands was tired of being the second in command of nothing. He felt like he had learned nothing. He had been disregarded and delegated to the most mundane of tasks. He had been treated like a buck private or the base mascot. All he knew was that there was a lot going on he didn't know diddly about and it was driving him crazy.

Any Theatre Commander of any worth would have removed Colonel Leon DeSilva for dereliction of duty; or duties, in this case, as he wouldn't attend to any of the daily administration, left troop orders to his captains, spent his middays at Club Naval and his afternoons at his villa. He fished. He played golf. He arranged and attended many soirees. He obstructed the regional President. He obstructed justice. In short, he was useless as a Post Commandant.

The election would be held in three days. After that, Lieutenant Colonel Alvarro Parros would, in his mind anyway, be called back to the mainland or become a refugee on a transatlantic yacht crossing disguised as a crewman, if he didn't get caught.

So, Alvarro saw a short window of opportunity; a window that might shed light on the most controversial thing he had learned about and that which was the most whitewashed of all; Atlantic Sun, the Habitat and Graciosa. From day one when he saw the map on the wall and realized that no contingent had been sent to the two islands, it had been a burr in his saddle. It was confirmed later by his meeting with Gustave Parcanto.

He printed out the order himself and held it up to reread what he had just penned and assured himself it was in the proper format. He affixed the signature he had come to know so well and applied the stamp to it. So armed, he grabbed his duffel and worked his way down to the city dock where the two cutters sat in the bay awaiting their next missions. They had been freshly painted with the red, green and yellow of Portugal's flag over the old red, white and blue stripes from their Coast Guard days.

Number four was the closest and it didn't matter to Alvaro which one he took. He saluted from the gangplank, requested permission to come aboard, received it and worked his way up to the pilot house where he handed the Lieutenant Commander the order. It read: 'Pursuant to this order, you are to forthwith escort Lt. Col. Parros to the Islands of Graciosa, support his reconnaissance of the complex and its holdings and assist him in any possible actions deemed necessary by him in the best interests of Portugal.' It was signed by Colonel Leon DeSilva.

"When would you have us depart, Sir?" The Lt. Commander seemed uncertain about the order, but he was facing a superior officer who was hand delivering the order to him.

"I would prefer we left immediately. As you see, I am prepared. "

"Fortunately, my crew is on board, Sir. I can get us out of here in about twenty minutes, with your permission."

"Granted."

Alvarro decided to sit directly back of the pilot house to monitor the situation. From the bench there, he could observe the Commander, the docks, the city streets, and even Club Naval on the other side of the harbor. By now, DeSilva would be at his villa, and by the time the departure was discovered, they should be well out into the Atlantic steaming northward past the eastern tip of Sao Jorge. It would take the balance of the afternoon, an overnight and the following morning's leg to arrive in Santa Cruz. Alvarro believed he would have them dock Number 4 directly on the resort's piers. He assumed they could easily handle an eighty- two footer.

Sixty miles out, they were beyond the range of radio communications. Not having any kind of air contingent, DeSilva could only send the other cutter after them or wait Alvarro out for his return. In any case, by the time all that could occur, the election would be over and Alvarro would be fairly sure of his upcoming fate.   In the meantime, he would play his role to the hilt.   He was, after all, a Lt. Colonel in the regular army, commissioned by the President himself and if he did not have any real authority, he had a significant amount of apparent authority.   That might let him find out what was going on up there and he might actually be able to say that this tour of duty was not a complete farce.   Wherever he ended up next week, he could at least feel he had tried to do something positive.

*

Jackie had returned from the big island a wreck.   She was emotionally distraught and needed some time to recover. She emailed both Brian and David about what had happened at the air strip and promised to meet with Brian the next morning to discuss it.   She also asked David what he would like her to do about the crash and the testing that was supposed to be accomplished but had ended so tragically.

She arrived promptly at nine a.m. as Brian had requested, meeting him at his fourth floor office in the administration building.   She had pulled herself together, but still did not look well.   She hadn't slept but a bit, the re-occurring nightmare still vivid in her imagination.

She started to apologize, but Brian cut her off.

"It's okay, Jackie, it's not your fault.   I didn't think it would work, anyway."

"Then why did you let this happen?"   She stammered.

"Because David was insistent that the tests be done.   I told him that we should try an exact replica in size and weight by auto pilot first; but he felt we were ready enough to go ahead with the pilot operated helicopter.   I don't know what happened out there, but something about the helicopter mechanisms, engines, rotation of blades, whatever, interfered with the beam."

"Two men died, Brian."

"I'm not responsible for that. It's not a good thing, but I'm not going to tell you that each of those men had PHDs and spoke eight languages. They knew what they were getting into. That said, it is David who takes sole responsibility here. It's his impatience that caused this and he'll have to answer for it."

"I haven't received any response yet from him, Brian, so I don't know how to advise you."

"You don't have to. I've had enough of David Deed's program. He's going to break this company and all we have built will go down with it."

"But, he has a grand vision. He is opening up new frontiers. He can change the dynamics of science and technology for decades to come."

"You still don't see it, do you? You forget I've known David for going on twenty five years. He has a vision, alright, but it's not what you think. He dreams of a Utopia. He told me about it après ski in Purgatory years ago. He read the Harrad Experiment in college and ever since then, has felt that a utopian system would be the greatest thing since sliced bread. He thinks the sanitation engineer should get the same benefits as the neuro-surgeon. He believes that the only way to accomplish this is to establish a Utopian system in the process of interplanetary colonization. "

"It's intriguing, I'll admit, but it has no basis in reality. He camouflages the whole thing by insisting that it's about science, about new discoveries, about trade and investment and maybe that actually will work, but he forgets that someone or something actually has to operate that Utopia. Can you imagine the decision making process if hundreds of colonists have to decide on everything? You know the classic definitions: a committee is an animal with one hundred stomachs and no brain; a group of people who by themselves can do nothing, but collectively get together and decide that nothing can be done."

"Sometimes a vision is just another altered reality, Jackie. Sometimes, a vision is a hallucination. In this case, I think David's hallucination here borders on nuts and I'm not taking part of it anymore. Hell, I've got my own Utopia right here. You don't see it, do you?   This is my escape clause, my parachute.   In fact, David approved my proposal last week.   The electronic signatures have been affixed and the fully executed documents are on their way.   I exchanged 95% of my equity in Engenuity for all this, as long as I share all scientific discovery.   I've got Moontracer, and the moored Grady-White; I've got an entire resort complex; a private villa on the beach; an eco-tourist mecca in the undersea habitat; and a unique arrangement with the government that gives me title and free reign.   Hell, I've even got my own airport, for all intents and purposes, and a customs house.   I have two jets. I can go anywhere I want at a moment's notice and I have an almost inexhaustible stream of revenue coming in and I still have some equity in your company, which might be okay if things go well."

"All I have to do is manage Atlantic Sun like the business that it is and treat people reasonably fairly and I have what David wants and can't have or experience in two generations."

Jackie was astounded at the simplicity of Brian's deduction and realized that David had probably gotten all he wanted out of the resort and of Brian.   He could move on from there.   This project was just a stepping stone for David, but there was still quite a bit left here to be done, unfinished business and tying up the loose ends, plus the dealing with the painful aftermath of the accident.

"I still have to complete my mission.   I have to meet with the Habitat staff."

"I had forgotten about that, Jackie, but, yes, go ahead and deliver what you must.   I don't know what your status with the company will be going forward and it's not my problem.   If David wants to continue testing, he'll have to find another venue or come to a new agreement on that.   In any case, I'll handle that and I doubt I'll allow that sort of thing here.   It's kind of bad for business. "

"Take a few days.   Finish your assignment, but if you stay here past next Friday, I'll be charging you full fare for your suite.   Understood?"

Jackie nodded.   In some ways, she had to admire the

man, but she still hated him.

*

Number four pulled up to the resort pier that was nearly finished for small cruise ships. They came unannounced. It was ten a.m. The dock master raced out to meet them when the boat came plowing in and two crewmen leapt off the cutter to tie it up. The dock master was about to chew out the Lt. Commander for such a brazen entrance, but as soon as he uttered his first words, a Lt. Colonel appeared with a written order in his hands.

"Orders from the Commandant of Acorean Command for a formal reconnaissance of the complex and its properties."

"May I see the order?" He protested.

"Certainly not. You will take it on my authority. If you have any problems with that you can call the Commandant himself." Alvarro waved to the rest of the crew to come to the landing. Once the contingent of crew came ashore, Alvarro had seven seamen to assist him. The eighth and the Lt. Commander stayed on board to cover the ship. He told the crew to fan out, take note of what they saw and report back by noon. He took the dock master along the pier to the sub's anchorage in hopes of getting a glimpse of the Habitat. Unfortunately, they had missed the tour by over an hour and the sub would not be back until twelve thirty. Instead, he would have to review the grounds and would take the Cliffside trail to get a close up view of the Barge to the north.

Meanwhile, in Ponta Delgada, Colonel DeSilva arrived at the office, did not see his second in command, but still assumed everything was in order until he arrived at Club Naval at his usual time, eleven a.m. From there, he could see across the bay from his favorite café seating and noticed cutter Number Four was no longer in dockage. That seemed strange for he did not recall any mission planned until the following week. Alarmed, he took the stroll to cutter Number

Three, which was still at the pier, a walk of about twenty minutes in the late morning heat that sorely aggravated the Commandant by the time he got there.   In discussion with the Commander of Number Three, he soon realized it must have been Colonel Parros who had ordered the boat out and now he had a problem and he believed he knew what it was.

He raced back to his office, even more aggravated, and made the call to Brian Deming.   He told Deming that he had a rogue officer who had countermanded his orders and who probably would be coming to Graciosa.   Deming informed him that he could see the cutter from his office window, now that he had bothered to look and that he would take care of it.   He did, however, let Colonel DeSilva know that he considered this to be DeSilva's problem and he would hold him responsible for this intercession.   It would be reflected in his monthly remittance.

Deming immediately called Captain Kane, who took four well-armed men with him.   They caught up to Alvarro Parros on the Cliffside trail at the promontory point, field glasses in hand.

Kane leveled his Glock at the Lt. Colonel.

"You're under arrest, Sir."

"You must be kidding.   I am Lt. Colonel Parros of the Portuguese Headquarters staff in Ponta Delgada.   I have orders to do a reconnaissance of this island and this complex."

"I doubt that.   Besides, the military has no authority here, by agreement with the government.   Move."

Alvarro attempted to wave the orders in front of Kane, but received only a machine gun nozzle in his ribs for the effort.

"The orders are signed by the Commandant."

"I doubt that, too.   He just called my boss.   But, we'll get you sorted out real soon."

They shoved Alvarro back down the pathway from which he came and propped him up in front of the administration building as Brian Deming came down to greet him.

"So, you have orders, eh?"   Kane had radioed ahead

to Brian. "Let me see them."

Deming took the orders from Alvarro and read them, noting the signature did indeed appear to be Colonel DeSilva's.

"One of you, or both of you, are trying to pull a fast one. I don't know why yet, but it was a damn foolish move on your part. Candy, put him in the Lodge and post a guard at each door. Have his stuff sent over there. Confiscate all his communications devices. He'll be treated like a guest with room service, but he won't be allowed to leave the Lodge. Have the crew remanded to their Commander and lockdown the cutter. It will not be allowed to leave until I say so."

Alvarro knew he had walked right into it; and he also knew that he had found out exactly what he wanted to know.

*

They decided to take the submarine tour to the Habitat. At two hundred twenty five apiece, it was a bit pricey, but Annie felt it was worth it. Where else could one see the ninth wonder of the world, as it was now being called and, after two days of lounging poolside by the waterfall, a new activity seemed enticing. They had to leave early to grab something to eat and catch the sub at the eight fifteen a.m. boarding time. They both dressed for a very casual trip, shorts and a halter for Annie and shorts and a Vee Tee for Chris, except at the last moment, he clipped on the Talisman Star.

"Why are you wearing that today?" Annie asked.

"I don't know. Just felt like it. Maybe, it's because this is a sea adventure and I thought I should. Besides, I believe it brings me luck."

They hurriedly grabbed a coffee and a muffin in the lobby and made their way to the sub, The 'Iguana', that made the two trips a day to the Habitat. It took an hour to get there, plus docking time at the Habitat's port, then an hour and a half tour, followed by an equal time for the ascent back to the resort, a four hour tour in all.

The Iguana carried eight passengers in comfortable seating, plus cargo in a hold, but it also had a jump seat in the back for a crew person and two seats for the pilot and a guide. As Wayne Trudeau was making the run down that morning, he played the role of the guide.   He introduced himself to his full compliment of passengers and then talked to each.   He approached Chris and Ann.   He could see them holding hands.

"Are you two married?" he asked politely

"Yes," Annie said and grinned, "But, not to each other."

Only a lawyer could say that and laugh. Wayne was a little shocked, but then burst out in laughter.   It would be a fun trip.

Across from them in the jump seat at the back, a dark haired, elegant woman with perfectly bronzed skin, dressed more formally than casually, gazed intently at them and turned away to look out the porthole.

Jackie realized it was the same two who were at the air strip three days ago.   That memory had been shelved behind the disaster and she hadn't given it the slightest thought until she had seen them board the sub for the journey to the Habitat.   Instinctively, she clutched at the portable hard drive in her pocket.   Who knew who these people were?

They submerged and glided gracefully through the calm sea waters.   The unique glass bottom allowed them to see the denizens of the not so deep;   tropical fish, striped with an array of colors, goliath grouper, an occasional barracuda, a few nurse sharks and as they went farther down and darker, larger fish, including a couple of great whites.   In the clear water, the sun's rays could almost make it to the sea floor, but the sub had to turn on its lights half way down to make its way to the Habitat.

At the 'Ferd', the sub docked and locked to the causeway shield and pumps began their chore of removing the water from the entrance.   When the green light came on over the side hatch, Wayne motioned for the passengers to move out into the causeway and into the first room of the Habitat where the tour would begin.

The room featured displays of the construction of the

'Ferd', the unique lab put in place and the astounding atrium that they would see later on. The history of the Habitat clearly indicated that this was to be the precursor for interplanetary colonization; the model from which new communities would be built in the new frontier. From that room, they entered a library containing hundreds of books and a computer station. The next two rooms were guest rooms, completely independent studios with bath, stove top, refrigerator and microwave. The next room was a hallway adjacent to utilities rooms. It then opened up to a garden nursery, a good four hundred square foot space. All along, Wayne explained how pods had been lowered into place by the barge and crews of robots and divers had connected them into the Habitat.

From there, the greatest achievement awaited them, the Atrium. Built with Structured Insulated Panels, Lego like structures locked and fastened on all sides along with specially formulated plexi-glass panels, this achievement was arguably the greatest creation of the Habitat. It was half the size of a football field and rose seventy feet into the sea upwards from the floor. It housed plant life of all kinds and a garden area. It was this that would be the central focus of inter-planetary colonization; living, working and open spaces in a hostile environment.

Jackie had wanted to see this, as it was something she could not have envisioned, but it was now time for her to excuse herself and make her delivery to Dr. George Preston. She made her way out of the Atrium to the connecting courtyard that led to the Lab at the back end of the Habitat.

In the two days following their meeting with Brian, Suzie and George had accomplished another dive with the aid of Neptune II and Big RED. Their findings weren't as spectacular, but still magnificent: a gold goblet, a complete ornate amphora and another smaller etui filled with wooden buttons and four needles. Still, the prize of both dives was the fluted medallion.

For some reason, she was enthralled by it. It had a familiar feel to it and she felt like she had seen it before, but, of course, that was impossible. She arranged all the artifacts as if on display. Wayne Trudeau was coming down that morning and had intended to take them back to the resort to be locked up for safe keeping. All the testing that could be done at the lab had been done and the work was to now keep the dig going to retrieve as many artifacts as would be possible.

As she pondered the relics in front of her, declining to think of their final fate, Jackie came into the Lab from the courtyard entrance. No one had been expecting her.

"Dr. George Preston?" She asked.

George looked up from his monitor, eyed her inquisitively and asked his own question.

"And who would like to know? And for what reason are you here interrupting our work?"

"I'm sorry, but I am here to deliver a hard drive to you from David Deeds."

George took notice. David was his employer, but to have sent someone in person was a bit odd, especially when he wasn't told about it. It put him on edge, thinking some high level of security was involved.

"I'm Jackie Guiterrez, Doctor. Vice-President in charge of marketing and operations. This is an encrypted hard drive of nuclear fusion formulas and tests. David entrusted it to me to give to you in person for you to proceed with experiments on your own. He did not feel comfortable in doing this any other way. He trusts you and he felt the lab here had the capabilities to follow up on this."

She handed him the hard drive.

"Ms. Guiterrez. I'm sorry you came all the way here to deliver this, but we don't have any time for that at all. We're a little busy here."

"What do you mean? I thought you were only building a desalinization plant and running a few tests."

"Brian didn't tell you? We're sitting on the greatest archeological oceanographic dig in the history of the world. We have uncovered artifacts eleven thousand years old. We are sitting on proof of the first vestiges of Atlantis. We'll be here for months working on this, others will be here for years.

I can't believe you weren't told before you came here."

"I wasn't told a thing. And, as far I know, David doesn't know either. I just got an email from him this morning. He didn't say anything."

"That's odd." Dr. Frost interjected. "Brian told us he was going to tell him days ago."

Jackie was beginning to get a different picture. Brian was keeping this under wraps until his deal went through and he never told the scientists a thing about the transfer. Jackie looked intently back at Dr. George.

"How can you be sure this is Atlantis?"

"Actually, Ms. Guiterrez, we can't. We can't even be sure it was called Atlantis, but myth has always been based on some spectrum of fact. What we have are eleven thousand year old artifacts; crafted artifacts from an advanced civilization. That is unheard of. We have a density of artifacts, indicating a settlement or an outpost. We have historical references dating back two thousand years. We have the perfect conditions and medium to examine. We also have our education and work experience that leads us to reasonable suppositions and the one I would put forth to you is the general understanding of mankind's longevity and geologic reality. Look at the civilization that has been created in the last five thousand years. Mankind has been here half a million, with more or less the same brain size and inherent capability. If the Egyptians said there were two advanced civilizations in 9000 B.C., why not? Wouldn't it be logical to assume that another advanced civilization could have been built from 14000 B.C. to 9000 B.C., a similar five thousand year period? And think about the 'cataclysm', what a five hundred or a thousand foot wall of water would do today to cities like London, New York, Paris; hell, half of the world. What would be left of civilization as we know it? How long would it take to recover?

We will find out here, Miss. We have found the Holy Grail of Archeology. We're just beginning to step forth with our imprint."

At another station, Dr. Suzie Preston had finally pulled herself away to engage in the conversation, then caught a glimpse of the tour group coming into the hallway on the other side of the glass partitioning that separated the Lab from the connecting annex on either side. Her face turned white. She gasped. She summoned all her strength to rise up and stumble over to the partition. She tapped on the window. On the other side, Wayne led the group of eight and Chris thought the woman in the white lab coat had gone mad. She was tapping on the glass, pointing at him. He mouthed 'what', but she kept tapping, then tapped her chest. She pointed at his chest. He clutched at the Talisman Star. She nodded vigorously and then waved them to come into the lab. Wayne finally caught on and led Chris and Ann to the entrance, ushering them inside. He took the rest of the group away to finish the tour. He would come back later.

Dr. Suz stared in disbelief. "Where'd you get that?"

"This? This has been in my family for years. If you could ask my Aunt, which you can't, she would say it has been in the family for hundreds of years."

By now, Jackie and the two men were paying attention.

"Could you take it off? Could I see it?"

"I guess." Ann helped him unlock the clasp.

Suzie took it over to the trays that she had prepared and lay the Talisman Star next to the fluted medallion. She slumped in her chair. She turned back to Chris and Ann.

"Could you stay here for a while? I'd like to run some tests."

"How long? We're supposed to leave in a half hour."

"Could you stay overnight? We have guest rooms?"

"What is there about the Talisman that you would need to do tests for?" Ann asked.

"Do you see that item in the tray next to it?" Dr. Suz motioned.

Ann and Chris both looked at them side by side. With the exception of the condition and the diamond crystal, they were identical.

"That piece in the tray is eleven thousand years old. Wouldn't you like to know about yours?"

Ann looked at Chris and he was clearly astonished and puzzled. But by now, she clearly knew now how to deal with him.

"Look, honey, this is an adventure worth having. How many people get to stay overnight in the world's largest undersea habitat? This is something we can tell our kids about."

"You want kids? This late?"

"I'm here for the full ride, Chris."

Snapping out of the segue that had derailed the original question, Chris came back to Suzie and smiled.

"Yeah, we'll stay."

"I'm staying, too," Jackie added and thought to herself: There's an awful lot of new information to digest with no shortage of secrets being hidden here and you all are going to help me figure it out.

Not ten minutes later, Wayne Trudeau returned and motioned to his former passengers to come along. Dr. Suzie waved him off, but he opened the hatch and entered the lab.

"What's going on?"

"These good folks have agreed to stay with us for the night so we might run some tests." George said.

"I can't authorize that."

"We did. It'll be fine. We have extra rooms."

"That's not the point," Wayne interrupted, "There's no authorization for anyone other than staff to stay here."

"We authorized it." Dr. Suzie added.

"George, you're in charge here, tell her we can't authorize that."

George looked at Suzie and understood very clearly her feelings on the matter.

"Suzie's in charge here. See you later, Wayne."

Suzie flipped him the bird.

*

Brian hadn't been to the 'Ferd' since the completion of the project before occupancy, but based on Wayne's visit after the morning excursion, he sensed there was an urgency and decided to take the trip down. It was too late to catch it that day and it was too dangerous to try at night, so he planned the trip for tomorrow. There would be no tours and the notice was posted at the hotel and at the dock that all sub tours for the day had been cancelled due to technical difficulties.

Brian had forgotten about Jackie's trip down to hand over the hard drive. That could be a problem. Jackie had to now know the extent of the work going on there and the finding of the artifacts from antiquity. She had probably had her ear bended with the Egyptian and Greek histories; of the many suppositions about Atlantis, but in his mind, that would probably not be much of an issue for Jackie. She understood business and she had a full understanding of the transfer of the complex. The details of how artifacts would be treated would be something that would be negotiated or tied up in court over a long period of time. She would know that, too. But, Brian would pre-empt those scenarios by moving all of the items to Zurich and have them vaulted.

The couple that had been invited to stay over was quite curious, though, and Brian wondered what in hell they had to do with the dig or the scientists. Wayne hadn't connected Chris's Talisman Star with the artifacts in the lab. He had missed the initial exchange and wasn't part of the follow up conversation, either. So, it was a mystery to Brian, but like all mysteries that occurred in his life, he would soon have the answers in hand.

*

The tests came back conclusively. The Talisman Star was the exact same piece of jewelry or medallion, or artifact, or whatever it was as the fluted medallion on the tray. The RCA test indicated it was twenty four years younger than the one in the tray, but the Talisman was still eleven thousand years old. It was in better shape; it had the full diamond shaped crystal imbedded in the center interior of the fluting.

After receiving permission from Chris, they gave the Talisman the same final cleansing bath the other piece had; and once completely cleaned, it sported the same rune like characters that clearly meant something, but no one in the Lab had any idea what the language or the symbols might mean.

"That doesn't surprise me," Dr. George Preston mused. "When they found the Phaistos disc on Crete, it had markings that dated back thousands of years. No one has yet figured out what they meant. And this is much older than that."

"Would you be willing to try another experiment?" Dr. Suzie was on the verge of begging.

"Maybe, what would it entail?" Chris wondered.

"I'm thinking phosphorescence, possible solar properties. I'm wondering if it can collect sunlight all day and provide some light at night. We can simulate that with this sunlamp here. It should work in a couple of hours."

It was already late, well after dinner, but no one wanted to retire. She prepped the experiment quickly and the group took turns going back and forth from the lab to the library or their rooms to pass the time. It was almost midnight when Dr. Suz felt they were ready. She turned off the sun lamp, dimmed the lights and held the Talisman Star up against a small screen. The crystal glowed in the dim light and cast discernible rays on the screen. Held closer, she thought she could make out some rune markings that must have been inside the Talisman itself. She was ecstatic. The Talisman had a specific purpose, to project some image or marking in the darkness, perhaps of great value; or perhaps, merely a parlor trick, as her grandmother would have said.

Still no one knew what it meant.

"How can a stone like that glow or cast sunlight?" Ann asked. "It's not some kind of solar lamp, is it?"

"Chuck is our geologic oceanographer. He can explain it better." George offered a sweep of his hand to his colleague.

Dr. Frost stood up like he was about to offer a lecture,

then decided he'd better sit back down and relax.   It was late.

"There are new scientific experiments with organic crystals.   By introducing aromatic carbonyls to form strong halogen bonds in the crystal, the molecules become quite tightly packed.   This suppresses vibration and heat energy so that the electrons are enhanced and fall back to a ground state.   This leads to a strong phosphorescence, aka sunlit reflection."

"That said, however, that is not the case with what we're looking at.   If that level of science existed eleven thousand years ago, they would not be using medallions or implements of this nature.   No, this has to be a naturally occurring phenomena intrinsic to this stone, this diamond crystal.   We wouldn't be able to tell exactly what that is without further testing of the stone itself and I don't think my archeologist colleague would want me to do that."

Suzie nodded her head.   Destroying the artifact to see what made it tick was out of the question.   They needed to know a lot more before any dissection took place, if ever.

Chris thought back to his childhood.   He remembered something.

"Turn it on its side, would you, and hold it to the screen."

By placing it in that manner and within four inches of the screen, an image appeared out of the bottom of the Talisman.   The circular image cast shadows of shapes to the left and right of the sphere, but also a small circular shape in the center.   It meant nothing to five people in the room, but Dr. Frost felt something click in his memory.

"Some of this shape, I know."   He said.

"My Aunt used to play with this, sometimes.   I didn't see her do it very often, but she liked to cast the shape on the wall.   I didn't remember any of that until you did this." Chris thought aloud.

"Since we are referencing an artifact that's eleven thousand years old and if I were to guess based on my memory," Chuck went on, "we would be looking at the shape of the Atlantic Ocean about fourteen thousand years ago. The shapes on the edges would be the continents and the smaller shape might be Atlantis."

"Then what would this be?" George asked.

"I think it might be some kind of sextant, some navigational tool, something that might help guide a sailor in the early evening, to help set a course for the night." Suzie offered.

"My family on my Aunt's side came from here. That's why I'm here. They came to the new world as navigators for the whaling ships out of New Bedford. Is it possible and I know this sounds crazy, but is it possible that this might have been handed down for centuries as a means to chart a course?"

"Anything is possible," George noted, "Just not probable. It probably traveled through thousands of hands to find its way back here. It's probably just an interesting piece of jewelry."

"Let's take that just a bit further," Suzie thought out loud. "Noah and his Ark escape from the flood. Hundreds of other boats just like that end up all over the world, creating or enhancing civilizations and a variety of legends. Clearly, it was not the end of the world, but a tragedy large enough to reshape societies. Every one of those boats had a navigator of some sort. Suppose some tried to go back to Atlantis. They would have needed a sextant, a compass to guide the way. They returned and found nothing left but volcanic islands, untillable and useless for human existence. The medallion was still useful for guidance, but the world for which it was made no longer existed. It/they fall into disuse, but for some reason, are still precious to navigators. They are considered lucky. They represent a guiding star. Now, the probability that it could have been handed down becomes a bit more enhanced, doesn't it?"

"My lucky star, my Aunt called it."

"Let's go even further," Dr. Chuck went on. "You mentioned the Phaistos Disc, George. It's true it hasn't been deciphered and there may be a reason for that. Some feel that the language on the Disc contains breakthrough information, such as the key to inter-dimensional travel. Theories exist that the Disc was actually created by Isis-Osiris and contains original knowledge.   I can't debate that and we'll probably never know, but the idea of using a unique precious artifact to house important and specific cultural knowledge of a civilization is not new. This could be the case here.   This is clearly a unique artifact, engaged for some distinct and important purpose.   Why not include precious knowledge and have it be cherished for generations?   Why not keep the chronicles of Atlantis alive in this medallion?"

"This is quite too much to think about," Ann pleaded.

"And it's awfully late," Jackie added, "And we need to get some sleep to be clear headed tomorrow.   We have to think about what we are all going to do about this."

All agreed and left for their respective quarters.   Chris and Ann had a double bed in a chamber designed for another married set of scientists like George and Suzie.   They lay down, frazzled from the long day and tried to get their minds to calm.

"I wish I had some drug, something to quiet down this runaway brain." Chris whispered.

"All these strange beds.   I've been sleeping in nothing but strange beds for weeks.   It's so hard to get to sleep in them, Chris.   And this is the strangest one yet.   The only constant is you."

"I know something that might help."

"Here, in this place?"

He looked lovingly into those beautiful eyes.

"It'll be something we can tell our grandkids."

*

I am being driven into the deepest recesses of my soul.   My spirit is being tested. I stare at the ceiling of my room and I am two hundred feet under the sea.   What do my ancestors know?   What are they trying to tell me?   What is the real reason I am here? Why me?   Why not me?
I have seen the past.   I have seen the future.   I have dreamed of disaster and it happened.   I know there is evil around me.   I know I am afraid.   Maybe, not enough.   So many strange events.   So much psychic activity.   Can

eleven thousand years be communicated in one day?   In one instant?   My being is swimming in the entirety of the Universe And this person, this person next to me, this person I have waited all my life for.   At my side through all of this with no complaints.
Please, God, love me just a little bit more.   Help me take care of her.
Help me get through this.

CHAPTER SEVENTEEN

Atlantic Sun

The submersion and trip to the 'Ferd' was set for ten a.m.   Brian decided that it might be a good idea to bring Kane along; he wasn't sure what action he might have to take. Wayne Trudeau would be going along and of course, the subs' pilot.   He would have plenty of room to escort whoever back to the resort.

In the Habitat, the three scientists and the three guests sat in the kitchenette adjacent to the Lab around the large round table that served as their dining room, café, and in many cases, the spillover staging area for the Lab itself.

The discussion over cereal, toast and coffee was about the disposition of the artifacts; the property, ownership, and rights to the finds.   Jackie was a bit vehement about it.   An old side of her was emerging.

"Anything found here has to belong to Portugal."   She stated flatly.

"However," George noted, "There are international salvage rights retained by the finders and their companies."

"Meaning all of this would now belong to Brian Deming?" Suzie asked.

"Precisely."

"I'm not so sure about that," Ann offered, somewhat reluctant to join in the conversation.

"Excuse me?" George interrupted.   His pompous arrogant side was about to assert itself.

"She's a lawyer," Chris added, "and a damn good one, too."

"I don't think Chris remembers too well," she added, "but I went to law school in Columbia.   I interned at the U.N. in my third year and went to work in their counsel's office my first two years out of law school.   That was before I went out to Denver to live with my brother and start up a practice out there."

"In any case, I think Portugal's situation is unique. Something about the continuous occupation of the Azores for five hundred years. You might recall that during WWII, the free government was in exile here. After the war, I believe that through the U.N., some special agreement was reached about possession of the sea lanes or the ocean surrounding the islands. I don't know what it was called, nor its provisions; I'd have to look it up, but I believe it provided some special protections."

"Then it's settled." Jackie said vehemently.

"Probably not that easily," Ann went on. "Courts have been tied up for years with salvage claims of private enterprises and competing jurisdictions. I think Spain is still trying to get back treasure spilled in the sixteen hundreds off the coast of Cuba."

"Regardless," Chuck Frost stated, "Brian had Suzie catalog all the pieces. They're scheduled for pick up today. In fact, I thought he'd be on the sub tour down here this morning and they're already late. They should have been here an hour ago."

"I guess we better get ready." Suzie started for the Lab. "He's going to vault the artifacts up at the resort."

They entered the next room, the Lab, and Suzie finished up the trays, ready now for export. She handed the Talisman back to Chris.

"Better take this back. I'd love to keep it here, but its' yours and you'll be leaving today. I wish you could stay. I did take a picture, though, for comparison later. Perhaps you could come back when we've done more testing."

"I'd like that," Chris offered.

"I wouldn't wear that, today," Annie chided.

Chris stuffed it in his pocket.

Dr. Suzie stacked the trays and prepared them for removal by placing them in a large vinyl traveling case, not unlike a pizza delivery bag.

They heard the sub hit the docking port and the causeway extension wind out. In less than five minutes tourists or Brian or staff would be by. They didn't expect Brian and Wayne to appear with the Security Chief, Captain Charles Kane.

Brian burst in followed by the other two. He was

295

clearly agitated.

"So, what's this business of uninvited guests staying over last night?"

Suzie stepped forward in confrontation.

"We invited them to participate in some of our experiments. Ann here is an archeological attorney and Chris is an artifact collector. We get bored down here, Brian, and we like to have some company once in a while. That okay with you?"

"What about you, Jackie? You didn't have any need to stay."

"Actually, I did, Brian. I had to explain the encryption of the hard drive. We needed to discuss the nuclear fusion formulas and what David expects from those studies. It was getting late. George and I were in a heated discussion about his performance standards and we were trying to resolve time and testing schedules. You know, we all have specific agendas here and there are demands on all of us."

Backed up enough, Brian cooled ever so slightly, but he was ready for his pick up and he didn't feel like discussing the matter any further.

"Everything here?"

Suzie nodded. Brian unpacked the bag, picked up the listing that catalogued the pieces, flipping the pages and examining the prints. He corresponded the list to the contents of the trays, detailing each closely.

"What's this piece here?" Suzie had forgotten to take the Talisman's picture off the JPEGs.

"That's not ours."

"Whose is it and where is it?"

"None of your business," Suzie retorted.

"The hell it ain't. Candy, search them."

"No, that's alright," Chris stepped up. He pulled the Talisman from his pocket.
"It's mine. It's been in my family for hundreds of years. That's what the Doctors wanted to test."

"A likely story. You've got nothing to do with that piece. That belongs here. Candy, take that."

Kane ripped it from his hands.

"You can't take that, it's mine," Chris yelled.

"It's on my property. I can take anything I want."

"Just like you took anything you wanted on the Western Slope, including the lives of my friends, you Son of a Bitch." Chris was astonished at his own outburst, but his anger had gotten the best of him.

If looks could kill, the look on Brian's face had already put a hole straight through the middle of Chris's forehead.

"Candy, arrest that asshole. Take the attorney, too."

Kane's pistol was already drawn and he waved the couple forward. He shoved Chris out the door. Ann followed him close behind.

"Damn it, Chris, if you were my client, I would have; I would have, in my girlfriend's words, I'd slap you nekkid."

Kane escorted them back to the sub. Brian Deming lifted up the case and hung it on his shoulder.

"You can't take those," Jackie blurted out. "They belong to Portugal."

"Am I going to have trouble with you, too?" Deming pulled his own pistol.

"You're leaving anyway. You might as well join the others." He handed Wayne the gun and directed her off.

George Preston stepped up. He had seen quite enough.

"I must protest, sir. These people meant no harm and they are quite within their rights. I demand you release them."

"You are quite well uninformed, Dr. Preston, as I now own this place. All of it. If you, your wife and your partner ever want to see sunlight again, let alone get off this Island, you had better do as I say. You'll continue your work here until I see fit to dismiss you. You would be well advised to get back to it."

Deming turned and walked out the door. He met Kane at the interlock.

"They all go in the lodge. Move their stuff, confiscate everything."

Joe's new plan was similar to his first plan, identical except that when he called for a reservation, he also reserved a tee time for six p.m. for a quick round. He would rent a set of clubs and a pull cart. The same instructions were given to Trevor and to Bill. If he were not back in two days' time, they knew what to do.

At the Lodge that afternoon, three new guests were being invited into their new accommodations. Kane escorted them through the front door and waved them in, the armed guards right behind him.

"Pick a room. Dinner's around six. Get used to the place."

One of the guards dumped their belongings in a pile behind them.

It was indeed structured like a traveler's hotel; one interior corridor with twenty rooms, a small office space, laundry, and a small dining area in front with four tables. At one of the tables, a uniformed man sat reading a magazine. He looked up at the new guests and was stunned. He dismissed the couple; he had never seen them before, but the woman with them, she, he knew.

Jackie did not recognize the younger man at all. Yet, he had a broad smile and his eyes were beaming. He was of medium build, but trim and looked like a Portuguese version of John Kennedy, Jr. He had wavy dark hair and intense eyebrows. He was incredibly good looking and Jackie couldn't help but be attracted to him. He was clearly an officer of some sort. Jackie had dealt with a lot of them, especially around the skunk works, and she could tell them apart rather easily, even though she was not familiar with this man's insignia.

There was no doubt in Alvarro's mind who the woman was. She had gotten only more beautiful, but the features had always been there. She had aged wonderfully. She had filled out as only a mature woman could and had grown in stature and presence. She was amazing and he was so very proud.

He couldn't resist a little teasing and rose to walk over next to her, a wink added to the ever present smile. He couldn't stand it any longer.

"Juanita, don't you recognize me? I'm your bag of stones."

"Oh, my God, Alvarro. Alvarro, Alvarro." She jumped at him and crushed him with a hug that didn't seem to end. He thought she would break his ribs. She kissed him on the cheek and pulled away from him, still in embrace.

"Oh, you are so handsome." And then, the situation dawned on her.

"What on earth are you doing here, and, what the hell is an officer of the army doing detained here in this place?"

"It's a long story, Juanita."

"It's Jackie now, but sit, little brother, and tell me all about it."

Ann and Chris didn't understand a word of the conversation, but they could tell this was an important reunion, so they excused themselves unseen, grabbed their bags and went down the hall way to pick out a suitable room. There was a larger room near the other end with a queen bed and they immediately took it.

"No telling how many more are coming." Chris said.

"Only if their hot blooded mouths get ahead of their brain," Annie spit back. She was highly disappointed that Chris got them into this mess.

"It'll be alright," Chris tried to sooth her.

"I'm not so sure, Chris. It seems pretty dire to me."

Joe took the water taxi over in the afternoon, checked into the hotel and got another first floor room. He only brought a large carry-on bag with room enough for a change of clothes, some toiletries and a laptop, which he did not currently possess.

At five-thirty, he made his way over to the pro shop, rented a set of clubs and a pull cart. He teed off at 6:07 p.m. He was the only one scheduled, so he wasn't paired up with anyone and he took off on number one. With good play, he would be done in two to three hours, the perfect time to head back.   Looking at the course map, he would have his best shot coming off number seventeen or straying off eighteen to close in to the administration building.

After a sloppy but fast paced round, he hit eighteen at quarter after eight, just as the sun was beginning to set out over the sea.   He made a beeline off the cart path and pulled up behind a palm near the building and left the cart, visible, in front of the palm.   He made his way to the fire escape, moved the rock again and took off his shoes and socks, stashing them under a fern.

Ambling up the wall and on to the escape, he made his way to the fourth floor office.   The window was still unlatched and he pried it open.

Inside, the office was the same, nothing out of the ordinary.   The laptop sat in the middle of the desk.   He disconnected it, wrapping the battery pack up and attaching it to the laptop with several pieces of scotch tape from the desk.

He heard footsteps on the stairs below.   He couldn't go out that way.   There was no way he could get down the escape with the laptop without making some noise, so he decided that the best plan was to toss it.   It landed in the shrubs four stories below with a whoosh and a rustle.   The noise distracted whoever had been coming and Joe waited patiently, peering ever so cautiously out the window.   He saw a guard walking toward the bushes and seeing nothing amiss, he turned to come back into the building.   Joe knew this was his only opportunity to get out, so he gently climbed out the window and navigated his way to the ground.   He quickly made for the bushes and grabbed his shoes and socks.   He hopped over to the bag and cart and was tightening his shoelace when a very large man came up behind him.   It was Captain Charles Kane.

"What are you doing here?"
"Golfing."
"Not over here, you're not."
"I had to go to the bathroom really bad.   I thought there might be one over here."
"There isn't.   There's one at the maintenance shed if

you can't make it to the pro shop.   Are you a guest here, Sir?"

Joe got up and brushed off his shorts.

"Yes, Sir."

"May I see your key?"

Joe produced the key.   Kane noted the coding and gave it back.

"Don't be coming over in this area again, Sir.   This is for staff only.   Guests should stay on the course."

There was no way Joe was going to get the laptop now. He quickly devised another plan as he made his way to the shop and then back to his room.

Kane continued his rounds and did a complete search of the building.   He finished at Brian's office.   There was nothing unusual there, but the laptop was gone.   That wasn't uncommon since Brian often took it to Moontracer or his private Villa.   Still, the stranger walking around the building gave him pause and he decided to give Brian a call.

Joe set his alarm for four a.m.   He would get up, get out by five at the dawn's earliest light, find the laptop in the bushes and catch the first taxi back to the big island.
He overslept.   At five thirty he was awakened by a light rattling at the sliding doors leading to the patio.   He quietly extracted himself from the bed and stood to the left of the curtain when the door slid open.   The same large man entered and Joe hit him as hard as he could, a right cross to the jaw.   Kane reeled for a moment, then swung a powerful leg kick to Joe's ribs.   It knocked the air out of him.   He doubled over and Kane's two interlocked fists came down on the back of his head and neck.   Joe went into the newly laid hard wood flooring head first.   He was out cold.

Twenty minutes later, Kane opened the front door to the Lodge and dragged the unconscious man into the dining area.   Jackie, unable to sleep, was already up, having a cup of coffee.

Kane dropped the man on the floor.

"Here.   Something for you to do.   I'll be back to talk to him later."

It wasn't even close.   In the hill towns of Braga, Vila Real, Visseu and Abrates it was two to one.   In the mountain villages of Braganca, Chives, Castelo, and Portelegre it was even higher.   The seacoast towns of Valencia, Sines and Caldes de Rahia were taken and the Algarve villages of Lagos, Palimao, and Faio were in his column, too.   Only in the two largest cities, Lisbon and Oporto was the race close, and there they were even.   Pedro Anabel Cavadas won the Presidency with fifty seven percent of the vote, while President DeSilva only garnered forty one.

At first, DeSilva demanded a recount.   But, the disparity in numbers was so great that the he finally dropped the idea.   A recount would not change the verdict.

There was a concern, though, that DeSilva might retain power by use of the military forces he created.   President elect Cavadas shared that concern and requested a meeting with the Defense Minister, Ferdinand Pechorro.   The reports given him over the months and his own views based on his personal investigations led him to believe that   Pechorro was an honorable man.

The Minister agreed to meet him and was waiting on the main floor when the President Elect arrived.   He personally escorted him to his office.

"It is a pleasure to meet you, Sir.   You ran an outstanding campaign."

"Thank you, Minister."

"Please call me Ferdinand.   How can I be of service to you."

They sat in two comfortable leather chairs in the spacious office next to a large picture window that looked out on the government plaza below.

"Ferdinand, I want you to be absolutely honest with me."

The Minister nodded.

"Would President DeSilva take over the government by

force?"

Defense Minister Pechorro sat deep in thought for a moment.

"It is not possible, Sir."

"How is that?"

"The military understands that for democracy to work, civilian control must be maintained. You can't have the military countermanding the will of the people. If you do, you don't have a democracy. The military supports the Office of the Presidency, not the person who holds it. No President is above his duties to his Office."

Pedro Anabel Cavadas had just gained a new found respect for Ferdinand Pechorro, but still he pressed the matter.

"How can you be so sure?"

"Sir, I am a former Major General in service to my country. I am, until you relieve me, still the Minister of Defense and I command the generals in that Army. I would never allow it, and they know it. Again, our loyalty is to the Office of the Presidency and to the Republic of Portugal. President DeSilva is not a bad man. He will retire with grace. I can promise you that."

"Ferdinand. Would you consider staying on in the cabinet?

"It would be an honor, Sir."

"I'm thinking of National Security Advisor. I think you'd be the best man for the job."

"I would gladly do it."

"Thank you."

Pedro Cavadas looked across the room at the large map of Portugal on the wall. Push pins had been placed at what appeared to be military installations. There was a separate inset of the Acorean Archipelago. There were two push pins on it, one in Horta and one in Ponta Delgada. That reminded him of the other thing he wanted to talk about.

"Ferdinand, do you have the power to grant commissions and offer promotions?"

"Certainly."

"I would ask a favor."

"Okay."

"You may remember my campaign manager, Alvarro Parros.   Surprisingly, he was recalled to service and promoted to Lt. Colonel, second in command at Ponta Delgada."

Ferdinand Pechorro tried desperately not to let the guilt he felt about that tactic appear on his face.

"I would like you to promote him to Brigadier General and place him in charge of all forces in the islands.   Would you do that for me?"

"I would, Sir.   I will sign the commission today."

"And send it email with follow up enclosure, a copy also to the President of the Regional Government, Gustave Parcanto.   I'm sure in the next three weeks while I'm putting together a cabinet, Alvarro can put to use the things he's learned there and provide a more positive administration.   It will serve him well on his resume as he is on my short list of one to take your job.   We will need him here and I believe you will find he is an outstanding citizen and will be a great champion for our country."

"I will be glad to do it.   I will find relief in doing it."

The last statement indicated to the President Elect that Ferdinand had more to do with the banishing of his friend than he may have let on, but had wrestled with it in his mind.   This, then, would be a good atonement for an act borne of perhaps necessity, but certainly not decency.

"Thank you, again, Minister Pechorro.   It has been a pleasure."

President Elect Cavadas left the meeting buoyant in his preparations for the future of good governance for the Republic.   Yet, late at night, slumped in his chair, he wondered at the monstrosity of the task before him.

I am President of my country.   It has not always been what I wanted to be, but one cannot make changes at anything less. Or so I thought.   We are so desperate: we have twenty one percent unemployment, we are broke and our debt ceiling is rising and we have no way to pay. Our religious strife and provincial violence have never been worse, our country on the verge of a police state. And, I promised change. I have been a radical all my life and my fight was to get here, to win. Now, I am here. How am I going to do this? So many promises, so many agreements. The journey was so much better than the conclusion. Pedro Anabel Cavadas is President. A blow for liberty. A recognition that Portugal will rightfully take its place in the world of great nations. Bullshit. I hope to get out of here alive and seeing the tasks ahead of me give me pause to think that I must have been out of my mind to think I alone can fix this. There's a new world order out there, run by multi-national corporations and as small economic countries, I don't know how to combat this. I knew how to combat my enemies thirty years ago; I shot them. That's pretty much out of the question, now. Nationalism is useful; Venezuela and Bolivia did it, but it is a painful process that can kill investment. So many solutions to find, so little time. God grant me the wisdom, the energy and the grace to do it well.

*

Brian faced a dilemma. All of a sudden, he had a not so harmonic convergence of meddlers and do-gooders interfering with his plans. Never, at any time, had he quite so many people trying to mess up his life, all at once. He had five problems over there in that lodge and another three virtually prisoners in the Habitat. The situation was very serious indeed. His laptop was gone and he didn't know where it was. He had no idea how much these people knew and the guy who stole the computer was still unconscious. Nonetheless, the conscious ones had all talked together by now and had probably filled in the blanks of each other's histories.

He had no problem in killing people. During the Gulf

War, he had actually enjoyed helping jihadists meet the seventeen virgins they were supposed to get after martyrdom. In his personal and professional life, a number of people had gotten in his way or stood as obstacles to his plans. Those that had sufficiently been obstructive had been summarily dismissed from planet earth.

It started with Luke, the dolt, who he had hired to help him set up that migrant worker twenty some years ago in order to rid himself of the damned wildcat miners. Luke had shot and killed the illegal farmhand and then, at the same time as those two goons blew up the bar in Silverton, managed to get himself busted in a petty theft of beer, cigarettes and cash at the seven eleven on the west side of Durango.

Luke was sent on an errand down to Farmington, New Mexico after his release. His car had been tampered with and he had a fatal accident coming over the mountains on Rt.160 on the return. Craig and Ron did their time and moved out to Las Vegas. Those two were especially dangerous, well versed in explosives and motivated to earn money the easy way after an eight year criminal record. Brian could ill afford to have them coming after him and when they did, that was a job he did himself, just to make sure it was done right. That gangland style hit left two bodies in a sand pit at an old construction site near Zion National Park. That was a cold case that he was sure would never be solved.

Then, the last of the wildcat miners were taken out in Montana. Brian could ill afford his past being discovered when he moved on to partnership in EngenUnity, and when Skip Conboy started nosing around in all of those cases, Brian sent a pro out from California to take a walk with Skip out past the ghost towns of Eureka and Howardsville for an impromptu visit to Animas Forks. The pro came back.

There had been a few others along the way, for other reasons; and as Atlantic Sun developed, a couple of nosy fisherman ran into bad weather and a particularly obnoxious boat captain had been escorted out to Davy Jones's locker fifty miles north of Graciosa.

The dilemma here was who should die and who shouldn't. It was clear to him that the Americans, Chris and

Ann, would probably have to be removed. The man probably had detailed information on him that should not come to light and the attorney would only help him do it. They could be killed in Santa Cruz by some idiotic armed robbery play. That might work. Jackie would be difficult. He would probably let her go back to the States.

She didn't have anything on him, save the findings of the dig, and that, he could stall on indefinitely. He lived in Portugal and would have to be extradited. Even if they could prove ill intent, it would take years. Besides, he could always get to her later.

The scientists were bottled up, literally and figuratively. He would let them go after he sufficiently tucked away the priceless artifacts in Zurich. Ownership of the property, the contract with Portugal, and the rights of salvage would most logically go his way in any court. He felt fairly confident about that.

The rogue Portuguese officer was, of course, a rogue. Something would have to happen to him; and it would be best if it happened to him in DeSilva's hands. He would have Kane take him when in custody by DeSilva, perhaps enroute to Ponta Delgada. Or, even better, in DeSilva's own jailhouse. That would be beautiful.

And finally, the WorldGreen agent and activist; he was definitely a goner. But, where there's one of those assholes, there had to be more. They would have to find the others and soon. He would send some Blackthorn guards out to the big island and maybe a couple as far as Sao Jorge and look for one of their ships. They might have a plane at the airport at Santa Cruz. He'd look there, too. Their plane or their ship needed to have a spectacular crash or explosion. That would be the most fun.

He sat in his swivel chair gazing out his window at the paradise he had built. He was rolling a quarter between his fingers. No one would take this from him. No one. He felt confident he had a reasonably good plan, but there was one other option. He could just kill them all.

CHAPTER 18

Home Invasion

When Joe regained consciousness, he was lying in a bed staring straight up at the most exotic woman he had ever seen. She was a Mediterranean beauty. Her long black hair draped sensuously over her shoulders, her dark skin and eyebrows gave her a slightly hardened look, but the smile on her face could chase away demons from your soul. Her large brown eyes spoke of compassion. She didn't have to say a word for Joe to understand that she had been taking care of him; that she was his personal angel.

"If I'm dead," he muttered, "then I'm in the right place."

"I think you'll be fine. We don't think anything's broken."

He attempted to sit up, got half way and his right rib cage howled at him.

"Maybe not broken, but one hell of a bruising. That son of a bitch kicked the hell out of me."

"That's Kane, Joe. He's a real bastard."

"How'd you know my name."

"Your ID, WorldGreen. It's very interesting you're here."

"It's a long story."

Jackie looked around her and back at Joe.

"I seem to have a lot of time."

Joe told her of his return from the aborted mission in the Aleutian Bay and how his crew had been brutally attacked. When asked, he explained to her how he had gotten into WorldGreen to begin with and how he dedicated his life to the cause. He told Jackie of the odd situation of significant private funding to examine what was going on in the Azores and of their well-planned and prepared, if not arduous journey on the Cormorant across the Atlantic and finally, the information they had gained from the locals and their own investigation into Atlantic Sun's activities. She had listened intently.

"Thank you, Joe, for sharing all this. And, based on what I've heard from the others and my own experience of late, I am getting a not so pretty picture of what I've been involved in here."

"If someone is determined to do wrong, Jackie, there's little you can do to stop them. You can't legislate morality. You can only expose what they've done and hopefully before too much harm has been done. These types of corporations are notorious for their disregard for people who get in their way. They don't care what happens to anybody and the collateral damage is accepted as the cost of doing business."

"You really do hate multi-national corporations, don't you?"

"In general, yes, with a passion. There are damn few that have any kind of ethical ground to stand on."

"I am beginning to see your point."

"Jackie, help me up. I need to speak to the others. We have to get ready."

"What for?"

"We're going to be rescued. It might be tonight at dusk. It might be tomorrow night. I don't know. It depends on what they decide, but it was planned on from the get-go."

They were about to leave the room when they heard Kane and another guard talking as they walked down the hallway. The door to the room was open and the two came in. Jackie stood up and pushed her chair back. Joe sat upright in the bed.

"Finally, sleeping beauty is awake." Kane grabbed the chair from Jackie and sat. "So where's the computer, sonny boy?"

"You know I don't have it."

"True. So where is it?"

"Since I don't feel like being beaten unconscious this morning, I will tell you I threw it in the bushes from the office. If you root around in there, I'm sure you'll find it."

"Fair enough, no beating for the moment. Where are the others?"

"What others?"

"Your WorldGreen buddies. You must have

associates with you, eh?"

"Nope, sorry, it's just me. I flew in a few days ago. We're stretched pretty thin and they didn't have enough money to send a crew all the way out here, so I'm it."

"I'll save your beating for later. That is, if I find out you're lying; and I will find out if you're lying, and, if you are, I will beat you to a pulp. Do you want to reconsider you're statement?"

"No, I'm telling you the truth."

Kane considered that he probably did tell the truth about the laptop and maybe he was telling the truth about a crew. He would make sure, of course, so he let it go for the moment.

"Alright, sonny boy, but I'll be back to see you."

Kane and the other guard left the room and the Lodge. Jackie helped Joe up and he hung on her shoulder down the hallway to the dining area where Alvarro, Chris and Ann sat at one of the circular tables. He introduced himself and explained to them what he thought was going to happen.

"I hope its tonight," he said finally, "It better be or I think I'm screwed. I think we all are. Jackie, if you could help me back to the room and help get me ready, I'd really appreciate it. I'm still a little weak."

In reality, Joe was feeling a lot better. He decided that he wanted her company as much as possible. This one was a keeper.

'I've never met any man like him. He is the exact opposite of all the men I have ever dated or ever cared for.

He is not a professional: not a lawyer, a banker, an executive, a corporate star, a hot shot agent. He is the antithesis of all of them.

He hates the world I come from. He detests the establishment with a passion.

He is my Pakistani cab driver.

He has lived a hard life. I see it in his face. And yet, there has been joy in it.

He stands for something. I stand for nothing in comparison.

311

He says he's incredibly boring, but I find him so terribly interesting.
I think I have been waiting for him.'

*

"In a situation like this, Bill, you don't wait. He should have been back an hour ago. That means they caught him. It also means they'll be looking for us, even if we don't think so. It means we have to pack up, lock up and get out there and get him. It's time for the golf bag."

Trevor retrieved the bag and emptied its contents on the salon table. He chose the long barreled Baretta with the suppressor for his handgun and put it in the side pocket with the golf balls.

"The thing is, Bill, that a silencer doesn't stop the sound. It only decreases it so like, you won't blow out your ears in a small room. This is what we'll use if we have to, but it will probably be heard, so we have to pick our spots and work around that."

"I thought it made a pfffft sound."

"Only in the movies. They're either using a BB gun with a silencer or they're muffling out the sound in the editing process."

He looked at the two Kalishnikovs and took the 104.

"This is lighter and has less recoil. We do not, however, want to be using this at all. If we are, that means we are in a spray fight and spray fights are messy. I don't like messy."

He then took the Barrett M107 .50 caliber and shoved that in the bag. He looked at the rest on the table, picked up a snub nose .38.

"Put this in your pocket. Use it only if absolutely necessary. It doesn't have a suppressor and unless there's a backhoe behind you, everybody will hear it."

Trevor put the rest of the rifles and pistols in the cabinet below the sink.

"There, I think we're set. You got a baseball hat?"
"No."

"Well, you're not going to look like a caddy with that damned Greek fisherman's hat, are you? Here." Trevor reached into the bag and tossed Bill a Calloway golf visor.

"Let's get the hell out of here."

They locked up the Cormorant and made their way to the water taxi at the commercial dock. They waited for the 4:10 p.m. boat that took twenty five minutes from dock to dock to get to Atlantic Sun. As Joe had noted, it was a local that piloted the boat. That was one less thing to worry about.

They got to the pro shop just before six and Trevor sent Bill in to get a scorecard. The legend showed the eighteen holes and their juxtaposition such that they could figure out how to get closest to the old hotel building and the maintenance sheds via the cart paths. Based on the discussions the three had the night before, these would be the logical places to lock someone up. For Trevor, it was simple. Wherever he saw armed guards around a building, that would be where Joe would be held.

The two ambled around the course, launching an occasional ball with a five iron Bill had stuffed in the bag, just for the hell of it. Bill figured to get a good laugh watching foursomes try to figure out who hit what. For almost an hour, they traveled the paths, avoiding the golfers, before they hit fairway number seventeen. The cart path wound within one hundred fifty yards of three major buildings. One was the Administration building. There was no one there. The other was the maintenance shed and while there was a lot of activity, Trevor could not make out a guard. The last building on the far right of the tee box had the 'Lodge' imprinted on it. There was a guard at the front entrance and as they walked further, another appeared on the far side.

"Bingo," Bill uttered.

They back tracked as if looking for a ball, then disappeared into the foliage. They found a good hiding place to rest and sat as the evening wore on. They would wait another forty five minutes for the sun to start its evening ritual and then make their move.

*

Chris had just listened to everything Joe Hackett had said. He understood it fairly well, but even as the situation was as dire as it was, he couldn't help how he felt.

"I still want the Talisman back. That son of a bitch had no right to take it."

"What the hell is more important to you?" Joe shot back. "Your life, or some damn piece of jewelry."

Chris thought for a moment.

"That's a good question. If I had to give up my life for something that had been so important to my family for decades; and would be for generations to come, I'm not sure I could turn away from it."

"Would it be worth your partner's life?" He looked directly at Ann.

Chris didn't hesitate.

"Hell, no. Not now, not ever."

"Then you have just placed your values where they belong. We need to get out of here alive and no amount of personal belongings, or artifacts, Jackie," he stared at the woman he had come to depend on, if not adore, with hardened eyes, "must deter us from that. All of that will sort itself out later, if at all. Our job is to escape, period. I think you made it very clear, Chris, that we are dealing with a cold blooded killer in Deming and I have no doubt about what Mr. Kane will do."

"How should we prepare?" Jackie asked.

"Tie your sneakers, be ready to run like hell, forget your bags, but get your passports."

Alvarro spoke to his sister. Jackie translated for the rest.

"My brother says we have to get to Ponta Delgada. He says the regional leader, Gustave Parcanto, will help us if we can get to him. He says we must not be waylaid by the military."

"Our only chance, then," Joe went on, "Is to make it to the Cormorant and ship out as fast as possible. We'll need a hell of a head start, it's just a trawler and it'll only do sixteen

314

knots, eighteen if we wind her up.   That's not going to get us there quickly."

"When will your guys come?" Ann asked.

"I pray it will be tonight and if it is, they'll be here within an hour, just as the sun sets. If they don't come tonight, I think we're done for."

*

"Maybe," Bill whispered, "You could create a diversion and I could sneak up behind him and knock him out."

"Bill, you seem like a decent guy, but you must understand that I am going to kill him.   At minimum, he's a thug, an ex-con, a mercenary who's killed a number of people. He's younger than you, stronger than you and he is probably well trained.   He may kill you with one well-placed blow.   He is guarding our friend, our partner, with intent to exterminate him at some point.   He isn't going to get a break or a warning shot."

Trevor pulled the pistol with the silencer from the golf bag.

"He won't be expecting this."   He leveled the piece over his arm and took careful aim in the last of the diminishing sunlight.   The wind was blowing in from the sea.

"With luck," he said, "We'll get an acoustic shadow and the other guard won't hear it."

"Thwunk".   The shot went straight and true.   The guard went down immediately, already on his way to meet his ancestors before he hit the ground.

Trevor got up and calmly clutched his golf bag and walked towards the lodge.

"Bill, help me drag that piece of dog meat over to the bushes there and if you want, get his ID."

"Whatever for?"

"So you can establish a scholarship fund in his name at his alma mater."

"Don't be such a bastard."

"Now, you're getting the hang of it, Bill. Grab whatever keys he has and let yourself in. I'll leave the golf bag here. Take the guard's rifle in with you and give it to Joe. I'll go around front and take care of the other fellow. Be careful."

In an instant, Trevor was in the shadows.

Bill let himself in and walked into the lobby where his skipper and four other people sat around a table.

"Thank God," Joe uttered. "I've never been so glad to see such a surly looking clod in my whole life."

Bill grinned from ear to ear. Within a minute, Trevor came through the front door, as if he were simply a tourist wanting to check in.

"Time to shit and git," he yelled. "My god, we have a coffee club, here."

"Just one merry band of incarcerated miscreants." Joe answered back.

Trevor looked over the fivesome and took in the beauty of the two completely different women.

"Merry indeed."

Bill tossed the rifle to Joe as they moved out.

"The plan?" Trevor asked.

"We get to the boat and get to Sao Miguel." Joe answered.

"They'll be after us within two hours. We won't stand a chance."

Jackie was translating to Alvarro and he had another idea.

"Alvarro says we should take the cutter. It's faster."

"Why don't we take them both?" Trevor offered.

Alvarro figured he could order the boat out, especially if he and four others were armed. It sat at the other side of the commercial dock from the water taxi, so there was little distance involved.

"First, let's get to the maintenance shed. You four swipe bags and carts. Take anything that will work. I'll keep them busy with questions about shipping my bag or whatever. Make your way to the south side of the hotel and dump the stuff and we'll meet you at the dock in about ten, fifteen minutes. I have a surprise planned for this crew." Trevor motioned Bill to follow him.

They managed to tie up two of the staff with an inordinate amount of conversation long enough for Chris, Ann, Jackie and Alvarro to make off with two golf carts. Once assured they had vanished into the coming darkness, Trevor and Bill thanked the young men and pulled their bag and hand cart off past the administration building to the watersports kiosk.

The lovely blonde was just locking up. Bill and Trevor waited a couple minutes and then Trevor set the C4 plastic with a two hour timer. Trevor hoisted the bag to his shoulder and Bill folded up the pull cart as they sauntered down the beach and in front of the hotel. They were right in front of the Beach Bar when Bill stopped them.

"Let's get a couple of beers to go."

"Now?."

"Yeah. If we end up taking the cutter, there won't be any booze on that bucket and I could surely use a beer right about now."

"Okay, let's do it.

They angled off to the bar, got four to go on a carrying tray and made off to the commercial dock.

"I would say, Bill, that this fairly well completes the tourist disguise."

*

Kane found the laptop in the bushes. The two men he sent to Santa Cruz to scour the docks and check out the airport came back in the late afternoon with nothing. There were a couple of American yachts there, but they were definitely not WorldGreen staffed. Of all the new arrivals in the past two weeks, there wasn't one that fit the description Kane had in mind. There was a Canadian fellow who had been asking around about missing boats or problems, but he was on a trawler sporting a Portuguese flag. Fellow boaters had indicated that was captained by a gentleman who spoke fluent Portuguese, albeit of the mainland dialect. Without digging much deeper, Kane assumed that Joe Hackett had been telling the truth. Ergo, there was no urgent need to go beat the pulp out of him, so he waited for his guards to make their evening report.

At nine thirty, the call did not come in. Kane waited an obligatory ten minutes, then decided that all was not right and made his way from the Security office past the maintenance buildings and fairway eighteen towards the Lodge. There were no guards posted. The doors were open and as he entered and scanned the dining area and hallway, immediately understood that no one was there.

It was too dark to go searching for bodies, so he decided that the escapees were his only priority. He called out an alert on his phone and rousted out all the off duty personnel. They would meet at security in ten minutes. It was then that the watersports kiosk blew all to hell.

Kane knew full well that he had been wrong. There were other WorldGreen activists out there and they knew what they were doing. He wasn't dealing with total amateurs here. He called Deming, who made his way down to the meeting while half the resort staff were battling the blaze and trying to save what equipment they could.

They were short yet another guard, the one who had been posted to the commercial dock. That instantly told Kane that his hostages were off the island. He took three of his men with him and asked Deming to hold the fort until all personnel had reported in and he had come back. What he found absolutely amazed him. Sitting at the farthest table from the beach bar and closest to the commercial dock was the Lt. Commander of the cutter and six of his crew.

"What in hell are you guys doing here?"

"We were boarded by the Lt. Colonel and three well-armed men. They kicked us off. Two of my men stayed. They powered up and took off well over an hour ago."

"Why didn't you report this to me?"

"See that man at the end of the dock? He has a high powered sniper rifle. They told us he would kill any of us who left the table. We saw the rifle. They were dead serious."

Kane nodded and left very carefully, making his way back around the tables and around the Beach Bar past the hotel towards the village. He took a quick right angle and made his way to the south side of the dock. He could get within fifty yards of the man, but then would have to sprint and hope for the best. It was dark and even with a good infrared scope, it would be hard to hit a moving target. He burst into a full run and was on top of the man in less than six seconds. The old man stared up at him in wonder and in fear as he saw the pistol leveled at him. He was leaning on his cane.

"What are you doing here?" Kane asked him angrily.

"Some guy gave me a hundred euros to sit here for a couple of hours and point my cane at the beach from time to time. It sounded stupid, but hell, I was here anyway for the sunset, so I said sure and he took off."

"Where'd he go?"

"Can't say. A bunch of people got on the water taxi and about ten minutes after that, that navy boat left."

CHAPTER 19

Sea Cruise

Joe had Jackie, Alvarro, Chris and Ann on the covered flybridge with him. The Cormorant had left the Santa Cruz docks just before nine p.m. Jackie sat in the other twin seat and Alvarro stood beside her. Chris and Ann sat at one of the two corner bench seats with a table in front of them. Behind them on the open deck sat the fake circular vent housing that held the .50 caliber machine gun.

Chris had his head in his hands, elbows on the table and shook his head like a dog flicking off water.

"Ahhhgghh. It just galls me to leave that behind." He gave himself a little slap and looked lovingly at Annie.

"I am so sorry, Annie, for all of this. This adventure has turned out to be quite a mess. Just think, less than three months ago we were sitting under the night sky at my fifth wheel, listening to the last train out of Silverton and the horses at the ranch next door. I couldn't have imagined then that we would be here, like this."

"Stop beating yourself up. Remember, I came willingly. And, no, I didn't expect this, but I'm still glad I'm with you."

"Let's hope we get out okay. By end of tomorrow, I'm sure we'll have been done with the authorities and can check into a nice hotel, minus all of our belongings."

"We'll have to buy all new stuff. That's not so bad, is it?"

"Thank God they didn't confiscate our wallets."

Joe turned from the pilot seat.

"That's only so they could bury your IDs with you. By the way, can any of you read charts?"

"I can," Chris said. "I did a little sailing in Narragansett Bay in my youth."

"Good. See if you can plot me a course around the east side of Terciera that will bring us into Sao Miguel on the north side directly across from Ponta Delgada."

"Won't that take us out of the way?" Jackie asked.

"Exactly. If they think we're headed to Ponta Delgada, they'll think we took the direct route around the west side and we'd cruise into the city from the south.   This way, we'd come into port at Fannais De Luz, then, go overland into the city. We should be able to disappear."

Alvarro was working the radio, attempting to contact Gustave Parcanto, but they were still out of range and it was late.   By morning, they would have a better chance.

"Nothing?" Joe asked.

"Not a peep." Jackie came over and rubbed him on the neck and shoulders.

"Doing okay?"

"For now."

Trevor stood at the helm of the cutter as it hit cruising speed of twenty six knots.

"You sure you can run this thing?"   Trevor asked Bill.

"It's an old Point Class ship.   We're undermanned and it's a damned good thing those two seamen volunteered to help us, but we'll be fine.   I may have to run around a bit, but I'm used to the critter."

"What about the weaponry?"

"Your golf bag there will do fine."

"No, you jack ass, the boat."

"The mortar's useless to us, unless we want to siege a fort, but the Brownings will defend us well.   Might be able to use that small cannon in the right spot, but basically the machine guns will do the job."

"You're familiar with this ordinance?"

"In the five years I spent in Okinawa, we could only run WWIII missile test simulations a couple of times a week. That left a lot of time to play with guns and we did.   We had two of these old point class ships out there at the base and would go out with them on some of the drills.   Yeah, I've played with these toys.   They're fun toys."

Reassured, Trevor summarized his plan.

"They won't try to get at us till morning and we should be in Horta by noon.   Then, we will have to blend into the populace and find a decent place to hide. We'll be waiting for a call and we'll figure out how to get to Ponta Delgada later. Meanwhile, see if you can get a couple hours of sleep and relieve me by three. I'll need some rest, too."

*

Kane sent a team into Santa Cruz by ten p.m. It took over two hours to search the village, the airport, the marinas and three of the outlying villages, Luz, Guadeloupe, and Santa Vicente. None of the escapees were on the island.

One plane had left for Ponta Delgada at 8:45 pm. The passenger list did not name any of the people Kane had sequestered. From the Dock Master, he learned that two boats had left the slips, one a seventy six foot Trawler and the other a hundred sixty foot Italian made yacht on its way to its new owners in Fort Lauderdale. The navy cutter had not come near the village docks and was assumed well out to sea.

Kane had no armed boats that could catch up to the cutter or the trawler with a three hour head start. Deming's cigarette boat could catch them in an hour and a half, but it was in dry dock at Santa Cruz for an overhaul, so it would be the helicopters that would have to intercept the two boats. He informed the pilots at one a.m. to be ready to leave at first light. That would give them about four hours sleep.

Deming was still up with him and was pacing in his office.

"They have to be going to Ponta Delgada. They'll be trying to get help." Deming was obviously worried.

"Maybe. They could also be on their way to Horta and seek protection from officials there. And, the cutter's gone. We don't know if they're all on the cutter or all on the trawler or a combination of both. I am going to assume the Lt. Colonel is on the cutter."

"It doesn't matter, Kane. Actually, that might be to our advantage. The man pirated the ship in the first place and we can charge thievery and murder here to boot, so I think we

322

should go after both of them and blow them the hell out of the water."

"It's your call, Boss. I have no qualms about rectifying this situation. I've lost three good men here and I don't like losing my men."

*

In Lisbon, progress in staffing a new cabinet was going well. Everyone on the short list for open positions had been contacted, save one. President Elect Cavadas had attempted to contact his new General in charge of forces in the Azores to no avail for the past four days.

Communications from Parcanto and Colonel DeSilva indicated that neither knew where Alvarro Parros was. That sounded insane to him and it gnawed at him so much that he called in the Minister of Defense.

"Ferdinand, I know you sent the appointment I requested. Everyone in the loop got copies, so I can't understand why no one seems to know where Alvarro is. I know the Islands are spread out, but it can't be that difficult."

"Understood, Sir, but if some people don't want him to be found, then it might be very difficult to find him."

"I thought of that. If I leave here for a few days, can you promise me that the country won't go to hell?"

"Things will remain stable, Sir."

"Then, I want to get a flight to Ponta Delgada. Do we have anything I can use?"

"You can't have the President's jet, not yet, but we do have another that the Vice-President uses as do other Cabinet Ministers when necessary. I don't think it is in use currently. There's not much call for official travel in between administrations, but I'll check on its status."

"How soon can I get out?"

"With luck, tomorrow morning. It's a three hour flight. You could probably be there by noon."

"Good. Let's make it happen."

"Sir, you are our President Elect.   You should have a detail assigned to you.   I would be remiss if I allowed this without proper protections."

"Give me an officer and a rifleman.   I can carry as well. That should do us fine. Okay?"

"As you wish, Sir."

*

At five thirty am, the sun shed its first daylight on the eastern shores of Atlantic Sun's Island.   The remote, self-contained thatched villas on the private and posh Gibralter Beach; the most recently built and reserved for only the wealthiest, most discerning guests and celebrities, were the first to catch the morning rays on the secluded shoreline.

At the heliport on the other side of the Island, the two Atlantic Sun emblazoned Huey helicopters took off, each with a pilot and a co-pilot and each headed in a different direction, each with their gun ports opened.

At one hundred and fifty miles an hour top speed, it took almost two hours to come within range of the navy cutter headed to Horta.   Unmolested, it would be there in another two hours, but Kane had guessed right.   One boat was definitely on a direct path to the city on Faial.

Trevor had also guessed right.   He knew the only way they could come after them was by air.   He had Bill prepare the arms as well as possible;   setting the cannon for altitude fire at a thousand yards, elevated twenty degrees and the Brownings at the same elevation, but ready to fire at a moment's notice.

They heard it before they saw it.   Bill was already at the machine gun turret.   The two seamen on board had been well advised to stay below and keep to the engine room. Trevor had his M107 on the bench next to him.

The Huey came out of a low hanging puff of a cloud and was within seven hundred yards when it started firing.

Trevor ripped the helm to the left, giving the broadside to the copter. The Brownings sat across from each other back of midship so Bill, on the port side gun could now take aim at their assailant. He cut it loose as it bucked and kicked with every pounding round tracing at the Huey. He might have hit it, but he couldn't tell because it swirled around behind in an instant and opened up on the Pilot House.

The copter's machine guns tore up the seats, the windows, the benches and the back of Trevor's legs up to his hips. He had been hit several times, either directly or from the ricochet of the lead off the boat. He locked the helm and hit the floor, fingering for his rifle as he did so. He got the Barrett down and steadied her. He aimed for the fuselage and got off six rounds before he passed out. He missed his target, but dinged up the tail prop enough to choke it.

Meanwhile, the cutter had turned in a slow circle and Bill abandoned the machine gun to run for the 20mm cannon on the front deck swivel pad. The Huey hung in the air for a moment as the cutter turned. Bill had only to adjust the cannon a hair and then let the curvature of the ship's motion bring it on to the Huey, which seemed like it was dead in his path.

Bill let it roll into the shot and fired. The crash from the cannon was deafening and the recoil enough to knock Bill on his ass, but his aim was as good as it ever was and the shell disintegrated the Huey in a ball of fire that exploded into a shower of flame, smoke and oil that cascaded into the ocean.

'Best skeet shot I ever made', Bill hummed to himself.

But, now he had another problem. The cutter was going in circles as he clambered up to the Pilot House. Trevor was a mess, blood all over the place. Bill got cushions from the benches and laid Trevor's legs up on to them. He tore his pants off and found five holes in the man; two in the left thigh, one shattered the right knee, one in the calf and another in the right hip. He got the Medical unit out from the cabinet and worked on all the wounds until he was convinced he had stopped the bleeding. It was only then that he considered the boat. He unlocked the helm and altered the course to Ponta Delgada. He would have to get Trevor to the Hospital soon or he would lose him.

Kane's second Atlantic Sun Huey flew directly to Ponta Delgada over the west side of Terciera. They found nothing on the way and circled the city overhead of the marina for a closer look, but did not expect to see the trawler. They should have seen it on the way. It was now eight thirty and there was no sight of it. They radioed into the Security office with their long range system and Kane directed them to fly back over the east side of Sao Miguel and then the ocean side of Terciera. He indicated also that he had heard nothing from copter number one, which should have reported back by now.

Huey number two headed out over the mountainous eastern side of Sao Miguel. The morning sun was now at an angle that drove blinding light and ocean reflection into their eyes, so they made a wide arc out over the sea to come back to the northwest towards Terciera. Thirty miles out they spotted what they thought was the trawler on a course southwest towards the center part of the north shore.

The Huey swooped down to buzz over the ship to get a good look, radioed back that there were five people on board, one, the Lt. Colonel and got back confirmation to shoot the boat down.

Chris looked up at the copter as it buzzed overhead.

"An Atlantic Sun Copter? What are they going to do, throw beach balls at us?"

Jackie looked at Chris with a frown.

"You don't know Brian Deming like I do."

The Huey came out of its rotation and settled in behind the Cormorant's stern at approximately three hundred yards, then leveled out. It opened fire at two hundred and closing. Bullets scattered about the Flybridge, pinging the deck, the fake ventilator cover and smashing into the back of the wheel house. Alvarro was hit on the first sweep, once in the thigh and once in the hip.

Joe bellowed at the top of his lungs.

"Get below. Fast. Girls, get Alvarro into the salon,

now."

Ann looked at Chris grimly.

"I told you it would unravel.   He's lost his mind."

"And we're right in the damn middle of it."

Jackie and Ann grabbed Alvarro and hauled him to the stairwell that led to the salon.   Jackie took his feet while Ann held him under his shoulders.   His blood was trickling on Jackie's face as they eased him down.

The Huey had circled and was coming in again.

"Chris, take the helm.   Start zig zagging."

Chris did as he was bid and Joe went to the ventilator cover, flipped up the latches and pulled the hood over.   The specially mounted Browning M2 was already belt connected to the two hundred link box, so Joe only had to flick off the safety and cut it loose.   He let the rounds fly as fast as the Huey's were coming in.   It was a fierce firefight for about forty five seconds and the Huey veered off planning to make another sweep.   Joe slumped to the deck.   He was hit in the shoulder.   He yelled at Chris.   Chris left the wheel and dragged Joe to his feet back into the covered fly bridge and sat him in the Captain's chair.

"I can hold the boat, Chris, but I can't fire the gun. You'll have to do it."

"I've never shot at anything or anybody in my life."

"You'll have to.   Otherwise, we die. We all die. You, me, Jackie, Ann, Alvarro.   Do you want that to happen?"

"Good God, no."

"Then, get your ass out there.   Shoot the bastards. Just aim it and pull the trigger. Now, go, get the hell out of here."

Joe held on to the helm with his good arm and kicked the boat hard to starboard.   The Huey shot across the bow of the boat and circled again, firing even as it did so.

Chris felt the gun on his shoulders, swiveled it back and forth a couple of times and looked up the nozzle between the protective plates.   If he could think of it as a video game, he thought he could do it, maybe.   The Huey rolled into position and opened fire.   Chris gripped the trigger and felt the kick of each round every split second as the bullets flared out at the target.   He imagined points on the screen as he lit up the copter with hit after hit.   If only it were a game, a real game, not this. The rounds were flashing out in rapid succession even as the bullets clanged around him.   He tried not to take notice, but kept firing until he saw the smoke pour out from the underbelly of the Huey.   It took a quick dive towards the water then landed with a thunk and a splash. Chris quit firing.   He saw two men rapidly toss an inflatable into the water.   It expanded almost instantly as they dove in to latch on.   The Huey was going under and by the time the men clambered up over the side, the last of the propeller became invisible in the rolling two foot swells.

The Cormorant was safe.

Chris went to Joe's side.

"Good work, Chris.   You might just have saved our ass."

"We've got to get you to a hospital, Alvarro, too."

"I've already set a new course.   We'll go straight into Ponta Delgada.   Get one of the girls up here and help me stop this bleeding."

Chris called out and Annie came up the stairwell.

"Alvarro's going to make it.   Jackie is tending to him now."

She looked at Joe.

"Chris, help me with him.   Let's get him wrapped up."

*

At the Security Office, Kane had gotten the last communication from Huey number two.   They'd been hit and were going into the drink.   They were thirty miles out from Sao Miguel and the Cormorant appeared to be headed around the Island to Ponta Delgada.   He turned to Brian Deming, who sat next to him, his hands folded and thumping lightly on the desk.

"I don't know what those guys had on that boat, but taking down a Huey is no small matter.   These people came prepared." He looked intently at Deming.

"We're pretty much out of options. I can only assume Huey number one is out of commission. That means we have nothing out there and nothing here to intercept them."

"We have the jet." Brian offered.

"Yes, at Santa Cruz. We still have to get over there and get off the runway. They'll be in the harbor in less than two hours, maybe an hour and a half."

"Load up. I'll get my hardware. We'll get them ourselves. Lord knows, if you leave it up to someone else, this is what you get."

Kane said nothing, but smiled and agreed.

"Candy, once airborne, we can be at Ponta Delgada in a half hour. We can run in ahead of them and get to the docks to greet them. Royally. I will take personal pleasure in exterminating every one of those son of a bitch, bitch, bastards."

Deming armed himself. He picked out his long barreled automatic pistol with the silencer. In the back of his mind, he knew his reactions were coming out of anger, out of his fierce determination to destroy all that opposed him, but in his rage, he still had enough sanity to understand that he needed to be able to escape from this mess and live out his dream life. He would have to kill them as silently and deftly as possible, then disappear.

He threw on a mid-length London Fog raincoat and the two of them headed to the commercial dock where a patrol boat waited. At top end speed, they were in Santa Cruz in less than twenty minutes. Kane had called ahead for a taxi that took them to the airport. They hustled up their pilot, secured authorization from the tower to use their own strip and within forty five minutes of having left the Security Office, they were on the tarmac, ready for take-off. By the time they landed in Ponta Delgada, it would be an hour and fifteen minutes. From the air terminal, they had to cross in front of the Fort de Sao Bras and the post compound past the city pools to the marina. It was going to be close.

*

Lisbon II took off at eight a.m.   President Elect Cavadas had two staff on board with him; Colonel Orlando Delacudra of the Chief of Staff's office was the officer assigned the task.   Delacudra was normally a liason between the Joint Chiefs and the Defense Minister.   Ferdinand Pechorro had decided that the President Elect needed a staff member of rank, a rank sufficient to command the attention of Colonel DeSilva, if need be.   The second, a Sergeant, Ricardo Serraipa, was a rifleman in the nineteenth infantry. He carried an M16, another exported US arms supply for the Portuguese army, and a sidearm.   The Colonel had a sidearm as well, and Pedro Anabel Cavadas had a pistol in a shoulder holster under his sport coat.

They cruised at twenty eight thousand feet.   It was a beautiful day and the sea was clearly visible through light, wispy clouds as they crossed the near Atlantic.   Pedro had never been to the Azores.   He was intrigued at the possibility of a pleasant stay for a few days where he might get to know, first hand, the remote Islands he would soon have to govern from the distance in Lisbon.

The flight would take a shade less than three hours and they expected to be on the ground by eleven a.m.   Pedro hoped he would find Alvarro by evening, such that they could have a fine dinner and a long conversation.   Alvarro was not only a potential cabinet minister, but a good friend, who had been with Pedro from his humble beginnings in politics in Braga.   He delighted at the idea of renewing that friendship and having his friend work in his cabinet.

They cruised at twenty eight thousand feet.   It was a beautiful day and the sea was clearly visible through light, wispy clouds as they crossed the near Atlantic.   Pedro had never been to the Azores.   He was intrigued at the possibility of a pleasant stay for a few days where he might get to know, first hand, the remote Islands he would soon have to govern from the distance in Lisbon.

They started their initial descent ninety miles from the airport.   It would take a half hour to land, taxi, dock and feel Terra Firma under the feet, so Pedro looked out at the increasingly closer ocean and the eastern tip of Sao Miguel in the distance.   He could see the famous Furnas Caldera high up into the mountain ridge.   He also thought he saw a flicker of silver coming at them from the North.

The President Elect's jet was cleared for landing and began its final descent when another private jet cut directly in front of it and screamed in for a landing at high speed. The pilot of Lisbon II pulled up hard and banked left, hoping to avoid the tailings of jet fire in his face. He nosed up fiercely, surprising his passengers to the point of alarm, and made the swing outward to redirect his landing. The radio chatter included an incredible amount of swearing by the tower, but he was finally able to obtain a new authorization and lined up for his strip.

"I would like," Pedro said to his Colonel, "to arrest that son of a bitch who just did that. Can I do that?"

"You don't yet have authorization, Sir." Colonel Delacudra answered. "But, I do, and I will authorize you to make such an arrest, should you so wish."

"I would wish that very much. I'm sure the fifteen extra minutes that it would take wouldn't present much of a difficulty for my friend, who doesn't even know I'm coming."

"Very good, Sir."

Deming's jet hit the runway intended for Lisbon II. The pilot pulled up to an open dock and shut the engines down. The hatch way opened. Deming came down the steps first, clad in his raincoat, followed by Kane and another Blackthorn agent. Deming wasted no time, walking just short of an Olympic speed pace as a Security Agent confronted him. The officer was about to pull his piece to insist that Deming follow him when Kane came up behind him and smashed his head with the butt of his forty five.

"Here, secure that, you asshole."

The man fell to the Tarmac.

Deming and Kane went into the terminal. The other agent stood guard by the plane. As soon as they had entered the terminal, Lisbon II came down. It too glided up to the terminal and set its hatch open and steps down. Pedro came out first, followed by the Colonel and the rifleman. He noticed the other jet right away and the three walked over to the guard who stood poised to act. However, in the face of a full Colonel, regaled with all manner of honors, he was hesitant to follow through. Pedro walked up to him and said.

"You're under arrest and this plane has been

confiscated. Sergeant, disarm this man and guard this plane. Here, give that rifle to the Colonel. Wait here for us. I will send assistance." He turned to the agent. "Where is your boss, your passengers headed?"

"To the docks, Sir." Was the reply

Pedro and the Colonel went after Deming and Kane, unaware of the nature of the men they were stalking. Those two had cleared the terminal and were on their way past the Sao Bras to the marina.

The Cormorant came into the commercial harbor and received instructions to tie up at slip two thirteen. Joe had indicated they had an emergency and that they would need to get to the hospital directly. They did not want and ambulance, fearing intervention by the police or worse, the military, but required only a taxi to take them from the docks parking lot to the medical center.

Jackie and Ann hoisted Alvarro on to their shoulders as they led him off the ship down the wooden deck to the main pier, while Chris helped Joe off the boat behind them. The fivesome hobbled to the concrete pier ahead and the taxi was waiting in the lot fifty yards past the private entrances to the marina's slips.

Joe asked if they could switch. He could see that the girls were having a hard time keep Alvarro aloft, he nearly a dead weight on both of them. Chris switched with Jackie and he and Ann were better able to hoist Alvarro upwards. Joe was doing fine with Jackie, actually much better, since he could walk on his own, but loved leaning into her. He put his head on hers.

"Thank you so much." He kissed her forehead.

They were within twenty yards of the taxi when they heard shots. Deming had slung out the pistol with the silencer from his raincoat and had begun firing at them from one hundred fifty plus feet plus away. The first salvo was short, but the second sprayed enough led to hit Ann in the shoulder. She instinctively fell, Alvarro going with her and Chris dropped him down to dive over and cover Annie. Joe immediately saw what was going on in front of him. He pushed Jackie away and pulled out his pistol. He was the only one in the group armed and he stood like a policeman, in a stance with his legs apart, elbow and arm locked, firing back at his assailant.

Deming was running out of time. He moved up quickly and hid behind an old Citroen, firing a third round from a new clip. If he were going to escape, he would have to end this soon.

Pedro and the Colonel had picked up their pace, waving off all potential intrusions and were not more than two hundred yards behind when they first heard shots. They closed some of the distance in seconds and Pedro could see the man in the raincoat, crouched behind a silver colored car, firing at five people, four of them already on the ground. The large uniformed man behind him held a forty five in his hand, but was not firing. He simply looked like a spectator. Pedro scanned back quickly. Of the four on the ground, two were women, fairly far apart and there were two men down, one in a Portuguese Army uniform.

"I can't be having this," Pedro yelled. "Give me the damn rifle."

The Colonel handed it to him.

Pedro dropped to his knee. He fired seven shots in rapid succession from the twenty magazine clip. The first two whizzed by Deming close enough for him to feel the breeze of them as they clanged into a truck beyond. He was aware he was being shot at for only a split second as the third round hit him in the stomach, dropping his head slightly, just enough so that the fourth shot grazed off his temple instead of burrowing into his brain. The fifth and sixth shots hit him in the right hip, the seventh went wide into another car. He went to the ground. The man behind him holstered his forty five, crouched and ran through the parking lot out into the Avenida Du Don Henrique and disappeared into the traffic and the melee that was now brewing.

Pedro Anabel Cavadas, President Elect of Portugal, the one-time highlands partisan, flipped the rifle to Colonel Delacudra, who looked at him in astonishment.

"Like riding a bicycle, Colonel."

CHAPTER 20

Resolutions

Leigh Deming got the email when he came home from his clinic.   A certified letter was to follow, but since it was coming from Portugal, there was no telling when that would arrive.

Leigh's pathway to adulthood varied a great deal from that of his older brother.   He left the family home in Durango to also go to school at Colorado State in Fort Collins and did his pre-med there.   He went to medical school at the University of New Mexico in Albuquerque and followed that with an internship at the University Hospital.

There, he met Sylvia from Guadalajara.   They married right after med school and she helped him get through it and the internship that followed.   They moved back to Durango for Leigh to join the staff at the regional hospital.

A few years later, they moved to Grand Junction to work at the largest regional hospital on the western slope and Leigh soon opened up his own small clinic.   It was a simple practice that featured a PA, an RN and two office staff, but it gave Leigh the freedom to make his own hours, assist at the Hospital and also donate some of his time at the VA hospital on the east side of town.

Most people thought that Doctors made fortunes. That was hardly the case.   After furnishing the clinic and its monthly obligations, there were staff to pay for and all the necessary fringe benefits.   There were colossal insurance costs, for the clinic, for malpractice and for his work at both hospitals.   After setting aside something for retirement, in hopes that it might ever come, a decent living wage was obtained, but that's all.   Sylvia had contributed heavily to the family's income with her career as a dental hygienist.   It allowed them to live well on a nine acre ranch just outside of Fruita, halfway from that quaint western village and Grand Junction, the biggest city on the western side of Colorado's Rockies.

The property abutted the Colorado River and had great views of the mountains to the east and south as well as the Colorado Monument to the west. That national park was a convulsion of twisted canyons and arroyos cut from the ancient sea bed by the great Colorado River and the streams and freshets that wound their way to the river valley below. Two thousand foot spires and small crested buttes rose up from the valley, imprinted with millennia of rock strata that gleamed, almost crystalline in the morning sunlight. The horse trails around the park and out into the valley were considered the finest in the State.

It was with great pride, then, that Leigh and Sylvia were able to get their oldest daughter, Helena, the palomino that she wanted for her sixteenth birthday. Not only did she have a fine scrub pasture to feed her horse on, but endless horse paths on which to ride right outside her own gate.

They led an idyllic life of modest means, slightly into the upper middle class and considered themselves to be three of the luckiest people around. Leigh loved the valley, loved the river and the mountains, loved the city that had grown modestly, but beautifully into a cosmopolitan center and loved the Village of Fruita with its lovely cafes and authentic western storefronts. Other than an occasional conference and the annual family vacation up north, Leigh had no desire to ever leave his sanctuary.

So, it was beyond disturbing that he should be forced to go to Ponta Delgada, Portugal, to identify his older brother and to make decisions about his life. And, it would be at his cost. He had been told, however, that as the only living relative and heir, he and only he, could make the life or death decision. Brian was in a life supported coma.

Begrudgingly, he left home from the regional airport to Denver, caught a non-stop flight to Dulles, from there to Boston where he caught a red eye to Ponta Delgada. After seventeen hours, six time changes and very little sleep on any of the legs of the journey, he arrived at the Medical Center of the Greater Azores bleary, irritated and distraught at the duties he had to perform.

He met the staff Liaison who handled translation at the

main desk and was ushered up to intensive care.   She led him down the hallway to a large private room where his older brother had been placed and entered to meet the physician in charge.   He could see the arrangement of IVs, the Intubator, and other supportive equipment that was keeping his brother alive. He looked down upon this man who had been a large part of his life and saw a shell of the vibrant human being he used to be.

The Doctor explained to him through the Liaison that there was a slight chance that Brian might recover; that it was remote, extremely remote, and that if he did recover, he would never have his full faculties again; and that he would probably require substantial care, should he even regain consciousness.   The Liaison left the room to give Leigh some time to sit with his brother and to think about what he wanted to do.

Leigh looked up at the attending Physician who had stayed behind.   The Doctor could not understand English. It mattered not to Leigh in the slightest at the moment.   He looked up at the physician, boyish pain evident in his face.

"You know, he was a miserable prick to me.   He teased me endlessly when I was little.   We lived about a block away from the Animas River.   When I was four and five, he would bring home snakes just to frighten me.   It scared the shit out of me."

Leigh paused for a moment and sighed.   "He knew I loved toads.   I liked to catch them.   He would take them, stick firecrackers in their mouths, light them and throw them in the air to watch them explode.   I would cry for hours."

"When I was nine," Leigh went on, "He shot me in the knee twice with a BB gun.   It hurt for weeks."

The Doctor looked at Leigh and recognized the pain on his face, but had no idea what he was talking about.

"When he was in High School, he treated me like a bag of dog shit.   I was a nuisance.   Then, he went off to college, became a big shot football player, a staff sergeant and came back home to start his real estate business.   Even the two years I lived in town, I never saw him.   He was too busy wheeling and dealing and rubbing every one's face in it.

337

Nobody got in his way.   He would chew them up and spit them out."

"You see, my brother was a first class bastard. He didn't care about anyone or anything, except himself and his ambitions.   He had good intuition, though, and made a huge success of himself, but I'm sure he burned a lot of people on the way."

"I wonder what he would do in my place?   Would he let me live?"   Leigh pondered for a few moments. "No, he would let me go.   I would be a burden. I would be in his way."

Leigh looked again at the Doctor, who was waiting patiently for a response he could understand.   Leigh knew he had been venting, but he needed to.   He took his finger and ran it across his throat.   He knew the Doctor could understand that.

The Liaison came back in.

"Have you decided what you want to do?"

"Pull the plug.   Let him go.   It's time for him to answer for his life."

Leigh handed the woman a card.

"I'll be flying up to Graciosa this afternoon.   I'll be staying at Atlantic Sun.   I have a free room.   You can reach me there when it's over.   In the meantime, I am going to drink at the bar, also for free, until I am good and drunk, the jet lag disappears, and I begin to look like a huge problem.   I'll come back in a couple of days to make sure he's dead and sign all the paperwork."

And with that, Leigh Deming forever parted company with his only brother.

*

Jackie sat at the desk of the executive offices of Atlantic Sun.   In front of her were the three copies of the fully executed agreement that transferred all of the properties from EngenUnity to Brian Deming. They came in three days after the firefight in Ponta Delgada that had left Brian in a coma. They awaited Brian's original signature.

In most courts of law, an electronic signature was not

considered valid or binding until an original signature could be obtained. Jackie had been advised by corporate counsel under David Deeds' guidance to package the documents up and send them back. It was if they never existed. EngenUnity would retain control of Atlantic Sun, the Habitat, the airstrip, the boats, the planes, the sub; everything in total.

David had asked Jackie to stay on and manage the operation until all the wrangling and investigations were completed. She agreed to do that under the stipulation that she alone would negotiate with the Portuguese government. It was no secret now that her brother was the General in charge of the military operations for the Azores and Blackthorn's presence had been replaced by a detail of the Federal Army under direct command of Alvarro Parros.

Commander Charles "Candy" Kane had overpowered the Sergeant guarding Brian's jet on the day of the fire fight and had rejoined his own staff at Atlantic Sun to make his escape. That was no surprise to Jackie; that man could overpower a tank and the corporate jet had returned within the hour of the shooting back to Graciosa. Kane had rounded up his team, packed all that was theirs and had left Santa Cruz on board Brian's jet two hours after his return. Late that day they were back in Zurich. Kane left the jet at the airport. He couldn't give a damn about what might happen to it. He simply reported back to Magruder for a new assignment.

When Blackthorn deserted Atlantic Sun, they left the artifacts in the safe. Apparently, that was an entanglement Kane didn't need or want, but Jackie was keeping that information to herself. In no way would EngenUnity ever take position of the findings of Atlantis. The artifacts belonged to Portugal and she would see that they stayed there.

That was not the only thing she didn't tell David Deeds. She would not return to the States any time soon, if ever. She had found her brother and that, to her, was the start of having a family. And, she had found Joe, the man completely opposite of any she had ever known. He had saved her life. She was sure of that. She had grown a great fondness for him and he for her.   She wouldn't leave him and he wasn't going anywhere, not from the hospital for a couple of weeks nor for months from the Islands.

Atlantic Sun would need a complete management overhaul.   That would take a great deal of time and there was no clear vision of what might happen with the Portuguese government under the new President.   It was good that Alvarro had his confidence.   It would cut through a lot of red tape.

Meanwhile, she needed to go back to Ponta Delgada that afternoon.   She had to see Joe and Alvarro would be heading to the mainland that evening.   She also had to return a certain item to Chris Eberhardt, as much as it pained her to do so.

*.

At the opposite end of the intensive care ward, across from the nurses' station, Trevor Hagan regained consciousness.   He had been out four days.   When Bill had guided the cutter to port with the help of the two navy seamen, Trevor had lost four pints of blood, which had to be infused immediately.   Of all his wounds, only two were severe and the one to the knee would take multiple surgeries to repair. He would remain at the hospital for weeks.

Bill came in to see him every day and noticed the name on his chart changed on the third day.   He had given the staff the Dylan Kerrigan IDs and that was the initial name on the chart, but since Trevor came in with multiple gunshot wounds, formal investigations were required and his true identity discovered.   He faced several counts of eco-terrorism in England going back twenty five years and they demanded his extradition.

Bill was allowed to see Trevor momentarily and speak to him as he awoke, but was hastily exited when Trevor became groggy again.   Staff would work him hard to keep him awake in the next few hours.

Bill moved on to Joe Hackett's room on the second floor.   Joe was recovering nicely and could be released in a week or so.   He entered the room to see Joe sitting upright, grimacing at the tray of food in front of him.

He looked up at Bill.

"Send me back to Galway and throw me in the Dubh. What'd I'd give for a decent sandwich and a cold beer."

"You want me to sneak something in here?"

"If you can manage it."

"Anything, Skip, just ask for it."

Joe nodded his head.

"So have you decided?"

"Pretty much.   I'm flying back tomorrow.   However, I'm packing up Renee and we'll be back here in a week. We're going to spend the winter here.   To hell with the damn cold.   Just thinking about it gives me the chills, and after seeing this place, it's no contest.   We'll do fine here. In the spring, I'll help you take the Cormorant back to Quebec, if that's what you want to do."

"They're not going to like you being gone all winter at HQ"

"Joe, I'll be seventy in March.   I don't give a damn. And, I don't need to work. You know why I like casinos?"

Joe shook his head.

"I won a nice jackpot years ago and I bought a farmette in southeastern Ontario right below Ottawa.   I rented it out and built it up.   We sold it as a small agri-business when wheat prices skyrocketed.   Renee is a prudent investor and we haven't needed to work for years.   I just did it for kicks. After this little adventure, I don't think I need any more kicks. I think we'll just sit back and enjoy them damn golden years."

"They let me use the computer this morning, Bill, and I was able to skype Quebec City and talk with Whiteford.   You know, when they told me that you were going to be assigned to me as my marine engineer, I was elated.   You were a bit of a legend at WorldGreen then.   Now, Bill, you are The Legend.   I think they'd let you do anything you wanted as long as they could say you were still affiliated with them.   And Bill, I'm glad you're going to be staying here.   I think I might need a best man."

*

On the second floor, at the other end of the Medical Center from Intensive Care, Chris sat in the most uncomfortable vinyl chair he could ever remember.   Annie had been in and out of sleep, recovering from her second operation.   Her collarbone had to be repaired, but she was recovering well.   She could be released in a few days.

Alvarro walked into the room.   Alvarro had healed the quickest of them all, his wounds only superficial.   He was sporting his new uniform, that of the Brigadier General in charge of all military forces in the Azores.

Chris and Ann were confused until Alvarro spoke.

"I'm glad you're doing so well, Ann."   He offered.

"You speak English?" Chris asked.

"Quite well, actually.   We had to learn it in High School and I also took it in college."

"Why didn't you tell us?" Ann chipped in, groggy, but still awake enough to be peeved.

"Look at it from my point of view.   I'm a Portuguese Officer.   I'm a prisoner at the Resort.   Four people get thrown in with me, one of them my sister whom I haven't seen in over twenty years.   I don't know any of you.   I don't know who you represent.   Two guys burst in with guns after subduing the guards and I don't know them either and neither do you.   I'm already in deep shit, anyway, and I don't know who to trust and I'm not even sure of my sister.   Wouldn't you hide behind a language for a while if you could?"

They both nodded.

"I've made the rounds," he added.   "And Jackie will be in later.   I have to meet her at the airport.   We'll get about fifteen minutes and then I have to board a flight for Lisbon. The inauguration is tomorrow."

"Will you be coming back?"   Chris asked.

"Yes, for a short time, but I'm going to be going on a

342

mission for Pedro. I'm sorry, I guess I should get used to calling him Mr. President. In any case, he won't tell me what it is yet. He wanted to confer with the Solicitor General. I do know it has something to do with what you and Jackie were talking about that night in the Habitat. Jackie put me on to it and we did a little research. It appears we do have some distinctly unique oceanic rights, but we'll see."

"I wish you the best in whatever endeavor you take up," Ann offered. "If I can be of any help, you can reach me through Chris. I don't think we're going anywhere for a week, at least."

"I was hoping we might call on you. We may need you both for our investigation. I have spoken with the others. Bill is down with Joe now and Trevor is here for some time, but we do have a problem with him. The English want him back."

"You can delay him, can't you?" Ann asked.

"A great deal, but perhaps not indefinitely. There will be a lot of legal wrangling."

"I would take his case. Without him, none of us would be sitting here. I won't let him be taken back. Besides, I believe there was an amnesty a few years back for all IRA activists and I don't think they can rightfully drag him back. I think they'll just put pressure on you till you give in."

"Pedro won't do that. He'll dig in his heels. But, are you sure you can do this?"

"You can take an international case from anywhere, but you have to retain a barrister in England to present it. We'd do all the work and it would be delayed through intermediaries constantly. We could tie it up for years. You and I together can probably keep him here for eternity."

"I like it. We'll make it happen. Thank you, Ann."

"Thank you, Alvarro. We are blessed to have met you and consider you as our friend."

Jackie hugged her little brother till her breath gave out. She didn't want to see him go.

"You know, sister, that my life is not my own anymore."

"I know. You belong to the country now."

"I must get on that plane.   They are waiting for me."

He kissed her cheek and walked out the causeway. She fought back the tears and left the terminal to take a taxi to the medical center.   There was another she would have to care for, and he needed her more.

She stopped by Ann's room.   She knew Chris would be there.   She knocked on the open door and was greeted by two warm smiles.   She walked over to Chris and sat next to him in another uncomfortable vinyl chair.   She handed him a paper bag.

Chris's smile got even bigger.

"The Talisman Star." He blurted out.

Jackie looked at him sternly.

"You know Dr. Preston wanted desperately to keep it, at least for a few months."

"Which one?"

"Well, both actually, but Dr. Suz was very vocal about it.   I told them it was yours and yours alone.   You would decide."

"Are they staying on?"

"Yes, they want to work the dig until it is complete. They say it's the work of a lifetime.   There was one caveat, though.   They refused to stay overnight in the Habitat one more day.   They wanted a suite at the Resort and be able to go back and forth at will.   I could hardly say no."

"Good," Chris said and laughed.   He looked at the Talisman in his hands.   It had been so important to his family all these years, these decades, these centuries.   Yet, he felt it now served a higher purpose and it might bring him more luck if he let it be what it was meant to be.

"I will leave it with you, Jackie, on loan, if you will personally honor it and give me something in writing I can take back to the Estate."

"I will do that, Chris, and thank you.   This means so much to the Scientists and to my country as well.   We will make it up to you, somehow.   But, now, I must beg your forgiveness as I must go see Joe.   I find I now have several men to care for."

Jackie smiled.   She was truly happy. She left the room

344

to go down the hall to see her new love.

Ann sighed.   She looked up at Chris, who was obviously affected by her mood.

"Chris, I've done a lot for you.   I've given up a lot.   I've traveled with you half way across this world and I've been with you through all of this.   But, I never expected that I would get shot and end up in a hospital.   There are things a person will do for another, but this is not what I would consider normal."

She paused and looked pleadingly at him.

"I think you owe me and I want you to do something for me."

"Anything, Annie."

"I want to go home.   I want to get out of here."

Chris slumped in his chair.   This was such a blow. He never expected it.

"You want to go back to Colorado."   It was exhaled as a sullen whisper.

"No, no, you adorable dimwit. I want to go to Jamestown."   She touched him tenderly.

"I want to go home."

Chris lit up like a bright, shining, sun drenched sea morning.

"I'll call June.   I 'll get her to make the place ready."

Annie kissed him on the forehead.   There were tears in her eyes.   There were tears in his.

*

Alvarro had never been out of the country before.   He had no idea a city could be this big.   He had been given detailed instructions on how to get to the UN by the new consulate.   She had worked several years at the UN as a staffer prior to her appointment by President Cavadas.   She had indicated he needed to forget about taking the subway or the train and instead had arranged for one of the Delegation's Mercedes to pick him up at the airport and deliver him directly to the UN Secretariat Building.

He stood in awe at the magnificent thirty nine story building in front of him. Hundreds, if not thousands of employees and delegates must have offices in that building. There were two wings adjacent to the tower that extended a full city block on either side. These, he had been told, housed the General Assembly and the Economic and Social Council. Before his week's assignment would be over, he would have to meet with both of them.

But first, he must meet with his own Delegation, now headed by Ms. Branca Moncada. As instructed, he waited in the great entrance hall until Ms. Moncada herself appeared carrying a sign with his name on it. The Major General was easy to recognize in his new dress uniform, complete with the additional star on his epaulet. Pedro and Alvarro had a lengthy discussion about whether he should wear a suit or his military trappings and in the end, both felt that the presence of a Major General lent authenticity to the proposals being proffered to the councils. Pedro was sure that if military action were necessary, the General who would be in charge of that action would sound much more convincing than a Minister in a suit.

"General Parros. It's wonderful to meet you." Ambassador Moncada graciously extended her hand.

"An honor as well, Ms. Moncada."

"Please call me Branca."

"Okay, then you can call me General. No, just kidding, call me Alvarro. I'm kind of new at this General business."

"And I'm new as a dignitary, so I'm sure we'll both stumble through it just fine."

"I hope so. Did you get the communique from President Cavadas?"

"I did. We have you set up for meetings in the order he requested. He did not tell me what proposals you were putting forth."

They began walking towards the elevators.

"You're first meeting is with the World Heritage Sites Committee. Tomorrow, we meet with the U.S. Delegation. Could you tell me what we are doing?"

"I could, but I think I will wait until after the meeting with the U.S. tomorrow. I'll have a clearer picture of how we will proceed."

They cleared the security check point in front of the elevator bank and took the lower floor elevator that would deliver them to the wing for the Economic and Social Council. The World Heritage Sites Committee would be meeting there and the two arrived ten minutes before the meeting began.

"Ms. Moncada, ah Branca, is Rhode Island close to here?"

"Two to three hours by train."

"Oh. That might be a bit much. I have friends there in Jamestown and I'd like to see them before I go back. I have a couple of free days if all goes well here."

"I can have our staff look into the arrangements and set it all up for you, if you wish. I'm sure we can accommodate you."

"Thank you."

Major General Alvarro Parros entered the meeting hall and approached the dais as bid, Branca Moncada at his side. She was clearly a pro and greeted most of the committee persons by name. It eased him into his delivery.

In the end, there was little else the Committee could do but to declare the Atlantis Dig a World Heritage Site. Portugal held all the cards on that. Ann had been right. The Acorean Atlantic Autonomous Zone had been created by the UN to protect the seas around the archipelago as a response to the nation's support of the Allies during World War II. The British held a lease on the airfield at Ponta Delgada and the Americans had the Lajes Air Force Base on Terciera. Without those two critical logistical positions, air support could not have been mounted for the Africa campaign or the invasion of Italy. The creation of the zone was completed in 1952 to honor Portugal for its dedication to the war effort.

That was the easy part. The tough nut to crack was the United States.

*

Jackie Guiterrez had left Lisbon the day before and had returned to Atlantic Sun. She refused to stay more than one night even though President Cavadas pleaded with her to negotiate from the Capital. She had explained politely that she did not want to leave Joe by himself, not that any harm would come to him, but that she couldn't bear being away from him. It had taken her so long to find him and she had no inclination of ever letting him go.

She had talked to her brother in New York and the first phase was complete. She now had to call David Deeds and lay it out for him. He wouldn't like it, but she thought she might have some ideas that would help David go along with it.

The time difference was a problem and so she waited until eight p.m. to call. It would be just after lunch time in California. He was returning with take out from one of the many carts on the street.

"David, you do know why I'm calling, right?"

"I understand the proposal that you sent. Would he really do it?"

"Yes, David, President Cavadas surely would. He feels that the management here violated so many laws, native and international, that he would find little disagreement or strong sentiment against his actions in anything he undertook."

"What about the science?"

"If you make the calls and prove that you are on board with this, the President will share any further scientific discovery with you, but will retain ownership of it. Is that clear enough?"

"Yes, but I have to say I am most displeased with your negotiations in this matter. We should have been better represented. I want you to prepare to come back here and continue your work with the shuttle."

"David, take a deep breath. It is nine minutes after eight by my watch. Effective this moment, I no longer work for you. And I would suggest that you do nothing untoward regarding Atlantic Sun. There is a platoon of regular army stationed here, directly under the control of General Parros.   If so much as one switch is turned off, there will be hell to pay."

"I must protest."

"David, you are in absolutely no position to protest or even negotiate.   Make the calls."

*

Alvarro hugged his friends goodbye.   He had two days of lobster rolls, clam cakes, stuffed quahogs, clam chowder and French fries drizzled in vinegar;   in short, all the delicacies of Narragansett Bay. The climate was certainly different than the Azores; winter was beginning to make its presence known and the time after the Holidays brought increasing cold and grey skies to the quaint New England Island.   Chris and Ann were beginning to hunker down for the next couple of months, he with an Estate to close out and Ann with an international case on her hands.   She enlisted the help of J. Willie Giles in Providence and he was coming through like a champion.

Alvarro flew back out of Boston, first to see his sister in Ponta Delgada, then on to Lisbon where he reported to his friend, his President, Pedro Anabel Cavadas.   He entered the President's office and received a warm welcome.

"Great work, Alvarro.   I wasn't sure you could pull it off."

"I think Jackie had a lot to do with it.   That and your reputation.   They all believed you would nationalize all of the Atlantic Sun Properties.   This way, everybody got something."

"So, do you have it?"

Alvarro reached into his computer case and handed the Charter to his President.

"I have the honor, Sir, of presenting to you the first United Nations Chartered independent World Not for Profit Corporation, The Azorean Atlantis Corporation."

Pedro looked at the charter with pride.

"This will be a great thing for our country."

"Especially as you designed it, Sir. A seven member board, four appointed by you, the Chair of the Corporation appointed by you, and three by the UN Security Council. That will ensure we have a majority. Your appointment of the Chair and The Corporation's separate reporting to the Secretary General creates a separation of duties that will insure transparency. Azorean Atlantis will be able to act independently as no other Corporation in the world can."

"And the Americans are happy?"

"With a 3.6 Billion dollar write off for EngenUnity as a donation and assurances that the Lajes Air Base lease will be renewed, they were very happy. I'm not so sure that EngenUnity was all that happy, but my experience with them was not so fun filled that I give a damn. Nevertheless, Deeds made the calls to the US President, the Congress and the delegation, so the support we needed was there."

"I am relieved, Alvarro, that I didn't have to send the Army in and make a big mess of it. However, we must now begin to learn to speak and act like diplomats. You, especially."

"Why, Sir?"

"Because," President Cavadas smiled, "You are now the Chair of the Azorean Atlantis Corporation."

"What?"

"There's no one better suited for it and no one I trust more. This is the biggest thing to happen to Portugal since the colonization of Brazil. And, you're more than familiar with it. You brokered the deal. You know the Islands. You'll need to get started right away. I've arranged for Colonel DeSilva's Villa, just recently acquired, to be used as the main office. The adjacent land can be used for the new museum. You can live on the third floor while the offices are being constructed."

"And what of Colonel DeSilva?"

"Per your recommendation, he has been reassigned pending a Tribunal. He currently heads a battalion in the Moelho region. If I can't persuade the populace that we will install an autonomous government for that region, I'm afraid Colonel DeSilva may never see that Tribunal. His ill-gotten gains have become the property of the Republic and I have assigned them to your corporation. You'll have an effective base from which to build your Not-for-Profit."

"How am I going to do this alone?"

"Alvarro, Alvarro.   You'll have a Board within the month.   In the meantime, your sister is running the operations for Atlantic Sun.   You'll need a first class administrator for an Executive Director, a good lawyer for general counsel, one with international law skills.   You'll need a strong Security Director.   The Scientists are already there, but you'll need a Maintenance Division, run by a decent engineer.   You've got a lot to do.   Do you think you can handle this?"

Alvarro thought for a minute, rubbed his chin and grinned.

"I think I already know just the right people."

The memory of it is dim.   It has improved with my extended time on earth and through the reoccurrence in so many dreams.   It has been with me all my life.   The house is small, tan or light brown, I think.   It might be stone, but that isn't so vivid.   The yard is not spacious, but very neat.   I remember lying on the grass.   There's a white picket fence.   It is not tall, but it goes all the way around the house.   And the blue flowers.   That's the most vivid memory, the blue flowers.   I know what they are now.

I don't think the cataclysm was so sudden. It just built up and up. The volcanoes were always present and they scared us to death when they shook and spewed.   I don't remember the end, but I think it got to the breaking point and could hold back no more. I feel that the seas finally rose up and took us in.

I have a house next to the ocean now.   It has a white picket fence, too.   It is larger than the other one.

I can feel the seas rising again.

ABOUT THE AUTHOR:

William J. Breidinger is from Little Torch Key, Florida. He and his family also spend summers in Central New York, based out of Cortland.

This second novel takes place in several locations around the world, notably, southwestern Colorado, Jamestown, RI, Canada and the Azores. The history of Rhode Island's sea faring culture also plays an important part in this thriller/adventure story.

Bill was the former Deputy Director of the NYS Dept. of State, Division of Community Services. During early retirement, he served as the first Executive Director of the CNY Living History Center from its inception until it began day to day operations in 2011. Bill is a Certified Community Action Professional (CCAP) Emeritus and served twenty years as a Commissioner on the National Association of Community Action Partnerships' (NACAA) Certification Commission.

Bill moved to Little Torch Key in retirement with his charming bride, Phyllis and their fur child AnnJean.

His first novel, Shadows of the San Juans, the definitive western on the life and times of Alfred Packer is available solely as a Kindle Book at Amazon.com

www.ingramcontent.com/pod-product-compliance
Lightning Source LLC
Chambersburg PA
CBHW071305200626
46813CB00015B/114